JAIL BIRD

Jessie Keane is the bestselling author of *Dirty Game* and *Black Widow*. Her most recent novel, *Scarlet Women*, the third in the Annie Carter trilogy, shot straight into the *Sunday Times* bestseller list. Jessie lives in Hampshire.

Also by Jessie Keane

Dirty Game
Black Widow
Scarlet Women

JESSIE KEANE

Jail Bird

HARPER

Harper
An imprint of HarperCollins*Publishers*
77–85 Fulham Palace Road,
Hammersmith, London W6 8JB

www.harpercollins.co.uk

A Paperback Original 2010
1

Copyright © Jessie Keane 2010

Jessie Keane asserts the moral right to
be identified as the author of this work

A catalogue record for this book
is available from the British Library

ISBN: 978-0-00-790984-1

Set in Sabon by Palimpsest Book Production Limited,
Grangemouth, Stirlingshire

Printed and bound in Great Britain by
Clays Ltd, St Ives plc

To Cliff, who still has a lot to put up with . . .

Acknowledgments

To everyone at HarperCollins for the hard work and creativity involved in making *Jail Bird* the stunning book it is, and to all my friends for their endless kindness and encouragement.

Prologue

The death woman was coming. Winston Collins's senses were befuddled with ganja weed, but he knew *that*. He thought he had done a bad thing, but he wasn't too sure what the bad thing had been. His mama had told him he shouldn't be bad, and he had always done his best to walk a good path. But now . . . he wasn't sure what was going on. Only that they would *pay*.

He was hyped on ganja and grief. But he could still smell blood and cheap nylon carpet, could still feel the heat of the sun being magnified by the big plate-glass window as he stood there, sweat-sodden back pressed tight to the wall. And he could still *see*. He could see the crimson-soaked horror in the chair. And he could see . . . oh yes, he could see *her*, just passing by the window, all unknowing, her blonde hair catching the sun like a bright banner, her walk quick, urgent, as she approached the door of Jack Rackland's office.

It was her. The death woman.

Praise God and don't worry, be happy . . . now how did

it go? He was so upset that he had forgotten the words of his favourite Bobby McFerrin song. Suki would know.

But Suki was gone.

There it was, nibbling away at the edge of his brain like a rat chewing on rotten meat. Suki was *gone*, and Bev was hovering between life and death; he might lose her too and he couldn't bear it, couldn't bear any of it; it was all *her* fault. Lily King had brought death into their happy home. Winston had always been peaceful, easy-going; but not now, not any more. Lily King and her sidekick had ruined his life, and they had to pay for it.

He saw it all again: Suki turning over the cards and her troubled gaze coming up to meet his, her sweet lips saying, look, this is Lily King's card; it's death. And him laughing, oh yeah, sure hon, and do you want this dinner edible or ruined? He didn't give all that tarot crap a second thought. Give Bev a shout, the dinner'll get cold, he'd said to her, brushing it aside, brushing that *look* in her eyes aside, that look of purest fear. *God* how he wished that he had taken her more seriously.

But Suki was gone.

He relived it. Suki turning away, saying yeah sure, but there was something in her eyes, a darkness, a terror. Because in her gut Suki knew about Lily King, she knew there was big trouble coming, and he shouldn't have laughed at her all those times when he did, he should have given her more attention, taken more notice.

Too late now.

Suki was gone.

The pain of it hit him all over again.

All that was left was the death woman. Dealing out vengeance, dealing out a world of hurt to Bev, who might even now be going about the hard business of dying, and Suki . . . Jesus, he'd loved that woman. Loved her to bits.

Now she was gone.

And all because of this woman, and her lust for revenge. *The fire. Oh Jesus, the fire.*

Somehow he'd got Bev out, and he'd been going back for Suki, all the while heaving and choking, the smoke – the horrible, rolling black *smoke* – snatching the air from his lungs; but the flames had been too much for him. The flames had driven him back.

Well, now he was here, and so was she. Lily King was opening the door, pushing through fast, and then pausing, freezing as she saw what was sitting in the chair. Winston's hand tightened on the bloody machete in his strong right hand. Now he was going to put an end to her evil ways. She moved in further, breathed out 'Jack . . .' and Winston was so close he could hear how fast and panicky her breathing was, and he thought, *Yeah. Now I've got you.*

He surged forward, raising his hand to strike her dead.

She heard the movement as he pulled away from the wall. Turned, her eyes widening.

Here it comes for you, bitch, thought Winston.

She liked revenge? Well, so did he.

Revenge was *sweet*.

1

1996

LEO

Leo King could never resist blondes. Ash, golden, strawberry, Nordic – he loved them all. Hell, he had even *married* one. Of course he loved his old lady, Lily. Of *course* he did. She was the mother of his children, he loved the bones of those two girls of his and he loved Lily too, but sometimes . . . well, he guessed it was a weakness, but sometimes he just got the urge to stick it in something *new*.

Like he was doing now. And it was being appreciated, too.

'Oh, *honey*,' the blonde he was humping doggy-fashion in the hotel bed was crouching on all fours, moaning and gasping, clutching the French headboard with long, elegantly manicured nails.

She's going to scratch the damned thing, thought Leo.

Which was okay, fuck it. But if this had been at home, in his own bed – and sometimes, oh yes, sometimes he did that, and he felt bad about it but he did it anyway – then scratching the furniture was a no-no. Because he'd felt just lately that Lily wasn't entirely in the dark about his little extracurricular bits of bedroom activity. Marks on the headboard would blow the whole thing wide open, and he didn't want that.

What Leo wanted was to carry on having his cake and eating it – this delectable little bit of fluff right here, who had been the first but who most certainly was not the last.

'Oh Leo *sweetheart*,' Adrienne screamed as he pumped away.

Actually she was a bit theatrical about sex, this one. Not like Lily, who was a real slow, sensual burn. He loved Lily, but this . . . ah, it was the thrill of the chase, the cornering of the quarry, the proof that he still had it, in spades.

Of course women never understood that.

They never appreciated that extramarital sex was simply *fun*, something a guy would do if he could, with whoever – the *whoever* scarcely mattered; it was just the doing of it that was the good bit.

Forbidden fruit, he thought. That's what it was. Forbidden, and therefore twice as desirable.

But now she was moving, he was slipping out. Fuck it, he'd just been getting into his stride there. She turned on the bed, great breasts, high and firm and brown-nippled, slim waist, brown pubic hair, so *not* a natural blonde, but who gave a fuck? She lay down on her back and clasped him with her wide-open thighs, smiling up at him dreamily.

'Let's do it this way for a change,' she panted.

That annoyed him. He liked doggy-style the best. He'd thought about why over the years and had concluded that he liked it best that way because the woman in the bed could be anyone, anyone at all, you didn't have to see her face, you didn't have to tell her you loved her (that came later, or earlier if she was proving resistant to all his other best lines), or have it rammed home to you that it *wasn't Lily*: doggy-style, you could be shagging anyone or anything, you could be putting it in a hole in the *fence*. It was simple, and it was – nearly – guiltless.

Okay, he was nearly there anyway. He pushed back into her warm wetness and she pulled him in close, skin to skin. She was a fabulous lay and so he was willing to forgive the interruption – this time.

'*Jesus!*' she was yelling in his ear now. '*Oh God – Leo!*'

And now she was applying those nails that had marked the headboard to his back.

'Ow!' he complained as she ripped the talons down his flesh. 'Jesus, take it easy . . .'

Marking him was completely out of order. She knew that. She knew the rules. No love bites, no tooth marks, no scratching. No evidence for Lily to find and start to complain over. Although Lily was a good girl, never really nagged. Lily wasn't an in-your-face sort of woman. She was quiet. Restrained.

A doormat? sprang into his brain.

No, not that. Was she?

Anyway, here was this stupid bitch Adrienne, breaking the rules, flouting them in his *face*, but oh Jesus, that felt so good, she was a fantastic lay; she was just the best.

'Arghhhh!' shouted Leo as he came.

He collapsed onto her, gasping.

'Jesus, you're heavy,' she complained mildly.

Leo was a big bull of a man, dark haired and dark skinned and tipping the scales at eighteen stone. Considerately, he heaved himself off her and collapsed onto the bed.

'That was *good*,' said Leo, eyes closed, a broad smile on his chops.

Jessie Keane

'Yeah,' she said, and cuddled up to him, smoothing her hand over his chest hair.

Knowing what was required of him – this was what they *all* required, after sex, he'd found – he dropped a kiss onto her cheek and gazed deep into her eyes. 'Love you, babes,' he murmured.

'Love you too,' Adrienne whispered, her eyes intense as they stared back into his.

He groped around for something else to say. She was waiting for something. He came up with: 'You're something special.'

'Hmm.' Adrienne knew she was special. She'd been his mistress for over ten years now, even since before he'd wed Lily. But now . . . well, what she had begun to suspect had been proved to be the case. Jack Rackland had done a thorough job and dug up a whole heap of dirt. She knew that Leo had been keeping secrets from her. From Lily, too. But then – Lily was no concern of hers.

She cuddled in against his chest. Her face grew serious. 'Do you really think that I'm special?'

'Sure you are.' Leo stifled a yawn. It always knocked him out, chilled him like nothing else, having sex.

'I think you're special too,' she whispered, her fingernails circling on his chest, her eyes fixed upon the little whorls she was forming in his dark chest hair. *And I'm sick of sharing you*, she added silently.

'Thanks, babes.' Leo's eyes were fluttering closed.

'That's why I've decided,' she said.

Leo heaved a contented sigh. 'Decided?'

'I'm going to tell Matt. Then you can leave Lily, and we can be together.'

8

2

1996

LILY

Usually Lily King loved a little me-time, a little girly pampering, but on this particular Monday to Friday break she realized that she wasn't in the mood to be relaxed and soothed at her favourite spa with her mates; she had too much on her mind.

She hadn't wanted to let the girls down, but by Wednesday she was pacing the grounds of the super-deluxe spa like a caged animal, and by Thursday she could see that it was hopeless. She couldn't just lay about any longer, fulminating over what the hell Leo had been up to, without a thought for good old Lily; dependable, quiet, *stupid* Lily.

Even a worm turns eventually, she thought, hurling her stuff back into her Louis Vuitton suitcase.

You could only heap so much shit onto a person's head before they finally came spluttering to the surface and said okay, *enough*. And – finally – here she was, a very domesticated and dull little worm, turning around at last. Going home.

'Miserable mare,' Becks had said with a cheery grin through a wad of chewing gum. Becks *always* chewed gum. Tall and lanky and sporting her usual blonde bouffant up-do, Becks had been swathed in a thick white towelling robe when she'd knocked on Lily's room door and found her dressed and packing her things. She swept Lily into a hug. 'You've had a cob on all week,' she said, pushing Lily back a pace and staring into her eyes. 'Anything you want to talk about?'

Lily shook her head.

She couldn't talk about it. She was sure that her husband was shagging around and it was painful even to think about, much less discuss. This break had been a mistake. She wanted to go home and have it out with Leo. They had things to discuss. *Important* things. She'd tried before, but he'd just said she was crazy, she was imagining things.

She *knew* she wasn't imagining things.

Sure, the marriage hadn't been perfect. They both knew it. But they'd both *tried* to make a go of it, after the first flush of lust had worn off. Well, she'd tried. Obviously Leo had been trying out *other* things, playing other games. Like hide the sausage.

'Well take care,' said Becks, and hugged her again. 'I'll have to make do with Hairy Mary for company, won't I? She's always in that pool. She's *still* in the bloody pool; she'll look like a prune by the time she climbs out. Pity Adrienne couldn't have come along. Or Maeve.'

Lily forced a laugh. Hairy Mary was in fact their good friend Mary, who was married to one of the East End's biggest drug dealers. She was a stunning little dark-haired hottie who went in for ultimate waxing; the only hair she had on her body was on her head. Maeve was Lily's sister-in-law, married to the middle King brother, Si.

10

Leo, Si and Freddy – they were a set; inseparable: brothers in arms.

As for Adrienne . . . well, Lily thought that Adrienne was probably busy. And she knew what she was busy *doing*, too.

'I think Mary does it to be streamlined,' grinned Becks. 'Less water resistance.'

So, Lily went home.

Home was a 1930s art deco mansion in deepest Essex, with both an indoor and an outside pool. Leo had fallen in love with the place when they had seen it up for sale. He liked the fact that Si's place – equally palatial – was just up the road. Lily had been pregnant at the time with Oli, and Saz had been a bumptious two-year-old, whining with boredom as they house-hunted. This was the thirteenth house they'd viewed, and Leo had said 'we'll take it' without hesitation, and promptly renamed it The Fort.

'How about The White Elephant?' Lily had joked with a tinge of acid in her voice, because it was huge, it was white, it was the *thirteenth* house they'd looked at, and wasn't that meant to be unlucky?

Besides, she was throwing up all day every day – *morning* sickness, what a laugh – and she was worried that she was going to heave all over the estate agent's suit if they didn't get a move on.

After they moved in, Leo saw to the installation of a new security system to turn The Fort into a modern-day fortress. Leo owned, ran and understood the security biz and had installed a security system so watertight that if a mouse so much as farted in the grounds, he'd know about it. It was a double system: if you cut the phone lines, he proudly told her, it would still function. It had everything – sensors both

11

inside the house and out, a secure entry system, and Leo added a high wall around the perimeter of the grounds. It was, truly, a fortress.

Lily learned to love The Fort too. She furnished it lavishly. They had a cleaner in twice a week, the man came and attended to the pools, and the gardener called on Thursdays to keep the grounds in pristine condition. It was only later, *way* later, when the girls were in primary school and Lily had begun to suspect that Leo was indulging in a little extra-marital lechery that she started to think that her 'white elephant' crack had been closer to the mark than either of them could have known at the time. Grandly appointed and heavily secured though The Fort was, Lily came to believe that they were not really owning the house, *it* was owning *them*. Or her, anyway. She felt trapped here – trapped, and unloved.

Oh, Leo had been fair about it. He'd put the deeds to The Fort in both their names, and she appreciated that. But increasingly she felt like a bird in a gilded cage. Leo was free to fuck around all he wanted – she had only recently become certain of the fact that Leo was playing around with Adrienne, wife of the firm's accountant Matt Thomson – but *where*, exactly, did that leave her?

She sighed deeply as she steered her Porsche 911 through the remotely operated electronic gates. She drove up the winding approach and there was The Fort. Lily looked ahead at the well-lit courtyard in front of the huge house and felt ridiculously proud of the place. All her friends were envious that she lived here.

Yeah, but then there's a downside, she thought.

She and Leo had been married a *long* time. Leo had started out a small-time crook, twocking motors, creating mayhem on the football terraces and running errands for the local crims all around Essex and the city. He had been her first real lover.

But not her first real love, she admitted to herself.

That prize had gone to Nick O'Rourke. Leo's closest friend. She had been hotly, obsessively in love with Nick as only a very young girl can be. Then Nick had turned his back on her. She had pleaded with him, *What's wrong? What did I do?*

He had been cold as ice. 'It's over,' he said.

That had hurt so much, pierced her to the heart.

But then Leo King had kicked in the door of her quiet little world, collecting her in his souped-up car from the school gates, impressing Lily no end and making all her gawky little school friends nearly shit themselves with envy.

Back then, Leo had seemed so grown-up, so exotic. He was a bad boy and – like Nick – exuded a potent, violent charisma. There was Greek way back in Leo's family some-where, and that came out in his dark, bulky good looks. Leo was charming and brutal in equal measures, always with cash to spare and attitude by the bucketful, and Lily's strictly boring, law-abiding parents – her dad a postman, her mother a cleaner – had clamped down on the budding relationship almost immediately.

But not soon enough.

Decimated by Nick's rejection of her, Lily had sought solace in the arms of Leo. And Leo had wasted no time in popping Lily's cherry and giving her a little something to remember him by. After that, Leo – being young and stupid, just as Lily was even younger and even stupider – had proposed. Lily's parents had softened towards him after that. There had been a white wedding – well, *ivory*, anyway. Lily had forfeited the right to wear white on the day she let Leo King deflower her in the back of his hot-rod car, as her sour-faced mother never tired of reminding her.

Nine months later, after twenty-four hours of agonizing labour, a little bundle of joy arrived and was christened Sarah. Three years after *that*, by which time Leo was making a big name for himself in criminal circles and they were living the life of Riley, another daughter turned up. Olivia. Oli.

Lily half smiled as she thought of her two precious girls. Yeah, there were downsides – being married to the-ego-has-landed Leo King was one, who by the way farted like a fibre-fuelled wart hog in bed, emitting smells that could almost lead a person to think that a rat had crawled up his hairy great arse and died there – but hey, here was an upside.

A *huge* upside.

Her two lovely girls. Sarah – or Saz as she was known to everyone – getting very grown up at just nine years old, and Oli who was just six. Saz was a stately little girl, prettily blonde and dainty, very much daddy's princess. Oli was the tomboy, the wild one, dark-haired like her dad and always faintly dishevelled. Lily adored them both, and so did Leo. He'd do anything for his girls.

Yeah – anything except give up chasing skirt, she thought.

Lily parked the car, turned off the engine and got out. The sensor came on above the front porch, further illuminating the drive where she stood in cold, bluish light.

Ain't it funny? she thought. *Crooks always expect other people to be crooked too.*

There were lights blazing out from the upstairs windows, a few left on downstairs too.

'Hey Leo!' she called out when she stepped into the hall. No answer.

Fallen asleep again with the telly on, thought Lily irritably.

He'd be laid out on the bed in his underpants, mouth open, snoring: *not* a pretty sight. She sighed and dumped her case on the hall floor. She put her handbag on the consul table under the big Venetian mirror. Her reflection stared back at her. It gave her a bit of a turn, looking at herself caught unawares. She saw not the happy girl she'd once been, but a woman weighed down by troubles. Yes, she was blonde and she looked good. Slender, dressed in designer clothes and wearing foot-fetish shoes, buffed to bronze with fake tan, sporting long acrylic nails and a lot of expensive make-up. But her face said it all. An unhappy woman stood there, her mouth turned down and her eyes, brown with tigerish flecks of gold, lacking any spark of life.

Lily looked behind her reflection at the vast hall, at the chandelier she'd sourced so carefully, the cream marble on the floor, the watered silk Dupioni drapes that had cost a bloody fortune, and she thought: *Hey, guess what? It's true. Money doesn't buy you happiness.*

Lily moved away from the mirror, not liking what she saw. She felt a huge sense of emptiness eating at her guts, a sense of complete futility. Tonight she didn't even have the comfort of Saz and Oli to relieve it. They were staying over nearby at Si and Maeve's for the week. If Lily was away, then that was just the way it had to be – Leo King didn't babysit kids, even if the kids were his own. That was women's work, not men's.

'Leo!' she called again. She couldn't hear the telly going in their huge lounge, or up there in the master suite. Maybe he was in the games room. He wouldn't be in the heated indoor pool: Leo was a morning swimmer.

No, it was late. He would be upstairs, asleep. Nice and

peaceful, the bastard. Lily gritted her teeth and thought again about the things she'd found over the last few months. The receipts for jewellery. A gold bracelet from Tiffany, a Patek Philippe ladies' watch that *she* had never received. Expensive bouquets of flowers that she'd never seen hide nor hair of. And a bill from a classy restaurant – *not* the sort of place he'd take his hoodlum mates to.

She'd phoned the number on the bill, saying she'd been there with Leo King on that date, and she thought she'd left her scarf behind. Had it been handed in? They told her no, but it was the manager's day off, they'd check with him tomorrow – and she'd be coming in as usual with Mr King, wouldn't she, next week? If the scarf was found, they'd put it aside for her.

'Thanks,' said Lily. She'd hung up and checked the calendar. Leo had last been to the restaurant on Wednesday lunchtime.

The following Wednesday, she drove there and sat outside in her car and waited. And there he was, walking into the restaurant – with Adrienne Thomson, wife of the company accountant.

Leo was taking the mickey, making her look a bloody fool. And now she'd had enough. Now the games were going to *stop*. She was going to lay it out for him, spell it out plain: either he stopped, or she was walking away, and she was taking the girls with her and he was going to pay, pay and pay again for making her look like such a total *schmuck*.

Grimly, Lily started up the stairs.

All right, marriage to Leo had for her always been a compromise. But she had worked at it, made a life, a family, a home. But this was the final straw for her.

Lily had never been the confrontational type. She had always felt she'd struck lucky, marrying a bloke who could keep her in style. She lived well. Lunches with the girls. Spa breaks. Holidays in Marbella and Barbados. The works.

She'd grown up poor, with parents who'd been forced to penny-pinch to get by. She knew it had scarred her. This life – *her* life – was so different. Her mum could never quite believe it when she called – and being Mum she was always quick with the snide remarks, the 'getting above yourself' lectures, all that sour inverted-snobbery stuff. What did she want, the miserable bitch? That her daughter should have to scrape along through life, cleaning other people's lavvies like her?

'Pride comes before a fall,' Mum would sniff, glaring disdainfully about at her daughter's opulent lifestyle. 'Salt of the earth, the working class, don't you forget that, my girl.'

Lily ignored her. She knew that she, Lily, had never changed, that she never had and never would put on airs and graces. She was still herself, still true to her roots – she was still quiet, awestruck Lily Granger, who had been painfully dumped by Nick O'Rourke and then been amazed that his pal Leo King fancied *her* and not any of the other, more exuberant girls in her circle. She was the same Lily Granger who had become Lily King, the biddable, reserved and faithful wife of Leo King.

Biddable.

Lily's lip curled in bitterness as she thought of what a prize idiot Leo had taken her for. Yeah, she might live in luxury, but she'd been made to look a twat. She was sure his mates and his business 'colleagues' would know what he was up to, would pat him on the back and think him a big man for cheating on his wife with poor Matt Thomson's old lady.

'You dog,' they'd say admiringly.

And if the boys knew, then her friends knew too.

Leo was a major Essex 'face', and he and his boys were behind many a heist. Leo, his brothers and Nick O'Rourke led a cadre of suited-and-booted villains, all deeply dangerous and mired in running 'front' companies. Lily didn't know much about their business, and she didn't want to. The money poured in; that had to be enough. So she'd put the blinkers on, kept her head down and ignored the rest.

There was always a price to pay in this life. She had come to know that over the years, shedding her girlish innocence as she got to know the man she'd married. There was a price to pay – and that price was her dignity. And just lately that price seemed too fucking high, by about a mile.

She was outside the closed bedroom door now, and her heart was beating hard with the tension of it. Because he would kick off. She knew that. Leo had never once hit her – he never would – but his temper was formidable, his rages seemed to fill up the space all around him, to suck all the oxygen out of a room. She didn't ever like to upset him, but now she'd been pushed too far.

Yeah, the worm's finally doing a U-turn, she thought.

'Leo!' she called again, wanting to wake him quickly, wanting more than anything to get this over and done with.

He'd deny it. She knew damned well that he'd deny it. But there were things she knew for sure now; there was *proof*, and she had right on her side.

'Leo, will you wake up? I want a word,' she said, nerves making her voice harsh and demanding as she swung the door wide open, crashing it back against the wall in her haste to get in there and get the damned thing said.

And then she saw the blood – splatters and loops and obscene thick *skeins* of blood – and the body with its head shot clean away. She stopped dead in the doorway, all the strength draining from her limbs in an instant, her lips mouthing words that would not come.

Her long nightmare had begun.

3

2009

Lily King was out. She was standing at the gates of Askham Grange nick, wearing jeans and a white t-shirt, a grey hoodie and white trainers, clutching a black bin bag full of her worldly possessions.

The first thing she knew of her friend Becks's arrival was the horn of the car. It blared out a merry eight-tone tune as Becks whipped round the corner in it. The second thing that announced Becks's arrival was the colour of the car. The daft bint had a *pink* open-topped car. Lily cringed a bit as Becks tore along the road, waving madly, her white-blonde hair whipping out behind her in the warm June wind. So much for hopes of a quiet departure. Becks never did a damned thing quietly. Lily should have known that.

'Lils, Lils! Hiya Lils!' she was hollering even before she brought the car to a screeching halt.

Becks was her best mate. Only Becks had visited her inside while she'd been down south in Holloway. And Becks was the only person who'd offered to drive all the way up to Yorkshire to pick her up now she was no longer to be detained at Her Majesty's pleasure. She'd offered her temporary accommodation too, to keep the probation officer sweet.

Becks is a very kind girl, thought Lily as the pink monstrosity barrelled to a halt right in front of her. *Barking, sure. Mad as a hatter. But kind.*

'Lils babe, jump in!' Becks was trilling over the loud thump and grind of the Foo Fighters. She grabbed the black bin bag and lobbed it onto the back seat. 'Jesus, it's so *good* to see you.'

Lily was clutched around the neck in a tight hug. Becks's jaws were working, chewing gum as always, and the scent of Wrigley's surrounded Lily in a haze of sweetness. She smiled into Becks's perfumed hair and then she looked up and stiffened.

A bull-barred 4x4 that had been parked across the street was slowly pulling out. As it drew level with Becks's car, the darkly tinted electronic window slid smoothly down. A bulky man was behind the steering wheel, a man with a shaven head, snub nose, cleft chin and piggy dark blue eyes.

Oh shit, thought Lily.

Freddy King, Leo's psycho youngest brother was sitting there in the driving seat staring right at her.

Becks felt her grow rigid and she drew back. Looked at Lily's eyes. Saw where they were directed. Becks looked around, following Lily's gaze, and saw Freddy there.

'Fucking hell,' Becks muttered under her breath.

Both women froze, wondering what the hell he was doing here, what the hell he was intending to do. Lily's heart was threatening to bust its way straight out through her ribs. Suddenly she wished she was back inside. She'd felt *safer* inside.

Now she was out . . . and here was Freddy.

Freddy started to grin. Lily felt her stomach tighten with fear. Freddy had a grin like a crocodile. It wasn't intended to convey warmth, only threat. He lifted his hand and pointed a finger at her, mimicking the pointing of a gun.

Lily gulped.

He was mouthing something now. Lily stared at his face, a face she had last seen twelve years ago whooping and hollering in triumph across a crowded courtroom. Big heavy features, pitted skin the result of childhood acne, black eyebrows that met in the middle. Freddy had never been the brains of the King outfit – and by God it showed – but he was certainly the brawn. He exuded an air of casual menace. Lily looked at that sneering mouth and tried to make out the words.

When she did, it gave her no comfort at all.

You won't see it coming, but trust me – it is.

And then he gunned the engine, and was gone, roaring off along the road.

'Creep,' said Becks with a shudder.

Lily felt as though someone had just stepped heavily on her grave. Leo's two brothers hated her, and they had reason. She just hadn't expected they'd make their intentions clear quite so soon. Her mouth felt dry and it was as if a cloud had passed over the sun.

She looked along the road. The 4x4 was gone, but the feeling of menace lingered. She took a breath, opened the car door, and slid into the passenger seat of Becks's ludicrous pink motor.

'Blonde joke,' said Lily. 'What's the first thing a dumb blonde does in the morning?'

Becks looked at her doubtfully.

'She introduces herself,' said Lily.

Becks raised a thin smile.

'And what's the second thing a dumb blonde does in the morning?' Lily asked.

Becks shook her head.

'She goes home.' *And where the hell is home, now?* she wondered.

Becks smiled obligingly, but her heart wasn't in it. 'You think he knew the day you were getting out, and followed me all the way up here?'

Lily didn't answer, but yes – she thought Freddy had done exactly that. For the sole purpose and pleasure of scaring the shit out of her.

'He was saying something, wasn't he?' Becks was frowning now. 'I couldn't tell what it was. Did you see what he was saying, Lils?'

You won't see it coming – but trust me, it is.

'Nah,' said Lily. 'Couldn't make out a word.'

She looked at the prison. Twelve years out of her life. Twelve *years*. But the nightmare had started before that, on the night she came home to accuse her husband of having an affair.

4

'What you thinking about, Lils?' asked Becks.

Lily came back to the present with a jolt. She forced a smile. Banished the image of all that blood, that huge *splatter* of blood, from her mind once again. 'Nothing much,' she said, realizing that she'd been back there again, reliving that awful night.

She was wrapped up in Becks's spare towelling robe, having soaked in the bath for ages. She'd washed her hair, scrubbed herself all over, but still she couldn't get the stink of prison off her skin. It was Friday evening, earlyish. Watch the soaps, go to bed. That was their grand plan. They'd eaten – just the two of them; Joe, Becks's lankily attractive husband, who worked for one of the East End mobs, had taken himself off somewhere – and they were now polishing off the last of the wine.

Becks flopped down beside Lily and looked at her, sitting there bolt upright, blank-faced. Becks popped a piece of gum in her mouth and chewed thoughtfully. Lily knew what her friend was thinking: that Lily had changed. The Lily Becks had known – before the Leo thing had kicked off – had always been quiet, smiley, not a hint of attitude on her. *This* Lily had grown a tougher skin, altered into something different, something alien.

Her best friend, thought Lily. She was sitting here with her best friend, and now she hadn't a clue what to say to her. She knew that her presence was starting to make Becks feel uneasy. Lily had just done twelve years for killing Leo. Sure, there were a lot of people who'd wanted to kill Leo – shit, they'd been queuing up around the block – but everyone believed that Lily had actually gone ahead and *done* it. Blown his head clean off. Becks had remained a friend despite that, over all this time, visiting, making an effort. But she *had* to be wondering how the hell anyone could do that, take a life, even if sorely provoked.

Becks was staring at Lily.

'What?' asked Lily.

'Nothing.' Becks shook her head.

'Come on.'

Becks looked back at Lily. 'I just . . . well . . . what's it like? Killing someone, I mean?'

Lily smiled faintly. 'You just point and shoot, I suppose. Easy.'

Becks swallowed. Lily was *really* making her nervous. The way she'd said that. So cool. So flippant.

'It can't be easy,' said Becks with a shaky laugh.

'It could be. Supposing you hated the person you were shooting. Supposing he had – for instance – been poking someone else. Or beating you up. Stuff like that.'

Becks nodded. 'Right.'

Becks had been at the trial. She remembered that the defence had used that, told the jury that Leo had beaten the crap out

25

of Lily on a regular basis, tried to lessen the sentence. Becks had doubted that was true; she still did. The defence counsel had been clutching at straws, but everyone could see that Lily was going down for a long stretch.

'You know what, Lils? You still look bloody good.' Then she grinned. 'Forty's the new twenty, y'know.'

Lily sighed. She'd always looked younger than her years. 'I'm not forty yet. Not till next April.'

'Mine hits next June,' said Becks. 'Scary, or what?'

Silence.

Then Lily said: 'Si and Maeve. They still living with the girls at The Fort?'

Becks shook her head. 'When Oli turned eighteen back in February, they moved out – back to their own place just up the road. The girls are still there, though.' Becks felt uncomfortable talking about this. Lily had lost her home. A con couldn't profit from their crime, so her share of the house – which would have been the *full* share had Leo died peacefully in his bed – had passed into a trust for the girls, administered by Leo's brother Si and his wife Maeve, who were appointed trustees and guardians of the girls by the courts.

Lily sipped her wine, but it tasted sour to her now. She was remembering all those frantic, tearful times when she had phoned out from prison. The very first time she had phoned The Fort, thinking that the cleaner or *someone* would pick up, Si had answered the phone, told her to fuck off, and put the phone down on her.

Becks was darting furtive looks at Lily.

'*Now* what?' Lily asked.

Becks shook her head. 'No, it don't matter.'

'Oh for fuck's sake, Becks, spit it out,' sighed Lily. She looked tired all of a sudden, tired and irritable.

Becks sighed. She knew she ought to listen more to Joe and what he told her. Joe was the epitome of sensible. For instance, he'd kicked off about Lily coming here, but Becks had *insisted*. And now she could see the error of her ways, because with Lily in such close proximity she found that she just couldn't keep this huge secret from her. It wasn't fair. Lily had been through enough.

She couldn't help remembering Lily standing there outside the prison gates, looking lost, her eyes blank, her expression hopeless. Her old mate, Lily. She'd stuck with her, because for God's sake this was *Lily*. They'd known each other all their lives. And if Lily – of all people – had blown Leo away, then she *must* have been goaded beyond all reason. So she owed the poor cow the truth, at least. Didn't she?

'I wasn't supposed to tell you,' said Becks.

'Tell me what?' asked Lily.

'About Saz's wedding.'

'You *what?*' Lily shot upright, slopping wine over the arm of the chair.

Saz! Her baby girl. She hadn't seen her or heard a word from her in twelve years. And now . . .

'Wedding? What the fuck're you talking about?'

'She's getting married. Tomorrow. And I'm not supposed to tell you that, you didn't hear that from me, okay?'

Lily sat there, gobsmacked. When she had last seen Saz, she had been nine years old. Now she was twenty-one. A fully grown woman. And she was getting *married*. Her eldest daughter. Her lovely girl.

'Where?' asked Lily. 'What time?'

'Oh, no,' said Becks, shaking her head. '*No*, Lils. Don't even think about it. The King boys see you within ten miles of *that*, they'll go apeshit.'

'There's nothing in my licence that says I can't contact the girls – or anyone else, come to that.'

'No! Lils, don't. The Kings . . .'

'Hey,' said Lily with sudden sharpness, '*I'm* a King. Remember?'

Becks was taken aback. The Lily she'd known had never snapped like that. *I guess becoming a murderess changes a person*, she thought with a shudder. And what the hell was she doing, helping a murderess out like this? Joe was right. She was mental to get involved. And now she'd opened her fat gob and put her foot straight in it. As usual.

'Freddy King said he'd kill you if he ever clapped eyes on you again,' Becks reminded her. 'He was outside the sodding jail, Lils. Think about this. He drove all that way and waited, just so that he could scare you.'

Freddy was hot-headed and stupid, Lily had always thought that. Not like Si. Si was a thinker. Leo had been smart too – but not, as it turned out, quite smart enough.

'Freddy King's full of crap,' said Lily.

'He'll do for you if you go there,' warned Becks seriously.

Lily shrugged and glugged back the last of the wine. She turned and looked Becks dead in the eye. 'Like I care,' she said. 'And Becks . . .?'

'What?'

'I didn't kill Leo.'

Becks gulped. 'You what?'

'I didn't kill him. I know you all thought I did. Everyone did. Including the police who investigated the case. Including the judge. No one bought that shit about him beating me up and me killing him being justifiable. People knew he was screwing Adrienne Thomson. They were convinced I cracked and killed him for it. But I didn't.'

Becks took a long swallow of her wine. She needed it. Was Lily bullshitting her? But why would she do that? She'd done her time, what would it profit her to start spinning fairy tales?

'So who the hell . . .?' she asked Lily.

Lily shrugged. 'Dunno,' she said.

She looked straight at Becks and Becks felt dread take hold of her. 'But I'm going to start with Adrienne. She was all over Leo's bits like a dose of the clap, ever since school days. She was Matt Thomson's missus, but he didn't do it for her, did he? We all knew that. Apart from firing blanks, poor bastard, she went round telling everyone he had a tiny dick.' Lily emptied her glass and grimaced. 'Yeah. I'll start with her.'

And after Adrienne, I'll go on to anyone else who might have done it, she thought. *And when I find them, when I finally find out who did this to me, then God help them.*

5

1997

Lily King was twenty-seven years old and standing in number one court in the Old Bailey. 1997, and no one believed that the Millennium Dome would ever come in on budget or that Princess Diana was going to be dead within months. Everyone, however, believed that one day soon Tim Henman would win Wimbledon, and for sure everyone believed that Lily King, wife of 'entrepreneur' Leo King, was guilty of his murder.

The jury were filing back into the court, and now here came the judge. A low, excited murmur buzzed around the jam-packed courtroom. Lily stared straight ahead, willing herself not to break down, not to cry. Terror gripped her, and disbelief. This couldn't be happening. Not to her.

The jury had reached their conclusion after just forty minutes of deliberation. Her brief had been reassuring when they'd spoken before the trial, but now when she tried to catch his eye, he was looking away. She'd put her blonde hair back in a French pleat and dressed in a sober black suit for the trial, on his recommendation.

'Don't look too glamorous. Keep it plain, keep it simple,' he'd said.

But Lily had the strong feeling that she could have been wearing spangles and a leotard, and she'd still be fucked.

The court clerk was taking the verdict form from the leader of the jury, and was now handing it up to the judge. Now there was no excited murmur. The whole courtroom was silent, waiting for the axe to fall.

Lily's eyes were fixed on the florid-faced judge in his sombre grey wig and robes. He put on his glasses, unfolded the paper and read it. Then he passed it back to the clerk, cleared his throat and started to speak. Lily didn't hear a word he said, over the roaring tumult in her head. Didn't want to hear what she feared the most.

When he stopped speaking, there was a moment of total silence. Then pandemonium broke out. Suddenly the whole court was in uproar, the press were storming toward the doors, Leo's family were stomping and yelling in triumph, Freddy and Si were glaring their hatred at her. Becks was sitting there, pale-faced and wretched. Nick O'Rourke was there too, silent amid the noise, as if carved from stone. The judge was yelling for silence, but nobody was taking any notice.

Lily King was going down for the murder of her husband, Leo King. She had blown Leo's brains out after finding out he was having an affair with Adrienne Thomson. Both motive and evidence pointed to Lily: her fingerprints had been on the gun – no one else's. Her charmed life was over. Her fate was decided. She stood there, dazed, as hell erupted all around her. Her eyes sought her brief's again, but he was looking away, tidying his papers.

Bastard.

How the fuck could this be happening?

But it was. A guard appeared on either side of her. She turned numbly. They led her back down to the cells.

6

Bright and early next morning, Lily was up, showered and dressed. It was either that or sleeping, and dreaming. She dreamed a lot. Last night it had been the court case. No, she'd rather be up and doing than asleep and at the mercy of the dreams.

Becks lent her the pink car and Lily drove over to where she wanted to go. It felt funny, being behind the wheel after so long inside, being free to just come and go – within reason. But it felt good. *Powerful.* She liked it.

She checked in with her probation officer first, a dour-looking, overworked woman with an office pallor, thin dull hair and a fistful of blackheads on her nose.

'All going well?' the woman asked, not unkindly.

'Fine,' said Lily, and told her about her plans to stay with Becks and to look for a job soon. A lie, but so what? She planned to be too damned busy to waste time becoming a wage slave.

'I'll need to visit you sometime soon at that address,' said the officer, and got out her diary.

Jesus, Lily thought, but this was the deal, she was a lifer out on licence, this was it for the foreseeable future.

'Fine,' she said, and they made an appointment for the following week, then Lily left to press on with the real business of the day.

When she banged on the door of the smart detached house near Romford, Adrienne Thomson opened it and her jaw nearly hit the floor.

'Fuck!' she gasped out, and started to shut it again.

Lily stuck her foot in the door and put her shoulder to it. Lots of gym sessions in the nick had made her harder, stronger. She wasn't weak little Lily any more. That Lily was gone.

'That's hardly friendly, Adrienne, is it?' asked Lily, forcing her way into Adrienne's neat and painfully clean hallway. 'Trying to shut the door in an old friend's face.'

If Adrienne Thomson had expected a visit from anyone, it certainly wasn't Lily King. No one had told her that Lily was coming out. In the back of her mind, Adrienne had known it had to be soon, but she had shied away from that, tried not to think about it. She didn't want to go there, not now, not ever. It had been bad enough at the time. The police had questioned her for hours on end and it had all come out at the trial. It had caused terrible ructions with Matt. She just wanted to forget the whole thing, and let it lie.

Only it looked as if she wasn't going to be allowed to.

Lily walked on into the big, sunny lounge and Adrienne followed slowly and stood just inside the door, wondering what the hell was going to happen next.

'What have you come here for, Lily?' she asked urgently. 'Matt's only just left, he could have seen you . . .'

Matt was the firm's accountant – bent, of course, and

clever as buggery at manipulating figures, moving money and generally keeping the taxman stumbling around in the dark while the boys enjoyed a very comfy lifestyle.

'I know he just left. I watched him go.' Lily turned to her old friend with a frigid smile. 'I know you wouldn't want him to see me. I respect that, Adrienne. Why rub the poor bastard's nose in it, eh?'

Adrienne at least had the grace to look ashamed at that.

Lily looked at her with disdain. Adrienne was still a very good-looking woman, Lily had to give her that. Long, thoroughbred legs, *almost* as shapely as Lily's own, and even longer. Her body buffed and golden, toned and tanned. Hair streaked blonde. Pretty dark eyes; nice straight teeth – due more to a dentist's skill than nature. Wearing a neat white t-shirt, figure-hugging jeans, a huge plaited leather belt slung low on her thin hips, and a lot of gold jewellery. But her face was a fraction too long for beauty, her jaw too pronounced. And she had a miserable face on her, as if life had proved a disappointment. Well, it probably had, married to a dull man like Matt, with his nose always buried in the accounts and – if the rumours were to be believed, and Lily thought they were – a prick like an acorn.

Adrienne had wrapped her arms around herself, as if feeling a sudden chill. It was warm, though: summer. Sunlight was beaming in on all the carefully dusted and polished furnishings.

'I . . . I never got the chance to apologize to you, did I?' Adrienne mumbled. Her eyes rose and they anxiously searched Lily's coldly set face. 'I'm sorry, Lils. Truly I am. That thing with Leo . . .'

'Thing?' Lily gave a bark of laughter. 'Oh, you mean your *affair* with my *husband*?'

'I know it was bad.'

'Oh yeah. But then that was you, wasn't it, Adrienne? Always ready to put out at a moment's notice.'

'That's not fair,' said Adrienne shakily.

'Oh, so now we're talking about what's fair?' Lily came up to the taller woman and glared at her. 'How about being banged up for twelve years for something you didn't do, Adrienne, what do you think about that? Do you think *that's* fair?'

'But you . . .' Adrienne's voice faltered. She bit her lip and lowered her eyes.

'But I *what*?' Lily leaned in close and Adrienne flinched and jerked back. 'What, Adrienne? Come on. Finish the sentence.'

'But you . . . you were found guilty. You . . .' Adrienne's voice trailed away again. She gulped convulsively. 'You . . . you killed Leo. They said so at the trial. That he knocked you about and . . . and had an affair with me . . . and that night, that same night he'd been with me, he went home, and then . . . you killed him.'

'And you believe that?' said Lily.

Adrienne nodded slowly. 'You were convicted. You did it.'

Lily nodded. 'And poor bloody Matt. The poor sod's still with you, after all *that*?'

'We talked it through. I said maybe we ought to split, but he didn't want to. So we made a go of things.'

'And you never did anything like that again, after Leo?'

Adrienne shook her head. She'd gone almost pale under her fake tan; it was giving her a jaundiced look.

'Pardon me if I fucking well laugh,' said Lily. 'Bet you've had more men than I've had hot dinners. You always were the gang bike.'

'Look, you've got *no right* coming in here, barging into

my home saying things like that to me,' said Adrienne, and her eyes were fiercer now, although bright with unshed tears. 'Your husband wasn't exactly fucking perfect, you know. And *you* couldn't have been all that, judging from how keen he was to bed *me*.'

'You *bitch*,' spat Lily, and slapped Adrienne, hard.

Adrienne grabbed at her burning cheek, and suddenly she looked frightened.

She didn't recognize this person. This wasn't the Lily she'd known years back. *This* Lily looked as though she really could kill someone in cold blood.

'You know, you ought to watch your step,' said Lily, pushing in even closer. 'You think I'm a murderess, remember? I do things to people, ain't that what the judge said? I'm a danger to society! You ought to remember that, next time you feel like reminding me of you and my old man dancing the horizontal tango.'

Now Adrienne was sweating. 'Look, I didn't mean . . .' she backtracked hastily.

'Yes you did. You meant every word. And to think he tried to deny it. Did you like the flowers, and – oh yeah – the Tiffany bracelet, the one he never gave *me*?'

Adrienne looked blank. 'What Tiffany bracelet?' she asked.

'Oh, don't give me all that old pony.'

'Leo never gave me anything like that.'

'Bollocks!'

'He didn't! What would have been the point? I couldn't wear it, could I? Matt would have spotted it straight away and asked where it came from, and I never wanted to upset Matt, not really, he was so good to me.'

'He was a bloody fool. Turning a blind eye to all your goings-on because he liked a nice, quiet, cosy domestic life.'

'Matt's a *good man*,' retorted Adrienne.

'Yeah, but boring as fuck. Or else why were you crawling into *my* bed and shagging *my* husband, Adrienne? With Leo constantly denying everything, telling me I was going nuts, and you know what? After a while I actually started to think he was right, I was just going crazy, I was paranoid, just like he said I was. When all the time I was *right*. Him and you were getting cosy, and all the time there I was being made a fool of. You and him. It makes me feel *sick* just thinking about it.'

'It wasn't like that,' blurted Adrienne, tears spilling over and streaming down her face, making ugly tracks in her foundation. 'I loved Leo. I'd have left Matt for him, I told Leo I would, but he didn't want that.'

'And what about *me* in all this?' shouted Lily in rage. 'Leo was married. To *me*. And he had two little kids. How the hell could you have done that, split up my marriage?'

'For God's sake!' Adrienne erupted, throwing her arms wide. 'You didn't even love him! You never got over your infatuation with Nick bloody O'Rourke, did you? So can you *really* wonder that he looked elsewhere?'

You didn't even love him, thought Lily.

'You know I'm telling the truth,' said Adrienne, pushing home her advantage when she saw Lily's sudden uncertainty. 'And it's not as if I was the only one.'

Now Lily stood frozen in shock.

There was a long, long silence.

Then she said: '*What* did you say?'

'I *wanted* to be the only one.' Adrienne swiped irritably at her cheeks, leaving blotchy streaks in her make-up and mascara stains under her eyes. 'I wanted him to love me like I loved him. But he didn't. There were *others* . . .'

Others, thought Lily in a daze. *What the fuck . . .?*

'What are you talking about? There were no others,' she said, drawing back, looking at Adrienne incredulously.

And suddenly Adrienne was laughing. 'Oh, Jesus,' she gasped.

'If you're getting fucking hysterical I'm going to give you another belt round the chops,' Lily warned her. 'Now shut it. And tell me what you're on about.'

'Oh Lily, and you talk about *Matt* being a fool. You were so innocent, so bloody little-wifey-indoors that you didn't even know what time of day it was, did you? You *still* don't. You seriously believe it, don't you? You seriously think I was the only one.'

'You're telling me you weren't? Straight up?'

'No *way* was I the only one,' said Adrienne, and she wasn't laughing now – in fact she looked sad. 'Sodding Leo.'

'Tell me about the other one, then,' said Lily flatly. She felt as though she'd just stepped into a new nightmare.

'Other *one*?' Adrienne shook her head and let out a guffaw. 'God's sakes, Lily! Other *one*! That's priceless!'

So Adrienne went on to tell her about the rest of Leo's 'girls', and how she'd hated that there'd been others.

'I tracked them down,' she said, and there was a glint of triumph in her eyes as she said that. 'I tracked them *all* down. I even had a list of their names and addresses.'

7

Freddy King was in the pub with his brother Si. There was an empty place at the table they always occupied in their local. It was Leo's place, and Freddy nearly choked with emotion every time he saw it. *No one* sat there, unless they wanted to start wearing their arse as a neck ornament.

'She's out,' he said to Si.

'I heard,' said Si, who was older than Freddy, and wiser. He watched Freddy, who was now tapping a beer mat on the table, *tap tap tap*. He was on edge, and who could blame him? She was *out*.

'So what we gonna do?' asked Freddy.

'Do?' Si lifted a finger and caught the barman's eye. He indicated their table. The barman nodded. 'What do you mean?'

Freddy leaned forward. 'You know fucking well.' *Tap tap tap*. 'That cunt wants sorting.'

The barman came hurrying over and put two more pints on the table.

Si nodded his thanks. Took a leisurely mouthful of beer. Looked at his brother. 'She's done her time,' he shrugged.

'She ain't anywhere near paying for what she done, and you know it,' spat Freddy angrily. He threw the beer mat down and it skidded off the wet table. 'Twelve years? What the fuck is that? – it's taking the piss! Our brother's *dead*; he ain't coming back and walking free like that bitch is.'

'All in good time,' said Si. He leaned in and lowered his voice. 'What, you want to get yourself banged up? Do anything right now and the Old Bill won't have far to look, will they, you tosser? You're always in a fucking rush, that's your trouble.'

Freddy's face worked, his jaw clenching and unclenching. He knew Si was right, but that made it worse. Like he had no control over any of this. Like that cow was in charge, not him, not the King boys.

Si reached out and clasped Freddy's meaty forearm.

'*Look*, Fred,' he said urgently. 'Wait a bit. That's all I'm asking. Give it a year, two years; you can do the bitch any way you want, but right now? Forget it.'

'*Forget it?*' Freddy leapt to his feet and shouted the words. Heads turned. Si gave him a 'shut up' look. 'No, *you* forget it, Si. I fucking well won't.'

And he was off, barging across the bar, bumping into punters in his headlong rush for the door. A bloke with a pint slopped all down him said, 'Hey! Watch it, mate,' and that was enough.

'I ain't your *mate!*'

Freddy started in, punching the man hard in the jaw. Glass and beer flew into the air. The man reeled back and Freddy piled in on him, punching, kicking, red-faced with fury. Si was there in a second and grabbed his brother, dragging him back, shoving him hard towards the door.

'Get *out* of it, you silly bugger,' he snarled, and Freddy

went, the red rage still gripping him – but this was Si, and he always took notice of Si.

They lurched, panting, out into the car park, wary punters skirting around them, shouts and curses following them out.

'Just keep walking,' said Si, hurrying towards the car, jumping in, starting the motor. He'd had three pints, but who gave a toss? Laws were for other people, not for him, not for the King boys. Freddy jumped in too. In minutes they were a mile away and Si was just clipping on his seat belt and telling his brother to calm down.

'You want to keep a lid on that temper,' said Si irritably.

He felt like he'd been saying that to Freddy ever since the silly git turned two years old. Freddy had never understood the word *subtle*, but Si did. Si knew that sometimes you just had to think things through and bide your time. He didn't want Freddy blundering about upsetting Saz and Oli. The bitch was their mother, after all. He had to tread carefully. He *would* act, but discreetly, choosing his moment with care.

'Hey! I got every right to be mad,' said Freddy. 'She's out, and now you're telling me there's not a thing I can do about it.' Freddy swore to himself that he was going to sort that cow. He owed it to Leo. Usually he paid attention when Si made his feelings clear, but not this time, no way.

Si sent his brother a sidelong glance as he tore through the lanes. *Crisis over*, he thought. Freddy seemed calm again. For now. And thank fuck for that, because tomorrow was the wedding, their niece was getting married. Si was giving her away. The last thing any of them needed right now was Freddy kicking off.

8

Lily was sitting in Becks's kitchen, her head in her hands. Becks put a mug of coffee in front of her, and sat down opposite.

'So what did Adrienne say? Was it bad?' asked Becks, chewing gum.

Lily dropped her hands. She stared at Becks.

Becks stopped chewing. 'What?' she asked nervously.

'Did you know about the others?'

A wary smile formed on Becks's lips. 'Others?'

'Leo's other women.'

Becks's mouth dropped open. '*What* other women?'

'Are you bullshitting me, Becks?'

'No! Absolutely not. What other women? I knew about Adrienne, shit, everyone did.'

Yeah, thought Lily. *Everyone did.*

The court case had brought *that* right out into the open. Adrienne's involvement with Leo had been all over the tabloids, along with photos of Lily, the wronged wife turned murderess.

Adrienne had told her that although the police had questioned her about Leo, she had never said a word to them or to anyone else about the other women in his life. The list was her private property, and the detective who had tracked down 'those tarts' was bound by client confidentiality, she'd told Lily smugly.

'You didn't think to tell me about Adrienne,' said Lily to Becks.

Becks looked pained. 'I didn't want to hurt you, Lils. I nearly told you a dozen times, but then I thought, would *I* want to know? And I backed off from it.'

'You mean you wouldn't want to know? If Joe was shagging about the place? Really?'

Becks shook her head, her jaw moving rhythmically as she chewed the gum. 'Nope. Ignorance is bliss, Lils, that's what I say. Not that Joe would do that. Not his style. And anyway, I'd have his balls for earrings if he did. But come on. My Joe? No way.'

Lily thought back to when ignorance had nearly driven her half mad, with Leo saying she was imagining it all and her own mind playing tricks on her; she'd got more paranoid and more miserable by the day. It hurt her that Becks had kept this huge, awful secret from her. But that was Becks. She'd been a great friend. She'd visited Lily inside – while she was in Holloway, anyway; always cheering, always cheerful, when no one else had bothered. Lily would never forget that. But sometimes, you only ever got half the story from her. And sometimes, you didn't get the story at all.

'So what are you saying? What, is there more than one?' Becks asked, curiosity eating her up.

'Keep going,' said Lily, sipping the hot, strong coffee.

'Two then?'

Lily shook her head.

'Get out. More than *two*?'

'More than three,' said Lily.

'Four?' Becks's eyes were huge with amazement, her jaw moving like a piston. 'You're having a laugh.'

'Try six,' said Lily.

'What the . . .?' Becks was gazing at Lily as if she'd gone mad. '*No.* You can't be serious.'

'Got it straight from the horse's mouth. Adrienne's, to be precise.'

Lily gave a grim smile even though inside she felt sick with the betrayal of it. To learn that Leo had been unfaithful to her with one woman was bad enough; to be told straight out that he was a serial adulterer was painful. All right, they hadn't exactly been love's young dream: Adrienne was right about that. Leo had been second-best for Lily, and maybe he had sensed that, who knew? But six women? That was *really* taking the piss.

Although, thinking about it, she supposed there was a pattern here. The three brothers, Leo, Simon and Freddy, had been sired by a philanderer, after all. Old man Bobby – or 'Bubba' as he was more commonly known – King had put it about all over the place, everyone knew that, right up until he fell off the twig. Leo was just following the parental example. Freddy was still single and fancy-free, he could do what he liked. But if Leo had followed his old man's example and cheated, then it was entirely possible that Si was doing the same, married or not.

If I was Maeve, Lily thought, *I'd have my eye on Si right now.*

She thought again of Leo, screwing around and then coming home to her. For God's sake! Their love life hadn't been all that, but she could have got a dose of *anything*, the selfish bastard. Anything at all. The thought of that repulsed her, gave her the dry heaves. And it filled her with rage, too. That he'd treated her with such total disrespect; treated her like an *idiot*.

Lily sipped at the coffee. Tried to get a grip even though she felt she was losing it. Six women. Not one. Six, including Adrienne.

And even if Adrienne's in the clear, any one of those others could have had a reason to blow Leo's brains to kingdom come, she thought.

'Adrienne had him followed,' said Lily as Becks sat there transfixed. Lily let out a harsh laugh. 'Can you believe that? She had a private detective on the job. His mistress didn't trust him. Didn't mind him shagging the wife, but anyone else? Forget it. Apparently she suspected there was another woman tucked away somewhere, and she wanted to know who. So she hired this guy and he turned up a whole stable of whores, of which she was just one.'

'Holy shit,' said Becks faintly. 'So who are these others?'

'I don't know yet. But it certainly puts a different complexion on things, don't it?'

'What do you mean?'

'I *mean*,' said Lily patiently, 'I didn't kill Leo, but *someone* did. And they were happy to let me do time for it.'

'You think one of these women . . .?'

Lily shrugged and stood up. 'Dunno.'

'Yeah, but Lily . . . look, if whoever did it was crazy enough to blow Leo's brains out, then . . . well . . . for God's sake, they could do it to you, too.' Becks raised troubled eyes to her friend's face. 'You know what? If I was you, I'd just let it lie. Let it go. It's all past now, anyway. Try and forget it. Move on.'

'I *can't* move on, Becks.' Lily's fist hit the table in frustration. Becks jumped. 'Not until I find out who stitched me up. Lost me my freedom. My home. My kids. Everything I had, they stripped it off me. And I've got to know who. And *why*.'

Becks was shaking her head, her face solemn. 'Don't do it. Don't start in on this, Lils. Bad things could happen to you if you carry on with this, I'm warning you.'

Lils reached over and patted Becks's shoulder. 'You're a good friend, Becks, but come on, get real. Bad things have already happened to me. And I think it's about time they started happening to someone else. Now, I need to use your phone, is that okay?'

'Sure,' said Becks doubtfully, and Lily went off into the hall, closing the door firmly behind her.

When Becks checked the landline later – Lily was in the bath again; Jesus, how many baths could one woman take? – she found that Lily had keyed in 1-4-1 before making her call, so that neither Becks nor her husband Joe could easily find out who she'd been in contact with.

When Lily came downstairs wearing Becks's spare bathrobe, her smile was hard and cold. Becks looked at her nervously.

'So!' said Lily brightly. 'What am I going to wear to this big wedding then? Hope you've got something suitable I can borrow.'

Oh Gawd help us, thought Becks.

9

'What do you think, Aunt Maeve?' asked Saz King, turning back and forth before the big cheval mirror in her bedroom, holding out her ruffled skirts, inviting favourable comments.

Saz was feeling pretty damned pleased with herself. She loved being with Richie and couldn't wait to be married to him. Richie made her feel special, adored. He was a little older than her – eight years – and sometimes she did think: *What's all that about?* Was she looking for a father figure because Dad was gone?

Well, maybe she was. Whatever, she felt happy today. She relished being the centre of attention and was eager to marry stoic, stable Richie because yes, all right, with him she felt *safe*.

Maeve King, Si's wife, looked at her niece and thought, *She's the most beautiful girl in the whole world but my God! – she's the spitting bloody image of her mother.*

Incredible to think that Saz was twenty-one years old, astonishing to think how fast the years had flown by; how one minute she'd been a bewildered and grief-ridden nine-year-old child, and then the next, pow! All grown up. And so eerily like Lily, too.

'Oh Saz! I think you look lovely,' said Maeve, choking back a tear.

She was determined to make this a happy day for Saz, the best of her entire life. She thought of what Si had told her last night, about his brother Freddy kicking off because Lily was out. Maeve thought that Freddy was mental, a bit of a mouth-breather. Si and Leo had always been the brains of the outfit. No one had told Saz that Lily was out. Si would have thrown a fit if they had. He had discussed it with Maeve, of course he had; but they'd agreed it was best that she didn't know.

'Do you think the veil's too much?' asked Saz.

'No, it's perfect,' said Maeve.

She thought that Saz couldn't have looked more exquisite if she'd tried. Money was no object, of course; never had been, not in the King family. If a King woman wanted something – a swimming pool, a diamond necklace, a designer wedding dress, *voilà*! It appeared as if by magic.

Saz was turning and preening in front of the mirror, smiling secretively at her reflection as sunlight poured through the big balcony windows, highlighting her shimmering loveliness in fairy motes of gold and silver.

'You got your garter on?' she asked.

Saz smiled and raised the ruffled hem of the dress to reveal white silk Jimmy Choos, white stockings and a blue beribboned garter. 'Right here,' she said.

'Don't let him twang it,' warned Maeve with a laugh. 'That's a family heirloom, that is.'

Think your mother wore it too, shot through her brain, then she wished it hadn't. She frowned. Why did she have to keep thinking of Lily today?

The answer was simple: she was taking Lily's place; so, even if Lily wasn't here, her spirit was hovering over the proceedings like a rotten odour. They'd all moved on with their lives. Maeve and Si had become guardians to their two nieces, and to lessen the upheaval for the girls they had rented out their own place just up the road and moved into The Fort. They had never used the master suite; too many memories, and all of them unsettling.

'Where's the car? Isn't it here yet?' Saz was now demanding fretfully, going to the window, looking out.

Saz might *look* like Lily, but deep down she wasn't like her mother at all. Saz was quicksilver, but Lily had been like rock: calm, immovable, a bit of a house mouse really, but with an aura of stillness and strength about her. Maeve could still remember the first time she'd ever seen Leo weave his testosterone-and-bling-laden spell over Lily. They'd all been crowding around his flash car after school – they'd all been mates, all familiar with each other – and the other, bolder girls, Mary and Becks, Adrienne and Julia, had been all over Leo and his pals like a rash: teasing, flirting, flashing their big smiles, their coltish legs and their pert, perfect teenage boobs. Maeve had joined in a bit, although she was no beauty, not like some of the others; but Lily had hung back, uninterested.

Maeve shook herself.

This was Saz's big day and she was going to make sure that she enjoyed it. It was not Lily standing there, but Saz, Maeve told herself firmly. But Maeve remembered that she had been a bridesmaid when Lily had married Leo in eighty-seven. Maeve had thought Lily might go for a Princess Di-type thing, all puff sleeves and full skirts, but Lily had stayed true to type and worn a simple ivory shift

– with a large bouquet of cream roses to conceal the bump of her pregnancy.

And here was the result of that pregnancy, standing before Maeve now. A beautiful full-grown woman who shared her mother's bone-deep and effortless brand of glamour. Lily had always looked good – Maeve had envied her that. Maeve had to work hard at looking good, particularly now an early menopause had hit her like a ton of shit and she'd gained two stone almost overnight.

Maeve had made a special effort today, because she was acting as 'mother of the bride', wasn't she? Today of all days, Maeve had to look good. So she had squeezed her short, dumpy form into pull-in pants and a fuchsia pink silk dress and matching jacket, with a little 'fascinator' clip-on water-fall of feathers and flowers sitting atop her streaked blonde new Judy Finnegan-type hairdo.

But looking at her lovely niece she had to admit that, beside Saz King, she just looked like mutton done up as spring lamb.

Jesus, just look at her, she thought.

Saz was wearing a tight-fitting pearl-studded gold satin bodice that showed off her full breasts to their best advantage, tapering down to display a neat waist before flaring out into a huge, impossibly full skirt that was a cascade of opulent cream silk ruffles. The train was small, balancing the massive length of the skirt. Saz's long blonde hair was swept up behind a pearl-encrusted tiara. Her face, with its neat nose, large, serious, navy blue eyes (now those weren't like Lily's, and thank God for it) and wide, smiling mouth had been professionally made up. She glowed with radiance. Suddenly she turned to Maeve and grinned.

'It's here!'

Maeve looked out. The Rolls-Royce Silver Phantom, cream and decked out with white ribbons, was coming up the drive.

'I'll give your Uncle Si a shout,' said Maeve, and took herself off to find him.

'And where the hell is Oli?' Saz shouted after her.

'You're not supposed to do that,' said Oli King sternly, pushing her dark curling hair out of her eyes and ignoring the almost unbearable, palpitating heat of desire that was sweeping over her. She sneaked a look out through the stable door when she heard a motor passing. 'And look, there's the damned car and I'm supposed to be in there helping Saz . . . no, don't do that . . .'

Oli was eighteen to Saz's twenty-one, and she thought that her sister Saz had been *born* old. She, however, had not. She wasn't planning on getting married, settling down, all that boring load of bollocks, not ever. She planned one day to live on the Left Bank in Paris and have a lot of lovers. Beyond that, she hadn't planned much at all. But then . . . then she had met *Jase*.

'Do what?' asked Jase, his fingers busy inside the terracotta-coloured silk bodice of her bridesmaid's dress.

'*That*,' she snapped, although the rough touch of his hands against her cool-skinned breasts and hard, urgently aroused nipples was driving her insane. 'Stop it. Or I'll tell Uncle Si on you.'

Jase worked for Si. Doing what, Oli was never entirely sure.

Ask no questions and you'll be told no lies: that was the family motto. Obviously it was Jase's motto, too, because whenever she'd tentatively skirted around the subject of what he actually *did* for Uncle Si, Jase was always evasive. He was

Head of Security at the family club, she knew *that*, but that wasn't all he did for Si and Freddy, she just knew it. There were too many nights away, too many hushed phone calls and delivering packages, too many times when he was distracted or distant.

Jase was gorgeous, though. Curly dark hair, big shoulders, narrow laughing dark green eyes. He looked great in the morning suit he was wearing, a white carnation in the button-hole. He'd said *she* looked great in the terracotta-coloured dress, too, and had promptly brought her in here and tried to get the damned thing off her.

Oli hated dresses anyway. She lived in jeans and t-shirts. High heels *killed* her. It was all very well for Saz, poncing about like Lady Muck, but she hated all this show. She was happier here, in the old disused stables, with Jase. If only he'd behave.

'You've got fantastic tits,' said Jase, popping one out of the top of the bodice to admire it more easily.

'No . . .' moaned Oli, but when he put his mouth to her breast, lapping the nipple with his tongue, she stopped protesting. She was absolutely smitten with Jase. She loved all this. She'd been terrified the first time, terrified and sort of *flattered* too. Because Jase had told her he loved her, and then he'd done it to her, and it had been her absolute first time, very quick, brutally sexual, and quite painful. And then had come the wait, the horrible, anxious wait, and the fear. *I could be pregnant*, she'd thought over and over, feeling sick with dread.

That was how she felt most times they did it now – sick with terror as well as desire.

'We've got time for a quicky,' said Jase, already lifting her skirts.

'No we *haven't*,' said Oli, thinking: *Oh shit, not again*.

'Yes we have.' He nuzzled into her neck. 'You let me last time. You liked it.' He took her hand, stroked it over the bulge in his trousers.

Oli groaned. She felt nearly incandescent with need now. She *had* liked it. But they'd used no protection, nothing, and she'd been *so* relieved when her period had come on. She looked down. He'd unzipped himself and now he was holding his naked penis, hugely engorged and aroused, in his hand. 'Come on, Oli. You know you want to . . .'

Oh, and how she wanted to. She was so lucky to have Jase for her boyfriend, she knew that. He could take his pick of the girls in their circle, but he'd chosen her, she was *such* a lucky girl and she didn't want him thinking she was a complete washout; she couldn't bear the idea of him going off her, going with one of the many others who were just waiting for their chance with him.

Sometimes in life you have to make instant choices, Oli knew that, and she was impulsive by nature, she *liked* to make her decisions quickly.

She made this one without any further hesitation. She tore off her knickers, leaned back, parted her legs, lifted her skirts.

'All right. But only put it in a little bit, okay?' She was panting.

He put it right in. *Way* in. She gasped as it slipped into her wetness like an eel through water. Oh, it was *good*.

But too quick, too quick again, leaving her throbbing, not sore but restless, *unfulfilled*. And afterwards she felt more sober. Her period was already late and she knew that until it came, she'd be in a state of horrible anxiety. An unplanned pregnancy didn't figure in her Bohemian dreams of the future. Not at *all*.

10

The bells were ringing and so was Si King's head as the Silver Phantom rolled up at the church, him and his lovely niece resplendent in the back, him wishing he hadn't bothered with the pub last night. Trust Freddy to start acting up because that bitch Lily was on the loose again. Jesus, his head was throbbing. He'd have to tap Maeve up for some aspirin. She always carried a stash of supplies in her handbag.

Patience was Simon's forte. It wasn't Freddy's, and it hadn't really been Leo's either. But Si always played the long game. And he was going to get Lily sorted, but not unless he could be one hundred per cent certain that he could fix it to look accidental. He'd been thinking about it, and he thought that maybe he could. He didn't want to upset the girls in any way, not if it could be avoided; there was always that to be considered.

'*Now* what the hell's Oli up to? She's going to ruin her hair,' said Saz from behind her veil.

Si looked. Oli was outside the vestibule with Jase, one of his boys. Jase and a couple of the other security guys were acting as ushers today. She was trying on his top hat, knocking her flowered headdress askew, laughing up at him as he grinned back down at her.

Si thought that Oli's hair was beyond ruining. It was wild, dark and curly, and nothing would tame it – a bit like Oli herself. He frowned as he gazed out at the handsome couple indulging in shameless flirtation. Maybe he ought to mark Jase's card for him today, tell him to back off a bit. He'd been considering this for a little while; he'd noticed the play between the two of them was getting a bit more serious. Jase was a smart youngster, a good worker, but a chancer; he'd see Oli as a good ticket to advancement in the King organization and Si could tell that he was working the old charm on his gullible niece like a pro. Yeah, definitely time to have a word. Didn't want the silly little git getting Oli up the duff or anything drastic like that. Then he'd *really* have to step in, and Jase would be sorry.

'She looks beautiful,' Si said smoothly to his flustered niece.

'She looks tatty, just like she always does,' fretted Saz.

'She looks lovely, and so do you. Now relax. Enjoy the day.'

The vicar was standing just inside the porch now. Jase had gone back inside.

Smart move, you little arsehole, thought Si, his headache making him irritable.

Oli was there by the vicar, patting her headdress back into place, rosebuds and bits of greenery tumbling out of it, her expression one of extreme innocence as she smiled over at her uncle and sister. Looking like butter wouldn't melt. Si wasn't fooled. Saz was cool; Oli was the hot one. He guessed that Saz's Richard wasn't in for much fun tonight, but if he'd been marrying Oli, it would have been quite another story.

The uniformed chauffeur was opening the car door.

'Well, here we go,' said Si, and gallantly helped his niece alight from the car. 'Time to get married, young Saz.'

It was a lovely ceremony. Everyone said so. All the mob boys and their wives were there, decked out in their best. The church was overflowing with cream floral arrangements to match Saz's dress, and when she walked up the aisle there were audible gasps from among the guests, she looked so astonishingly beautiful. Many of them thought, *so like Lily*, but they would never have said that aloud. Some things you just didn't mention, not on a day like today. Not unless you wanted to get your teeth back in an ashtray from one of the King boys. The Kings were crim royalty, you didn't upset them, it wasn't wise.

Richard stood at the altar, beaming with pride as Saz walked towards him. His smile remained all through the reading of the vows, which he stumbled over endearingly. But Si – and Oli – caught the slight frown of irritation on Saz's brow as he did that.

Little Miss Perfect, thought Oli. *Jesus, Saz was such a spoiled madam.*

Maeve stood there beside Si and watched the whole thing with a tear in her eye. She'd caught the frown too. She knew Saz had been spoiled, far more so than Oli, because Saz had been more affected by what had happened all those years back. She'd been older; she'd understood more of what was going on. And so Maeve had tried doubly hard to help the little girl come to terms with her loss. Tried to give her as normal a life as she could.

Then came the signing of the register, and the newly married couple emerged from the vestry looking so happy.

'She'll have his bollocks on a skewer before the year's out,' muttered Freddy King to his mate.

Richard was a quiet guy who did small jobs for Si and Freddy; he was a good worker, but needed to grow a backbone. You only had to look at Saz King to see she was a ball-breaker *extraordinaire*. Gorgeous, though. But Saz's mum was a nut job. How far could the apple *really* fall from the tree?

Organ music was echoing around the church and now the couple were walking back down the aisle, smiling at their friends and relatives, Saz looking as stately as a queen, nodding around at the sea of faces like a ham actor taking plaudits.

'How long do you give it?' hissed Freddy.

His mate shrugged. 'Six months? Maybe nine if she drops a sprog quick.'

Saz and Richard went out into the sunshine, the guests piling out behind them, throwing confetti. Saz was giggling and picking bits of multicoloured paper out of her hair when she saw the figure standing nearby, very still, just watching.

The woman standing there had Saz's own face, but it was calmer, sterner, older but no less beautiful. She was shabbily dressed in a creased and rumpled cream linen suit that fitted where it touched. It looked as though it had been made for someone a foot taller than her, and it hung around her like a shroud. She was perched on high white stiletto heels that had sunk into the grass and were now muddy from the soft earth. Her blonde hair was scraped back into a careless ponytail. She wore no make-up.

Saz froze. The woman smiled slightly. Saz went sheet-white.

Richard was looking at her, wondering what had happened.

She'd gone from laughing to dead-faced and looking on the verge of fainting away, all in the space of seconds.

'Saz? What's up, sweetheart?'

'Oh my *God*,' mumbled Saz, clutching at her throat, looking like she might actually throw up.

'What . . . ?' Oli had come forward, wondering what sort of drama-queen act her big sis was putting on now, Jase trailing behind her. Si and Maeve came out, chattering and smiling, and then abruptly the chattering and smiling ceased, and the only sound was the bells ringing, and even that sound was no longer cheerful and joyous. Now the bells sounded like death knells: ominous, threatening.

'Jesus, it's *her*,' hissed a woman in the crowd.

The whole party stood stock-still and looked at the woman standing there, her eyes full of desperate love, her face naked with longing as she looked at the beautiful bride, the stunning bridesmaid.

Lily felt tears start in her eyes as she looked at them. *Her girls! Her lovely girls!*

Oh God – they were so grown up! But she knew them; she still knew them. And they knew her, she could see it in their eyes. But . . . they didn't look happy to see her. It hurt so bad, to see the horror and the . . . yes, the *disgust* on those beloved faces. But she was going to get over that. She would have to do hard work, win them over, make it all right again. They thought – they had been *duped* into believing that she had killed their father. Somehow, she was going to have to show them that it wasn't true. That she was still their mother, that she loved them.

Tentatively, she started forward. She could see Si King and his wife Maeve standing a little behind Saz, and Freddy was there, staring at her with hatred in his eyes. Well of *course* he hated her, he thought she'd done it, but she hadn't. She hadn't. Somehow she was going to show them all, prove it to them.

Somehow.

She walked forward, her heart thudding in her chest like a bass drum. Her hands were clammy. Becks's high heels were too big for her and the pointed heels kept sticking in the ground, so she staggered slightly, but she kept that faint smile on her face, determined to reassure her girls, not to frighten them. No, she would never do that, but she had to make them see that she was still their mum, she still loved them.

Saz shrank back as Lily approached.

Abruptly the bells stopped pealing and the silence was shocking. Lily stopped walking and stood there, two paces away from her daughters, her eyes going from one to the other, a tear slipping down her face as she looked at them with an expression of hope and wonderment.

'My beautiful girls,' she said, her voice cracking with emotion. 'I've missed you so much.'

Saz moved suddenly, startling everybody. With a shriek, she hit Lily with the huge and exquisite bouquet she was carrying. Cream roses flew, pulled loose by the impact. Lily fell back, raising an arm to shield herself, her expression almost comical with hurt and bewilderment. Saz hit her again, and again. Trying to protect herself, Lily saw Oli make a half-gesture towards Saz, maybe to get her to stop, maybe to help her beat her own mother, Lily didn't know. She staggered back, hobbling, one heel catching in the turf. Ignominiously, she fell, pitching backwards onto the ground, all the wind knocked out of her.

'*Murderess!*' yelled Saz as Richard tried to hold her back.

'Jesus, Saz, stop it,' he said, his face a mixture of embarrassment at his new wife's behaviour, and disbelief that *she* should have the brass neck to show up on a day like this.

'I won't stop it! She killed him! She killed my dad!' Now Saz was sobbing, struggling, still trying to reach Lily, still trying to inflict damage.

Trembling, Lily knelt up on the muddy turf. Her hands were dirty; there was a smear of mud on Becks's linen dress. She got to her feet and found that one of the heels on the white shoes had snapped. She hobbled lopsidedly, a pathetic figure before a huge crowd of hate-filled onlookers.

Lily swallowed and swiped at her eyes, leaving a trail of mud on her cheek. She could take hatred from the others, but from her own girls? From Oli? From Saz? But that was what was written clearly on their faces. They hated her.

Now her eyes were searching the crowds, seeing the expressions that were a mixture of horror and obscene delight. Some of these bitches would be dining out for a month on this day. No doubt about that. She saw Maeve there, not far behind Saz, looking oddly triumphant, and there was Freddy, looking at her as though he would like to slit her open right now. Looking at her as if she was a marked woman, living on borrowed time. Which she was. She knew she was, but she didn't much care. Doing stir got you like that. You just got through it. Somehow, she had. And now all she cared about was proving to her girls that she was not their father's killer. Anything else, she didn't give a toss.

Then she realized that she could no longer see Si in the crowds. Anxiety was suddenly gnawing at Lily's innards. Lily had always thought Si was like one of those big spiders you see sometimes on your bedroom wall – so long as you could see where he was, you felt okay. Worried, but okay.

But when Si slipped out of sight, you had to wonder *now what the hell's he up to?* Si was all secrets and schemes. Freddy would be dangerous if he had half a brain, but at least he'd always come straight out with it. Si was the true danger.

She shouldn't have come here. Becks had been right. She was aware of how shabby she looked, wearing ill-fitting borrowed clothes and shoes. She knew she'd been so long inside that she'd forgotten how to present herself to the world, how to behave. She knew she'd made a wrong move. She knew she'd have to pay for it, too.

She stood there, tears streaming down her cheeks, flinching from the look on Saz's face, all twisted up with hatred, and her eyes came to rest on Nick O'Rourke's face in the crowd – Leo's best man, his best friend, his business partner. Dark hair, nearly black eyes with a hard, unforgiving expression in them. Tall and broad-shouldered and wearing a morning suit like he'd been born to it. He stared back at her, and very gently shook his head.

For God's sake, his eyes said. *What the fuck are you doing?*

Lily bowed her head, defeated. She didn't know what she was doing. That was a fact. Her own daughter had just assaulted her; she was cringing inside with hurt and horror. Saz hated her. She glanced up, looked at Oli. Against her dark hair, Oli's face was blanched white. Her eyes were resting on her mother, but not with warmth. She was staring at Lily as she would at a deranged stranger, likely at any moment to freak out and inflict damage.

Lily thought miserably, *That is exactly what I've done here. I've ruined Saz's day, she'll never forgive me now.*

Not that there had been much chance of that anyway. But she had to try, didn't she? Even if she'd got off to a disastrous start. Supposing she got the chance, after this?

Her eyes searched the crowds. She still couldn't see Si. That was worrying. That was *frightening*.

'I'm sorry,' she said loudly, the words half choked with tears. 'I shouldn't have come. I'm sorry.'

And she turned and limped off, feeling their eyes boring into her back, feeling their hatred, feeling like *shit*.

11

'So . . . how'd it go?' asked Becks.

Lily looked up from the kitchen table and gave her friend a mirthless smile.

'How does it *look?*' she asked bitterly. She had come back dirt-smeared, limping, sobbing her heart out. Talk about stupid questions! Seeing Becks's recoil of hurt, she added: 'Sorry.'

Lily dragged her hands over her head, rubbed at her tired, teary eyes. 'Sorry, Becks. I shouldn't take it out on you. It was a fucking disaster. And I'm sorry, I've ruined your bloody shoes too. I've ruined everything.'

Becks sat down opposite. She reached out and patted Lily's hand. 'Bugger the shoes,' she said, unwrapping a new pack of gum. She popped it in her mouth. 'Don't matter a bit. They were only cheapies. But I told you you shouldn't have gone.'

'Oh, thanks a bunch for *that*, Becks,' snarled Lily. Then she shook her hands in front of her face, clutched at her head. 'Sorry, Becks. I'm sorry. I just had to see her, today of all days . . . Jesus, Becks, my own daughter's wedding and I didn't even know the damned thing was happening, how do you think that made me feel? Like a fucking reject, that's how. Which is what I am. I'm a bloody pariah. They looked at me . . . shit, they all looked at me like I was unhinged. Like I was going to cut their throats or something. And the girls. My girls . . .' Lily's voice trailed away. She shook her head. She couldn't even get the words out.

'Did . . . Si King see you there?' asked Becks cautiously.

Lily looked up at her friend's face. 'Yeah,' she said, fighting back more tears. 'Oh yeah, he saw me. And Freddy too.'

'Shit,' said Becks, her chewing going into overdrive. 'You gotta watch them two, Lily. You've got to be more careful.'

'Why?' Lily gave a mad laugh. 'I ain't done anything! And even if I *had*, I done the time for it. I done someone else's time, Becks. Not mine. Someone else's. Do you think that's right?'

Becks shook her head.

'No. Well neither do I.'

'But Lily,' Becks's voice was tentative, her expression uneasy, 'what can you do about it? It's all too late now. It's done. And you know what I think? I really think the best thing you can do is . . . take off somewhere. Just go away. Somewhere new. Start again, make a new life for yourself.'

Lily looked at Becks in surprise. 'What?' she said at last. 'Just . . . go away? Forget my girls? Forget that some *arsehole* fitted me up for all this? You ain't serious.'

'I am,' said Becks, leaning forward and stabbing the table with a French-manicured fingernail to emphasize her point. 'I'm completely serious, Lils. If you stay around here . . . what will you do? How will you live?'

'I've got plans,' said Lily stubbornly.

'Lils, listen to me for the love of God. The Kings got it in for you. You know that. It's only a matter of time before they make their move, and . . .' Becks's voice faded. She stared at the table.

'And what?' prompted Lily.

'And . . . look, I'm sorry, Lils, but Joe . . . he's not happy about any of this. He don't want trouble with the King brothers. Who'd want that? You'd have to be mental to upset that pair.'

Lily was staring at Becks's face. Her eyes were still averted, avoiding contact with Lily's own. 'So what are you saying, Becks?' she asked, but she knew, she *knew* what was coming.

'Joe thinks, I mean, *we* think, that . . . oh fuck it all, Lily, we don't think you should stay here any more. I'm sorry.'

Lily's face was a mask now, hiding her hurt, hiding her shock. This was *Becks*, after all. Her best friend in all the world.

'They've talked to Joe, have they?' she asked, and her voice sounded small, strained – not her own.

Joe was on the firm: *everyone* in their circle was on the firm. Antagonizing the Kings was not a sensible option.

Becks said nothing. She nodded. Lily saw it then, in Becks's eyes – the fear. She didn't mind helping Lily, but there was a line and Lily had crossed it. It was all very well to help a mate in trouble, but when that help put you in bother with the Kings, then you had to say, *enough*.

'I don't mind if you want to tell the probation people you're still staying here,' said Becks hurriedly. 'I talked to Joe about it – he don't mind doing that much. We'll cover for you, if you want.'

'Right,' said Lily. 'Yeah. Okay. Thanks for that. I've got an appointment to see her here next week . . .'

'No probs. You show up, I'll be here, it'll be cool.'

'Right.'

The perfect end to a perfect day. Her daughters hated her guts and now Becks was turfing her out the door. Lily was dry-eyed now, numb with the shock of it all.

The doorbell rang.

'I'll get it,' said Becks, glad of the interruption. Lily could see the relief etched on her face as she bolted from the kitchen and along the hall. She heard Becks talking to someone, a man's voice, light and husky. For a moment her heart leapt into her throat and she thought: *Si King, oh God help me, or is it that lunatic Freddy?*

Becks came back into the kitchen. She didn't bring the Kings with her. Lily, pale-faced and wretched, looked up at her. Becks's expression was awkward, her glance slipping away from Lily's.

'It's the private detective bloke,' she said. 'The one you phoned.'

Lily had forgotten she'd made this appointment. She'd forgotten everything, in the excitement of getting to the church to be humiliated, rejected. An image of Saz's white, horrified face came into her brain again and she squeezed her eyes shut to block it out. The pain was awful.

She opened her eyes and stood up. She was still wearing the cream linen; it was creased to hell now. She hadn't even had a wash since she'd got in, she'd been too shocked, too hurt. She scuffed on her trainers and left the kitchen, shutting the door behind her. She went along the hall to speak to Jack Rackland, who she hoped could work miracles. Somehow, she doubted it.

12

He wasn't what she had expected. Actually she didn't know *what* she had expected, some seedy old weasel of a bloke with thin hair, a raincoat and a dewdrop hanging off the end of his nose maybe, but the man who stood at the door in no way matched that description. He looked to be about thirty-five, and he was bulky but not fat, medium height, neatly turned out in a well-fitted suit, shirt and tie. He had a good head of straight dirty-blond hair, a tanned intelligent face and very direct heavy-lidded light blue eyes. He was a good-looking man, and that surprised her. Not a weasel at all.

And here I am looking like shit, thought Lily, embarrassed.

'Mrs King?'

'Yeah, that's me.' Lily made an awkward gesture back at the kitchen. 'Look, we'd better walk, my friend's busy . . .'

She didn't want to take him in the house, not after what Becks had said. She had some pride left – not much, admittedly – and she wasn't about to infringe on Becks's territory when it had just been made clear that she wasn't welcome there any more.

'Okay.' He looked faintly surprised, but he turned back toward the gate and started walking. Lily came out, shut the front door and walked alongside him. In silence they went along the street, heading for the park. It was a gorgeous day and Lily should have been at her daughter's wedding reception, mother of the bride, happy as could be.

Instead she was here. Ousted from her friend's house. Talking to some dubious bloke who was probably going to tell her things she didn't even want to hear about her late husband. Mud-stained and teary from Saz's attack on her. She looked a mess. She *felt* a mess. She felt as if all the strength had drained out of her and she was glad when they reached the park and sat down on a bench beneath the shade of a big chestnut tree. They were close to the paddling pool, and they sat there in silence for a few moments, watching the kids splashing around, carefree, having fun, their mothers flopped out on the grass, relaxed but ever-watchful. Lily couldn't help remembering her two when they'd been little. Happy days. All gone now.

'I wasn't sure I ought to come,' he said.

Lily turned her head and looked at his face. He was a big man. He took up a lot of the bench. She'd got out of the habit of men, she realized, banged up with a load of hormonal women. 'Oh? Why?'

He shrugged. 'It's an old case. I worked for Mrs Thomson, gathering information about women she suspected a particular man to be involved with.'

'And you know that man was my husband, Leo King,' said Lily. 'And Mrs Thomson was "involved" too. With my husband.'

He looked at her. There was a brief flare of something like amusement in his eyes. 'Look, whatever the ins and outs

69

of it, the client's always right, Mrs King. The client's paying for the privilege.'

Ah yes, payment. She hadn't thought about what he'd want for this. She hoped he wouldn't ask for anything up front. She had a little cash from her prison work, but it wouldn't be enough, she knew that. Nowhere near enough.

Did that slapper Adrienne have some brass neck, or what? she wondered angrily. *Behaving like a betrayed wife and tracking all Leo's other whores down.*

'Have you kept the records? I mean, you found them all. But have you still got their details on file?' she asked him.

'Twelve, thirteen years ago?' He shook his head. 'Unlikely. I don't even *remember* that far back. Or not much, anyway. There was a nurses' hostel, maybe. Something involving nurses, anyway. I've thought about it, racked my brains, but no good.'

Shit.

She wondered whether he was telling the truth. If he had to find them all over again, it could be costly for her, and a nice little earner for him. Being in the nick made you doubt people. Made you cover your own arse at all times.

'You bullshitting me?' she asked him bluntly.

Again that glint of humour. 'I wouldn't dare, Mrs King. You blew your husband's head off. You've just got out of stir. You've got a face on you like the wrath of God. Do you think I'd want to upset you?'

Lily looked at him. Their eyes locked. He didn't look the type of man to be fearful of anything, much less a shabby-looking blonde. She'd always thought she was a good judge of people, but fuck it, look where *that* had got her. But . . . she thought she could trust him. Just a bit. Maybe. But she had to keep her guard up, keep any hint of weakness hidden away.

70

'Could you find them again?' she asked. 'Could you get me their names – which might be different now, I suppose. And maybe their old addresses?'

'The woman I worked for . . . she was mentioned in the court case, wasn't she?'

Lily nodded. 'Adrienne Thomson's an old friend of mine, we go way back.'

He let out his breath. 'You want to choose your friends a bit more carefully, Mrs King.'

Don't I bloody well know it.

'I'll need a down payment, get me started. Three hundred ought to do it.'

'Dream on,' said Lily. 'I'm short of readies right now.' And no *way* was she going cap in hand to Becks, not now.

'I've got to live, Mrs King,' he said, his eyes still holding hers. 'I've got exes, just like everyone else. And I've got to say, no cash, no deal.'

'I didn't say I couldn't get some,' said Lily. 'Soon, anyway.'

'Soon? Like, when?'

'Like a few days' time.' And she wasn't looking forward to *that* event, not at all.

'Are you bullshitting *me*, Mrs King?'

'I never bullshit, Mr Rackland. Never.' Her eyes were steady on his. 'Do you believe me?'

He was silent, his eyes searching her face. 'You know what?' he said finally. 'Funnily enough, I do. Which might make me a fucking fool or a sucker for a pretty face, but there you go.'

'Are you married, Mr Rackland?'

'Jack. Call me Jack. We're separated, me and Monica.'

'Who cheated? You, or her?'

He paused for a beat, looked down, away. 'Her,' he

said. 'Said I was working too much, didn't pay her enough attention.'

'Hurts like fuck, don't it?' Lily smiled grimly. 'But not as much as being banged up for something you didn't do. Not as much as losing your husband, and your home, and your kids, and doing twelve long damned years for something someone else did.'

'Are you really saying you didn't do it?'

'Got it in one.'

He let out a low whistle. 'If that's true . . . if that happened to me . . .' He shook his big head, leaned forward, rested his elbows on his knees.

'Yeah, what?'

His head came round and his eyes met hers. 'I'd want to kill some bastard. And I'd make it nice and slow.'

'Jack,' said Lily, 'I do believe we're reading from the same page.'

He nodded and stood up. 'You'll get me those contact details? Then I'll get on it. I can wait a week for the money, no longer. Then I'm dropping this like a hot potato, that's a promise.'

'I think that's fair,' said Lily. She stood up too. They shook hands. 'I'll be in touch.'

He turned and walked away, back across the park.

Lily paused there, looking at the happy scene in the paddling pool. Happy kids. *Her* kids would be dancing at Saz's reception now, Saz and her groom – Christ, she didn't even know his name! – would be cutting the cake; there would be speeches, toasts, love and laughter. And here she was, standing alone, watching other people's families having fun, not sure whether or not to go back to Becks's place at all. She wasn't welcome there. Fuck, she wasn't welcome *anywhere*.

She thought of her parents. Dad was gone, but Mum was still standing, so far as Lily knew. She'd live to torment, that one. She could call on her – if she really wanted to endure another hour or so of prune-faced bollocking, which was all she ever got from her mother; all she had *ever* got, come to that. Mum had visited her, just once, after she'd gone down for Leo's killing. Just once, shortly after she'd first been put inside.

She'd been new to prison life, terrified, depressed. And Mum had come in and said – God, would she ever forget those words? – 'This is where I always thought you'd end up, Lily. You're a bad 'un. They always say the quiet ones are the worst, and by God you've proved them right.'

Did she really want more of that? Answer: no.

She walked off across the park, going back toward Becks's place. She'd pack up her stuff and bugger off, that was all she could do now. Find a little B & B or something. Sleep in a doorway if she had to. Anything was better than staying at Becks's when Becks had made it plain she was surplus to requirements.

She crossed the road and started walking back along the rows of houses toward Becks's place when a long black car pulled in to the kerb. A man jumped out of the back, grabbed her arm, and yanked her off-balance.

'Hey!' she yelled, but her feet went from under her and she was half carried, half pulled into the car. She found herself lying across the back seat with a man on either side of her. Fear shot through her like a hot knife through butter.

Oh shit, she thought, *Freddy King*.

'What the . . .?' she gasped out.

One of the men, a huge bruiser, lifted a thick finger and pointed it at her. She remembered Freddy, outside the prison, pointing his finger at her like a gun. Yeah, this was Freddy's work all right. 'Shut up,' he said.

Lily shut up. The car zoomed off. She was trapped. She was *finished*, even before she had properly begun.

13

There were four of them in the car, and she thought they were just going to drive her somewhere, hurt her, then finish her off. She could hear her heart beating like a trapped animal's, she was so scared. Her bowels felt liquid, her stomach was churning into knots. Oh God. She didn't know how she was going to get through this.

How you get through everything, she thought. *Alone.*

Her eyes filled with tears; it was weak but she couldn't help it. She really was alone. Completely alone. Her friend had abandoned her. Her daughters, her lovely girls, had rejected her. She would never, ever forget the expressions on their faces when they'd seen her at the church. Hatred. Fear. Loathing. It was more than any mother could take.

And now, this. The end of it *all*. She was terrified, but she was also sort of relieved. It would be over. All the suffering. All that time she'd done, and all for nothing. All for someone else's crime. Now she was tired, and so alone. She didn't mind dying; but she hoped they didn't hurt her too much first.

She thought they would. She saw it again, Freddy King outside Askham, aiming his finger at her, mouthing the words: *You won't see it coming.*

And guess what? She hadn't. He'd got *that* right.

The light was going as the car crunched onto gravel and skidded to a halt. Sudden silence descended. Into Lily's mind came Saz's face, filled with hate and horror. She screwed her eyes tight shut, held back the tears. She'd wanted so much to make things right, and now she wouldn't get the chance. That stung her, hurt her bad. Her lovely girls. Lost to her forever.

They flung open the car doors and she was manhandled out onto the drive of a big house. She noticed nothing else about it, only that it was big. She was nearly shitting herself with fear now. Why had they brought her to a house? Why hadn't they just driven her off into the forest, topped her there?

She was bundled into a hallway; big again, huge – maybe Victorian, she hadn't a clue. Terror was freezing her brain like dry ice. Then into a room with an empty fireplace – it was summer, too hot for fires – but a *nice* room. Sofas in it, the smell of polish in the air. She was shoved down onto one of the sofas.

'Wait there,' said one of the faces.

Jesus, the King boys are going to drag this out, she thought numbly. *They're going to get their money's worth out of this.*

The men left the room. She sat there, swallowing hard, trying not to succumb to total hysteria. She glanced over at the long closed curtains. Perhaps there were French doors there, an escape route?

The inner door opened.

'It's locked,' said a low, masculine voice. 'All the windows are locked. In case you were wondering.'

Lily turned her head.

Nick O'Rourke stood there, leaning casually back against the door, a big and threatening presence with his dark hair gleaming in the subdued light of the room, watching her steadily with his nearly black eyes, his gaze very intense. He still wore the black morning coat he'd been wearing at the church, but he'd removed his tie and opened his shirt collar.

Lily braced herself. She hadn't known Nick was in tight with Freddy and Si. He'd been best man, best friend and business associate to Leo, but his relationship with Leo's brothers had – she thought – never been anything other than cool. Obviously she thought wrong.

'What the hell . . .?' she said weakly.

'What the hell is right, Lily.' Nick O'Rourke walked forward and flopped down into an armchair. 'Like, what the hell are you playing at?'

He stretched out his long legs and his calf brushed against hers. She flinched back as if burnt.

'I don't know what you're on about,' she said. She looked at the inner door, knowing that any minute now the heavies were going to come back in and start working her over. New alliances had been made, alliances she knew nothing about. Ignorance wasn't bliss at all. It was going to be the death of her.

Just get on with it then, she thought. *Let's have it done.*

'What I'm on about is this,' he said, and his voice sounded strained, as if he was making an effort to control his temper. 'Are you stark, staring mad?'

Oh, so first he wanted an apology for something. 'You mean, turning up at Saz's wedding today?' she asked, having to cough to get the words out, her throat was so parched from fear. 'Okay. I admit it. It was a stupid thing to do. All right?'

'*Stupid?*' The dark, dark eyes widened as he stared at her. 'Oh, no Lily.' He gave a bark of laughter, but he didn't sound at all amused. 'You've gone way beyond that point on the road. You passed *stupid* right back at the last fucking round-about. Now you're driving through *mad*. What the hell were you thinking?'

Lily swallowed hard, blinked back more panicky tears.

'I wanted . . .' she gulped. '. . . I just wanted to see them. Saz getting married, how could I miss that?'

He was shaking his head, his eyes moving over her. Lily cringed, very aware of what she looked like: mud-spattered, crumpled, tear-stained; a complete and utter wreck.

'And look at the fucking state of you,' he said in irritation.

As if that's going to matter now, she thought.

'I just . . . had to be there,' she said lamely.

'No, Lily, you didn't. Si was there. Freddy was there. You *didn't* have to be there at all, are you totally insane? Do you for one single minute think that your daughters wanted to see you there today? Do you think they *behaved* as if they were glad to see you? I suppose that silly cow Becks told you about it?'

Lily shrugged. She wasn't going to drop Becks in it; she couldn't grass up a mate – even if Becks had made it clear to her that she wasn't welcome any more. That wasn't her fault, anyway. Becks was just frightened, and she was *right* to be frightened: her and Joe didn't want trouble with the Kings.

'Yeah, I bet it was,' he went on. He looked exasperated. 'Fuck it, Lily, how long you been out?'

'Yesterday. I got out yesterday,' said Lily.

'And today you've upset the whole bloody applecart. Jesus, that must be some sort of record.'

Lily swallowed hard. All right. She knew she'd messed up. But she'd been desperate, couldn't he see that?

'They're my girls,' she said, and her voice was a little fiercer, a bit stronger.

'They. Don't. Want. To. Know. You,' he said with brutal emphasis.

'*No . . .*' Lily shook her head, denying it, blanking it out even though she knew he was right.

'*Yes*, Lily. It's the damned truth. How would *you* feel, if your father's murderer pitched up at your wedding?'

Lily was still shaking her head, biting back more bitter tears. She'd dated Nick O'Rourke before she got involved with Leo but now she wondered why. He was such a *bastard*. Leo had been all flash, gold rings winking in the light, thick gold chains around his neck, everyone's big brother, the one with the barrel chest and the big booming laugh; you could hear him in the next street, doling out cash and champagne and bonhomie to all and sundry. But Nick . . . Nick had been her very first love, her forever regret in life. She'd been seriously and hopelessly in love with him before Leo had come on the scene. Seeing him in the years that followed at parties, weddings, christenings, always with a new girl on his arm – Nick the playboy – had hurt badly at first, but the hurt had been dulled over time. And then he had married the exquisitely beautiful Julia, Leo's cousin. That had hurt Lily, too, but only distantly; the pain wasn't so fresh, she wasn't a besotted young girl any more. Life had gone on; they had taken different paths. She had accepted that.

Nick was so different to Leo. Quieter, darker – cleverer and more cunning, she had always thought. If Leo was sun and brightness, then Nick was the magnetic pull of the dark. Nick didn't put all the goods out in the shop window for all to see; he kept something back. He was a thinker. It made him more dangerous than Leo could ever have hoped to be.

And who better to get Leo out of the picture? thought Lily suddenly. *His business partner. His oldest and best friend. Suspicion would never fall on Nick, but Leo could have screwed him on a deal. Nick was a brooder; he remembered every slight inflicted upon him back to the cradle. Nick could have decided he'd had a gutful.*

'You're such a bastard,' she said it out loud, felt better for it.

'Yeah, but I'm the bastard who's pulled your arse out of the crap today,' said Nick, unmoved by her words. 'Freddy went ballistic when you showed up, he was saying he was going to do all sorts.'

Lily stared at him. 'And you thought you'd come in on your white charger and whisk me away, did you?' Her voice was trembling with emotion. Most of it was rage. He'd scared her witless, him and his bloody boys. And now – was she hearing this right? – he was saying that he'd had her snatched, brought here, just because Freddy King was mouthing off as usual?

'Something like that.' He gave a thin smile.

'Freddy's *always* threatened all sorts,' she said.

'Lily, he meant it. You're staying with Becks and Joe, yes?'

'Not any more. She's told me to go.'

'That's a damned good idea, for them and for you. Where, though?'

Lily shrugged and slumped further down into the sofa. She felt exhausted with the aftermath of all this shit, and bewildered by Nick's motives. And bloody *angry* too: he'd really scared her.

Nick stood up and went to the empty hearth. For such a big man he moved with a panther-like grace – silent and deadly. Which he was, she knew that. He was a hard man and a dangerous one. He'd grown up – like Leo – delving deep into the protection rackets and dabbling in large-scale bootlegging. Then he'd graduated to the criminal equivalent of the Premier League, working with an elite network of tough, trusted men at the highest level, and running rings around the cops and Customs & Excise.

There was a set of keys on the mantelpiece. Nick picked them up and they jingled.

That sound.

One of the older cons had told her she would feel like this. *'Just the sound of a set of keys jingling is gonna make you jump out of your skin for the rest of your life. You heard how men used to come back after World War One, shell-shocked from the Somme? Anyone so much as popped a cork near them, or a car backfired. They just dived for cover. And that'll be you, Lily girl. Every time you hear a set of keys.'*

Nick tossed the keys into her lap. Lily flinched.

'There's a safe flat across town. The boys'll take you back to Becks's place to get your things, then take you on over there. All right?'

'What you doing this for? Guilty conscience?' asked Lily.

'What?'

'Did you . . . *you* didn't have anything to do with Leo's death, did you?' she stumbled out.

Nick looked surprised. Then he laughed. 'That's a good act, Lily. And that's a really good line to take, particularly with Si and Freddy King after your blood. So let's get this right – you were an innocent, banged up by mistake? It was a miscarriage of justice? Someone else did it? Me, maybe? Oh Lily. That's a bloody good one.'

Lily stood up. She'd been frightened, abused, accosted by her own kin and now the bastard was *laughing* at her.

'It's not *funny*,' she snapped.

His laughter stopped suddenly. He moved forward and stood facing her. Suddenly she felt very small.

'Oh, too right it ain't. It's far from that.' He was staring at her face. 'Twelve years in stir and you're still fucking beautiful. How'd you manage that Lily King? So beautiful. And so bloody *deadly,* too.'

'I didn't do it,' said Lily through gritted teeth.

'Yeah, that's a good one. I'd stick with that if I were you.'

Now Lily was getting mad. She lashed out, wanting to wipe that smirk off his face. He caught her wrist, held her there.

'Now *don't* start that with me,' he advised. 'If you hit me, I swear to you, I'll hit back, and you know what? I can hit a lot harder than you. So don't do it.'

Lily was silent, fuming, her eyes glinting with temper. He was hurting her wrist, but she wouldn't say so. She'd die first.

'I didn't do it,' she said again. 'And I'm going to prove it's the truth.'

'Ha! Lily, you did it. I knew you. You were a shy, quiet girl and all I can think is that Leo pushed you too far, pushed you beyond reason, and you finally snapped.'

'You think I killed your best friend? Truly? Then you ought to hate me for that.'

'Yeah.' Nick was staring at her thoughtfully. 'You're right. I should.'

He pulled her into his arms and kissed her.

Lily didn't struggle: she was too stunned to do that. She kept very still and tried not to respond. She couldn't afford to let him see even a tiny bit of softness or pliability in her; she had to stay tough, stay in control. But – hell – it was difficult. It had been a long, dry time in prison. And if Nick was helping her – God knew why, she'd try to figure it out, if she could – then maybe she'd be wise to exploit any weakness for her he might still have.

He pulled back, and stood there looking at her from inches away. 'You know what I'd like to do now?' he said.

Lily gulped. Her lips were throbbing, and other parts were too. She shook her head.

'I'd like to take you upstairs,' he said, then his mouth tilted up in a cynical smile. 'And I would – if it wasn't for fear that I might wake up with what's left of my brains splattered all over the room.'

'You bastard,' said Lily. 'I *told* you . . .'

'Yeah, that you didn't do it.' There was a flicker of uncertainty in his eyes. He let go of her wrist, pushed her firmly back, away from him.

Lily told herself she was glad about that. *Keep strong*, she told herself. *Keep focused*. It was hard though. 'I'll show you,' she said. 'I'll prove it.'

'Look, Lily, don't show me anything and don't try to prove anything to me, I'm not biting, okay? Just keep out of trouble, or I promise I am going to give you *such* a seeing-to one of these days.'

Promises, promises, thought Lily. Then she clamped down on the thought, clamped down on the feeling. Her blood was fizzing from that unexpected kiss, but she didn't want that. She didn't want to get mixed up with *anyone*. Getting involved with hot, dodgy men had got her into this mess. She wasn't going to go there, not any more. Even if Nick wasn't Leo, Leo of the dazzling charm and the secret stable of tarts, he was still a bad 'un and he was best avoided.

'Now,' he went on, crossing to the inner door. One of the bruisers, the one who had told her to shut up on the joyride over here, was standing there. Nick turned back to Lily. 'Keep out of Si's way. And if you see Freddy coming, for the love of God leg it fast in the opposite direction. Okay?'

Lily nodded slowly, although she knew that she was planning to do only one of those things.

'Nige'll drive you,' said Nick, looking expectantly at her. 'A thank you would be nice,' he said.

'Fuck *you*,' said Lily, and the last thing she heard as she and Nige headed out of the house was Nick bloody O'Rourke laughing his bollocks off at her. Again.

14

It was her first day in Holloway. She thought she would choke with terror at the sensation of being hemmed-in, shut away. A prison officer at reception checked and logged her belongings, then allowed her to buy two phone cards with her own private cash.

'Should be just one,' said the officer. 'But as you're new in, two, okay?'

Then she was strip-searched for the first time, adding indignity to fear, and locked in a room with six other prisoners. Three of them were heroin users, one of which had turned on her violent boyfriend, nearly braining him with a candlestick, and she joked that his head was so hard it had broken the bloody thing, and she was sorry about that because the candlestick had been a gift from her mother.

One of the others was an intimidatingly tall, twenty-stone Jamaican woman with dreadlocks and a bass-baritone voice, called Mercy. She'd been done for importing cocaine and spoke in a fast patois that Lily at first struggled to comprehend. After a while, she developed an ear for it, and could *talk to Mercy and understand her fully. Mercy had three kids at home in Jamaica, and had taken the coke with her on her first-ever trip to England because she had been told that if she didn't, her eleven-year-old son would be killed.*

'Do you know if he's safe now?' Lily had asked her later on.

'He's in hiding with his grandma,' said Mercy, and Lily thought then that her own life had been a picnic compared to this poor woman's. After that, they each had a rudimentary health check and then Lily was pronounced 'processed' and was put on D3, the intake wing, in a four-bed dormitory.

Like boarding school, *she thought.*

'It true you killed your old man?' asked one of the heroin junkies in the dorm. The girl had told Lily she'd decided not to sign on to the methadone programme because she said they were all loony-tunes in the hospital wing: she'd tried it before and she wasn't trying it again. She'd rather go cold turkey.

Lily didn't answer. She was blank-faced with shock at finding herself here, inside.

The heroin girl took her silence as an admission of guilt. They'd all read about the case in the papers; many of them had been the victims of violent husbands, boyfriends, pimps, and Lily had turned the tables. Struck a blow for the sisterhood.

'Hey girl – respect,' said her cellmate with a grin.

15

Lily sprang awake next morning wondering: *Where the hell am I?* She'd dreamed again. Back inside. *Fucking* dreams. But now she was lying in a comfy double bed, and sunlight was filtering through the closed curtains, and her first thought was that this was a different dream, another illusion, and that at any moment she would *really* wake up, and she would be in stir, forever in stir, on a hard bunk bed with a stained mattress and scratchy blankets and snoring cellmates for company. Ready to face the indignity all over again. The degradation, the dire prison food eaten at trestle tables on cheap, uncomfortable chairs, the need to fill the day before lights out and the sweet release of sleep.

But no. Here she was. She was *out*. Her mind ran back over the events of the past two days. Becks telling her to go – and the relief on her face last night when Lily and the boys had pitched up and collected her things. Joe skulking in the background – keeping out of it; not wanting to get involved. And who could blame him? Jack Rackland, sitting on a bench with her in the park, watching kiddies play . . . oh, and *her* kids, her beautiful girls, and then – and this was so painful, so awful – Saz's face twisted with hate as she'd launched herself at Lily, knocking her flying.

Lily turned over in the bed, groaning, pulling the pillow over her head, trying to block out the image.

Oh, and more of them. Nick O'Rourke laughing at her last night, Nick O'Rourke kissing her. She paused over that. Relived for a moment the old, delicious sensations. But no. She couldn't trust him. She couldn't trust *anyone*. So what if he'd ferried her off to this neat, unshowy safe flat? So what if the kitchenette cupboards were well stocked with food. So what if she found wearable women's clothes in the wardrobe, and a man's, too – what was this, a little love-nest for Nick and some tart? She thought his marriage to Julia had ended long since, she'd heard that somewhere. Probably from Becks.

All right, he'd done all this for her, but she *still* couldn't trust him.

Furthermore, she was potless. She hadn't a bean. Very soon, she was going to have to get her hands on some substantial cash, set herself back up on her feet, get Jack paid and pointed in the right direction. It was going to be a challenge, but she thought: *I can do this*.

A buzzer went off, very loud. Lily stiffened and emerged from beneath the pillow. *What the fuck?* she thought, her heart freezing in panic.

The buzzer sounded again, not muffled by the goose-down pillow this time. Very loud indeed. Lily sat bolt upright, pulling the long faded lavender-coloured t-shirt she'd grabbed out of the closet to wear in bed further down, hunching her knees up to her chest. She looked around her with wild, frightened eyes. Where was it coming from? It sounded again, and she pinpointed it. There was a telephone intercom on the wall. Someone was downstairs, leaning on the doorbell.

Oh shit.

Who the hell could it be?

She glanced at the clock beside the bed. It was ten past nine: she'd slept late. She'd been worn out. Now her pulse was hammering away as the fear picked up where it had left off last night. It would be Freddy or Si; they'd tracked her down and if she opened the door they'd kill her.

The buzzer sounded again.

Gulping, crossing her arms over herself for comfort, Lily left the bed and went over to the intercom. Yeah, it would be them. For sure. They'd found her. But . . . what if it wasn't them? What if it was Nick, how big a laugh would that give him, hard-hearted murderess Lily King quivering with fear from a doorbell?

She stood beside the damned thing and took a deep, deep breath. She reached out, feeling sick with terror, and picked it up.

'Hello?' she said unsteadily into the phone. 'Who's there?'

There was silence. Traffic passing by, someone breathing.

Oh God oh help, it's them, it's them . . .

'Hello?' she repeated, feeling cold sweat break out all over her body. Because she'd just told them, hadn't she?, that she was there. She shouldn't have spoken. Shouldn't have picked the damned thing up. What was she thinking? Was she completely mad?

There was nothing to be heard but the breathing. Fast, frantic breathing.

Oh for God's sake just say or do something, she thought. *Break the bloody door down, just get it over with. I don't care any more.*

Then an unsteady female voice said: 'It's . . . it's Oli. It's Oli.'

Lily sagged against the wall in shock. Oli, her baby girl . . .

Then she had a nasty thought. 'Are you alone, Oli?' Maybe she had Uncle Si with her, maybe this was a blind, a way in, Oli playing Trojan horse for the King brothers. Maybe Oli hated her just as much as Saz did. And why shouldn't she? God knew she had reason.

'Of course I'm alone,' said Oli, in a voice that sounded on the edge of tears.

Do I believe her? thought Lily. *Do I dare?*

She leaned back against the wall beside the intercom. Reached out a hand, pressed the release. She had to take the chance. She *had* to.

'Come on up,' she said, dry-mouthed with fear.

The first thing that Lily thought when she opened the door and saw Oli standing there – alone, and thank God for that – was, oh my God, my baby, how she's grown up. She felt an almost overpowering urge to hug Oli, to hold her close. Lily's second thought was that Oli looked distraught, and that she didn't look as if she wanted to be held or hugged. In fact, she looked like she was about to freak. Lily held herself firmly in check.

Oli came inside and Lily shut the door and locked it after her. Then she turned, leaning against the door for support, thinking *my baby, my baby* as Oli turned and looked at her with Leo's dark blue eyes, eyes that were only just this side of crazy. Oli's dark hair, long and wildly curling, was dishevelled. She was wearing pale denim jeans and a white puff-sleeved blouse and had about her that same old aura of litheness, of intense nervous energy.

Oli the tomboy. She'd always favoured trousers over dresses – unlike the more stately, feminine Saz – and was always off climbing trees, playing cowboys, camping out in the garden, doing wild, boyish things, while Saz petted her pony and shot clays with Leo.

Lily took a breath. 'Why don't you sit down?' she said, and Oli nodded absently and flopped down into the nearest chair, immediately starting to pick at the arm of it with long, nimble fingers. Her nails were bitten, Lily noticed as her gaze moved avidly over her daughter, taking in every precious inch of her. Oli's skin was still fine, lightly tanned, a smattering of freckles over the bridge of her turned-up nose. Her pouting rosebud mouth was unadorned by lipstick. Her lashes were long, her brows black and slightly bushy. She glanced up at Lily and Lily thought, *Oh she's so pretty. Those beautiful dark blue eyes are going to break a few hearts.*

Leo's eyes, she thought more soberly. Saz had been the real daddy's girl of the family, but Oli had loved her dad too, so much. And what must she think of her mother, who she believed had killed him?

Lily sat down cautiously, quite a way from Oli; she didn't want to panic her, make her bolt for the door. Oli looked as if she was on a knife-edge, not certain whether to stay or go.

'How did you find me here?' Lily asked her.

Oli made a flicking movement of her hand. 'I followed you. I . . . I wanted to see what you . . . I've been trying not to, but I wanted to see you, so I went over to your mate Becky's place after I'd heard Uncle Si and Aunt Maeve saying you were staying there . . .'

Jesus God, thought Lily. Oli had found her so easily. And so had Si and Freddy.

'And when I got there, I bottled it.' Oli stopped talking and clutched at her head with both hands, mucking up her hair even more. It was sticking out in all directions. 'I just . . . I couldn't come in. I sat in the car. It was getting darker. I didn't know what to do. And then you arrived with some men, and you all went in there, and I still couldn't get up the nerve to come in . . .' She gulped and rubbed the heels of her hands over her eyes like a tired child. Then she dropped her arms and looked at Lily. 'It's funny, I thought if I ever saw you again I wouldn't know you, but I did, I knew you straight away when I saw you standing outside the church. Don't you think that's odd?'

Lily didn't answer.

'When you all came out of Becky's, I followed the car. At a distance. I was careful the men didn't see me. I parked over the road. Then they went away, and the lights were still on up here, so I thought, I'll go over, she's alone, I can talk to her, ask her why she did it.'

'Oli—' said Lily.

'But I couldn't!' Oli let out a wild little laugh. 'I bottled it again. Then the lights went out. And I thought, all right, I'll wait until morning.'

'You've been sitting out in the car all night?' Lily asked.

Oli nodded, wrapping her arms harder around her body, her feet tapping on the floor, her movements frenetic, jittery.

Again Lily had to quash the urge to hug her. Instead she stood up. 'Let's have a cup of tea, and some toast, and we'll both start to feel a bit better.'

She went into the little kitchenette and made the tea, found bread in the freezer and put four slices in the toaster. Then she found butter, jam, milk, cups, plates, cutlery, put it all on a tray and came back into the small sitting area. She put the tray on the coffee table, poured out the tea, buttered the toast and slathered jam on it. Then she pushed a mug and plate over to Oli.

'Here. For God's sake eat something and drink some tea, you must be frozen.'

'What, playing mother? It's a bit late for that,' said Oli sharply.

Lily flinched, but she knew how Oli must be hurting. She had to soak it up. 'Better late than never I s'pose,' she said lightly, and started in on the toast although she was almost choking with nerves. Her daughter, her lovely little Oli, was sitting right here in front of her, looking as though she might leg it at any second, but she was *here*, thank God, she was here.

Lily swigged down some tea; it steadied her a little. She could see the food and drink having a similar effect on Oli, although she was only nibbling at the toast, she was too uptight to relish it.

'They said . . .' Oli's eyes suddenly filled with tears as she spoke. 'Aunt Maeve said he was having an affair with that horrible woman, that Adrienne Thomson. And that he'd been hitting you.' A tear spilled over and ran down Oli's face. She pushed her hands into her hair. 'You know, I don't remember much of what happened when Dad . . . when he died, or when you were taken away.'

'Much?' queried Lily.

'All right, I don't remember *anything* around that time. Except that you were both there . . . and then you were gone.' She threw her half-eaten toast down and shoved the plate away. 'I can't eat this.'

Lily pushed hers away too. Her throat had closed as she saw the misery in Oli's eyes. 'Oli,' she said urgently. 'I didn't do it.'

'*What?*' Oli was looking at her open-mouthed. Then she shook her head. 'You were tried and convicted. You were *found guilty.*'

Lily was shaking her head. 'No . . .'

'*Yes,*' said Oli, shouting now. Now the tears were falling, she was sobbing, nearly hysterical. 'I never saw him hit you. Not once. Saz never saw that either. That was a lie.'

'Oh Jesus, Oli . . .' Despite herself, Lily found herself reaching out, trying to bridge the huge, horrible gulf between them.

'Don't you touch me!' Oli snapped, cringing back.

Lily held up both hands and slowly drew back. *Okay, okay.* 'I didn't do it, Oli. That's the truth. Someone fitted me up for it. That's the truth too. I would never, ever have done such a thing to you. I would have slit my own throat first, Oli. I promise you that.'

Oli was silent now, watching her. She swiped a hand over her eyes. Picked up the mug of tea and sipped it, tried to gather herself.

Poor little cow, thought Lily. *How the hell has she managed to cope with this?* No mother. Her father dead. And the horror of knowing what had happened to bring all that about. Oli was eighteen, a young adult now; but in her eyes Lily could see nothing but the frightened, bewildered child she had been back then.

'The silly thing is,' said Oli finally, 'I want to believe you.'

Lily took a gasping breath. Oh, Jesus, could she make this right? Could it really be possible? She didn't dare believe it, not yet. But she could see that Oli was having doubts. And if she was clever enough, *cunning* enough, then she could open that tiny crack in Oli's armour, get inside and win her daughter back.

Saz would be quite another matter. But Saz wasn't here.

She'd have to face that particular battle later, and she wasn't looking forward to it at all.

'They on honeymoon? Saz and . . . what's his name, the groom?' she asked.

'South of France. Only for a week,' said Oli, her eyes fixed on Lily's face. 'Richard's got work to get back to: he works in the business for Uncle Si and Freddy. Him and Saz are going to move into our place when they get back.'

'Ah.' Lily knew that 'the business' covered a multitude of sins – literally. Ask any of the King brothers or Nick O'Rourke where they earned the vast amounts of dosh to pay for mansions, fast cars, holidays in the Caribbean and extremely high-maintenance blonde girlfriends and wives, and they would say 'import and export'. It was only true insofar as 'the business' was a blind for other, more lucrative and less law-abiding activities.

'Oli,' said Lily. 'I'd like to come home.'

Oli stared at her mother, her expression at first puzzled and then, as she took in the full meaning of what Lily had just said, horrified. 'You *what?*'

Lily decided it was time to start milking it. 'I can't stay here. It's strictly temporary, one night only, a favour from Nick. Becks and Joe don't want me there. I've got nowhere to go to, Oli. Nowhere at all.'

It wasn't true, and she hated lying to Oli, but fuck it. She wanted to go back to her own home. She *had* to go back there. She was prepared to kick any obstacle out of the way to achieve that goal, too. Up to and including Maeve and even Si King – somehow. She didn't know how yet. Si King wasn't so much an obstacle as a fucking great concrete wall, but somehow she was going to have to break the bastard down. If he didn't break *her* down first.

Oli jumped to her feet. 'You can't be bloody serious,' she burst out. '*Home?* You ruined our home, destroyed it. How can you, how do you fucking well *dare* say that to me?'

'I've got nowhere else, Oli,' said Lily. She was going for the sympathy vote, exploiting the softness she sensed in Oli, the willingness to be persuaded that her mother wasn't a murderess after all.

She *had* to get back into The Fort. It was essential; everything depended upon it.

'Forget it,' snapped Oli, shaking her head in disbelief. 'I don't . . . I really don't know why I came here . . .' she said, dragging a hand through her hair.

'You came here because you wanted to see me,' said Lily. 'And because you don't believe I was guilty, not really.'

'You were *convicted*.'

'I was framed. I didn't do it. And I need . . .' Lily hesitated, choosing her words carefully now . . . 'I need to come home, Oli. I need to be home with you.'

In Oli's eyes, Lily could see despair, desperation. Oli wanted her mother back. Oli had missed her. She could see it. She hated playing with Oli's emotions this way, but it had to be done.

Oli shook her head.

'Oli . . .'

'No! I can't talk about this now,' said Oli, and ran to the door, and was gone.

And there went that chance. Lily sat there, feeling shattered and frustrated. To see Oli so close . . . but so distressed, so tormented. She'd blown it; all her soft words hadn't worked. She felt tears start in her eyes, tears of anger and self-pity, and blinked them away. She *refused* to cry. She sighed deeply, stood up, started gathering up the breakfast things.

She had other things she had to be doing. She was going to have a long shower, dress in someone else's clothes and go and have another chat with her late husband's mistress. *One* of them, anyway.

16

'You know what? That ain't enough,' said Tiger Wu.

Freddy King stared at the man. 'You what?' he asked. 'You're having a laugh.'

They were standing in a clearing in Epping Forest, way off the beaten track, both of them dressed as ramblers in dark green hoodies and walking boots. Freddy felt a cunt but it was important that they weren't seen to be out of place here. They had to blend right in to the background in case anyone was about. There was stillness all around, and summer greenery and birdsong, all that nature shit. Freddy hated it. He liked the Smoke. Plenty of action, noise, people. Silence always made him jittery.

Duncan 'Tiger' Wu shook his head. He was half-Chinese, half-Scot. He had the sallow skin and exotic eyes of his mother, and his dad's height and strong Glaswegian accent. He wore his blue-black hair pulled back in a ponytail. He was much feared and revered around the East End, known as a good refuse collector – in other words, he got rid of people, for a hefty fee.

The fee was getting heftier by the minute.

Tiger prided himself on keeping his ear to the ground, knowing who was inside or out, who would have need of his services, who were the movers and shakers among the East End mobs and the Essex boys. He knew that Lily King had done her husband over, and that Si and Freddy King had been chomping at the bit ever since, wanting to do the cow a bit of harm in return. Freddy more than Si. Si was a reasonable man, within limits. Freddy was a headcase. Tiger knew that. But he was a *rich* headcase, and that made this whole conversation really interesting as far as Tiger was concerned.

'Five up front and five when the job's done; that's not a bad day's pay,' said Freddy.

'Does Si want this?' asked Tiger.

Freddy puffed himself up, his face reddening angrily. 'Si ain't doing this deal, I am.'

'Only I wouldn't want to tread on Si's toes,' said Tiger.

'Understood. Si's agreeable, okay?' lied Freddy. *Fuck* Si and his let's-wait-until-doomsday speeches. He wanted this bitch sorted, soonest. He would have done her right after the wedding, but Si had said, no, wait. That was all Si ever said – no, wait. Freddy was sick of waiting.

'Okay. So seven, yes? Seven thou up front, seven when it's done.'

'Go and piss up your kilt,' said Freddy with a snort of disdain. He had ten in his pocket, but if Wu stopped at six and a half, he'd be pleased with the deal. Wu had a reputation of being keen on the money and was the butt of a lot of Scots jokes around the manor because of it. Rumour was he'd skin a turd for tuppence. 'Six. That's all I'm prepared to go to, we either shake on it now or I walk,' Freddy relented, spitting in his hand and holding it out to seal the deal.

Wu was hesitating. 'Six and a half,' he said.

'Done. And don't forget. No comebacks, no way to trace it back to me. You got that?' Si would have his guts if any mud came flying their way, Freddy knew that. He didn't want to go upsetting Si.

They shook hands; the contract was agreed. Tiger Wu was going to get rid of Lily King.

And not a fucking minute too soon, thought Freddy, paying Tiger his wedge and tramping back through the mud to where they'd parked up. He was smiling. He felt better already.

17

'So what you got?' asked Jack Rackland from behind his desk, stretching and running his hands through his dirty-blond hair, when she pitched up at his modest little office in a quiet road off the busy High Street later that same day.

'All sorts,' said Lily, sitting down gratefully. Her feet throbbed and she was getting a headache in the summer heat. Pink or rainbow-coloured, suddenly she missed Becks's horrible motor. Bloody buses. Packed full, airless, never on time; you had to wait fucking hours for the things, then walk a mile to get to where you really wanted to go. She'd dressed in a borrowed pair of jeans and a white t-shirt, dug out her old trainers. Heels were great, but sometimes you had to move, sometimes you had to *walk*.

'And the payment, how's that coming along?' He was looking at her with his keen blue eyes, anticipating deception. He was wearing a pale blue shirt, the sleeves rolled up. Strong, well-muscled forearms. Altogether a good-looking man, and she had been a sucker for attractive men in the past. She had a fine appreciation of beauty in all things but in men in particular, and look where that had ended; so she wasn't going to start all *that* old crap over again.

'It's coming along,' lied Lily. He was *right* to look at her like that, but it galled her. She'd pay him when she could; she wasn't a rogue like Leo with his dodgy deals and his crooked ways. She didn't screw people over, particularly not people who were trying to help her.

'I said a week, then you pay up,' he reminded her.

'I know that's what you said,' Lily replied evenly.

'Just so long as we're clear.'

'Crystal.'

His expression was amused. 'No good looking at me like that, Mrs King. We have to be honest with each other.'

'Yeah,' said Lily, and put the list that Adrienne Thomson had reluctantly given her two hours ago on the desk.

Adrienne hadn't been keen to hand the list over. Had said she'd have to hunt around for it, she didn't know where it would be, could Lily come back later? Lily had said that she could. Maybe when Matt was in, then they could talk it over, all three of them, together. And miraculously Adrienne had turned up the list in five minutes flat.

'Oh Jesus, Lily, you ain't going to start raking over all this rubbish again, are you?' Adrienne had said, looking worried as she handed it over.

'It may be rubbish to you, Adrienne, but it's important to me,' Lily had told her.

Now Jack Rackland was pulling the list over towards him, looking it over.

'That's their names, and their last known addresses,' said Lily. 'I don't know why she kept the list, but she did. She's an odd sort, Adrienne. Didn't think a thing about going behind my back. But when Leo started cheating on *her* – I suppose that's how she saw it, the twisted mare – she went off her flipping head. But I have to say – her filing system's a lot better than yours.'

He glanced up at her with a glint of humour in his eyes. 'Have a heart, girl. I don't know of any company that keeps records on file for over twelve years. Jesus, even the bleedin' *taxman* only goes back six.'

She knew he had a point. But she was hot, tired, still upset over her unsatisfactory early morning meeting with Oli, still shaken by Nick's boys snatching her last night – and yes, she was irritated that Jack had reminded her again about the money, and she was now wondering just how the hell she was going to get her hands on it. She had to. She *had* to.

'Call me Lily,' she said. 'Mrs King don't sound right any more somehow.'

'Not after you killed off Mr King?'

Lily stood up, her chair crashing over on its side. 'That's it. That's *enough*. I told you I didn't do it, but you don't believe me. I told you you'd get your money, but you don't believe that either. So this is just a fucking waste of time, Mr Rackland. Give me back that bloody list, I'm going to sort this out on my own.'

'Whoa, whoa.' He held up his hands, half laughing. 'Don't fly off the deep end, I was only winding you up.'

'Well *don't* fucking well wind me up,' yelled Lily. 'None of this is funny. I've got the King brothers loitering around, my daughters are like strangers to me, I'm fresh out of stir and, you know what? Somehow your little jokes ain't going down at all well, Mr Rackland – don't ask me why.'

'Okay.' He stood up, came around the desk, righted her chair. 'Come on,' he said more gently. 'Let's calm down and be friendly. I'm sorry, okay? I didn't mean to upset you.'

'Bullshit! You *did* mean to.'

Jack looked at her. 'All right. Admitted. I wanted to get a rise out of you, see how you'd react in the heat of the moment. Mrs King – Lily – all I've got is your word for all this.'

Lily stared at him, reassessing. He might look like a big lummox, but there was a sharp brain in there, clicking away. He'd baited her deliberately, and got the response he wanted.

'Come on,' he said. 'Sit down.'

Breathing hard with temper, Lily sat down again. She felt like storming out the door, but she needed his help. She knew it. He sat down too and returned his attention to the list.

'Look, here's what we'll do. We'll be methodical about this, okay?' He looked up at her.

Lily took a deep, calming breath. 'Okay,' she said at last.

'We'll start at the top of the list and work down. Adrienne Thomson hasn't included herself on this roll call, I see.'

Lily shook her head.

'I have to tell you, though, Lily, that these women could be anywhere and doing anything after all this time. They could even be dead. You understand?'

Lily nodded.

'All right then. Who's number one on the list? Alice Blunt. Oh yeah.' He sat back. 'This is the one I thought I remembered. I told you, right? A nurses' hostel. I knew nurses were involved somehow.'

'She's a nurse?' asked Lily, curious despite herself, thinking, *Oh Jesus, Leo had all these women, all these damned women and I didn't have a clue.*

He was shaking his head. 'No, she's not a nurse. She was in a home *attended* by nurses. Well, a hospital really. Jesus,

I do remember her.' He looked up at Lily's face. 'She was crazy. Bandaged wrists, I remember that, it's all coming back to me. She'd tried to commit suicide. When I found her, she was in a psychiatric unit.'

18

Her head was whirling by the time she left Jack's office. *Alice Blunt*. The name meant nothing to her, nothing at all.

Fuck it, Leo, was this down to you? she wondered. The woman had slit her wrists and been admitted to a mental institution. She'd been seriously unstable, Jack had remembered that much.

'She was spooky to talk to. Sort of locked into herself, you know?' Jack had said.

Spooky and unstable.

'She could well be dead by now,' Jack had warned Lily. 'But I'll check, okay? I'll start in on this, and you start in on getting the cash together, all right?'

'Yeah,' Lily had said, and left. Thinking, *Oh sure. I'll get right on that. Go straight down the Post Office, get out a few thousand, how will that be?*

She didn't have money to hand, not the sort of sums he was talking about. She had a roof over her head for now, thanks to Nick O'Rourke, and she couldn't understand his motivation for that yet – but that was about it. When she thought of Nick, there was that nagging suspicion bothering her again. What, did he feel guilty because he'd done Leo, let her take the rap? Was all this unexpected kindness towards her just about him, feeling he owed her something? But . . . Nick and Leo had been as close as brothers. So Nick should *hate* her, just as Si and Freddy did, if he truly believed she'd killed Leo – shouldn't he? Right now she was almost too tired to think about it, and she had more to do before day's end, much more.

She went back to the flat to pick up her rucksack, got the bus to where she needed to go, and then another bus; and it was getting dark but she didn't care, she was on a mission. She then walked about a quarter of a mile as the night closed in around her, to get to the house. Finally, footsore and weary, she walked into the little gravelled turning and stood in front of it.

It was full dark now. Owls hooted back in the nearby woods. Off in the distance, a fox barked. She clutched at the cold metal of the big closed security gates, put her head in between the bars and stared up the drive. The big white shape of The Fort glimmered faintly in the gloom.

Lily drew in a shuddering breath.

She knew every inch of that house. Fifty steps on the main staircase, five strides to the master suite, ten steps from the front door to the indoor swimming pool room. *Her* house. Only it wasn't. Not any more. Although she and Leo had owned the house together, as 'joint tenants', a murderess could not be allowed to profit from her crime. And so the house – *her home,* she thought fiercely – had passed to the girls.

Si had filled her in on these facts when she had called out time and again from prison, telling her with grim delight that the courts had appointed him and his wife Maeve as guardians of Saz and Oli and trustees of their considerable fortune, which would come to them when they passed eighteen. Oli had celebrated her eighteenth birthday in the February just gone, and Saz was twenty-one; now, they owned The Fort. Not her.

Lily stared up at the house.

There were a few lights on up there. It was just the same. Big, imposing.

The last time she had come here . . . oh Jesus, nearly thirteen years ago! . . . she had been determined to confront Leo because she knew he was knocking off Adrienne behind her back. And then . . . she screwed her eyes tight shut. Blood. That awful great gout of blood – and the numbness; the disbelief. Leo – big tough brawny Leo, who had always seemed invincible, a Sun King, undying and ever undimmed – was dead.

Deep in shock, she'd picked up the gun and then stumbled, half falling, gibbering, down the stairs, and called the police, something she had never done in her life before. Something she – with hindsight, and wasn't hindsight a wonderful thing? – probably shouldn't have done at all.

And she'd stayed there alone in the hall, the rifle in her hands, until the police came and she said, he's dead, someone's killed him, and they looked at her as if she was crazy and might at any second start shooting *them*, and they said, okay, yes, Mrs King isn't it? Their faces had been white and fearful in the porch light. Put the gun down now, that's right. Put it down on the floor. She had forgotten that she was still holding it. Couldn't think why she had picked the damned thing up in the first place. But when she opened the door to the police she was standing there in the hall, blood – Leo's blood – dripping from her clothes on to the lovely chequered marble tiles she had once picked out with such care.

Oh God, such a nightmare.

And then the trial, the horror building, the whole thing developing like some foul growth. The evidence all piling in against her. The arguments people had overheard, and one in particular when she had shouted: *You bastard, if you've been playing away I'll kill you.* Not meaning it. Never meaning it. But she'd said it; it had been heard by the cleaning lady. The prosecution had laid it all out, it was plain as day. She had come storming back from the spa on that fatal Thursday to confront her husband. She knew the key to the gun cabinet was kept in the desk drawer. Leo was always punctiliously careful about locking the guns away, and he had a licence; everything was kosher. She had opened the cabinet in his study, loaded the rifle – her prints were the only ones on the gun – and then she'd gone upstairs and blown his head off.

She could hear the prosecution shouting these words at her, accusing, snarling, while she stood there flinching, thinking, *No, no, it wasn't me, I didn't do it, someone please help me.*

To be fair, the defence counsel had tried. Encouraged her to plead guilty, lessen her sentence. She was going to get a sentence – that went without saying. They had to try to do damage limitation, really: there was nothing else they could do. So she said Leo had beaten her. He never had, but dazed and confused and wondering what the hell had happened to her life, what was going to happen to her girls, she agreed to say he had. She was frightened of prison, being locked up – she wasn't a criminal. Desperation took over. She pleaded guilty, just as her brief advised. She'd screamed at him that she was innocent, but he had explained it to her; don't be a fool. You have to play the system. Admit guilt and you'll get a lighter sentence. Guilty, but provoked. And he was right. Her sentence was lighter than it could have been.

Not nearly light enough, though.

Twelve long, hard, bitter and painful years.

Now she could hear a car coming along the lane, could see the headlights beaming ahead into the darkness, lighting up the overhanging trees. It was a nice, quiet lane, never much traffic, just the odd car or two, and this one was coming at speed.

Too fast.

The noise of the engine was piercing, drilling into her skull. She turned, pressed herself back against the hard, cold metal of the gates. Then – *Jesus!* – the car came screeching around the turn of the road and headed straight towards her. It was going to go past, she knew it was, but she cringed back against the gates. Who was driving at that speed along dark lanes: a lunatic?

It was going to go past.

No. It wasn't.

She watched open-mouthed with horror as the car swung wildly to the left and came roaring straight at her, sending gravel flying, the headlights blinding her. She could see the huge shape of the 4x4 now, could see the outline of the bull bars at the front. She screamed, but she couldn't hear herself screaming above the massive roar of the engine.

She was going to die, mangled between the bull bars of the car and the thick metal of the gates. She was going to die right here and now, and she was never going to know who did this terrible thing to her, she was never going to know the love of her daughters again.

No, she thought fiercely. *Please God, no.*

Then there was a shriek as the brakes slammed on. The car roared to a halt, just centimetres away from the front of her body. The engine was idling. Lily could hear herself sobbing with shock. The headlights were a screen of white light, she was blinking, screwing her face up, holding a hand up to her eyes and . . . *oh shit* . . . now she could see the man behind the wheel.

She could see him. Freddy King, sitting there grinning cruelly at her.

She waited for him to get out. She couldn't move; she was trapped, almost half falling over the bonnet of the damned car; she was *fucked*. As she watched, Freddy raised a finger at her and wagged it slowly from side to side as if saying, *Naughty, naughty.*

Lily gulped, trying to draw in air, her heart beating crazily. She could feel heat radiating off the bonnet of the car; her nostrils were full of the stench of petrol. He was going to drag this out, relish it; this was the last thing she was ever going to know.

All right then, you fucker, she thought, *come on. Come on and finish it.*

Freddy threw the car into reverse.

Lily stumbled to her knees, the gravel striking through her jeans, but she barely felt the pain. This time he was going to do it, get her good. She got ready to push herself to her feet at the last minute. She would wait until he gunned the engine again, then make a run for it, take off into the woods; she was fit, she could run. Hours in the prison gym had honed her body down to its fighting weight. She was pretty sure she could outrun heavy, muscle-bound Freddy King. She wasn't going to make it easy for the bastard, that was for sure.

She waited on the ground, gulping, gasping.

Freddy sat in the car on the road for a heartbeat; then he gunned the engine and roared off into the night.

Oh sweet Jesus.

Lily slumped forward. She couldn't believe it. He'd had his chance, right there; and he hadn't taken it.

Because he loved to toy with her, as a cat toys with a mouse.

She fell sideways and lay slumped on the gravel, listening to the car getting further and further away. Heading for Si's place, probably. He'd followed her here, the bastard. He was *never* going to let this go. And now another one was coming, just passing through, or – oh God – was it him coming back?

She was going to throw up. Breathless, sobbing, she leaned back against the gates, closed her eyes, fought down the surge of vomit. Her head was spinning. Suddenly the aftermath of that cataclysmic fear hit her legs and she couldn't get up. She just lay there, powerless.

But the engine note was different. This was another car, smaller. And then the car – going slower than Freddy's, but still heading straight for her where she sat outside the gates – turned in onto the gravel, blinding her in the glare of headlights once again. Lily put her arms over her head for all the damned good it would do; she was going to get flattened now, this was it.

The car braked hard. Lily lowered her arms and squinted into the headlights' hideous blue-white glare. She saw a low, sleek car, a red sports coupé. And someone was jumping out

112

of the driver's seat. She thought, *Oh shit, here we go. Eyes down, look in.*

'Mum?' said Oli's voice. 'What the hell are you *doing*?'

And as her daughter hauled her back to her feet, Lily started to laugh, and then she started to cry.

19

'Shit, I could have *killed* you,' said Oli, putting a mug of coffee in front of her mother as Lily sat, shaking with the aftermath of shock, at the big, marble-topped island in the huge kitchen of the house.

Well I got my wish, thought Lily dazedly. *I'm in.*

But the question was, how long could she *stay* in?

Oli rummaged in a cupboard – the cupboards that Lily herself had chosen – and found some brandy. She added a splash to Lily's coffee, hesitated, then added some to her own too. Lily sat there, in her own damned kitchen, feeling distinctly strange. Feeling that somehow she had slipped sideways in time. Everything was the same, on the surface. But nothing was the same, not really.

'You scared me witless,' said Oli, sitting down.

Briefly Oli sank her head into her trembling hands. Then she looked up at Lily with angry and bewildered eyes. Her mother was here. The woman she'd cried for throughout her young life was sitting right here in front of her.

She'd bundled Lily into the car, brought her inside The

Fort. Acted totally on impulse. And now . . . now she hadn't a clue what to do. Lily was bad, guilty, a terrible person. But Lily was her mother and, much as she might fight it, Oli felt the pull of Lily like a powerful magnet, drawing her in.

'What the hell were you doing, squatting on the flipping ground outside the gates?' she demanded.

Well, what *had* she been doing? Lily wondered about that herself. Revisiting the past, mostly. Looking at what she had lost. It was both painful and alluring, doing that. Seeing all that was old and dear and familiar to her – her *home*, The Fort – when times had moved on, when she was no longer welcome here.

All she wanted was for the decade never to have happened. To rewind the tape of life, to go back to that night when she had found Leo dead, but in this version, *her* version, he would not be dead, he would be alive, and they would argue. He would be sorry for what he'd done – for fuck's sake, Adrienne Thomson of all people! – and there would be only Adrienne, only one mistress and not a veritable legion of tarts there to do his bidding. Leo would grovel (and this was unlikely, she knew it was, because she had never seen Leo grovel in his entire life, but this was *her* fantasy and that was the way she wanted it to play out), and all would be forgiven, and life would go on.

But it could never have worked out that way, because Lily didn't do forgiveness and because she had never loved Leo in the hot, heady way she had once loved Nick. Her and Leo had sort of suited each other, though: he was loud; she was quiet. He liked splashing the cash; she had enjoyed spending it. They had the girls to unite them. For a while it had been enough.

Only . . . then she had found out about Adrienne, and any

feelings of affection she'd had for Leo had vanished overnight. They'd just evaporated like mist, leaving her with nothing but bitterness. Truth was, after that he could have had ten mistresses or even a hundred; to her, it was a moot point. The damage was done.

The nip of brandy was steadying her. She felt a little less shaky. She glanced at Oli, who looked even worse than she did. 'I'm sorry if I scared you,' said Lily.

'*Scared* me?' Oli let out an ironic laugh. 'You didn't just scare me, you freaked me out! I thought you were lying there *dead* or something, I was . . .' Her voice caught, there were tears in her navy blue eyes. She blinked hard . . . 'Swear to me you'll never, *ever* frighten me like that again.'

Lily had to fight the urge again to reach out, touch Oli's hand, embrace her. She just nodded, feeling choked up herself as she looked at her daughter's face and saw the impact Leo's death must have had on her. It was very clear that although Oli might hate her, be suspicious of her, she was still Oli's mother and Oli feared the death of another parent. No matter that the parent was no good, a murderess, a lifer out on licence, the worst scum that ever crawled the earth; deep down Oli was terrified of Lily dying, as Leo had died. The early years had scarred her badly, left a deep mark.

'I'm sorry,' said Lily helplessly, hating Oli's pain.

'Well, what on earth were you doing?' demanded Oli. She cupped shaking hands around her mug of coffee.

'I just . . . wanted to see the place again,' said Lily. It was the truth, after all. Or part of it, at least. This was her home.

'What, lying on the *ground*?'

And what was she supposed to say now? That Oli's Uncle Freddy had been there, threatening to crush the life out of her? That she had collapsed with fear? She looked at Oli's

116

sheet-white face. No, she didn't want more shit going Oli's way. She knew she was going to have to make some waves but, for as far as possible, she was going to shield Oli – and Saz – all she could.

'I got upset,' she said. 'Seeing the place again . . . I didn't realize how much it would throw me.'

Oli nodded and sipped her coffee. Then the intercom buzzed on the wall beside the marble-topped island and Oli dropped her mug. Hot coffee spilled out, splashing over her white top, running onto the floor. The mug handle snapped off.

'Fuck!' said Oli loudly.

'I'll sort that out,' said Lily, going to the sink, her sink, the Belfast sink she'd selected from the catalogue, the one she'd taken such pride in. God she must have been in a trance or something in those days, living the ideal life, living a total lie – and she wrung out a cloth then came back to the island as Oli flipped on the intercom. A male voice said: 'Hi, Ols.'

Lily busied herself with the mopping up, one ear cocked towards the intercom. Oli was looking at her mother, her body language radiating awkwardness.

'Jase!' Another glance at Lily. 'Um . . . come on in.'

She held down the tab to open the front gates. She looked unhappy. Lily went back to the sink and rinsed out the cloth. Turned and looked at Oli.

'You've got visitors, I'd better go,' she said.

'No! It's okay.' But still she looked unhappy.

'Who's Jase?' asked Lily. 'Boyfriend?'

'Yeah. Sort of,' said Oli, then fell silent.

'Been going out long?' *Speak to me, Oli, come on, I'm your mother for God's sake.*

'About six months,' said Oli. She raised a hand to her

mouth and chewed at a hangnail nervously. Lily saw that all her other nails were bitten too, down to the quick. 'He works for Uncle Si and Freddy at the club,' she said suddenly. 'Um. Should I tell Jase you're here? Maybe he shouldn't see you.'

So Oli knew Freddy and Si were a danger to her mother. And – thank you, God – she was even making tentative moves to protect her from them.

They both listened to a powerful car engine coming up the drive.

'It's okay,' said Lily. 'I'm a fact of life, Oli. Si and Freddy are going to have to live with that.'

She sounded braver than she felt. Inside, she was quivering with nerves. Freddy had just demonstrated clearly that her arse was going to be fried at some time of his choosing. And while Si might be more subtle, he was no less dangerous. She knew she was in the shit. It was just a question of whether she could haul herself out of it before one or both of Leo's brothers pushed her under.

Oli looked uncertainly at her mother, but she went to the back door and opened it. The car pulled up outside, the engine was cut and a door opened and slammed shut. A very handsome and extremely muscular man in his twenties, with black curling hair, clear olive skin and laughing dark eyes came in and swept Oli up into his arms.

Jesus, he's stunning, thought Lily. And Oli looked like jailbait – only of course she wasn't, Lily reminded herself. Oli was eighteen years old, an adult, although she looked younger. She'd turned eighteen on the twenty-seventh of February. Lily would never forget that date, it was imprinted on her mind. Every year in stir she had marked that day off on her calendar, had got the phone cards, phoned out, asked Si – who had taken up residence with bloody Maeve in *her* home – if she could speak to Oli, wish her a happy birthday. And Si, the bastard, had always said no, Lily, you can't. Fuck off and die, why don't you?

Jase grinned and kissed Oli before he realized they had an audience. Then, gently but firmly, he pushed her back a step. His grin faded.

'This is . . .' Oli faltered.

'I know who it is,' said Jase, his eyes unfriendly now as they rested on Lily, standing there by the marble-topped island. 'I saw her at the wedding.'

'Hiya Jase,' said Lily with more bravado than she actually felt.

He nodded; very cool.

'Jase . . .' began Oli.

'Jesus, Oli, you're putting me in a bad position here,' said Jase, shaking his head, pushing a hand through his hair. 'You know how Si feels about all this.'

'Yeah, I do. But . . . she's my mother.'

'Who killed your father. What the hell are you doing, letting her in here?'

'Jase!'

'Well, it's the truth. She's got no right to come here. And it might not be safe for you. You don't know what the crazy bitch is going to do, now do you?'

Lily straightened, pushed herself away from the island. She stared at Jase with hostile eyes. She wanted to say that she had every right in the world to be here. But she was smart enough to know that if she smacked Jase down, Oli might then have to defend him, and she didn't want to alienate Oli, not when she felt she was making just a tiny bit of progress with her.

'I'll go, Oli,' she said, and made for the door, pushing past Jase.

'Yeah,' said Jase. 'Do that.'

'Wait!' Oli caught her arm, turned her. 'How are you getting . . . I mean, look, hold on. How are you getting back to where you're staying?'

She'd nearly said 'home, how are you getting home'. But Lily *was* home. Nick's flat was just a roof over her head, nothing more than that.

Lily shrugged. 'Bus.'

'*Bus?*' But for God's sake, it's miles to the nearest bus stop. And,' she glanced at her watch, 'it's too late anyway. All the buses are gone.'

'Then I'll have to use your phone, call up a cab,' said Lily. *Although I don't have cash enough for that.*

'No, don't be silly. Look . . .' Oli was hesitating.

Lily held her breath.

'Look,' said Oli finally, 'Jase can drive you.'

'Fuck *that*,' said Jase.

Oli sent him an angry glance. 'All right then, *I* will.' Oli was frowning. 'Or . . .'

'Or what?' *Come on, sweetheart, come through for your Mum*, thought Lily, hardly daring to breathe.

'Well, you could . . . you could stop here. Just for tonight.'

Jase turned away, exasperation in every line. 'You are seriously *mental*, Oli King,' he groaned.

Lily felt her eyes start to swim with tears. Oli didn't believe she'd killed Leo. She *didn't believe it*. Or she would never have extended the invitation to stay, she'd have been too afraid. For a minute Lily couldn't speak at all, she was too afraid that she would break down and cry.

Oli was looking at her worriedly, casting anxious glances

at Jase. She desperately wanted that young man's approval, it was obvious. But she was digging her heels in, making a stand for her mother. Lily felt unbearably touched.

'Well?' Oli said. 'Mum?'

Lily gulped hard. 'Yeah,' she nodded. 'Thanks. Okay. I'll stay.'

20

Becks had visited her in Holloway, under the 'hand-in' system for newly convicted prisoners; this visit was permitted within forty-eight hours of being incarcerated. Lily had been marched down with a group of others to the visits hall. There she – and they – were frisked and searched. The things in her pockets – including her two precious phone cards – were taken off her.

'I'll get them back though, won't I?' she asked the screw anxiously. She wanted to call the girls. She had to call them, hear their voices, tell them it was all a mistake, that it would all be put right somehow.

She would never forget the last time she'd seen them before she was banged up. The way they had stood there, looking at her, when she wanted to hug them, reassure them. Si and Maeve had been in the room, both of them standing behind the girls, holding their shoulders; Si and Maeve, guardians of the girls. Si looking at her like she was dirt on his shoe, Maeve's expression smug. Si held Saz, Maeve held Oli – and it was a little time before Lily realized with a sinking heart that Si and

Maeve were not holding the girls to stop them running to their mother; they were holding them to stop them fleeing the room altogether.

Now, after Becks's visit, she got her cards back and went and found the phone and joined the queue. When she finally reached the front and dialled out to The Fort, Si answered. She asked if she could speak to the girls.

'No, you can't,' he said. 'Haven't you done enough damage, you evil cow?' And he put the phone down.

She dialled again, shaking, crying. She had to speak to them.

But this time, there was no answer at all.

21

When Oli tapped on the bedroom door next morning she found her mother sitting up on the side of the bed, clutching her head. She'd given Lily one of the seven bedrooms the house boasted, every one of them large and en suite: Oli occupied one at the front; and Saz – Oli had told Lily last night – had a suite to herself at the back on the ground floor overlooking the gardens, which was going to be knocked through and converted into a completely self-contained apartment for her and Richard one of these days.

Lily had crept out of bed during the night and tried the door of the master suite she had once shared with her husband, but found it was locked.

Fuck it, she thought, and went back to bed, only to lie there in the dark, unable to sleep, thinking only that she was back, she was right here where Leo had lost his life. She had achieved this much. She knew she had a hard road to travel now, and if she got to where she wanted to be then it was going to cost her; but she was determined. And – and this

124

was the best of all – Oli didn't seem to hate her too much. Not at the moment, anyway.

When she had finally slipped into exhausted slumber, the dreams plagued her again. She was inside, desperately trying to contact Oli and Saz. Only she couldn't.

It was a relief to wake up.

'Mum? What's the matter?' asked Oli, seeing her mother hunched over, clearly in pain.

'Migraine,' groaned Lily. 'I get them something awful, they started just after – ' Lily paused for dramatic effect – 'just after I got locked up.'

Lily kept her eyes on the carpet. She saw Oli's feet in FitFlops moving past, going to the bedside table. Then over to the curtains, pulling them back.

'Ow,' said Lily as the light hit her.

'Is it really bad?' Oli's voice was sweetly concerned.

I am a terrible person, thought Lily. *I am beyond redemption.*

'Awful,' moaned Lily. 'Makes me feel sick. In fact . . .' and she dashed off to the en suite, closing and locking the door behind her – she didn't want any mishaps. She made elaborate throwing-up noises, flushed the loo, splashed water over her face and hands, and dried herself on a towel, not meeting her own eyes in the mirror.

Then she unlocked the door and went back into the bedroom and flopped down, gasping, onto the bed. There was a cup of strong tea on the bedside table. Her daughter was sweet, so thoughtful and so gullible. She hoped Oli wasn't this wide-eyed and innocent when it came to dealing with Jase.

'Can I get you anything? Paracetamol?' offered Oli.

'No,' said Lily, wincing with imaginary pain.

'Look . . . I have to go out,' said Oli anxiously.

'You go,' said Lily, waving a limp hand towards her daughter. 'I'll just rest here.'

'Do they last long? These migraines?'

'About three days, usually. I get the bad ones, flashing lights, nausea, dizziness, the lot. I'm sorry about this, Oli. Really I am.'

'Only I could give you a lift back to the flat,' said Oli.

'I can't move just now. And the flat was only for last night, I'll just have to go back there and get my stuff together and move on.' *God, I'm such a liar.* 'And I will, when I feel a bit . . . oh shit, sorry, Oli . . .' And she was off to the bathroom again. Locking the door again. More spewing-up sound effects, flush loo, run water, splash face, dry on towel.

Lily staggered back into the bedroom and collapsed onto the bed. 'I'm so sorry about this, Oli,' she said weakly. 'When you've been so good.'

'Look, I tell you what, you just rest there,' said Oli. 'I'll be back lunchtime, check you're okay, all right?'

'Thanks, Oli.' Lily had her eyes closed but she sensed Oli still hovering nearby, uncertain whether to go or stay. 'You go, I'll just try and sleep.'

And Oli went. She heard her close the bedroom door softly behind her, and move off along the landing and down the stairs. The front door slammed. Seconds later, Oli's little sports car gunned into life and tore off down the drive.

There was silence in the house.

Complete, utter silence.

Game on, thought Lily, and sat up and drank her tea.

She took a quick shower, dried her hair, put on yesterday's clothes, and trotted off along the landing to the master suite.

She tried the handle again, but it was still locked. She went downstairs. She knew this house like the back of her hand; she went straight to Leo's study – which was *still* laid out as a study, but looked pretty much unused. Her eyes went around the walls of the smallish room. There was no gun cabinet there any more. Someone, obviously, had taken it as too strong a reminder of what had befallen Leo, and hadn't wanted to go on looking at all the twelve-bores, air guns and beautiful, hugely expensive Purdeys, all lined up there, gleaming and treasured, after one of them had been used to kill Leo.

So, no gun cabinet. Lily sat down in the dark blue leather captain's chair behind the desk and thought about that, mulled it all over in her mind once again as she had done a thousand, a *million* times, while she had waited out the hours spent inside. The gun cabinet hadn't been broken into that night. The *house* hadn't been broken into either, which had told the police that whoever had done this had easy access to the inside of the house, or had somehow gained that access. Whoever had killed Leo had known that the household keys – to the gun cabinet, the cellar, spares for the main doors, sets for the outbuildings, had all been kept right here in this desk.

Lily thought of Leo's tarts. That was the only way she could think of them, the only way she could bring herself to let them enter her mind. *Leo's tarts*. One in a lunatic asylum – Alice Blunt; the others she didn't know about yet. She wondered if Leo had brought Adrienne Thomson back here and screwed her in their bed. Could he really have done that to her? If he had, it was more than possible that he had brought others back here too, up to and including the one from the loony bin. Who must have been a desperate, unstable woman. Who maybe had freaked and decided to blow Leo's brains all over the master suite.

Maybe.

But there had only been Lily's prints on the gun.

She hoped Jack Rackland was busy fulfilling his part of their deal, because she was certainly trying hard enough to fulfil hers. She sifted through the drawers, hoping that she would find what she was looking for.

She did. In the bottom left-hand drawer she found a pile of old photos. She looked through them, grabbed one, pocketed it. Underneath the photos were the keys, some of which she remembered, a couple of which she didn't. She went out to the shed first, and noticed that things were slightly different at the back of the house. There was decking now, and a large seating arrangement with a patio heater. Si and Maeve had clearly made themselves very comfortable while staying at The Fort, in *her* house. She unlocked the shed, stepped around the ride-on mower and the neatly stacked paint tins and gardening tools. She selected the tool she needed and relocked the shed, then went back indoors.

As she passed through the hall again she glanced at the clock. It was nearly ten thirty and Oli might be back at twelve or even before that for lunch, so she had little time. She hurried back up the stairs, collected the rucksack from the room she'd slept in last night and, with shaking hands put the key in the lock of the master suite and turned it. She stuffed the bunch of keys into her jeans pockets and stood there, suddenly fearful.

Her life had fallen apart the last time she went inside this room. Time had moved on, but in her head there was still a horror movie playing out inside it. Her walking in, angry, wanting a fight, wanting to get it over with, hyped up with adrenaline; and then the shock, the God-awful shock of seeing the body, *his* body, lying there, the head blown away, the blood, the brains and the gore everywhere. And then the police coming, and the slow sick realization that they thought she'd killed him.

Then, prison. Oh shit, so long in prison. Seven years in Holloway, two in Durham, one in New Hall, then the last two in Askham Grange. Being confined without everything she knew, everything she loved. Her kids torn from her, the boredom and the low, simmering anger because she *knew she'd done nothing*. She'd contacted her brief, asked should she appeal? He'd said certainly, yes; but the appeal had been turned down. So she stayed there, powerless, marking off the days, the weeks, the years.

And – finally – freedom. But not the total freedom she craved; this was a freedom still hemmed about with limitations. Seeing probation officers. Walking on eggshells, not wanting to do anything that might take her back inside. She was still not completely free, not free as she defined it. She was going to have to win that freedom for herself, bit by painful bit, piece her life back together and find the bastard who'd done Leo and let her hang out to dry for it.

Now she was outside the door to the master suite once again. And even though logic told her that there was nothing inside there that could hurt her, no ghosts, *nothing*, even so she stood there and felt sweat erupt all over her body at the thought of going inside.

But she had to. She *had* to.

Lily gulped and steeled herself to do it. She reached out and opened the door. With a moan she pushed it wide open, expecting the horror to replay, Leo lying there, what remained of him, unrecognizable, but unquestionably Leo. Gold rings on his stubby fingers, the familiar old white scar on his left wrist, the thick gold chain around his neck mingling with the blood and the bits of mangled flesh.

But there was nothing.

She stepped inside. Before she could lose her nerve and run she quickly relocked the door from inside. Then she turned and looked around the room she had once shared with her husband, the blood buzzing in her ears and her heart beating so hard in her chest that she thought it was going to break straight out through her ribs.

Nothing.

The bedding was different. Not what she would have chosen. The curtains were different too. But the bed was in the same place, the thick white carpet was . . . no, it couldn't be the same one. Those stains would never have come out. It had been relaid.

All remnants of Leo's death had been wiped from the room. Light streamed in through the windows. The atmosphere was peaceful, not troubled. Lily walked slowly into the centre of the room, laid the rucksack and the tool down. Then she looked at the wall behind the bed. Different colour. It had been cream when she was here, now it had been repainted in a stylish dark red. Red like Leo's blood had been as it poured out of him. Shuddering, Lily started shoving at the bed: it moved easily; it was on castors. She shoved it hard, pushing it out into the middle of the room, away from the wall.

Panting, she paused. Then she took up the pickaxe. It was damned heavy. She swung it back over her shoulder, pictured Si King's pudgy, self-satisfied face in front of her and let fly at the wall.

Whack!

It was hard work, hacking through the plasterboard. Leo's boys had done a bloody good job on relining this wall: *too* bloody good. Soon she was streaming with sweat but the clock on the wall over the dressing table told her that time was running on, there was no time to rest.

Whack!

She kept belting away at it, picturing Si there on the wall before her, Si her enemy, Si bloody King.

Take *that,* you bastard!

She was glad now that she'd spent time in the gym during her confinement; before prison, she wouldn't have had the strength to attempt this. Now new muscles – and hatred – powered her.

She kept hacking away, through a blooming haze of plaster dust, with arms that grew heavy and aching. She was wet through, gasping, and – oh bliss – soon she started seeing small orange bits of insulation material, then a larger section of the stuff as big chunks of plasterboard fell away.

Jesus, she was making such a mess, plaster and dust and shit everywhere, and she didn't know how she was going to explain any of this to Oli, but then the door had been locked and she guessed that neither of the girls ever came in here. The memories, the feelings evoked, would be too awful. And thank God for that. Because there was no way she was going to be able to clear all this crap away before Oli got home.

Finally she'd made a big enough hole in the board. She dropped the pickaxe and got in there with her hands, pulling at the itchy chunks of insulating fabric with her hands, yanking it out, throwing it aside. And now she really, really hoped that Leo hadn't let her down. That it would all pan out just as years ago he had assured her it would, telling her that if ever they needed it fast, it would be there, safe and sound. She dug deeper with her fingers, her nose itching as flakes of the fabric flew all around her, her skin itching too; Jeez, she hated this stuff. But then . . .

'Oh holy *shit!*' she said, and laughed out loud.

Because it was there. She couldn't believe it, hadn't *dared* to believe it, but it was. Her first glimpse of the wads of fifty-pound notes, all neatly bundled up and covered in polythene, was the most beautiful thing she could ever have imagined. She stepped back from the wall, went into the en-suite bathroom and splashed her face and hands to relieve the itching. She cupped her hands and gulped down an icy, delicious mouthful of water.

Then she went back into the bedroom, threw the empty rucksack onto the bed and unzipped it. She started to fill it with Leo's emergency stash. Bundle after blessed bundle. Leo had told her there was a hundred thousand behind the wall. She took the whole lot and stuffed it into the bag.

Once all the money was out, she rummaged around in the cavity, determined to get everything, not wanting to pass up a single package, grinning now because Leo had come through for her even from beyond the grave, God bless his cheating arse. Now she was going to be able to pay Jack Rackland, get the ball rolling. Suddenly her hand encountered not more money but two different items.

She pulled out the first, her grin fading and a frown forming in its place. What the . . .?

She was holding a cream-coloured cloth bag. She opened the pull-cord at the top and tipped the heavy item inside out onto the bed. It was something wrapped in oilcloth. She sat down on the bed and uncovered it.

'Jesus,' she breathed, staring at the thing on the bed.

It was Leo's Magnum. What had he always said about it? Yeah. She remembered. 'A hand cannon,' he'd said. 'Blow you to fuck, this thing would. And it's got a kick on it like a mule.' There were two boxes of bullets there, too. All neatly stashed.

In case of emergency.

Well, wasn't this an emergency? She was in the crap up to her neck, and that was a fact. If that wasn't an emergency, then what the hell was? But she had signed the Firearms Act when she got out of nick. If she was ever caught so much as in *possession* of a firearm, she'd be back inside faster than you could say knife.

She stared dubiously at the gun. But Freddy. And Si. She was in danger here. *Real* danger. And here was Leo, reaching out to her from beyond the grave, saying, *Here, Lils. Take it. You might need it.*

And she might. She knew she wasn't supposed even to handle things like this, and she wouldn't, she swore to herself that she wouldn't. Unless she absolutely *had* to.

She cautiously rewrapped the Magnum and the boxes of bullets, and tucked the whole thing into the side compartment of the rucksack. Then she looked at the remaining item. It was an old, unmarked videotape. She stared at it, and suddenly heard a motor coming up the drive. Oli's car, she recognized the engine note. And – shit, that was another car not far behind it. Maybe Jase again?

Quickly, she tucked the tape into the top of the rucksack, ran across the room, unlocked the door, stepped out onto the landing, relocked it. She heard voices in the downstairs hall as she pocketed the key. She hurried back into the spare bedroom where she'd passed the night and threw the rucksack down beside the bed, peeled off her jeans. Footsteps on the stairs now. *Fuck it, hurry up!* She yanked off her t-shirt and threw herself back in between the sheets. When Oli knocked lightly and then opened the door, Lily was doing a very good impression of someone fast asleep.

'Um . . . Mum?' Oli said softly.

Lily made a great play of waking up. 'Hm . . .?' she asked groggily.

'Um,' said Oli awkwardly, looking unhappy and resentful. 'You . . . you *lied* to me. You said you were only able to stay at Nick's flat for a night. I spoke to him and he said you could have stayed there as long as you liked, and he also wanted to know where the hell you were right now . . .'

'Ah,' said Lily.

'Ah?' burst out Oli angrily. 'You *lied* to me.'

'Oli—'

'No! I don't want to hear your excuses,' she snapped, turning away. 'Uncle Si's here. And Aunt Maeve. They want a word with you.'

Lily's guts clenched. Oh shit. Whatever that word was, she doubted it would be *welcome*.

22

'You really have got some balls, coming here, Lily King,' said Maeve.

As she joined Oli, Maeve and Si in the big downstairs living room, Lily could tell that the atmosphere in here was subzero, which came as no surprise at all.

'Hi to you too, Maeve,' said Lily, sitting down on one of the couches, beside Oli.

'And turning up at the wedding like that! You've got a bloody nerve.'

Lily shrugged. Whatever verbal Maeve dished out, she didn't give a shit. She was more worried by Si's presence. Maeve might yap at her like a terrier, but any *real* threat would come from Si himself. He was just sitting there staring at her, and if looks could kill she'd be toast.

But even while she sat there worrying over Si's threatening glances, she knew that he wouldn't start anything major in front of Maeve or Oli. They were her safety net. For now. But they wouldn't always be there, she was very aware of that; aware that Si would like to rip her guts out and that one fine day he still hoped to get the chance to do it.

She had the money now. She could function, buy transport, clothes, people, whatever she needed. *Thanks Leo*, she thought. *You old bastard.* So she felt a little less shaky, a bit more as if she was on solid ground. She'd grown used to the cushion of money when Leo had been alive, and without it she'd been anxious. Now, she could settle. Now, she could get on and clear her name.

She thought again of Leo's Magnum. What the hell was she going to do with that?

'What you got to say for yourself?' demanded Maeve. 'What you doing, showing up like this?'

Lily looked at her sister-in-law coldly. 'Wouldn't you have turned up, Maeve, if you heard your daughter was getting married?' Then Lily rolled her eyes and slapped her thigh. 'Oh no. *Sorry.* Forgot. You couldn't *have* kids, could you? Maybe that's why you were so fucking happy to grab mine when you got the chance.'

Maeve coloured up. Lily knew she'd hit a sore spot. The family grapevine had always said that Si was a Jaffa – seedless. Maeve had tried hard to get pregnant, but it soon became obvious that it was never going to happen.

'That's a damned cruel thing to say,' shot back Maeve, jumping to her feet and advancing on Lily in a rage. 'And it's completely bloody beside the point. *Someone* had to look after the girls when you did what you did and got locked up for it. And now you've got the gall to sit here in Leo's home—'

'*My* home, too,' Lily cut in.

'Yeah, the poor misguided bastard was fair to you, wasn't he? Put both your names on the deeds, Si told me. And you . . .' she glanced at Oli, who was staring down at her hands, clenched white-knuckled in her lap . . . 'Well, I won't say it. It's evil. *You're* evil.'

Lily was silent for a beat.

'Well, that's true,' she said at last. 'That is, supposing I'd done it, of course. Which – by the way – I didn't.'

Maeve gave a cynical shout of laughter. 'Oh come *on*. You pleaded guilty, for Christ's sake. You're having a bloody laugh.'

'Am I laughing?' asked Lily.

'Look,' said Maeve, now hovering over Lily with clenched fists. 'You done your time. Now why don't you just bugger off? Disappear back into the hole you crawled out of.'

Lily gave the enraged woman a thin smile. '*This* is my hole, Maeve,' she said flatly. 'This house. Oli has no objection to me staying in it – do you, Ols?'

Lily had to hold her breath at this point. She was shoving Oli's limits, shoving them hard, and she knew it. It was true that she'd lied to her about Nick's flat. And about the migraine – and Oli must have noticed by now that she didn't seem ill at all. She'd lied about quite a bit, actually. She didn't have a clue how she was going to explain about the master bedroom – or what was left of it, now she'd taken a pickaxe to the wall behind the bed. Lily knew that Oli loved her Aunt Maeve and her Uncle Si; they had been a permanent fixture in her young life when her mother and father had vanished off the scene. She must have grown close to them.

Lily felt a stab of insane jealousy at that. Those fuckers. They'd been here, watching *her* kids grow up, enjoying a family life that wasn't theirs.

Now Oli was all grown up, and there was Jase, too; Jase had reacted strongly – and badly – to the sight of Lily in the house, had hastened to tell Si, and here Si was to sort her out. Oli wanted Jase's love and approval. Would Oli now side with Maeve, with Si, with Jase, against her own mother? Lily really didn't know the answer to that.

'I . . .' Oli looked around at them all, her expression uncertain. She looked at Si, who hadn't said a single word since Lily entered the room, then at Maeve. Finally, her eyes came to rest on Lily.

Oh come on, Ols, thought Lily. *Don't let me down now.*

'I think I'd like Mum to stay,' said Oli unsteadily.

'Oh for God's *sake*, Oli!' said Maeve loudly, turning away, exasperated.

'Motion carried,' said Lily, standing up. 'Unless you feel like grassing me up to the authorities, telling them I've moved house and not told them . . .?'

She knew they wouldn't do that. No one in their circle ever ratted to the police.

'No. Didn't think so,' said Lily.

Maeve turned back to Lily, red-faced with rage, suddenly raising a hand to strike. Instinctively Lily grabbed Maeve's wrist and shoved herself up hard against the front of the bulkier woman, then hooked a foot in between Maeve's thick calves and heaved. Maeve's expression was almost comically surprised as she toppled backwards and hit the shag pile with a thud. Si came to his feet in one swift movement, his eyes fixed venomously on Lily.

Lily froze. Would he really do anything in front of Oli? For a moment she wasn't sure; he looked furious. Then he turned aside, helped his wife up.

'Now I'd like you both to get the fuck out of my home,' said Lily.

'You bitch,' said Maeve, gasping and flustered as she scrabbled upright.

Si gave Lily a twisted little smile. 'This ain't over,' he said softly, and ushered a limping Maeve out into the hall.

The two women listened as Si and Maeve crossed the hall and went out of the front door. The car engine started up and they drove away. Silence descended.

'Holy shit,' breathed Lily. She looked at Oli. She felt tears start in her eyes, tears of sheer relief. Oli had defended her, had come down on her side, not Maeve's. She held out a hand to her daughter. 'Thanks, Oli. Thanks for supporting me.'

'That don't alter the fact that you lied to me,' said Oli, standing up, her face sullen and averted. 'Look,' she said, 'you can stay here, but I don't want to talk to you. Okay?'

And she pushed past her mother, ignoring Lily's outstretched hand, and left the room.

23

Next day Jack collected Lily in his beat-up old car ('Good for surveillance work,' he told her when she did a double-take at the rusty old heap) from The Fort. Jack did a double-take of his own when he saw the house, the gates, the security system.

'You live here now, yeah?' he asked as she got in the car.

'Right,' said Lily.

'The bill for my services just went up.'

Lily looked at him.

'Joke,' said Jack, and started the engine and drove them over to the Lime Trees Clinic.

Alice Blunt, one-time mistress of Leo King, looked like a puff of wind would knock her clean off the Lloyd Loom chair she was sitting in. She was stick-thin, wearing a shapeless white dress and a cream-coloured cardigan; there were muddy white trainers on her big, bony, naked feet. Her hair, once no doubt vibrantly blonde, was like bleached straw. Her face was blank, her nose beaky, and her eyes – a pretty China blue, the only remnant of the woman she must once have been – were without interest or expression

140

as Lily walked into her room with the buxom dark-haired nurse.

'Visitor for you, Alice,' said the nurse cheerily. 'You remember Lily, don't you?'

Don't think she remembers too much, the nurse had told Lily when she'd arrived. *Don't get any visitors apart from her mother and brother. You're an old friend, you say? Been abroad for some time, you lucky thing? Oh, Australia? God, I could use some of that, soak up a few rays on Bondi. Well this is good. Maybe this is what she needs, a different face, give her a little jolt.*

But Alice didn't look jolted. She went on staring out of the window, out across the manicured lawns down to the big lake with its huge massed shrubs and grasses that danced in the sun and the wind.

Lily began to feel bad about this. It was obvious the woman was out of it. She was glad now that she'd left Jack Rackland, freshly paid and pretty damned happy about it too, sitting down in reception. She felt embarrassed on this woman's behalf – squirmingly so: there was a snail-trail of food stains down the front of the white dress. And unless Lily missed her guess, that was an adult nappy bulking up Alice's lower regions. The room smelled sour, of sickness and bad ventilation.

'Hi Alice,' said Lily. She could feel a stupid talking-to-an-invalid grin pasting itself all over her face, but she couldn't help it. 'I'm Lily, remember me?'

Of course she don't, thought Lily. *She's never clapped eyes on me in her life before. And look at her. The poor bitch don't even know which way is up.*

Lily looked doubtfully at the nurse, who would have ejected her straight from the room if she'd known what she had really come here for – to find out if Alice Blunt had shot Leo. One look at the wreck in the chair made it clear she wasn't going to find out a damned thing, not here. And seriously – could this slight, pathetic piece of human flotsam ever have had the strength in her, the *passion* in her, to fire a single shot?

'Take a seat and talk to her,' said the nurse. 'Might jog her memory.'

'How long's she been like this?'

'Oh – ten years or so. Since before I came here, anyway.'

'What, she just sits here like this? All the time?'

'Sometimes she's a little naughty, aren't you, Alice?'

No answer.

'Sometimes she goes off down to the lake by herself, but that's okay, we always know where to find her. Alice likes the lake – don't you, Alice?'

Alice said nothing.

'Messes up her trainers, gets them all muddy. She was down there after tea yesterday: look at the state they're in. I seem to spend half my life cleaning off Alice's trainers.'

Nothing.

'Go on,' said the nurse, 'talk to her. I'll be right along the hall if you need me.'

The nurse left the room, leaving the door wide open. Lily took off her backpack but held it close to her. It was still stuffed with all the money and with the videotape. The Magnum – that damned thing scared her half to death – she'd concealed back at the house. She had considered hiding the money there too, but she was too anxious about it, too reluctant to be parted from it, to do that. If she got stopped by the Bill, the money would be hard enough to explain, but the Magnum would be impossible. She didn't want to fall foul of the law, but it was sort of nice to know it was *there*, just in case.

Alice was still staring out of the window. Lily wondered if the woman was even aware that someone else was in the room. She cleared her throat. She had a prickly feeling that the nurse was listening out there in the hall somewhere, worried in case anyone upset her patient and earned her a verbal kicking from the suits in charge.

'You remember me, don't you?' she tried. 'I'm Lily. And . . . and you knew Leo.'

At the word 'Leo', Alice blinked.

Lily leaned forward in the chair and said the name again, more softly. 'Leo.'

Another blink.

'Do you remember him, Alice? Leo King?'

Lily felt excitement building in her gut. Although Alice's expression hadn't changed, she thought that maybe she *did* remember Leo. And now she wanted to ask more, much more, such as, *Did you blow my husband's brains out, did you flip and kill him and let me take the rap for it, you stupid cow?*

'Look,' said Lily, and she dug out the snap of Leo that she had lifted from the study while searching for the key to the master suite – Leo in his prime, taken on a Lanzarote golf course, Leo wearing white golfing gloves and a sun visor, his five-iron held casually over one meaty shoulder, Nick and some of the other guys there too, all grinning in the sunshine. She held the snap out to Alice, pointing out Leo among the group. 'See that, Alice? That's Leo.'

Alice extended one bony hand and took hold of the photo. She stared at it. Then she clasped it to her chest.

What Alice did next was the last thing Lily expected. She

opened her mouth wide – she looked like one of those crazy-golf clowns, scary wide-open red mouths painted on hardboard around a gaping black hole. Lily had time to think that; the ones that swallow your ball and look like they would swallow you too, given half a chance – and then Alice started to scream like a fire bell.

Lily almost fell off her chair.

'Holy *fuck!*' she gasped out, while Alice just went on screaming.

Instantly the nurse was back.

'What happened?' she demanded, running to Alice. 'What did you *say?*'

'I just . . .' Lily was almost in shock. The noise, the freaking *noise* the woman was making, it was deafening.

The nurse was shaking Alice's shoulder. 'Alice?' she was shouting. *'Alice?'*

Suddenly, just as abruptly as she had begun, Alice stopped screaming. Instead she started to cry, great wracking child-like tears, turning in her chair and clutching at the front of the nurse's mint-green uniform, pouring snot and salt water all down the front of it.

'There, there, Alice. There, there,' cooed the nurse. She turned suspicious eyes on Lily. 'She hasn't done anything like this before. Not in ten years.'

Well maybe it's time she did, thought Lily. Maybe this was a watershed for Alice Blunt. Maybe the sight of Leo would pull her out of the strange state she was in.

Lily stood up. 'Look, I'm sorry if I upset her.'

The nurse's eyes softened, just a little. 'That's okay. I'm sure you didn't mean to.'

'I hate to ask, but Alice's relatives – could they get in touch with me?' she asked. 'It's just . . . I'd like to know what happened to Alice, if they can fill in the blanks? When I knew her she was so different. I'd like to talk to them, if they're agreeable. Could I give you my phone number, and could you ask them to call me?'

The nurse was staring at Lily. Assessing her. Finally, reluctantly, she nodded. 'Yes, okay.'

Lily stood up, gathered up her backpack. The nurse found a pad and pencil and noted down The Fort's number with a promise to get one of Alice's relations to call. Lily left the poor sad shell of Alice Blunt sitting there, clutching the nurse, as a child would clutch a mother. She didn't ask Alice to give back the photo; she didn't think Alice *would*.

24

Lily got a shock when she dived into The Fort's indoor pool that afternoon and the water hit her like an ice pick straight between the eyes. *Freezing!* Whose bright idea had it been to turn the pool heating off? Did Oli like swimming in cold water?

Lily didn't. She remembered very well that *Leo* hadn't, either. He had always kept the indoor house pool at subtropical temperatures, with steam rising off the surface. Leo had loved the heat, the sun, the warmth. Hated the outdoor pool, even though that was heated too. Not hot enough. Too fucking *cold*.

Shivering, Lily briskly swam a length. She was wearing a borrowed one-piece swimsuit – navy blue, very boring and a couple of sizes too big for her – that she'd found in the changing cubicle at the far end of the pool. They'd always kept a small selection of swimwear in there for visiting guests attending Leo's famous parties . . . . Jesus, the parties they'd had in this house, way back when. Dancing and drinking and diving into the pool in full evening gear, big shoulder

146

pads on all the women's dresses, mullet hairstyles, Duran Duran and Spandau Ballet blaring out of the sound system, the laughs they'd had – all those bad boys doing their dodgy deals and discussing their moody goods; all the sparkling, glammed-up girls . . .

And of course thinking about the laughs made Lily think about the tears, too. And how empty those days had really been – oh, filled up with shopping and manicures and spa breaks, but still empty at the core. Empty and unhappy.

She pushed those thoughts away, because thoughts of losing Leo had prompted other thoughts, thoughts of Alice Blunt sitting there in a chair day in day out, speechless, dead-eyed. And then, those unearthly screams. Shuddering, she swam another brisk length: what the hell, it was cold, but it was a pool, *her* pool, and the sheer luxury of it almost overwhelmed her. She'd had nothing like this, nothing nice, nothing worth a monkey's fuck really, for twelve long years. She had a lot of catching up to do. In terms of living. And in terms of making peace with her daughters. And she knew that that would only be truly possible if she could find out who had really killed Leo.

Not Alice Blunt, surely. Alice had looked so frail, and that frailty had seemed bone-deep, not merely a result of illness, depression, whatever the hell it was fashionable to call it these days. Lily hoped the relatives would take the opportunity of phoning her, talking to her.

She wanted to know more about Alice. Even though it still – stupidly, she did realize that – stung a bit, to think of Leo shagging half the female population. Not only Alice, but also Adrienne. Not only *them*, but a woman called Reba Stuart. Jack had phoned again and said they were going to pay this 'Reba' a visit, was that what she wanted?

'Only I know you were upset after seeing Alice,' he said. 'You sure you want to go on with this? You can bail out any time, you know. You don't have anything to prove.'

'Except my innocence,' Lily replied stonily, going on the defensive because he was right, seeing Alice *had* upset her, and she hated that he had taken note of it. 'And who the fuck are you, my father?'

'Hey, I'm just saying . . .'

'*Don't* just say. I'm paying you, okay? I don't need a nurse-maid, I just need you to do your job, all right?'

There was silence on the other end of the phone. Then Jack said: 'All right. Fine,' and hung up.

She'd hurt his feelings. She knew it, and regretted it. She was getting to like Jack, and to depend on him. But liking and dependency were weaknesses she could not afford. She had to keep strong.

In actual fact, she would rather have had her arse rubbed with a *brick* than pay a visit to another of Leo's tarts. But she had to do it; there was no way around it. So yes, she was going to meet Reba Stuart tonight. What a treat.

So cold in here.

She swam another length, then another, and warmed up just a little but not enough. She was going to tweak that heat up later on, make it nice and toasty-warm for tomorrow's swim. To hell with being stone-cold.

She was making for the steps at one end of the pool, ready to get out, get a hot drink down her, when she saw that Si was standing there, silent, patient, and waiting for her.

A fizzing thrill of panic rippled all the way from Lily's head to her toes. It settled in her chest, clutching at her heart.

Fuck it, where did he come from?

Instantly she thought of her rucksack, stowed away for now in the changing cubicle with a hundred thousand pounds tucked inside. Safe. A damned sight safer than *she* was right now. Si the spider had emerged and she was a tiny fly. Damn it, she should have pushed forward to get the locks changed the minute after they'd gone yesterday, but Oli had been upset, doubtful – and she hadn't wanted to push her too fast.

Now, she could see that her error was going to cost her dear.

Si was there, watching her, smiling, his usual dark bespoke suit covering his bulk. In his hand he was holding the long pole with the net on it, used by the pool man to fish debris from the surface of the outdoor pool, when leaves and insects got blown in.

Lily kicked hard for the side but he moved and was there, waiting for her. Si gave a little smile. Then he put the net end of the pole against her breastbone and pushed her back into the cold water.

'No,' he said, 'just stay there.'

Stay here and I'll bloody well freeze, thought Lily, feeling a deep shiver course through her body, clamping her teeth together to stop them chattering with the cold and the sudden fear.

'I'm not very happy with you, Lily King,' he said as Lily moved back into the centre of the pool.

'Oh? Really?' Lily forced out. She was trying to clamp down on her rising panic, keep calm, keep thinking. But it was hard. She made for the steps again, but *again* he moved, blocking her path out of the freezing water, pushing her firmly back with the pole.

'Yeah, really. It's not on, girl. Really it ain't. You doing Leo. Turning up at the wedding and ruining Saz's day. Pushing

149

back in here, messing with Oli's head. Showing Maeve up like that. Not on.'

Lily swam over to the other side of the pool. He was there.

Now she was really starting to panic. She found it hard to catch her breath, it was so cold in here. Doggedly she swam another length, trying to keep her body temperature up with exertion, and when she got to the far end, he was there, too. She couldn't get out. He was going to keep her in here until she drowned.

'I didn't do Leo,' said Lily, and now her teeth really were chattering.

'Yeah you did,' said Si calmly.

'No, I didn't. Someone else did it.'

'Did they fuck. *You* did it.'

Lily made for the steps again – and this time Si came ankle-deep in the water with the pole, and *this* time he meant business. The end of the pole connected with her neck and she was abruptly submerged, forced under as he bore down on it.

The world was suddenly bubbling and blue-green and she was choking, swallowing mouthfuls of chlorine-laden water. Lily kicked back, away from him, and came up spluttering and gasping in the centre of the pool, her eyes stinging, her throat burning, shivers wracking her body.

Now Si had moved and was reaching towards her with the pole again; it struck her arm, not violently, but hard enough to knock her off balance. She realized that he was doing his best not to mark her; he wanted to make this look like accidental drowning. She fell sideways and was again under the water. She came back up, coughing, blinking, seeing him standing there watching her with that smug, triumphant half-smile on his face.

150

Bastard.

'What's going on?' asked an anxious female voice.

Lily's head whipped round. So did Si's.

Oh thank Christ. It was Oli. She was walking towards Si, looking at Lily in the pool, looking at the pole in his hand. Her eyes were questioning, worried.

'Oh, Lily was in a bit of difficulty,' said Si smoothly. 'Just helping her get to the side. Ain't that right, Lil?' And he turned and smiled at Lily with hatred in his eyes.

'Sure,' she said, cold through to the bone now, and frightened too, scared *shitless* in fact.

Now he held the pole out to her.

Lily ignored it. She swam to the steps and hurried up them. She snatched up a towel from one of the loungers and wrapped it round herself quickly. Then she turned and looked at Si, and at Oli standing there uncertainly, frowning. Oli knew something had happened here. She *knew*, even if her face clearly said that she didn't want to believe the truth of it.

Lily could almost hear Oli thinking: *Jesus, was he trying to push her under with that thing?* She thought that Oli knew the answer to that, in her gut. And if Oli hadn't shown up, he'd have done the job and the verdict would have been accidental drowning.

'People shouldn't swim on their own,' Si was saying to both of them, and now he looked genial, completely convincing. 'It's not safe.'

You can say that again, thought Lily.

She looked at Oli, still standing there with that frown on her face, and wondered what she thought of her kind Uncle Si *now*.

25

'Blonde joke,' said Lily as she walked along the shops up West with a reluctant Oli in tow the following day. 'What do you call a fly buzzing inside a dumb blonde's head?'

Oli looked at her, perplexed. Then she sighed. 'Okay, what?'

'A space invader.'

Oli almost cracked a smile. Almost. She'd been subdued ever since she'd come across Lily and Si in the swimming pool room yesterday. Lily had a feeling there were about a thousand questions queuing up in Oli's brain, all waiting to be asked.

She looked at her youngest daughter, thinking again how gorgeous she was, and how young, how vulnerable. Her heart twisted with pity for all that Oli had suffered, but she was going to make damned sure someone paid – in blood – for that.

Lily had suggested this shopping trip. What they called a bonding session, and where better to 'bond', she'd said to Oli earlier, than in 'Bond' Street?

'Shopping's so inane,' said Oli. 'And very un-PC, think of the credit crunch.'

Fuck the credit crunch. Lily had been reading the papers, she knew all about the banks crashing and shares plummeting through the floor. But she'd been undergoing her very own personal credit crunch for the past twelve years; she had come out of nick dressed in shit order, jeans and t-shirt and a sodding hoodie and trainers, and she had always been a dressed-up sort of woman, her style had always been classic and classy. Well, now she was going to restart her life. Reclaim her style. And she was starting *today*.

Where to begin?

She was like a kid all of a sudden, staring at the sweeties in the shop window, and – oh thank you, Leo, thank you – now she could buy the entire fucking sweetshop, if she chose. They passed by De Beers and Cartier, Lily lingering and admiring, Oli silent and trudging along at her heels. It was busy; there were crowds of people, tourists, shoppers milling everywhere, black cabs honking up and down the street, traffic moving at a snail's pace. It was great. Lily looked around her and soaked it all up, the smells of coffee and bread baking, the exhaust fumes, everything – she felt newborn. And the people – black, Asian, pale-skinned English, all going about their lives, all *free*. Unaware of what a luxury that freedom was. There was an Oriental man moving ahead of them, crossing the street, talking on a mobile phone, his blue-black hair pulled back tight into a ponytail. She loved it all.

They went into Chanel, Miu Miu and DKNY Jeans, then took a leisurely hike through Armani – oh, Lily *loved* Armani, but Christ her hair was a dreadful mess, she could see it in all the mirrors: chopped about, flattened, pale blonde flecked through with – oh fuck – the odd wiry grey hair. The sheer beauty of the clothes and accessories she was trying out showed up her own deficiencies. Bad hair, tick. Bad *nails*, oh yes indeed. Hard, calloused feet, too.

Then they were into Savile Row for a dive into Abercrombie and Fitch. Starting to feel a bit footsore, they went on to Conduit Street for a trip into Rigby & Peller to be properly measured and fitted for new underwear. Oli did cheer up a little in there, admiring a purple basque, fingering pale pink chiffon thongs and luscious pin-tucked and ribboned bras. They lurched outside, festooned with bags, did a quick recce in Moschino, and then gave it up, both worn out. They stopped for coffee and cake.

'I want to talk to you,' said Oli when they had been seated in a booth and had ordered. 'Seriously.'

'Seriously? What about?'

Oli stared at her mother. 'Well, about all this bloody *money* you've got for a start.'

'Ah. That.'

'And come on. Be honest now. Please.' Oli looked down at the table, started shredding a napkin. 'He was trying to hurt you, wasn't he? Uncle Si?'

Lily blew out her cheeks, not sure how to answer.

Oli sat back. 'You still do that. I *remember* that.' She mimicked what Lily had done. 'You always did that . . . when you were trying not to answer a question. Like, oh,' and now Oli was smiling a little, 'like, Mummy, where do babies come from?'

'Yeah, do you know the answer to that one yet?' Lily quipped. She was touched that Oli remembered her little foibles. She remembered Oli's, too – they were forever branded on her brain. Like the strawberry birthmark on Oli's upper right arm, and the vertical frown-lines between Oli's dark brows, very much in evidence now, signalling her determination to get an answer on this subject.

'Answer the frigging question, Mum. This is all fun, and it feels really strange but sort of nice doing this with you, just girly things like shopping and stuff – and you haven't explained yet about the cash, and don't think I've forgotten that – but it's just a smokescreen, ain't that the truth? So come on. Tell me. Was he . . .?'

Their waiter was back with two Americanos and cupcakes.

'What is that all about?' wondered Lily aloud. 'A thousand types of coffee, when all a person wants is strong and black . . .'

'*Mum.*'

Lily looked at her. 'Okay. Yeah. Si believes I did it. And he thinks twelve years of my life ain't enough to pay for the loss of your father. Straight enough for you?'

Oli stared at her. 'I'll speak to him,' she said.

'No,' said Lily.

'*Yeah*, I will. And I'll say that if anything happens to you, I'll know it wasn't an accident and . . . I'll go to the police.'

Lily sipped her coffee, troubled. She didn't want Oli going head to head with Si and that nutter Freddy. And no daughter of hers was going to turn into a grass if she had anything to do with it.

'Look, Oli—'

'No you look. I lost Dad. And now . . . now I've just got you back. I can't lose you too.'

Suddenly Oli's eyes were full of tears.

'Hey,' said Lily, reaching out, patting Oli's hand. 'Hey, it's all right. Nothing's going to happen to me.'

'No?' Oli swiped angrily at her eyes. 'Fuck me, Mum, how

155

can you say that? You've been banged up in prison for twelve years and you tell me it was all for nothing. That the person who killed Daddy is still out here, still walking the streets, free as a bird. Maybe I'm stupid to believe what you say, but I do. I don't think you killed him, and if that's so, then Uncle Si has no right, no right at *all*, to start threatening you.'

Lily was silent. She picked at her cupcake. Then she said: 'Do you think we should get the security codes and the locks and everything changed at The Fort?'

Lily could see that Oli was thinking again about the scene she had interrupted by the swimming pool. Lily there, shivering in the freezing-cold pool, and Si with the pole, keeping her in there.

'Yeah,' she said finally. 'I think we should.'

'What about Saz? What will she make of it?'

'Saz ain't here,' said Oli, tilting her chin up. Saz was her big sis, the boss of their little tribe – Lily knew it would take guts for Oli to stand against her.

'Well, okay. We'll get that organized, yeah?'

'Yeah. Okay. Sunstyle Securities come and test it and maintain it. I'll phone them, they'll do it.'

'Good.'

'And now the money,' said Oli, and that frown-line was still there as she reached for a lavender-iced cupcake and removed a sugared violet from its centre. 'How can you have all this money?'

'Ah yeah . . . about that.' And Lily told her about Leo's emergency stash behind the wall in the master suite, and that she had . . . well, accessed it.

'Accessed it how?'

'With a pickaxe. So we're going to need a builder as well as the security guys.'

156

'You did that when you were supposed to be ill with a migraine,' said Oli accusingly.

'I lied about the migraine. Sorry, Oli. But I didn't know how far I could trust you. I just had to get into the house and get that money, and then I could start to rebuild my life, start to find . . .'

'Find what?' Oli was diving into the cupcake but now she stopped and stared at her mother's face.

'Find some peace of mind,' finished Lily, when she had almost blurted: *Find out who murdered Leo.* She didn't want Oli getting involved in this crusade of hers. She wanted Oli safe, and once they started down this road she knew damned well that safety could no longer be guaranteed.

Oli was staring at her. Lily had the uncomfortable feeling that she was not quite believing what her mother was telling her any more.

'You know what?' said Oli. 'You're devious.'

'Oli . . .' She was going to say, no, no Oli, I'm not, please believe me, baby, but sometimes life throws shit at you and you need to duck and dive to miss it.

'Yeah, you are.' Oli was sitting back, nodding thoughtfully, staring at her mother. 'You've changed. You were never devious *before*. You were just . . . you were just my sweet quiet mum, until they took you away. I asked for you, you know.'

'Oli – oh sweetheart.' Lily felt as though her heart was breaking into a thousand tiny pieces when she looked at Oli's lovely face and saw the pain there.

'Yeah, I did. I asked to see you. I didn't understand, but they told me you'd done a bad thing, a terrible thing to Dad and we'd lost him, and now you had to pay for it. I didn't understand. How would a six-year-old kid understand all that shit? And I couldn't remember . . . it was just awful, I couldn't remember what happened when Dad died. I *still* can't. But I cried for you night after night, Mum. Every night, I cried. And for him too, for Dad. But neither of you ever came back.'

She was quiet a moment, looking down at her half-eaten cupcake. Lily said nothing. There was bugger-all she could say: all the damage had already been done and all she could hope for now was that she'd be allowed to make up for the crap Oli had been forced to endure in the past.

Oli's eyes flicked up and she stared at Lily. 'Uncle Si and Aunt Maeve told me and Saz that you didn't want to see us.'

Bastards, thought Lily, the news cutting her like a knife, even though it failed to surprise her.

She thought of those impassioned phone calls she had made on the girls' birthdays, at Easter, at Christmas; always hopeful, always trying, but hope dying by slow degrees as the barriers sprang up, as Si said again and again: *No Lily, you can't speak to them, why would they want to talk to the bitch who'd done their father? Fuck off and die, why don't you?* Si could have got the house number changed, but he hadn't. Lily guessed that he enjoyed turning her down, making her suffer. Change the number and he'd have to find other ways to get his jollies.

Lily found she had to clear her throat and blink hard before she asked the next question.

'Did . . . did Saz ask for me too?'

Oli slumped forward, pushing the remains of the cupcake and the cooling coffee aside. She leaned on her elbows, pushed her hands deep into her wild curling mop of dark hair, and looked at her mother.

'No,' she said. 'Saz never asked.'

'Oh.' That hurt a lot.

'It changed her,' said Oli sadly. 'It changed her, big-time.'

'How do you mean?'

'Just . . . oh, she's a bit wild sometimes. A bit out of it.' Oli gave Lily a wan half-smile. 'I think she's scared herself a couple of times and that's why she's married Richard. He's so straight, so flipping *boring* really, but a really nice man. He's a sort of anchor for her.'

Lily straightened, perturbed by what Oli was telling her, but knowing she had to put it to one side. She tried not to think about Saz's anguish, or Oli's, not now. It wouldn't help. She had to keep strong, keep focused. She picked up her coffee cup and drained it. 'You know what I need?' she said.

Oli shook her head.

'A bloody good hairdresser,' said Lily. 'And another coffee.'

26

You'll never see it coming. But it is.

Lily remembered Freddy's mouthed words to her outside Askham. They drifted through her brain at the weirdest times, like now, when she had left Oli at the table with all their bags, and asked the waiter where the loo was. He directed her into the back of the coffee shop, and she went down a corridor and turned right at the bottom, and all at once she had a feeling that someone was behind her, walking steadily in her footsteps, and then she could *hear* a heavier tread behind her, a man's footfalls.

You'll never see it coming. But it is.

Terror rocketed up from her heart to her brain, and all the time she was thinking, *Don't be stupid, it's just one of the staff*, and she tried to chide herself, to make herself look round, but she couldn't, she was too afraid that it would be Freddy, huge, shaven-headed, pug-nosed, cleft-chinned Freddy with the cruel laughing eyes, and he would catch her and kill her, all the while saying, *You see, Lily? You see it now, don't you? Now it's coming. Now it's here.*

160

She quickened her step and she was at the loo door now, reaching a trembling hand for it. There was a little thing on the cheap brown wood-effect door – a white stick-on plaque depicting a dumpy little skirted cherub peeing into a pot. What a tacky, ridiculous thing to become your last memory of life on earth.

She was turning the handle, moving quickly, but she knew she would never be quick enough. It was Freddy, he'd come for her, this was it. A big hand clamped down on hers and she was spun round. Another hand went over her mouth, stifling the scream that was starting there.

Jesus. Oh God, help me.

'Lily King,' said Nick O'Rourke, his black-on-black eyes glinting with fury, 'what the *fuck* you playing at, girl?'

Lily sagged back against the loo door. Nick took his hand away.

'What the fuck am I doing? What the fuck are *you* doing, you arsehole?' she snapped, feeling giddy, her heart beating crazily with the fright he'd just given her. 'Jesus! You nearly gave me a sodding seizure!'

Nick looked mad enough to spit. He leaned back against the wall and stared at her like he was debating whether to wring her neck or jump her bones. Lily found to her annoyance that she was still finding him fiercely attractive, with his dark hair and his intense face and his good height, shown off really nicely by a slick suit that looked like Hugo Boss if she was any judge.

All right, enough, she thought. She'd been banged up for too long and it had made her bloody rampant. But did she really want to start down *that* road again, lusting after high-powered bad boys and ending up in the sort of trouble she couldn't hope to deal with?

161

'You ain't got a clue, have you?' He was staring at her in wonderment.

'A clue about what?'

'You're being *stalked*, you silly cow.'

'*What?*'

'You've got Tiger Wu tracking you up and down Bond Street – didn't you even fucking well notice?'

'Tiger . . . Tiger *who*?' Lily stammered. What the hell was he talking about?

'He's a removal man, Lily. Oriental in appearance, with a ponytail. And what he removes is people.'

Oriental in appearance with a ponytail. *Jesus!* She'd seen the man out there, crossing the road in front of her and Oli.

For God's sake, what the hell was happening here? Nick was saying she had some git on her tail, and therefore on Oli's tail too.

'What the hell are you thinking of?' Nick demanded. 'Don't you think you should have *told* me where you were going when you decided to check out of the safe flat, so I didn't think some damned thing had happened to you – like Freddy King going off on one and whacking you, or getting some other cunt to do it for him?'

Lily cleared her throat. Her mouth was suddenly dust-dry. Good God, first Si had a pop at her, and now it looked as if Freddy was having a go. None of this was good news.

'Is he still out there?' asked Lily, thinking of Oli, her precious Oli, sitting alone in the coffee shop.

One of the waiters was coming down the corridor. Nick gave him a glare. 'It's out of order, pal,' he said with a face like thunder.

The waiter looked at Nick's expression and backed quickly up.

'No, he's not still out there,' said Nick, turning back to Lily. 'Good job I had someone keeping an eye on you. My boys have taken him for a little trip.'

Lily let out a heavy breath of relief.

'Word on the street is you're back at Leo's place,' said Nick.

Now Lily's eyes flashed. 'It's my home, Nick.'

'You think they're going to stand for that?'

'Don't look like it – does it?' sniffed Lily. He'd scared the crap out of her. And for fuck's sake, what made him think he could pile in here and start playing the big I-am? She was her own woman. Oh, she never used to be. She *used* to be quiet mousy little wife Lily King, ruled and practically bloody *owned* by Leo – and look where *that* had landed her. Now she was going to stand on her own two feet. Fuck men.

'I don't know what the hell you're playing at, Lily,' said Nick. 'But I don't like it.'

'And who died and made *you* God, Nick O'Rourke?' she demanded. 'I don't have to answer to the King brothers, and I *certainly* ain't going to start answering to you.'

Nick straightened. She could see he was royally pissed off with her now, but she didn't give *that*. Fuck the lot of them, what had they ever done for her?

Had she been in a calmer state of mind she would have admitted – if only to herself – that in fact Nick had done things for her, quite a few things really. Got her into the safe flat. And now, he had – apparently, but she only had his word for that – saved her from a contract killer.

But she was too angry to be grateful. Because gratitude was what they always wanted from you, wasn't it, these men? Be grateful and then do as you're bloody told, wasn't that always the way they wanted to play it?

Well, not now. Not with *this* girl. She'd been there and done that – and got caned for it.

Nick stared at her with those cold, cruel dark eyes. He shrugged. 'If that's the way you want it to be, fine. You go ahead. Only don't come crying to me next time the King brothers cut up rough.'

'Don't worry,' said Lily, and she brushed past him and walked off, back up the corridor to the coffee shop, even though she'd been dying for a pee. Her pride wouldn't let her take one, not with Nick O'Rourke loitering outside the door. 'I won't,' she threw back over her shoulder.

27

Oli went out that afternoon. 'You going to be all right?' she asked Lily worriedly before she left.

'Sure,' said Lily, but she felt jumpy. She hadn't told Oli about Tiger Wu, or Nick's intervention – fortunately the coffee shop was large and it had been packed with punters, so Oli hadn't seen Nick passing through. But soon it would be evening, and she knew that Si could get in here any time he damned well pleased – and so could Freddy, too.

'You phoned the security company to get the entry codes changed, and the locks, everything?' asked Lily.

'Yeah, it's done. They're coming tomorrow morning.'

It couldn't come soon enough as far as Lily was concerned. For tonight she was going to sleep with Leo's Magnum under her pillow and fuck the Firearms Act. Which reminded her. 'Hey, Oli, is there a VHS recorder in the place?'

Oli looked wide-eyed and smiling at her mother. 'A *VHS* recorder? Mum, that's really old shit. Seriously, that's so over. It's all flat screens and Blu-Ray now.'

'Right,' Lily sighed.

'But I think there's a load of old stuff, video recorders and cameras, things like that, in the study somewhere.'

'Oh.' Maybe she was in luck after all. 'So what are your plans today, Oli?'

'Nothing much. Just hanging out with the girls.'

'Well, have fun.'

And then Oli was gone. Lily sat there and thought over all that had happened since she got out of prison. She really felt she was making progress with Oli, and that was nothing short of a miracle. She was still pissed off with Nick. She didn't understand him at all, but then she never had. Sometimes she had the feeling that he was on her side, then he started laying down the law and her back went up. Shit, if he knew what she was *really* up to, he'd be even more put out. Because he knew her of old. He knew that once she started chewing on a thing, she wouldn't let up until it either squeaked or died. But maybe . . . and this was an uncomfortable thought . . . maybe he was just trying to throw her off the scent. Maybe Nick had an idea what had really happened to Leo. Hell, maybe *Nick* was the one she should be looking into more closely. Who the fuck knew?

A sweet memory drifted into her brain: her and Nick dancing at a youth club do, just smooching head to head, so close, so cosy – but then Leo had cut in; Leo *always* cut in. Maybe Leo had cut in in other ways, too – screwed Nick on a deal. Nick might be a pretty straight shooter, but she had always known that greed was good in Leo's eyes. Wave a fat wedge of cash under his nose and he might have been persuaded to do the dirty on anyone. Not Lily. Not the girls. Not Si or Freddy. They were family. But anyone else? Even Nick? She couldn't swear that Leo would have always trod the line the way he should.

The house was silent around her, waiting. No ghosts here, though, only memories. Not just bad memories, either. Leo might have been a cheating heel, and – all right – there hadn't been much love lost between them; but he had cared for his family and treated them well, on the whole.

She went out into the hall and into Leo's study. Looked around. There was a TV in the corner and an oldish computer on the desk. There were still big storage cabinets built into the far wall and she went to those. Leo's love life might have been a mess, but in business and where cash was concerned, she knew he wouldn't overlook the tiniest detail. She started throwing open doors, pulling out old encyclopedias and books and folders, none of which looked as though they'd been touched in years.

No good.

She went to the next set of cupboards beneath an impressively bulging bookcase (Leo had never read a book in his entire life) and she looked in there too.

Nothing.

Another set of cupboards, old golfing trophies in here, Leo had loved his golf. She dragged some of the silverware out onto the floor, tossed out some dusty old back-issues of *Pro Golfer* and found a VHS recorder sitting there with a Scart cable wound up on top of it.

'Oh yes,' she muttered, and pulled it out and went over to the TV in the corner and started fiddling with the connections. When she thought she had it right, she went up and fetched the tape and came back down again and switched on both TV and player. Then she started playing with the remotes. There was Sky on the thing; it was linked in to satellite. Everything had changed so much since she'd been put in the slammer.

She sat there and fiddled with the damned thing until she felt like shrieking and hurling all the remotes right across the room. Then she got it. Keyed in the aerial connection, bypassing the satellite dish. Pressed 'play' on the video, and it was playing.

First just white noise, a snowy screen.

But then the white noise stopped.

The screen cleared.

Suddenly, Leo King was in the room.

'Hiya Lily girl,' he said.

Lily's legs turned to water. She flailed backwards and sat down hard on the captain's chair at the desk.

'Holy fuck,' she moaned, feeling all the blood drain out of her face with the shock of it.

Leo was there, on the tape. Leo wearing a red open-necked Lacoste polo shirt, and she could see the thick gold chain around his brawny brown neck. His hair was cropped short, the way he always liked to wear it, his eyes were clear dark blue, brilliant against his tanned skin. It was the Leo she'd known, lived with, given children to, alive and well and sitting in – yes, he was sitting in the very same chair she was sitting in now, with the cabinets lined up behind him.

'Oh Jesus,' mumbled Lily, feeling the room spin around her, wondering if she was going to throw up or faint or both.

'Well, Lily girl, if you're playing this tape, I'm dead.'

She didn't throw up. But the room went black, and then she was gone.

She came round with her face scrunched down into the Berber rug. It was scratchy and it was hurting her. She pulled her head off the rug, wondering what the hell happened, where she was, was she still inside?

But she could hear Leo's voice – loud, booming, just like always. She must be going mad. Then she remembered the tape. She took a gulping breath and prised herself up from the floor, flopped back up onto the chair and looked at the screen again. Leo was still there but he had stopped speaking. She pressed the pause button with a shaking hand and sat there, looking at the frozen, flickering image of her dead husband. Tears slid down her face unheeded. All right, he'd been a bastard. But he was *her* bastard. And now he was gone forever.

Taking a gulping, teary breath she rewound the tape. Pressed 'play'.

'. . . if you're playing this tape, I'm dead. Also, you've got hold of the emergency stash and the gun. That's good. Take care of the girls, Lily.'

Take care of the girls. Not knowing that she wouldn't be given a chance to do that. Not knowing that she'd be fitted up with his murder.

'Oh, Leo,' she groaned sadly.

'The boys'll look after you,' he went on.

Christ, if only you knew, thought Lily. She put a hand over her mouth. Felt like she was going to hurl.

The phone was ringing. She glanced at it, then back at the screen. It kept ringing. She stopped the tape, switched off the TV. Snatched up the phone from the desk. Had to swallow several times just to get a word out. 'Hello?'

'You know Alice Blunt freaked out when you showed her that photo of Leo?' said Jack Rackland's light cockney voice.

Lily sighed, her mind still focused on Leo, looking so vital and alive when now he was dead, just bones lying in a cold grave. She rubbed at her eyes, pushed back her hair, tried to think straight. 'Yeah,' she said. She didn't think she'd ever forget that little episode with Alice.

'Well this one shouldn't do too much freaking – she's a tough nut. I'm free this evening, we can give her a visit.'

'And what was this one's name? Reba, was it?' *This one.* One of many women that her husband had been shagging while she'd been raising his kids, tending his home.

'That's it, Reba Stuart.'

Lily stood there feeling sad and so alone. She wished Leo was here right now, if only because he was familiar to her, a fixed point of reference. Right now she had no one to turn to. And another four women to find after this: women who thought nothing of sleeping with someone else's husband, who maybe thought nothing of *killing* someone else's husband too, and letting someone else get stitched up for it.

'Mrs King? Lily? You still there?' asked Jack.

'Yeah, I'm here.'

'You want to do that? Tonight?'

'Yeah,' she said on a sigh. 'Let's do it.'

She put the phone down and pressed 'play', and listened once again to her dead husband talking to her. It was oddly comforting.

28

Tiger Wu was hanging upside down in a garage under the railway arches, on one of the meaner streets of Peckham. There was a winch in here for lifting car engines out; they were heavy as a bastard, so it had been no problem at all hoisting Tiger up with the chains – he was a feather by comparison. His ponytail was brushing the floor. His face was suffused with angry colour. His hands were tied behind his back. He was in serious trouble.

He knew he was in serious trouble because Nick O'Rourke was standing there with a few of his boys. It was like a solid wall of muscle in here.

'You were following Lily King,' said Nick.

'No I wasn't,' gasped out Tiger.

One of the meat-headed seventeen-stoners standing around passed Nick a claw hammer.

'Yes you were,' said Nick, and his eyes were like cold black pebbles in his stony face.

'All right!' Tiger's eyes were fixed in panic on the claw hammer. 'All right, I was.'

'Better,' said Nick. 'Now, Tiger. Perhaps you don't know it, but Lily King's my friend's wife, and long ago – when we were just boys still wet behind the ears – you know what I promised him?'

Tiger shook his head hard.

'I promised him I'd look after Lily.' Nick went over to the workbench and laid the hammer on it. Tiger visibly relaxed. 'And now, what do I hear? That a removal man's on her trail. That's you, Tiger. Following Lily King. And now I've got a really important question to ask you, and you'd better answer it straight.'

'Ask me,' panted Tiger, straining against the rope binding his wrist, twitching about there on the end of the winch chain like a fish on a hook. 'Anything, just ask me.'

'Okay. Here we go.' Nick leaned in close to where Tiger was suspended. 'Here's your starter for ten, Tiger. How much?'

'Mm?' Tiger was sweating, droplets plopping onto the concrete beneath him.

'How much, Tiger? How much to off Lily King. Don't make me ask again.'

'Thirteen thou,' said Tiger quickly. 'Six and a half when I took the job, six and a half when it's done.'

Nick nodded thoughtfully.

'I wasn't going to go through with it, though. I was just making it look good. I was gonna take off Saturday with the cash, leave it.'

'But you were following her,' said Nick.

'To make it look good, I told you. Just for show, then I was gonna do a bunk.'

Nick was shaking his head now. 'You're a removals man, Tiger. That's what you *do*. You got a reputation as a good solid worker. You ain't – to my certain knowledge – ever

172

shafted anyone on a deal. So do yourself a favour and don't give me any bullshit.'

'But it's true!'

'It ain't true, Tiger. Don't try my patience, for the love of God. What you think I am, some kind of tosser? Now, who paid you?' Nick thought he knew the answer already, but he wanted to hear it from Tiger's own lips. Tiger was a vicious and unscrupulous little tick: he'd off a baby and cheerfully do his own grandma for the price of a bottle of Jack Daniel's. No way would he pull back from completing a contract.

'Come *on,* Tiger, I'm getting pissed off with this now,' said Nick as Tiger seemed to hesitate. 'Give me the name.'

Tiger let go then. 'That *bastard* Freddy King. He's a nutter. I only took the fucking job because I was afraid if I said no he'd do me because I was in the know. I don't go in for offing women, Nick.'

Liar, thought Nick. Tiger had only confirmed what he had suspected. Si was too shrewd to get anyone else involved at this early stage, but Freddy was a loose cannon. Freddy wanted Lily dead, and he was getting itchy to see it done. While Lily, of course, was swanning about the town like Paris Hilton, spending like a man with no arms – or rather sponging off Oli's allowance, no way could an ex-con lay hands on enough money for the posh shops she was doing – and making a good clear target of herself.

The silly cow.

He didn't know who was winding him up more – Freddy King, Tiger Wu or Lily herself. All three were treading pretty close to the edge with him right now.

'Tiger,' he said at last, 'I appreciate your honesty. I really do. But I hope you understand the reasons why my boys here are going to give you a smacking.'

Tiger Wu thrashed on the end of the chain like a fresh-caught salmon. 'Jesus – wait! Listen . . .' he cried out.

'I'm done listening,' said Nick, and turned away and left.

The boys closed in and soon Tiger Wu's shrieks echoed around the building, scattering the pigeons out in the wet, windblown street.

29

'Good Christ,' said Jack Rackland when they stepped inside Reba Stuart's place that evening. 'Talk about shagarama.'

Reba Stuart had a place in Soho, not just *a* place but apparently *the* place. The best not-so-little massage parlour in the whole town. There were eight or ten girls in the front room when Lily and Jack were shown in there, and they all looked like film stars.

'One hundred and fifty an hour,' said Reba proudly to Jack. 'And by God they're worth it.'

A gorgeous green-eyed brunette sauntered past Jack, giving him an enticing smile.

'Yeah, but sadly I'm not a punter,' said Jack, his eyes out on stalks. To Lily he added: 'Monica would have my balls for breakfast if I hooked up with any of *this*.'

'I thought you and Monica were history.'

'Hey, tell *her* that. She rants down the phone at me morning and night, like it's *my* fault she went and did the dirty on me.'

'Maybe it was. A bit.'

'Oh don't start. Jesus, the mouth on that woman, and she's barely five feet high.'

To Lily it sounded as if Jack still loved Monica, but she had her own worries right now – like Reba Stuart.

Reba looked like everyone's idea of a brassy barmaid. Big hourglass figure with cleavage prominently on display above a red glittery top, which was pulled in tight at the waist above a plain black pencil skirt. Too much make-up, fag-smoker's lines around the overpainted mouth. Shrewd blue eyes, and white-blonde hair, dyed to a crisp and swept up on top of her head, instant facelift. Despite that, Reba looked a decade older than her forty years. Her face was hard and businesslike; all fake smiles and cold calculation.

Leo liked blondes, thought Lily, feeling faintly sick.

'You said you wanted to talk about Leo King?' said Reba, leading the way through the totty-packed room and out into another, smaller, less lushly furnished. There was a table and chairs. She sat down, gestured for Jack and Lily to do the same. The harsh overhead light showed her lines up. She stared across at Lily. 'And who's this? Your assistant?'

'Yeah,' said Jack.

Lily glanced at him. He was good. Start calling it like it was too early and Reba might just clam shut on them.

'I knew Leo years ago,' said Reba, fishing out a packet of Dunhill's and a gold lighter. 'You don't mind if I . . .?'

They both shook their heads.

Reba lit up and inhaled deeply, exhaling plumes of smoke through her nose. She coughed once, sharply. The wrinkles in her face deepened. Lily felt glad she had never cultivated the nicotine habit, not even to while away the hours in prison. But by God she could have used a drink right now. To think of Leo in bed with this . . . and then coming home to her. It made her feel sick to her stomach.

Maybe Becks was right. Maybe fidelity really *was* too much to expect from the type of man she'd married. She should have learned the rules and played the game. She'd taken it all too seriously, felt he was holding her up to ridicule among their circle of friends. But after all, he'd only hurt her pride – he hadn't broken her heart.

Thoughts of Becks reminded Lily that she hadn't heard from her in a little while. Maybe Becks still felt bad about having to turn Lily out in the cold. She decided she'd find the time to call her, patch things up. Maybe arrange to meet up with all the girls for lunch, just like they used to back in the good old days. She *missed* those times so much. But then . . . *what* girls? What friends did she really have left?

There was Becks. There would *always* be Becks. And Hairy Mary; yes, she could still be called a friend, Lily was sure of that. But Maeve was her enemy now – and, as for Adrienne, who she had once believed to be a pal, well, why on earth would she want to sit at a table with that back-stabbing cow grinning across at her?

'First time I saw Leo King was . . . let me think . . .' Another thoughtful puff of the ciggy. 'Nineteen eighty-six. Late July. We were all sitting around watching Fergie get hitched to Prince Andrew at Westminster. Leo called right in the middle of it all, and some of the girls moaned on a bit. Like watching a fairy tale, that was. Then he calls and in they come, all the boys, and the romance of the day was sort of ruined, know what I mean?' Reba winked. 'They'd just come back straight from Amsterdam and they were loaded.' Reba was staring at Lily, hard enough to make her feel uncomfortable. 'I think we all know what Amsterdam and large amounts of money adds up to, don't we?'

Drug money, thought Lily. Yeah, she knew. Turned a blind eye to all that, but she knew. She even thought she remembered him making the trip. And instead of coming straight home to her – yeah, and she'd been watching the wedding too, who hadn't? – he'd concluded his business with the Dutch and come here instead to treat the boys, and, of course, himself.

Just boys letting off steam.

High-octane danger could do that with men. Do a moody deal, you half expect to get shipped back in a body bag. And if you *didn't*, if some bastard didn't off you or rob you or double-cross you before you made it home, there was a sense of release, a sense of needing to celebrate your success, to celebrate *life*. Because you still – against all expectations – had it.

So Leo had come to a knocking-shop instead of to her. They'd been engaged then, her and Leo – not even married. The first flush of lust should have been on them, but she had still been pining over Nick, still trying to come to terms with losing him, and Leo had preferred to bed a tart. That just about said it all.

''Course, they got it easy out there in clog land,' said Reba. 'Legalized prostitution. Must be heaven on earth. Not like here, with the Bill always sniffing around. Oh yeah, I remember Leo King. He was great in bed.'

Lily was glad she wasn't smoking – she'd have choked at that point. Jack sent her a quick look, but twelve years inside had taught her to keep her face straight and her head down.

'I didn't run the gaff then, I was one of the workers,' Reba elaborated. 'We had a big selection of girls then, just like now. Asians, Swedes, blacks, all beautiful. The men could pick and choose, double up, whatever. Leo picked me, he liked blondes.'

Lily felt bile rise into her throat. She swallowed it. *Willed* her face to stay blank.

'And Jesus could that man perform. He kept on coming back for more . . .' Reba blew out smoke, her eyes suddenly dreamy . . . 'I remember the last time he came here. Another Amsterdam trip. Our last night. *His* last night. I saw it in the papers later that week. He was dead. The most alive man I ever met, and he was stone-dead. Only it wasn't another *gang* killed him, as you might expect. It was his ever-loving wife.'

Reba was staring at Lily again. Now she started nodding. 'I know who you are. You're not his assistant. You're Lily King,' she said. 'You're the bitch who did poor Leo.'

Lily felt her blood run cold.

'What?' Lily sat there, open-mouthed, startled.

Reba was still nodding her bleached-blonde head. 'Yeah. You're Lily King. Saw you in the papers and on the telly when the trial started.' She took a contemplative drag on her ciggie then said: 'Girl, you ain't aged a *bit*.'

Well, you've aged about a hundred years, thought Lily.

'Was it just business then?' Lily asked slowly. 'You and Leo?'

'What, you gonna blow *my* brains to fuck too?' Reba gave a snort and angrily stubbed out her cigarette in a glass ashtray. 'I can't believe they let you out already. You should have *died* inside.'

Part of me did, thought Lily. *Maybe the best part.*

'Well I didn't,' she said. 'I'm alive, Leo's dead and here's the latest bulletin – I didn't kill him.'

'The fuck you didn't.'

'Ladies,' said Jack, holding up his hands.

'Did *you*?' asked Lily.

'You *what*?'

'You heard the question. Did you kill Leo? Was it a bit more than business for you? Did he take you home, to *my* home, and did he give you a line or two of something, a nice little bonus from clog land. Did you have a downer and turn nasty?'

'This ain't getting us anywhere,' said Jack.

'Yeah, he took me back there, gave me the guided tour. That was some place you had, you and him. You were a lucky cow and I doubt you appreciated it one little bit. He had a good deal going on, a big carousel scam, he told me about it. Pillow talk.' She gave Lily a sour smile. 'Look at your fucking face. You don't even know what a carousel scam *is*, do you?'

Lily didn't. She'd never known a thing about Leo's business: that was the way he wanted to play it and that was just fine with her. But this news burned her like a hot branding iron pressed against her flesh. He'd kept her in the dark and fed her bullshit, okay, she'd accepted that. But meanwhile, he'd been telling all his whores the juicy details? That hurt.

'Why don't you enlighten us?' asked Jack, shooting looks between the two. He didn't want a ruck; he knew that once the fur started flying there'd be nothing achieved here. But Lily and Reba were eyeing each other like gladiators in a Roman arena.

'Look, it's simple,' said Reba. 'It's the sweetest swindle you can imagine. You bring your goods into Britain and you're supposed to pay VAT to the taxman and then charge it to whoever bought the goods. If they were re-exported, the exporter claimed a rebate. With me so far?'

Jack and Lily nodded. Lily's teeth were gritted; this smug cow.

'The thing is, Leo never paid VAT in the first place, but he still claimed the rebate. He had a thing going where he imported and exported the same stuff – phones and computer stuff mostly – over and over again. Top dollar. I mean, really. We're talking millions here. Course you can't do it now, the taxman's got clever. Brought in a new system, plugged the loophole. But while it was good, it was *really* good. Leo made a *packet*.' Reba looked at Lily with contempt. 'And you spent it I suppose. And then you went and topped the poor bastard. Talk about killing the golden fucking goose.'

'Hey – *smartarse*,' Lily leaned forward across the table, her lips pulled back in an expression that was more snarl than smile, her eyes fierce. 'Didn't you hear what I said? I didn't do Leo. But by fuck I'm going to find out who did. And my best guess so far? One of you *slags* he knocked about with.'

'Oh yeah, sure. You getting yourself banged up for it was all a big mistake, that right?' Reba affected a bored yawn but Jack could see that Lily's last comment had hit home.

'Listen, you cheap cow—' said Lily.

'No! *You* listen: what did you think, you were marrying a saint in Leo King? Fuck's sake, get real. Image is what matters to men like that. A mistress is a status symbol, show off to your mates, prove how much money you're pulling in.'

'Mistress?' Lily scoffed. 'Hardly that, luv. Just a *tart*.'

'Yeah? Why'd he keep coming back then? *You* couldn't have been keeping him fully occupied in the bedroom department, that's for sure. Look, a man like that needs a woman on his arm when he's out on the town. It's a nice bonus, on top of the four-wheel drive and the luxury home in Chigwell in a couple of acres, the lovely kids and the *wife* who's not too bright and don't suspect a thing – a wife who's happy to take the cash and not question where it comes from too closely. Am I right or am I right?'

Not too bright.

The words clanged around Lily's head like a struck gong. Yeah, that was how everyone must have seen her. The little woman indoors. Meek and dim, happy to get down the shops and splurge while Leo was having a *splurge* all of his own with tarts like Reba, sad clingers-on like Adrienne and head-cases like Alice Blunt.

She'd only suspected Adrienne. Hadn't had a clue about the rest of them. And there were more. More she hadn't met yet. She felt sick now, really sick.

'You smug bitch,' she said, low-voiced, furious.

Reba's eyes flashed. 'Listen, I never hurt anyone in my life, but let me tell you, lady, Leo King was a diamond, so I'm willing to start with you.'

Reba jumped to her feet and was half across the table when Jack caught her around the waist and pulled her back, away from Lily.

'Now take it *easy*,' said Jack, grappling with Reba like an all-in wrestler.

Lily stepped around the table. 'No, come on, let her go,' she said. She'd dealt with some lairy old lags inside, she wasn't afraid of Reba Stuart.

'No, I *ain't* letting her go,' said Jack, and he looked angry now. 'Go and wait outside, Lily, for fuck's sake.'

Lily took a deep, shuddering breath. Then she turned on her heels and walked back through the lounge, still packed with the bevy of bored-looking beautiful girls. They watched curiously as she went out of the front door and slammed it hard behind her.

She waited, breathing hard with suppressed fury. That low-life *bitch*. Suddenly she felt weighed down, weary to her bones. She could search and search forever, but was she ever going to find any answers? Suddenly it all seemed hopeless, impossible. She couldn't win, and she ought to just admit that, give it up.

Jack came out within five minutes.

He stood there, looking at her with concern.

'You okay?'

'I'm *fine*.' Lily's teeth were gritted with the effort of keeping control of her emotions. Her whole life had been such a mess. Losing Nick. Losing Leo. Years in stir. And now, nothing but fighting and struggling, and she was tired, just sick and tired and worn out and sad.

'Don't act like such a hard-arse. You're not fine at all, you're in bits.'

Lily started to walk away, back to the car. Jack followed, caught her arm; turned her back to face him.

'Listen, Lily,' he said gently. 'It'll all work out. We'll make it, okay? I'll help you. Be a friend to you. But don't keep pushing me away. You've got to trust me.'

Lily stared into his kind blue eyes. She could almost believe he meant it; that all he wanted from her was her trust. But she doubted she could even remember how to do that, just blindly *believe* that someone had her best interests at heart.

'You poor little bint, you've really had a tough time of it, ain't you?' he said, and smoothed a big rough hand over her cheek.

And that was it; that was enough. The floodgates opened

and, finally, after twelve years, she let it all out and cried bitter broken tears over the front of Jack's best suit for the wreckage of her life and for the late lamented Leo King. That *bastard*.

30

You could buy snacks at the prison canteen once a week. You could also spend the remains of your weekly cash limit on coffee, tobacco, stationery, phone cards (although Lily eventually gave up on those: the girls were lost to her, what was the point?) fruit and batteries – one only, apparently you could make bombs with more – for a radio.

Becks had brought her in a bum bag, an item Lily had never possessed but now found invaluable. All her precious items – the most precious being a photo of her with her two lovely girls – she kept in there.

She soon got to know that if you left anything lying about or even in your locker, it was likely to go missing. So Lily quickly learned to keep all her goods on her person. She developed a prison persona. Hands in pockets. Head down. All femininity forgotten. Her and Mercy became a team, blocking out the rest of the prison world. She became numb, faceless, one of the crowd. After a while inside she didn't bother wondering if she'd ever get her life back. Without hope, without her home, without her children, without everything dear to her, she schooled herself not to care.

31

Lily slept with the Magnum tucked under her pillow – just in case; she wouldn't use it, she would *never* use it, or at least she didn't think so, but until the security codes and the locks were changed, better safe than sorry. The clothes she'd purchased were still in the bags in the far corner of the room, and the rucksack full of the remaining huge stash of readies, and Leo's video, was right there beside the bed.

When she woke up – starting awake, as always, from dreams of prison, from the belief that she was still in there, that she would *never* get out – she reviewed last night's meeting with that rotten hard-faced whore Reba, thought about how she had shed tears outside and how she'd been made to look like a complete fool.

Nothing new there, though.

Leo had been making her look a fool for years – she just hadn't known it.

She got up, showered, dressed, stashed the gun and the rucksack, and went downstairs feeling about ninety years old. Oli was in the kitchen, and there were two strange men wandering around the house looking at the alarm sensors.

'They're here from Sunstyle to change the settings and stuff,' said Oli brightly. 'Coffee?'

Lily nodded and sat down.

'You want anything to eat?'

'God no,' said Lily with a shudder.

'Oh yeah. You never ate breakfast,' said Oli. 'I remember now.'

Lily smiled faintly at her daughter. So odd to see her there, full-grown. So odd and so wonderful, too. But she worried over Oli and Saz. They were rich. All right, the money they had in abundance, and this house, were all ill-gotten gains – but try proving *that*, Your Honour – and they were rich enough never to have to work, never to have to *strive*.

That couldn't be good for them, could it? Certainly it hadn't been good for her, going from a lowbrow school to a kept – although married – woman, with no thoughts of a career, no ambition other than to play house.

'What you going to do with your life, Ols?' she asked, curiously.

'Oh! God, I don't know.' Oli paused and looked at her mother. 'I'd like to have a year in Paris sometime, I suppose, just living there, soaking up the atmosphere, you know. I just want to . . . have fun. You know.'

And meet bad men, thought Lily. *Men like Jase.*

'And where does Jase fit into these plans?' she asked.

Oli shrugged. 'Maybe he'll come too,' she said, and turned away to pick up the cafetière and two mugs.

And maybe he won't, thought Lily. The boys had their own rules, they did what they damned well pleased – and that wouldn't include following a girlfriend abroad if she chose to go. Girls were ten a penny to men like these anyway – Reba Stuart had made that clear to her. Bad boys exuded testosterone; they attracted female attention without even trying. The girls were forever buzzing around them, like wasps round jam. And why buy a book when you can join a library?

Jesus, I'm bitter, thought Lily as Oli pushed a full mug towards her.

'Tell me about Jase,' said Lily.

'What's to tell?' Oli shrugged. 'He's Head of Security at the club.'

'Kings,' said Lily thoughtfully. 'That's still going then.' Kings club had been started way back by Leo, Si and Freddy. Leo hadn't lived to see the place get properly established, and she was slightly surprised to find it was still in existence, without Leo's dynamic drive powering it along.

'Yeah, it's great,' said Oli enthusiastically.

'He worked there long?'

'What is this? An inquisition?'

'Nah, just curious,' said Lily lightly, and snagged one of the security guys as he passed by. 'Is this going to take long?' she asked.

'About an hour, that's all,' he said.

She nodded and he hurried on. 'Oli,' she said, taking a sip of the coffee. It was hot, strong, pungent. Delicious. You never got decent coffee in the nick. 'About Jase.'

'What about him?' Oli asked warily.

'I hope . . . I just want to say I hope you're being careful.'

'What?'

'*Careful*, Oli. As in not ending up with a fat belly.'

'Oh God.' Oli let out a little laugh and her eyes slipped away from Lily's. 'This is embarrassing.'

'It'd be even *more* embarrassing to find yourself knocked up at your age,' said Lily. 'Embarrassing and bloody inconvenient. I know. I've been there.'

Oli's eyes swivelled back to her mother's face. 'What, you're saying Saz was an inconvenience?'

'I'm saying you don't want to limit your choices in life, Oli. You're lucky, you have plenty. Don't just throw them away when you could take a few sensible precautions to prevent that situation arising.'

Lily spoke from the heart. She knew what finding yourself up the duff at a young age was like. If she hadn't been pregnant pre-wedding with Leo's baby, she herself would still have had those magical things called *options*. She could admit to herself now that she had always known in her heart of hearts that Leo was a bit of a shit. And if she was really, brutally honest with herself – which in those young, innocent days she'd mostly managed not to be – she'd already known that he was unlikely to be faithful. But there had been the baby, the pressure from her shocked and ashamed old-school parents, her fear of being alone, a single parent . . . so, no options. No options at all.

'Yep, *very* embarrassed now,' quipped Oli, but she was, she really was, Lily could see her cheeks had turned pink.

'You on the pill then?' This issue had been troubling Lily for a couple of days and she wasn't going to mince her words now.

'*Mum* . . .'

'Are you?'

'No I'm not.' Now Oli's cheeks were flaming. 'I had bad periods when I was younger. Tried the pill for that, but it just made me sick so I stopped taking it.'

'But you *are* sleeping with him?' Lily just knew that Jase

was not the type to act the monk. He'd want sex with Oli, and seeing the two of them together had already convinced her that their relationship was physical.

'I'm not having this conversation,' said Oli, getting up from the table and taking her mug over to the sink, where she emptied the contents angrily.

'Because, Oli, there's a certain point past which a man just can't stop, you do know that?'

'I'm out of here,' trilled Oli, heading for the door. 'I'll buzz to get back in, okay?'

'Get him to use a condom!' shouted Lily after her.

The door slammed behind Oli. A different security bloke wandered through, looking a question at Lily. Oli's car started up outside.

'Kids,' she said.

'Tell me about it. We're nearly all done here.'

'Good.' She hated strangers wandering about. Didn't know them. Could be anyone. Could be working for Si. Or Freddy. Now she was getting paranoid. And jumpy. When the phone on the wall beside the sink rang, she nearly fell off her stool. With her heart hammering, she went over and agitatedly snatched it up.

'Hello?' she snapped.

'Mrs . . . King?' asked a hesitant female voice, rough-edged and cracked with age. There were birds chirping in the background.

'Who wants her?'

'I'm Mrs Blunt, Alice's mum.'

'Oh yeah. Thanks for calling.'

'You wanted to talk about my girl Alice.'

'Yeah.' Lily thought quickly. 'Can we meet up?'

'I don't get about much,' said Mrs Blunt querulously. 'And

. . . your name's King, have I got that right? You're not . . . you're no relation to *Leo* King, are you?'

'None at all,' Lily lied. 'I'm just an old friend of Alice's, that all.'

'Well . . . I suppose it'll be all right then . . .'

'I'll come to you, okay? I won't take up much of your time,' said Lily. 'Just give me your address, I'll come over.'

Mrs Blunt gave her the address, on a council estate in Stepney.

'Give me an hour, okay? I'll be there.'

She tried Becks's number before she left, but Becks wasn't answering.

Mrs Blunt was so old she looked fossilized. She was skinny and bent double, and wavered uncertainly on a stick, peering myopically at Lily when her son let her in, before collapsing back into her chair. A dandelion fuzz of white hair stood out around her wobbling little head and her mouth was tooth-free.

There was a tray on a small table beside the chair, with a half-eaten crustless sandwich and a cup of tea on it. On the other side of the chair was a large metal cage, containing four budgies; they were making a lot of noise and scattering feathers in all directions.

The son was a bulky, crew-cut redhead in t-shirt, stretchy tracksuit bottoms and cheap trainers. He looked like he'd swallowed a lot of Big Macs, and probably the odd small sofa too. His expression and his manner were surly.

'She gets these things into her head,' he said as soon as Lily showed up on the front step. 'Won't let them go. She wanted to see you because you were a friend of Alice's, but let me make it plain – I didn't want you coming here. It only upsets her, talking about all that.'

191

As welcomes went, it wasn't much. The trip out hadn't exactly been great either. When the security guys had left, giving her three new sets of keys and a raft of bewildering instructions on how to set the new alarms, she had booked a taxi. The driver had talked all the way over, in a language she neither knew nor understood, then the jerk had massively overcharged her, and Lily had looked out at the rainy day and thought, *Is this worth the effort?* The driver was still out there, parked up at the rubbish-strewn pavement; the bill for all this was going to be astronomical, and no doubt he was going to want to chat all the way home, too.

Now the son was acting up.

'She's having her tea,' said the man, seeming to fill up the small, overheated front room with his size and bad temper. 'You could have picked a better time.'

No time would have been better for this one.

'You'll have to wait a bit,' he said, and Lily said yeah, okay, and sat down on the sofa. *Golden Balls* was on, roaring away – Alice's mother was obviously deaf as a post – and when she had been sitting there for ten minutes watching the damned thing, the son came bustling over and changed the channels, just in case she'd been enjoying it, just to make his point that she wasn't welcome.

Point taken, thought Lily, getting tired of all this. But, finally, she was granted an audience.

She went and sat in the armchair opposite Mrs Blunt. Mrs Blunt looked at her as if she was wondering why she was here.

Yeah, thought Lily. *Me too.*

'I don't want her upset,' said the son, removing the tea tray and going off into the kitchen with it, where he crashed the plate and cup into the sink. *And fuck you too*, thought Lily.

The birds sang on, irritatingly loudly.

'Do you let them out much?' asked Lily, unable to stop herself. She was surprised at how distressed it made her feel, to see them caged there.

'They don't like to come out,' said Mrs Blunt. 'Do you, little ones?' she cooed at the birds. 'I open the door, but they don't come out,' she told Lily.

Lily could understand that. Inside was safe. Outside – who knew?

'Mrs Blunt,' she said, 'can you tell me what happened with Alice?'

'You won't get any sense out of her,' shouted the son from the kitchen.

Lily looked at Mrs Blunt. She didn't look stupid, only old. And she had used the phone and given Lily her address with no difficulty at all.

'Alice,' Lily repeated clearly. 'I went to see her.' She hesitated, looking assessingly at the old woman. 'Mrs Blunt, I wasn't entirely truthful with you on the phone. I *am* – I mean I was – related to Leo King. I was ... married to him.'

Mrs Blunt stared at her. 'But ... they said his wife shot him. She got sent down for it.'

'I didn't do it, Mrs Blunt.'

'Hold *on* a minute.' The son came full-speed in from the kitchen. Before Lily knew what was happening, he'd grabbed the back of her collar and hauled her out of the chair she was sitting in. Lily's heart shot straight up into her throat with the shock of it. The budgies screeched and hurtled around the cage, flinging themselves against the bars. Feathers drifted around like a Christmas snow scene. Mrs Blunt cried out as Lily dangled, her feet off the ground.

'You're *her*, you're that fucking psycho,' he yelled, shaking her like a dog with a rat.

'Malcolm!' yapped Mrs Blunt.

He froze. Mrs Blunt was staring at him. After a tense second or two, he dropped Lily.

'She's a headcase,' said Malcolm defensively.

Lily gulped and tried to get her wind back. He'd startled her badly. She sank back into the chair and kept her attention focused on the old lady.

'That man,' said Mrs Blunt, her gummy mouth working with emotion, 'Leo King. He was bad. He ruined our Alice. *Ruined* her.'

'Yeah,' said the son, nodding sharply and still glaring down at Lily. 'You're a bad lot, all of you.'

Oh fuck me, thought Lily, trying to get her heart rate back to normal. *Wouldn't it be easier to keep a bloody Rottweiler than to have this oversized idiot about the place?*

'You were inside for years, that right?' the son was going on, his expression sneering as he stared at Lily. 'You done him, that's it, right? Well – bloody good job too. Wished I'd done it myself, lots of times. He upset our Alice.'

'And just when we thought Alice was getting on better, too,' said Mrs Blunt. 'What with the not-eating and everything.'

'She was anorexic?'

Mrs Blunt's eyes were suddenly bright with tears. 'She went off the rails, our Alice.'

'She was fucking mental,' snorted the son. 'Always was, always will be.'

And now you're flavour of the month, right? thought Lily, glancing at him.

'You your mum's full-time carer?' asked Lily.

'What's it to you?'

'Nothing at all,' Lily shrugged. Nice cosy job, no getting

up for work in the mornings. Just look after your old mum, hold her like a prize trophy, because your sister was mental and you were top of the heap. Sibling rivalry with a particularly nasty edge to it.

'Then mind your bloody own,' he said, and went back into the kitchen.

'She was always frail,' Mrs Blunt went on. 'Then she stopped eating much. Some girls teased her at school, something like that, she'd never talk about it. She was hospitalized once, she was bad with it. But then she got over that and got a job in one of his offices.'

'Yeah, your bloody husband,' the son chimed in from the other room.

'And?' prompted Lily.

'She was mad about him. Just *mad*,' said Mrs Blunt, her eyes dancing in her bony head. 'He used to send her flowers, and posh presents; there was a gold bracelet in a little blue box . . .'

The Tiffany receipt, thought Lily sickly. After all these years, finally she knew who'd been the recipient of that gift. Alice Blunt. Poor, weak girl, with her head turned by a rich and powerful man.

'Alice loved him, *adored* him.' Mrs Blunt's gummy mouth twisted in disapproval. 'Went crazy when he told her it was over between them.'

'How long did it go on?' asked Lily, although it pained her to do it.

The bony shoulders shrugged. 'Few months. But she was a highly strung girl, our Alice. She couldn't take it.' Suddenly the old mouth was trembling. 'She tried to do herself in. Slit her wrists. I found her . . . just in time. But she was never right after that. Needed round-the-clock care. He should never have let her down like that, she couldn't take that sort of thing.'

Lily cleared her throat. 'Yeah, but he was married. Didn't she know that?'

'We don't like you going near Alice,' said the son, rejoining them and looming over Lily like a threat. 'Who the fuck knows what you might do?'

'Malcolm! Language!' said Mrs Blunt.

'Sorry, Ma.' Suddenly he looked like a little boy slapped down by an adult. But immediately the truculent bruiser was back. 'But it's true, innit? She might want to do Alice too; she's a nutter.'

Lily bit her tongue to keep back a sharp reply. But something had been bothering her and she was going to ask it, no matter what. 'The clinic,' she said.

'Yeah? What about it?' asked the son.

'Who pays for Alice's keep? It must cost a small fortune.'

He shrugged. 'Government, I s'pose. We can't afford it, for sure.'

But the clinic was lovely; a really nice place. Not the sort of place she'd envisage an NHS patient on her uppers being shipped to indefinitely.

She looked at the son, and wondered. Wondered just how far he would go to please the mother and gain her approval. Wondered if Mrs Blunt had said at the time: Look, son, he's upset our Alice, upset her bad, what are you going to do about it? She'd have been looking at him all pleading and cunning, knowing how to manipulate, knowing which buttons to press. And did he then charge out into the night, bent on revenge, and kill Leo?

But there'd been no break-in. The alarm system hadn't

196

been breached. So . . . had Leo let the son in, had Leo in fact *known* Malcolm, since he knew Alice?

She stood up. Felt so tired that she couldn't bear to think about it any more.

'Thanks for seeing me, Mrs Blunt,' she said, and went to the door, the son dogging her heels.

'I don't want you coming back here,' he hissed in her ear as she opened the door.

Lily opened the door and paused there, looking out at the rain.

'Yeah, but you know what? We don't always get what we want,' she said, and walked off down the path to the waiting taxi.

32

That evening Freddy King was sitting at the bar in Kings, the family club. He was seriously pissed off at what Jase was telling him.

'No one's seen the little fucker for a while. We put the word out like you said, but no one knows a damned thing,' said Jase, eyeing Freddy warily.

Freddy the Freak, he was called among some of the boys. Jase wasn't one of those. Careless Talk Costs Lives was his motto. He knew Freddy could blow at a moment's notice and take your fucking head off, and he wouldn't want that, not when things had been starting to look so rosy.

Also, there was Si. Treated with even *more* deference by Jase. For obvious reasons. But now there was this thing with the door. Si was talking about a new system, a little experiment where one person ran the door for a fortnight, then another person took over. Jase on first shift, and then – and *then* – Brendan Gibbs.

That was the worst blow of all. Jase knew of Brendan Gibbs. All the boys did. Brendan Gibbs had a reputation around town as the hardest of hard nuts. Brendan was a thinker, like Jase. He was no brain-dead mound of muscle like some of the guys were. And now Jase was wondering, was this a quiet way of edging him out, off the scene? Was this what they called the thin end of the cunting *wedge*?

If it was, where the *fuck* did that leave him? He felt affronted. He had always done a good job on the door, tossed out the unlicensed dealers, protected the ones who were in the club on Si's say-so. He'd restricted the numbers of partying masses coming in to a couple of hundred max, and he'd turned down a *fortune* in bribes from punters wanting to jump the mile-long queues outside or be sneaked round the back.

Jase was starting to get an uneasy feeling. He felt he was being disciplined. But for *what*? For getting in good with Oli? Jesus, was Si saying that he, Jase, wasn't *good* enough to mix with his niece? Because if so, Jase was going to have to do a major rethink. He'd thought he was a contender for the future throne, had felt that Si liked him and was grooming him for success. But maybe he'd misread the signals.

Of course he had contingency plans. He'd been at Oli night and day, shagging her brains out, and he knew she wasn't on the Pill. Oli was sweet, eager to please; he'd had her doing things that her dear old uncle Si would have been shocked at. Early on, he would have worn a condom if she'd insisted (although he'd have cooked up some excuse to phase it out), but she was so fucking grateful for his attention, she'd been making cow-eyes at him for months before he made his move, so he knew he had the upper hand there and he had formulated a brilliant plan, and so he'd said right from the start, no condoms, he hated the damned things.

So he was having himself a real shag-fest with Oli – and

a few others, of course, that went without saying – and wearing nothing but a smile. Oli was so obliging. Sucked him off, tried anal, anything, but she liked missionary the best and that was good, because that was when a woman really took it on board, wasn't that right? On her back was best, and anyway he liked doing her that way, splayed her legs wide open, tucked a little pillow under her hips, kept her there, pumping away at her while she moaned with pleasure, then *bang* and off the little swimmers went to do their good work. He always tried to give her an orgasm just as he came himself; that helped get them up there, apparently. He'd read up on it. Wanted to get it right.

One of these days he was going to score a direct hit – if he hadn't already. She was going to be up the duff with his kid soon, she *had* to be. And Uncle Si might rant and rave for a bit, but then Jase would tell him how much in love they were, him and Oli, and he'd have Oli talk to her Aunt Maeve, crying buckets all over the ugly old mare, and then it would be wedding bells and he would be inside the inner sanctum, *really* on the firm. He'd been working towards that ever since he came out of school and started kicking off, wearing the old claret and blue scarf on the terraces at Upton Park when West Ham were playing. That was how he'd come to the attention of Si's boys, that and a little National Front demo work. It was time he moved forward and up. He was *ready*. But now, this. This little thing that didn't quite fit right with him. This feeling that he was being slapped down.

'There's been a bit of trouble on the door,' said Jase now as Freddy threw back a stiffener.

'So? It's your door. Sort it. Ain't that what we pay you for?'

Freddy was on a downer. All his boys were telling him

that Tiger Wu had vanished into the ether. They didn't know where or how or any damned thing, they knew fuck-all – and all *Freddy* knew was that the little cunt had six and a half grand of his money in his pocket for a job that would never be done, and that made him *seriously* annoyed. If he got hold of Tiger any time soon, that greasy bastard was going to be eating through a straw for a *month*.

Meanwhile, there was Lily King. Who'd been out of stir no time at all and had already moved back into the house, into *his dead brother's house*, after doing a measly twelve years for offing him. It just wasn't good enough. All very well for Si to say, wait, give it time, but Freddy didn't want to and by Christ he wasn't going to either.

The club was filling up – *their* club, his and Si's. It was a fantastic club and it easily rivalled the Ministry of Sound over in Gaunt Street. Poor fucking Leo had never seen it really take off, but they had, him and Si: it was a great place. Strobes whirling and lots of raving punters jigging along to the DJ's mixes, dropping a little E to get them in the mood, buying high-priced drinks, the place had a real good vibe. And now, what was Jase saying, that he was having trouble on the *door*?

'Fuck's sake, Jase,' snarled Freddy when Jase hovered there, seeming not to want to drop it. 'Get the sodding hell on with it. That's your job.'

Jase had thought he was on top of it. As Head of Security in the club, he was in a position of trust, but could he trust Si in return?

He'd dealt with Si honestly. Well, honestly in business. Granted, he was shagging himself senseless with Oli, but who wouldn't, given the opportunity? But in business, he had played it straight down the line. Now Si was playing silly buggers.

It wasn't on.

Jase was fuming. He thought maybe Freddy might drop a word in Si's ear, if he spoke to him in the right way. He decided to try it.

'It's just that I don't like this rotation plan, Mr King,' he said. 'Not at all. I built up this team of boys: they're the business. And that's *my* door.'

Freddy looked at Jase in disgust. 'Look, *fuck* your door, sonny,' he snapped, coming up off the stool and glaring into Jase's eyes.

Steady, thought Jase. Freddy was built like a tank; he didn't want to start anything with him.

'Why don't you piss off and make yourself useful?' said Freddy, pushing a meaty digit into Jase's chest. 'Go and see to your frigging door, boy. Or go and find me Tiger fucking Wu, that tosser. Or better still – go and do that bitch Lily for me, okay?'

Jase went up to the office after that. Better talk to the organ grinder, not the bloody monkey. Si was there behind the desk. Jase was a tough, fit young bastard, but seeing Si always gave him the squits. Si was sitting there like a brick outhouse, staring at him as he knocked and came in – staring at him with that cold, unblinking gaze he knew so well. There was something almost reptilian about Si. The stillness there was about him – but then when he moved, when he *struck*, he struck fast.

'What's up, Jase?' he asked, not looking very interested.

'Mr King,' said Jase, his voice sounding high-pitched and breathless. 'I wanted to say ... well, you know me. I'm a good worker. That's my door. I've done a good job on it, wouldn't you say?'

Si stared at him with that flat gaze. Then he sat back in his chair and stared some more.

'Yeah,' he said at last. 'I'd say you done good, Jase.'

'Then why the change, Mr King? The boys told me about Brendan being moved in, the new shift arrangement. Me on for a fortnight, then him . . . well, it can't work that way. That's *my* door.'

Si stared blankly at Jase until he started to fidget. 'Sorry,' Jase added, aware that he had raised his voice to Si King, and you didn't do that. Not if you were fond of living. But he was pumped up on steroids, bursting with aggression. Right now, he felt he could *kill* Si King with his bare hands – fucking around with his door, for God's sake – and enjoy doing it too. Still, he tried to swallow his rage. Tried to hold it down.

'It's just a thought,' said Si, with an easy shrug. 'We like to try new things, adjust the system now and then.'

'But I . . .'

'Brendan's a good man,' said Si.

'I don't know him. I know *of* him, everyone does,' said Jase, feeling his temper building to dangerous levels. 'But look, Mr King. Straight up. The door's mine. The boys I got working it are *my* team.'

'Correction,' said Si, 'they're *my* team. They are in my employ. Just like you are.'

Jase clenched his fists. He'd worked like a slave to get that door operating smoothly. He knew what this was about. Bloody Si. All his hopes and dreams, everything he'd planned for, was crashing around his ears, he just knew it. Si was shutting him out. Out of the firm, out of Oli's life, out of the *family*.

'This is about Oli, ain't that right?' he blurted out.

'Oli?' Si's expression didn't change.

'Yeah, you're slapping me down 'cos you don't want me and her together.'

'Jase, Jase,' said Si, gently shaking his head. 'Whatever makes you think such a thing?'

But Jase was right. He *knew* it.

He unpinned his security tag and threw it onto the desk.

'Fuck this then,' he said. 'I'm gone. I resign.'

Now Si King would weaken. Jase knew it. He was a *good* worker, the best.

'No, you ain't resigning,' said Si. 'Because I've just fired you. Clear off out of it, you little shit.'

33

Next morning the builder was in, repairing the damage Lily had done to the wall behind the bed in the master suite. Lily made him a cup of tea and took it in to him. Oli watched from the door and, as Lily turned back towards her, she could see that Oli's eyes were all over the place, darting around the room as if it might contain some horrible gremlin that might pounce on her in an instant.

'All right, Ols?' she asked her as the hammering and banging commenced.

Oli straightened. 'Yeah. Sure. I've just ... never been in here, not since before it all happened ...' Her voice tailed away. She wrapped her arms around herself, her face clouding.

Lily nodded. She was standing by the bed, over which the builder had thoughtfully draped a dustsheet. 'You can come in, Ols,' she told her gently.

Oli shook her head. 'Nah.' Her tone was light, there was a smile playing around her mouth, but it didn't reach her eyes. She looked as if she was going to burst into tears.

'It's just a room, Oli. That's all.'

'It's not just a room,' said Oli, shaking her head firmly.

'There's nothing in here. Truly.' Even as she said it, Lily was remembering her first foray back into the master suite since she had last seen it over twelve years ago. *She'd* been shit-scared, too. She joined Oli in the open doorway and Oli stepped gratefully back, out into the hall, and moved away, towards the head of the stairs.

'Oli, you all right?' asked Lily, hurrying after her.

'Fine!'

Lily caught her arm at the top of the stairs. 'No you're not. What's going on?'

'I hate going anywhere near that room,' gulped Oli. Now Lily could see that she was near to tears, genuinely upset. 'I thought I'd try it, but . . . I hate it. It's creepy.'

'There's nothing there, Oli,' repeated Lily firmly. 'What, you think your dad would frighten you, hurt you? He never would, not while he was alive, and not now either.'

'But I've . . .' Oli bit her lip and turned away again, made to hurry off downstairs.

'Yeah, what?' Lily prompted.

'Nothing, it's nothing.'

'Yeah it is. Go on. What were you going to say?'

Now Oli turned back towards her mother. Her face was distraught.

'You're going to think I'm mental.'

'*Oli.*'

'All right, all right. I've . . . *heard* things. Okay?' And Oli was off, haring down the stairs and into the sitting room.

Lily hurried after her. Shut the door behind them to give them some peace from the noise.

Oli was sitting on the sofa, arms crossed over her middle, staring at the floor.

Lily sat down beside her, prised loose a hand and held it tight.

'Oli? You've heard things? What the hell . . .?' Lily was staring at her and starting to feel very worried, very *spooked*. 'What have you heard?'

'Noises.'

'*Noises?* What noises?'

'Um – well . . .' Oli let loose a little bubble of laughter. There was more than a note of hysteria to it. 'Voices.'

Lily sat back, her eyes fixed on Oli. She was aware of her heart, beating very fast, and that her stomach was rolling over like a fairground ride.

Voices?

What the . . .?

'But the room's kept locked, Oli,' she reminded her daughter.

'I know. So it don't make sense, does it?' Oli glanced at her, a glance full of desperation and puzzlement. 'Unless . . .'

'What, unless what? Unless there's a ghost in the room? Come on, Oli. Get real.'

'I know what I've heard.' Oli was speaking through gritted teeth.

'All right. So you've heard it. Or you think you have.'

'I *have*.'

'Recently?'

'No. Not recently.'

'When was the last time then? Tell me.'

Oli shook her hand free and jumped to her feet. 'God, can we just stop this?'

'Just tell me the last time.'

'Oh . . . about three weeks ago, I was coming in late, coming along the hall, and I heard it then. It was horrible.' Oli shivered. 'Frightening.'

'More than one voice?'

'No. Just one. It was like . . . like a child's voice. Oh, look, can we drop this now? It really freaks me out.' She glanced quickly at her watch. 'Look, I've got to go. Got a busy day.'

Lily reluctantly let it go. For now, anyway. 'What's on the agenda, then?' she asked, trying to keep it light when Oli had in fact scared her.

A child's voice in that room? For God's sake, what was that all about? She looked at Oli and thought, *Is something wrong with her?* And that frightened her very badly. Worse than the prospect of any ghost. Had what happened here in fact *unhinged* her lovely daughter, was she – and, oh fuck, now she was seeing Alice Blunt in her mind's eyes, Alice with her adult nappy and her scarred wrists and vacant eyes – was she showing early signs of some awful mental illness?

Please God no. Not Oli.

'I'm having a hot paraffin wax manicure,' said Oli, seeming relieved by the change of subject. 'They're great, you tried them?' And then she realized the stupidity of what she'd just said and stood there looking awkward. 'Oh damn, I'm . . .'

Sure I've tried them, Oli. We lags get manicures all the time.

But she just smiled. Oli was upset, she wasn't thinking straight.

'No,' said Lily. 'But I will.'

Oli nodded soberly.

'Got your keys and everything?'

'Yeah, got 'em.'

'I'll catch you later then.'

Looking embarrassed, Oli nodded and quickly left the room – leaving Lily sitting there and wondering if her daughter, her darling precious daughter, was in the first throes of madness.

34

Just after the builder left, saying that the plasterer would be in within a week to skim the wall, Jack phoned. She picked it up in the kitchen.

'Money's running out,' he said.

'I'll see you right,' said Lily. Money – thankfully – was the least of her problems.

'I know you will. You okay now?'

'Yeah. Fine. All things considered.' Lily still felt embarrassed that she'd weakened in front of Jack. 'You?'

'So-so. Monica's still giving me earache; nothing new there.' She could hear a smile in his voice.

'You ought to get back with her,' said Lily. 'If you still love her. Which I think you do.'

'Maybe. You could be right. But only after we've wrapped this case up.'

'Wasn't that the trouble in the first place? You working too hard?'

'Hey, what do you want? Me romancing Monica, or helping you?'

'Helping me,' she sighed.

'That's all I needed to hear. Because I've got another one,' he said. 'Another one of Leo's women.'

Lily sat down. 'Right,' she said.

'Listen, I've been thinking this is maybe not such a good idea, you talking to these women on your own, or with me. Maybe I should talk to them first, what do you think?'

After I nearly took Reba Stuart's head off, thought Lily, filling in the blanks.

'Whether it's a good idea or not, I'm doing it,' said Lily, although she wanted to end this; she felt weary and worried the whole time, and the strong feeling of distaste – even sickness – she felt as each new flaw in Leo's character was revealed, was draining her of strength.

'I talked to Alice Blunt's relatives,' she said.

'Okay. And?'

'And Alice was anorexic, needy and mentally weak. To Leo it might have been a fling, a bit of light relief, but for her it was serious. Probably she clung on too hard and he said, whoa, what is this? It broke her when he dumped her, Jack. Broke her in two.'

Jack was silent.

'You think the government's putting out the loot for the clinic?' asked Lily. 'Only it's nice. Good furnishings, nice grounds, even a lake. I just wonder.'

'I can try and find out.'

'Can you do that?'

'Sure.'

'This other one . . .'

'Oh. Yeah.' He sighed. 'This one's a bit closer to home, Lily. Might cause trouble.'

'What, more than I've had already?' Lily was almost smiling at that. Was he *serious?*

Leo'd had Reba Stuart, and dull Matt the accountant's wife Adrienne, and he'd had poor deluded little Alice Blunt who'd worked in one of his offices back in the day. *Now* what?

'What is it, some girl who worked in the club?'

'It's worse than that. You'd better brace yourself.'

'Oh yeah?' She was thinking that he was just building up his part, getting ready to stiff her with an ever-bigger bill.

'Yeah. We're talking shitting on your own doorstep here. *Not* very clever.'

Now Lily wasn't smiling. She straightened and clutched harder at the phone. 'Who is it?'

'You know Julia, Leo's cousin?'

'Yeah, I know her. Of course I do.' Leo had a large extended family, all fairly close-knit. Unlike her own. All she had left – apart from Oli and Saz – was her mother. She thought again that she ought to call the old bat. But really, she admitted to herself, it was the last thing she wanted to do. She had liked Leo's big family when they'd first got married. Felt she was getting not just a man, but a whole clan too. Then, when it all hit the fan about Leo's death, there had been a whole raft of drawbacks. You crossed one, you crossed them all. You killed one, they wanted you dead too.

'Well – it's her. It's Julia.'

Julia was the beauty of the family, with long, thick, ash-blonde hair, a terrific figure, stunning blue eyes. She was like Nicole Kidman's twin, Lily had always thought, whenever they had spotted her at family weddings, christenings, birthday parties. Julia was so arrestingly beautiful that people stared in the street. Her parents had fawned on her too much, and as a result her petulance and vanity were legendary.

Julia was strictly high maintenance, but then most of the women in their group were. These men – bad men, hard men, the sort of men who were used to running the show and pulling no punches – expected high maintenance from their women. Keeping a woman in an expensive manner was all part of the game, giving them extra kudos with their mates. If your wife or mistress was driving around in a Beamer and flaunting her designer labels, then you obviously had the biggest balls in Essex and your pals would pat you on the back and say, you old dog, good going. And what's she like in the sack?

Lily had always found Julia to be tediously self-absorbed and thin on brain matter. She was like a great painting – fabulous to look at, but no better at conversation than a block of wood. A pretty *thick* block of wood, at that.

But men weren't interested in conversation when it came to mistress material. Shit, they could get that from their mates. With women it was the looks that counted, and Julia had those in spades.

The last Lily had known, Julia had married Nick O'Rourke. Nick had been a bit of a playboy in the years after Lily, so when he settled suddenly for Julia, their whole social circle had been in a state of shock. Were they still married? Lily didn't know and she didn't want to think about it. She'd felt hurt when Nick married Julia, and the hurt had surprised her; she'd believed – all right, she had *forced* herself to believe – that the feelings she'd had for him were dead and gone.

So Leo had been boffing Nick's wife. And if that wasn't a motive to blow his brains out, what was? Nick had been sidelined by Leo over Lily. And now over Julia, too? How would any man take that, coming from a friend?

'I've got to think about this,' said Lily, feeling bewildered.

'Yeah, well, take all the time you want,' said Jack with a sigh. 'So long as the payroll's sweet, and you're comfortable to continue with this, I'm in.'

And he hung up. At the same moment, the buzzer beside the sink started ringing off the wall. Someone was at the main gate. Lily stood up and walked towards it, her pulses picking up speed. It could be anyone. Si. Freddy. That contract killer Tiger some-fucking-thing-or-other. But she was safe now, wasn't she? Safe behind large gates and a total lockdown system that could be activated at a moment's notice. The only thing she *didn't* have in here was a panic room.

Lily flicked the switch and spoke unsteadily into the mouth-piece. 'Who's there?'

And an angry female voice came back loud and clear. 'This is Saz. Who is *that*?'

Oh Jesus, thought Lily. After a moment, she flicked the switch and let Saz in the gates.

35

Lily held the kitchen door open and Saz came storming in like a force ten hurricane. Her new husband, Richard, followed behind in silence.

'What the *hell* is going on here?' demanded Saz furiously. 'Where's Oli?'

Well, Lily had known this was coming. It had come sooner than she expected, though.

'I couldn't *believe* it when Uncle Si told me what was going on,' Saz raged.

Ah, so Si's responsible for this, thought Lily. He'd rung Saz and she'd come back to start world war three. Good old Si. You could always depend on that sneaky arsehole to put the knife in when you least expected it.

'Well, believe it,' said Lily calmly. 'Because it's true.'

'You've got some damned front coming back here,' said Saz.

Lily squared up to her daughter. Even as she did so she thought, *My little girl, my lovely Saz*. But all she saw in Saz's eyes was hate. In every twisted line of her lovely face was

214

disbelief, dismay, horror. That cut Lily like a razor, hurt her deeply.

I can do this, she thought, I can deal with it. I've dealt with worse. But the sheer hatred that was radiating out from Saz, from her own beloved daughter, was already sapping her strength, making her feel tired and hopeless.

'And what's happened to the gates? I couldn't open the damned gates,' Saz was ranting on.

'That's because we've changed the security codes,' said Lily.

'You *what?*'

'You heard me, Saz,' said Lily, struggling to keep her voice low and even. 'I've moved back in.'

Saz's jaw nearly hit the floor. 'Are you *mad?*' she demanded. 'You think you can just swan back in here when you, you *killed* Dad, you shot him dead?'

'Catch up with the latest, Saz,' said Lily. 'I didn't do it. Somebody else did.'

'As if I'd believe that,' snorted Saz.

Lily stared at her daughter and frowned. 'Why would you *dis*believe it, Saz? Is it so easy to think that I'm a villain?'

'I don't want you here,' said Saz, quivering with rage.

'Saz . . .' said Richard. Lily thought he was a handsome young man, with treacle-coloured hair flopping over his kind blue eyes. He looked awkward and unhappy. She almost pitied him. It was easy to see who was going to wear the trousers in *this* relationship.

'Oh shut up, Richie,' Saz snapped. 'Stop being so bloody reasonable.' She turned her attention back to her mother. 'And as for *you* . . .' Saz was literally twitching with rage. '. . . I want you out of here, right now.'

Lily felt anger start to ignite in her gut. *I want you out* from Saz. *I don't want you coming back here* from Alice's brutish brother. *What the fuck are you playing at* from Nick O'Rourke. *Stand in line and wait your turn* from the screws inside.

That's how they all see me, she thought. *As someone who'll do as she's told.*

The old Lily, the sweet, accepting Lily she had once been, *that* Lily would have said yes, okay. But twelve years inside had changed her massively. Yes, she had been a model prisoner. Stayed out of rucks, mostly. Kept her head down. Railed against the injustice of it all, but only to herself, only *ever* to herself. Wondered all those long days and nights, *who did this to me?* But she had stayed out of trouble inside and she had done the time. Now, she was *out*. And where had being the nice, biddable little woman indoors ever got her?

No-fucking-where.

Well, she wasn't about to make that mistake again. That old Lily had died inside. This new one was Lily reborn, remade, forged in the fires of misfortune. And this Lily was *not* about to take any shit, not from anyone.

'You want me out?' Lily put her hands on her hips and stared at her daughter. 'Okay. Here it is. Let me lay it out plain for you. Oli *doesn't* want me out, and she owns half this place. So I'm staying.'

Saz surged forward. 'You cow,' she snarled.

'Saz . . .' Richard made a restraining move, but Saz sent him a poisonous glance and he backed down.

'No, Richie, I've got to say this,' she said, whirling back to face Lily. 'You never once got in touch to say sorry or to explain what happened, or to plead your innocence.'

'I tried to get in touch lots of times, Saz,' said Lily wearily.

216

She'd already had this conversation with Oli. That fucking rat Si had a lot to answer for.

'Oh yeah. Like hell.'

'I *did*. Si fielded all my calls.'

Saz looked at Lily as if she was something nasty she'd just stepped in. 'That's a lie. You're *lying*. Uncle Si wouldn't do that. He told me that you never once tried to get in touch with me or Oli. *That's* the truth.'

Lily shook her head, suddenly feeling exhausted. This was starting to really wear her down. 'Your Uncle Si's a bastard,' said Lily. 'And rotten to the core. If we're talking truth here, what about that?'

'You *bitch*,' said Saz, and half turned and grabbed at something behind her on the worktop.

When Saz turned back towards her, Lily saw what was in her daughter's hand.

It was a *knife*.

For God's sake. Lily stood there, dumbfounded. Couldn't react. Couldn't even *think*. Her daughter had attacked her first with a bouquet of flowers, knocking her off her feet and onto her arse amid crowds of onlooking wedding guests, and now she was trying it with a *knife?* She couldn't even begin to take it in. And not believing it, not wanting to believe it, made her slow.

Saz was coming at her with the knife raised.

Richard grabbed Saz, pulled her back. 'Saz, no!' he yelled.

Fuck's sake, thought Lily dazedly. *She meant to do it. She was going to cut me.*

The pain of the knife going into her flesh could not have been more painful than what she felt now. That her daughter, the beautiful girl she'd carried for nine long months and finally, amid sweat and blood and tears and agony, given birth to – her daughter, her lovely Saz, had been going to knife her.

'Let me *go*, you bastard,' shrieked Saz, struggling to get out of Richard's grip.

Poor Richard, thought Lily faintly. *Is he wondering what he's getting into here?*

'Not until you *calm down*,' panted Richard, having to work hard to hold his new wife still.

Saz was red in the face and fighting to get free, but Richard was strong enough – thank God – to stop her. Finally she just collapsed in his arms, the knife dropping to the floor with a clatter. She started to sob, screwing up her face and staring at her mother through a haze of rage.

'I *hate* you,' she gasped out. 'You bloody *bitch*.'

And that was enough for Lily. She left the room, ran up the stairs, flung herself into the room where she'd been sleeping, threw herself on the bed. Then, and only then, did she allow herself to weep.

36

Jase knew he'd made a mistake taking Oli back to his flat after that meeting with Si. He wasn't in the mood for shagging, not after that. Wasn't in the mood for anything much, really, except possibly getting rat-arsed on his own. Should have gone off down the gym, done a few bench presses, worked it off.

'What's wrong?' she kept asking him.

Oh nothing, except that your fucking uncle has fired me, after all the effort *I put in with you, you cow.*

Well, he couldn't say that. But by God he thought it. And when Oli started in again with the oh-what's-wrong crap, is it something I said, are you okay, all *that* . . . well, he'd lost it slightly, just for an instant, and given her a sharp one across the chops.

Damned steroids, he was going to have to cut back on them one of these days; he was always pumped up and roaring, an aggressive outburst just *this* far away. So he'd lost it with Oli.

Not that it mattered much now. All his plans were in the

shit-heap anyway. He was crazy-mad about it. Oli should have had the sense to leave him the fuck alone, not go whining on about didn't he love her any more, all that jazz, when he was trying to think of a way out, trying to dream up another scheme.

She stood there in the little kitchen of his flat, her hand to her reddening face, and stared at him.

'Sorry,' he'd said straight away, but she'd just gone on standing there, staring.

So he'd belted her one. So what? Nothing to make a big deal over. It was a one-off. He'd been pushed past his limits by that bastard Si King.

Oli left shortly after that. He thought he'd maybe got away with it – she was mad for him, after all. Then he went down to the gym – where he should have gone in the first place. He lifted the weights again, again, again, muscles straining and bulging, sweat streaming from him like a river; and he thought: *Fuck this. That door's mine. I'm going to take it back. You see if I don't.*

And then he thought of Freddy King saying, Do Lily King. Jase paused, eyes widening.

Do Lily King.

Please Freddy and you'd please Si too. Maybe if he did *that*, like Freddy had asked him to, then maybe he could start to get everything back on track. Yeah, it would be sweet. That's what he would do.

He would kill Lily King.

Oli couldn't believe that Jase had hit her. She couldn't believe it, and yet she couldn't really say that it had surprised her that much. Jase had changed over the last few months. He had become steadily more aggressive, with a shorter and shorter fuse. She didn't like it. That wasn't *her* Jase, the one she knew and loved. She thought that . . . well, she suspected that maybe he was *on* something. Some drug or other. She knew he'd once smoked a little weed, didn't everyone? And then he'd stopped the weed, and before she knew it he was down the pub every night, drinking ten pints and a couple of shorts besides, and what good was that for him? She'd made it clear to him that she was not pleased about that. That he'd ruin his health.

'Darlin', you want me to stop the drinking, I'll stop,' said Jase, the old Jase, the one she adored.

Not knowing, of course, that Jase *had* to keep her sweet if his plans were ever going to bear fruit.

Oli knew he had his faults. But he was always trying to please her; she loved him for that. So he went on the health kick, always down the gym, toning up, *bulking* up, he seemed to expand in size almost overnight, his neck thickening, his arms growing dense with muscles, his thighs as big around as her waist. Could that be right?

'I'm taking a few isotonic drinks, that's all,' he shrugged when she questioned him about it.

Oli didn't think isotonic drinks would bulk anyone up as fast as that, or make them so . . . well, so damned aggressive. She suspected Jase was taking steroids to build up all that muscle. She didn't question him any more about it. But when he stood there sulkily in his little kitchen, clearly upset, she'd asked him had she done something wrong, what was it?

And then . . . then he'd hit her. Not hard. But hard enough. Her front teeth had mashed against her lip and her lip had bled a little.

This was *Jase* who'd done this.

Oh, he'd apologized. But so what? It was done. She reeled

out of his flat and sat in her car, shivering and crying. Finally, she'd steadied down enough to drive herself home. Only to find that Saz was back, raging about how could she have allowed all this to happen, how could Oli have let *that woman* back in their home, and what was wrong with her mouth, it was bleeding, didn't she realize?

Oli said nothing. She just went to bed, and lay there in the dark with her lip hurting and her eyes wide open, picturing Jase, Jase who she loved so much, Jase who had hit her. Somehow, eventually, she fell asleep.

37

Some evenings there was 'free association' for the lags, a real luxury. Lily and Mercy would wander around the wing, chat to people, shower, read papers. Lily became a bit of a gym bunny, worked off some of her frustration that way, but more often she'd just sit and watch some TV with Mercy.

'You killed your old man,' said Mercy while they slumped there, inert.

'Yeah,' said Lily.

She had long since stopped protesting her innocence. And she had learned that her reputation as a killer gave her a certain kudos inside; it made others keep their distance. She wasn't about to let that small advantage go, not even in a private conversation with a friend.

'And you got kids with the man,' said Mercy.

'Yeah. Two girls.' Lily showed Mercy the photo of her and Oli and Saz; all together, grinning happily. Leo had been behind the camera. She'd shown Mercy the picture before. This was a little ritual of theirs; it comforted them both.

Mercy looked at it. 'They're so beautiful. I got kids too, you know.'

'Yeah, you said.'

Lily glanced at Mercy. Tears were snaking down her cheeks, dripping off her chin.

Lily reached out and squeezed her hand.

There was nothing she could say that would make Mercy hurt less, nothing at all.

38

'Jesus! Your lip's cut, Oli. What happened?' asked Lily the next morning.

She'd made some phone calls and had been sitting in the kitchen alone, enjoying – or trying to – a solitary cup of coffee, and wondering what the hell else was going to kick off today. She'd slept badly again; the dreams still plagued her and she wondered if they always would. Then Oli walked in, her hair wild and her eyes looking as if she hadn't slept in a month. She was wearing dungarees and a flowery top – and her lip was cut.

Lily started off her stool, alarmed. Oli made *calm down* motions with her hands, and helped herself to a coffee.

'I fell over on the driveway,' she said with a half-smile. The smile quickly became a grimace as a spasm of pain lanced through her mouth.

'It looks awful. Does it hurt?' Lily was peering closely, wanting to do something to help. 'Did you put anything on it?'

'Yeah, some cream. Look, what can I tell you? I drank a

bit too much with Jase last night and after he dropped me off I stumbled and fell. It's nothing.'

It didn't look like nothing to Lily. And what was Oli talking about? She had heard Oli's car coming up the drive last night, not Jase's flashier, faster motor. Oli was lying to her. But the closed, obdurate expression on her daughter's face made her drop it.

'Did you know Saz is back?' she asked instead.

'God, yes. Saw her last night. She wasn't meant to be coming back until today.'

Lily's mouth twisted. 'Your Uncle Si phoned her and gave her the glad news. So she cut the honeymoon short. Couldn't get in of course because we've changed the security arrangements. She gave me a right earful.'

And came at me with a knife, added Lily silently.

Would Saz really have done her damage? She wasn't sure, and that hurt. She thought of all the grinding, horrible years inside, of how she'd dreamed one day of seeing her girls again. She'd known that Si and Maeve would taint them if they could, would try their hardest to turn them against her. She'd managed to get Oli onside. But Saz . . . Saz wasn't Oli. Saz took up a position and defended it to the end. If Saz was your enemy, then she'd probably *stay* your enemy until her last breath.

But I'm not her enemy, thought Lily with piercing sadness. *I'm her mother.*

'Saz . . . took it all very hard,' said Oli, frowning. 'You know how close she was to Dad.'

Yeah, Saz had been the daddy's girl of the family. Always hanging on Leo's coat-tails, sitting on his lap when he was at his desk in the study, shooting clays with him in the grounds, being twirled around by him as he threatened to dunk her in the fish pond, both of them laughing and wrapped up in each other. Saz and Leo. Funny how things divvy up in families. Saz and Leo, Oli and Lily. Two different teams occupying the same camp.

Yeah, Oli was the easy part, thought Lily. *Saz is something else.*

But she could do this. She told herself that, over and over again. She could do this. Believing it was half the battle. Doing it was the other half. And she would.

'So what's on the schedule today?' she asked Oli.

Oli shrugged and frowned. 'Dunno.'

Something had really taken the wind out of Oli's sails. Lily waited, but nothing else was forthcoming.

Oli sipped gingerly at her coffee and sighed. Then she glanced up at her mother. 'Think I'd better hang around here in case Saz does any more kicking off.'

'Okay. But that's unlikely, 'cos I'm going out.'

'She'll want to change the codes back again,' fretted Oli.

'She can't do that,' said Lily. 'Unless you agree to it.' She neatly sidestepped the fact that *Oli* had already changed the security codes without Saz's say-so.

'She'll try.' Oli looked uneasily at Lily. 'This is really awkward for me, you know. I don't want to upset Saz. But . . . I think she's wrong about you.'

'I'm pleased you think that.'

'I do.' Oli's face pinkened. 'I . . . I love having you back. I don't believe you're a bad person. I *can't* believe that.'

Lily smiled softly. Those were the sweetest words she'd ever heard from Oli.

'But,' said Oli with a frown, 'if I side with you against Saz . . . well, I can't do that. We're really close, Saz and me. We had to get that way, I suppose, after it all kicked off with you and Dad. I'm . . . I'm really worried that I'll lose her, over this.'

'I don't think you'll lose her,' said Lily, trying to reassure. 'She loves you.'

Oli gazed at Lily. 'She loved you once, too.'

Lily couldn't answer that; she felt too choked up. Instead she swallowed and said: 'Look, if Saz tries to alter anything, talk her out of it. You can do it. Convince her that all she'll succeed in doing is making a prat of herself.' Lily had already had a word with Sunstyle Securities, telling them that if anyone tried to alter things, they were to check the new password, the new secret address, security codes, *everything*, with Oli or her, no one else, at which point they would quickly discover that person had no authority to act.

So they had that covered. And now Lily was going to have a day out. First into town to get her hair and nails sorted, and then on to a lunch appointment to get something else sorted. Something that could maybe solve the mystery of who killed Leo.

39

He was waiting at the restaurant. As she came in and the maitre d' showed her over to one of the best tables, by the window overlooking the river, he stood up and Lily thought: *Yeah, he's just as hot as he ever was. Maybe even more so.*

She was glad now that she'd made an effort today, dressed in her new sharply tailored and scoop-necked navy Gucci suit and high-heeled gladiator sandals, and carrying a quilted Chanel bag. Her naturally golden-blonde hair was freshly highlighted and fell in soft, shining waves onto her shoulders, her make-up was light but faultless, her gel nails gleamed; she felt good for the first time in . . . oh, twelve years. And she looked good too. The expression in Nick O'Rourke's eyes confirmed it.

Lily was seated, and Nick sat back down too. They looked at each other.

'Lily King, you look fucking wonderful,' he said in that deep, gravelly voice of his.

'You too,' said Lily. It was true enough. He did look great. Black suit, sharp white Turnbull and Asser shirt, discreet tie.

Black hair trimmed and tamed into gleaming submission. Clean-shaven. *Strong* face. Dark and swarthy skin. Perfect teeth revealed in a smile. His eyes swept over her, settled on her lips – as if he was thinking of kissing her – and then they lifted to meet her eyes. Oh, he was more than handsome. Distinguished. The waiter came with the wine Nick had ordered, took their food order, and left. Silence fell between them.

'So . . . why the summons?' asked Nick, his eyes resting on her face. 'I thought I was *persona non grata* to you at the moment. After all, you threw my safe flat back in my face. And when I told you that you were being stalked up and down Bond Street, you seemed more angry at me than at that little fucker Tiger Wu.'

'What's happened to Tiger Wu?' she asked, curious.

'Oh now come on. Do you *really* want to know the answer to that?'

No. She didn't. Lily took a sip of wine. It was like nectar. She thought of the contraband hooch she and her mates had supped in prison, real gut-rot stuff. Everything was so fresh, so new. So *wonderful*. The fine restaurant, Nick sitting there looking so damned irritated and so *hot*. No, she didn't give a stuff about what had happened to Tiger Wu.

She remembered that Leo used to bring her here, back in the day. Pop stars and celebrities came and went, table-hopping and being feted by the chef and the owners. The diners way back then had been affluent, civilized. They still were. But dark, brooding Nick was sitting opposite her now, not big, ebullient Leo. The background was the same, the situation completely different.

'I had to talk to you about something,' said Lily, wondering how best to broach the subject.

Jail Bird

'Well that makes a change. Usually you don't want to talk to me at all.'

'It's serious.'

Nick opened his mouth to speak, but the waiter was back. They ordered and the man departed. Nick took a taste of the wine and sat back, watching her expectantly.

'Okay then. Go on,' he prompted.

'Julia.' Lily took another gulp of the wine. Suddenly, her mouth was dry. 'Julia . . . and Leo.'

Nick's gaze was very steady on her face, his eyes unblinking. He pursed his lips and nodded his head, very slowly. 'I didn't think you knew about that,' he said at last.

Lily let out a breath. 'I didn't. Until yesterday. What – you mean you *did*?'

Nick was silent for a beat. Then he said: 'I divorced her as soon as I found out about it.'

Lily stared at him. 'I'm sorry,' she said.

'For what? Leo was the first, but I'm sure there would have been others.' He was twirling the stem of his glass around on the table.

Lily looked at his left hand. *No wedding band*, thought Lily. *Should have noticed that earlier.*

'Julia was in love with herself,' he went on. 'One man – or even two – was never going to be enough for her. She had to have constant admiration and attention. It gets wearing, let me tell you. Very wearing indeed. And at least,' he added with a tight smile, 'I did the civilized thing. I didn't just blow her bloody brains out.'

Lily looked at him steadily. 'You really think I did that? Blew Leo's brains out?'

'Only under extreme provocation. And Lily, if you didn't, who did?'

231

'Now let's have a think.' Lily paused and made a great play of looking deep in thought. 'Oh yeah. You?'

Nick threw back his head and laughed. 'God in heaven, what an imagination you've got there.'

'You've got to admit, him boffing your wife's a pretty good motive,' said Lily.

'I suppose it would have been, had I given a toss either way by then.' Nick poured them both a little more wine. 'Which, by the way, I didn't. Julia might have been wonderful to look at, but I'm telling you, the woman was boring as tits.'

'You must have loved her once.'

'Yeah. I suppose I must have.' And he looked at her so intently that Lily started to feel awkward, as though she had missed something important.

'And there was no jealousy about it?' she asked. 'None at all?'

'Not on my part,' said Nick, his dark eyes boring into hers. 'How about yours? You sure you didn't know about Julia and Leo at that stage?'

'No, I was pretty much in the dark,' said Lily with a tight smile, 'about Julia, and about all the others. You did *know* there were others, didn't you?'

Nick nodded slowly. 'Leo was a player. Everyone knew about Adrienne. And there were others, a *lot* of others. Leo liked variety. I thought you understood that when you married him.'

'No,' said Lily, 'I didn't. Stupid, uh? I thought it was going to be just me and him. No fireworks, no big deal, just him and me and the girls – a team. How barmy was that?'

'I think he really loved you,' said Nick.

Lily gave him a sceptical look. 'He really loved me, but he had to screw a whole collection of tarts?'

232

Their starters came. Smoked salmon for Nick; grilled halloumi cheese for Lily. She suddenly felt as though eating would choke her.

Lily picked up her fork, looked at the food, then up at Nick and said: 'You know how I felt when I realized he was boffing Adrienne? Do you remember Princess Diana, getting out of that carriage and floating up the steps of St Paul's in that fabulous Emmanuel dress? Well, you don't know or care about dresses, but I do, and I just remember her emerging from that carriage like a chrysalis turning into a butterfly, all the creases coming out of the silk, her veil lifting in the breeze. I couldn't get over how stunning she was, how happy, how she thought she was marrying a one-woman man and everything was going to be fine. And then of course she realized she hadn't married that at all. That's how I felt. That the life I had with Leo – and okay, it was never hearts and flowers, never the big romance, but that was okay – was all a lie from start to finish. That it happened to some other woman, some other poor, dumb, gormless bitch who had all these ridiculous happy-ever-after dreams in her *stupid* head.' She threw her fork down with a clatter. 'He made a fool out of me. Everyone laughing behind my back. Poor old Lily, she don't know her arse from a hole in the ground.'

Nick leaned forward, eyeing her intently. 'Nevertheless,' he said flatly, 'Leo loved you. Prized you beyond all those others. Some men... look, some men just can't hack monogamy. Leo was one of them. Oh, he wanted the little woman at home, the comforts, the kids... but he wanted more, too.'

Just boys letting off steam. That was what Reba Stuart had said. Now Nick was telling her the same thing. Only she wasn't buying it.

'I can't believe you're sticking up for the bastard,' she snapped, pushing her plate away. 'Not when he shafted your own *wife*.'

There was bleak humour in Nick's eyes now. 'Do you know how long I knew Leo King?'

Lily nodded. 'You met in primary school.' Leo had told her that, many times.

'That's right. We did. We were friends ever since then. Whereas Julia . . . oh, I knew her for about two years. I met her properly at your wedding to Leo, in eighty-seven, actually, although I'd seen her around before that. And yes, she was stunning. But, sadly, she knew it. I was soon disillusioned with her. And when she started playing away, well, that was it.'

They had both been cheated on. Nick had been cheated on by both his friend *and* his wife. That was hard to take, surely? But Nick hadn't been fitted up – *she* had.

'I can't eat this,' said Lily, feeling sick inside because it was all such a mess. She had never truly loved Leo, and now she was thinking that he must have sensed that, and taken comfort in the arms of – possibly dangerous – strangers. And if that was the case, then Leo's death really was down to her; she hadn't shot him, but her lack of real warmth for him had maybe put him in harm's way.

'Yes you can,' said Nick, starting in on the smoked salmon. 'Leo's dead, but we're alive. And that's bloody good food going to waste there, by the way.'

Lily managed a slight smile. Then she thought of Saz waiting at home, Saz who was so mad at her, and how she had been tipped off by that reptile Si. Her smile died.

'What now?' asked Nick, buttering brown bread.

'Saz came back early. Si told her Oli was letting me stay.'

'Jesus God.' Nick sat back. 'Well, even more reason to keep your strength up. To face the battles ahead.'

'Oh thanks,' said Lily sourly, 'for nothing.'

'What about Oli? Is she really onside now?'

He was eating again, as if neither of them had a care in the world. Lily wished that was true. *So* much.

'I think so. Although it's tearing her in half to have to take sides with me against Saz. She hates it. Oli was always going to be the easy one,' said Lily with a sigh, drinking more of the wine.

'And Saz was always a little madam,' he said. 'Like Leo in that. Always has to be centre-stage. Just like him.'

'She detests me,' said Lily quietly.

Nick put down his knife and fork. 'She does. For now. That's what I mean about the battles, girl. You've got a fight on your hands, and you don't start a fight from a position of weakness. So eat up.'

'Oh Jesus, what is it with men and their sodding stomachs?' groaned Lily, but she pulled the plate back towards her and, slowly, she began to eat.

They were leaving the restaurant when it happened. Anticipating a liquid lunch, Lily had caught a cab there, and Nick had a minder with a Bentley. They were just beside the car when *another* car screeched through the car park at speed, and there were noises; it was several seconds before Lily realized that someone was firing a gun. Everyone scattered. The heavy pushed Nick, Nick grabbed Lily, and they all ended up in a tangle of arms and legs on the tarmac as the car sped away and was gone.

It happened so quickly and was finished so fast that Lily wondered if it had really happened at all.

The minder was back on his feet, staring after the car. Lily was flat on her back on the tarmac, and Nick was on top of her.

'You all right?' he said against her mouth.

Lily looked up at him in a daze. His first instinct had been to protect her, covering her body with his own. Yet, she reflected again, if he thought, if he truly *believed* she'd killed Leo, he should hate her guts.

'I'm fine. You can let me up now,' she suggested shakily.

'Yeah.' Nick gave her one last searching look, then took his weight off her and got back to his feet, pulling her up after him.

'Fucking *hell*,' he said as he saw what had happened to his car.

The heavy was looking at the Bentley too. All down one side, it was pockmarked with holes. Lily sagged against the car bonnet and wondered if she was going to pass out.

Drive-by shooting.

You read about these things happening. You just never thought in a million years that they were going to happen to *you*.

'You sure you're okay?' Nick was asking her, still holding her, rubbing his hands slowly, soothingly over her upper arms.

She nodded dumbly.

'Sure?' He was very close, gazing at her with intense concern.

Suddenly, Lily felt choked up. The last person to show her such consideration had been Jack, but that had been so different; an offer of friendship and support, nothing more. This was something else. As Nick held her close she felt a shudder of molten desire rip right through her, as fierce as a spring tide. She sagged against him, allowed herself the luxury of being held and reassured, enfolded in his strength. It was not what she was used to. It was . . . *wonderful.*

'Did you catch the plate?' he was asking the heavy.

'Yeah, but it won't be no use,' said the man-mountain glumly, still eyeing up the damage to the car. 'Thing'll be false, and the car was an old shit-heap, you know what that's for.'

Nick knew. 'Didn't see who . . .?'

The heavy shook his head.

'No. Me neither,' said Nick grimly. 'Call up the boys, get another motor here and get the car towed soonest. Come on, Lily,' he said to her, very gently. 'Let's move away.'

'Were they after you?' she asked him unsteadily, her mouth dry and her voice cracked with the tangled aftermath of fear and arousal.

Nick stared at her for a beat. 'Probably,' he said.

Liar, she thought.

40

Jase drove the car out into the wilds of Kent, found a long, deserted lane beside a field of vivid yellow rape. He parked beneath a stand of oaks and sat there in the driving seat for a moment, looking at his gloved hands shaking on the wheel. He felt sick.

Jesus, he'd really fucked that up.

He'd followed her when she went out in the cab. Saw her going into the restaurant and thought, okay, time to spare, and he needed to go and have a crap; he was nervous, hyped up. This wasn't his usual type of job. Also, he needed to take his pills. So he had buggered off for an hour or so, then stationed himself in the car near the restaurant's entrance, and watched and waited. Got the window inched down just enough. Got the gun ready. The instant he saw Lily King's bright blonde hair and distinctive long-legged walk, he gunned the engine, shot forward and peppered the area where she was standing with a good number of shots. Shit, *one* of them should have taken her out at least, but she hadn't been hit and he knew it. He'd looked in the rear-view mirror and seen

238

them all getting back to their feet. She wasn't hit. She was fine. And so – thank God – was the geezer with her.

Yeah, she fucking well would be, thought Jase. *Bitch had the luck of the devil.*

His head drooped forward until it was resting on the wheel. He could hear the hard, nauseating thudding of his heart as he lay there, shaking, sick to his stomach. He pictured the scene all over again. Lily with a man, and that man had a minder, and the car was big, black and expensive, probably a Beamer or maybe even a Bentley, and he had shot past, *zoomed* past after he'd fired the shots that should have taken out Lily King, but not before he had time to see, to realize, who that man was.

Nick O'Rourke.

He'd fucking near done a hit on Nick O'Rourke.

And that was something you never, ever did. Not if you were fond of going on breathing.

'*Shit!*' he groaned, pounding the steering wheel with his fists.

He took a breath, tried to calm himself down a bit.

It was okay. It would all be okay. Because Freddy had fixed him up with the car, two-tone, rust and dirt. It was a clapped-out old Nova, fast but near fatal collapse, and the plates were fake. And . . . they couldn't have seen him. He'd gone by there flat out. They *couldn't* have seen him, no way.

He gulped down more breaths and the furious thumping of his heart seemed to steady a bit.

Yeah, it would be fine. Only . . . no. It was far from fine, because Freddy had wanted Lily offed and Jase had failed to do that. Jase had so *needed* to do that, because then Freddy would have put a good word in with Si. Freddy would have said that he was a sound worker, a good bloke. Then maybe

239

Si would have taken him back on the firm, given him his door back, and maybe then he'd soften about this Oli business too, and *then* all Jase's dreams – no, his *plans* – would come true.

But he had fucked up.

Now, there would be no recommendation from Freddy. Now there would be a right royal kicking instead – if he was lucky. And God help him if Nick O'Rourke ever found out that Jase had nearly topped him. Then it would be curtains for sure.

It was all going wrong. *Everything* was going wrong.

He could hear somewhere, away in the distance, a tractor moving.

'Oh fuck . . .' he said on a shuddering breath, and stuffed the gun into his coat pocket, threw open the door, went stumbling round on the mud-spattered road to the boot. He opened it, got the can of paraffin out, unscrewed the cap, and went back to the driver's seat and doused the whole thing in the stuff. The chemical stench of it hit his nostrils and he gagged. Spattered a load of the stuff across the passenger seat, and in the back too. Shook it out until the can was empty. Then he stepped well back, rummaged around for his ciggy lighter, flicked it. Flame danced in his hand.

He threw the lighter into the car. A warm *whumph* of air hit him as the paraffin ignited. He stepped back further, stumbled, nearly went into the ditch. The tractor's engine sounded louder, closer. He started back off down the road. Didn't want the carrot-crunchers spotting him. It was a long walk back to the nearest town, but he was going to have to do it.

He was fifty yards away when the petrol tank blew.

Jesus!

The noise of it was shattering. He stopped, turned, looked back at the blazing remnants of the car. Well, that was one job he hadn't arsed up. He'd destroyed the evidence. The Bill would never get DNA or any forensics shit out of *that*.

He turned and walked on. Felt tired. His chest hurt. He wondered if maybe he ought to ease off the steroids a bit. Maybe he would, when he'd straightened out the mess he was in. Got everything back on track again, running like it should. He knew he could do it.

He walked on.

41

Now how did this happen? wondered Lily. She was in Nick's house, in Nick's bed. *How?*

But she knew. The shooting and Nick's tender consideration after it had shaken her. She knew she could just as easily have been dead right now. Not lying in Nick's big, cosy bed with him but on a slab in a morgue. In her weakened state, she had come back to Nick's with him, accepted a brandy, and then a kiss . . . and then, well, the rest was history.

Of course she knew how it had happened. She'd been vulnerable. Also, she'd always, always been massively attracted to Nick. She couldn't believe it had never happened before, really.

She lay there in the middle of the day, wrapped up in his arms, and knew there'd been another factor too: twelve long years in prison; long dry years when she had struggled to damp down any urges she might have. She didn't want to take the lesbian route, although a lot of girls inside did. She kept herself to herself, exercised hard, kept her head down. Did her time.

'You're quiet,' said Nick sleepily, dropping a lazy kiss onto her brow.

'Blonde joke,' said Lily.

'Oh God.'

'What do you call an intelligent blonde?'

'A golden Labrador.'

Lily sat up, feigning outrage. 'You've just ruined my punch line.'

'Don't do that,' he said, half smiling.

'Don't do what?'

'Tell jokes against yourself. You're not a dumb blonde. But I know what it is. It's a defence. You always were a shy girl. Always fending off admiration with a joke or two.'

Lily flopped back down. Yeah, he was probably right. She ran a hand over his chest, over the dark curling hair there. He was so gorgeous. Better looking than Leo, he always had been. But Leo could charm the birds out of the trees, could fill a room with his loudness. And she *had* been shy in those days, repelling attention, Nick was right about that.

Now she looked at Nick and wished he'd tried harder. Competed for her instead of stepping back, growing cold towards her, when Leo started to take an interest. If he had fought for her . . . then, oh how different her life could have been. Couldn't it?

Or would it have been the same with minor variations? Nick was no saint. Would he have cheated on her, played up to the boys, just like Leo did, once she was safely knocked up and tucked away in the marital home?

She sighed.

'And what was that for?' asked Nick, rolling over.

'You're crushing my left tit,' complained Lily.

'No I'm not. There you are, you see? Humour as a defence.'

'You're so bloody clever.'

'And you're so bloody lovely,' said Nick, and kissed her hard enough to take all thoughts of the next joke clean out of her head.

'Nick . . .' she whispered against his mouth.

'Hush,' said Nick, and kissed her again, and made love to her all over again, and it was wonderful, so much better than it had ever been with Leo; Leo had been all wham-bang-thank-you-ma'am, but Nick took his time, made her shudder and cry with the intensity of her orgasm.

Oh God, all those years, she thought with deep wrenching sadness. *All those wasted bloody years.*

Again they lay quiet, sated, twined together.

Finally Lily drew breath and opened her mouth to speak.

'Not another blonde joke, please,' said Nick, eyes closed, lips forming a smile.

'Do you think Julia would speak to me?' she asked.

Nick turned his head, opened his eyes and stared at her. 'Don't know. I haven't seen Julia in years. And I don't know that it's a good idea you seeing her, either.'

Lily stared into his dark, dark eyes.

'Those bullets weren't meant for you, were they?' she asked.

He lay back, shrugged. 'I've got a few enemies.'

'Seems I have too.'

'I don't like you doing all this.'

'All what?'

'Seeing people. I know you've been seeing people, Lily.'

'People?'

'Like a private detective. Like Reba Stuart. And Adrienne Thomson . . .'

'And Alice Blunt?'

He opened his eyes and looked at her. 'Yeah, her too.

You're looking for answers to something, and maybe somebody out there doesn't like it.'

Of course he knew what she'd been doing. Nick had always been the gleaner of intelligence. If you wanted to know anything, you asked Nick. He kept his ear to the ground. Had a network of people beavering away. He wanted to know everyone's secrets – but he kept his own close to his chest.

'Look,' said Lily, propping herself up on one arm and staring down at his face. 'I've already got an address for her. And yes, the private detective – that's Jack Rackland by the way, but then I bet you already know that – he's found it for me. But I thought I'd talk to you first.'

He shrugged. 'It's nothing to me whether or not you talk to Julia. But I don't want you placing yourself in a dangerous situation. Pursuing some sort of stupid vendetta that's going to land you in trouble.'

'Hey, it's not up to you to be my nursemaid,' pointed out Lily.

'Well, pardon me for giving a shit.'

'I have to talk to Julia.'

Now he sat up, looking truly exasperated. 'Look. I'd rather you didn't,' he said.

'Oh. Why?'

'Haven't I just told you why? You're going to wind up in a heap of trouble, and what for? Lily – you're *out*. You're *free*. Why not just let it go now? Why not just appreciate it?'

Lily looked at his broad, well-muscled back and thought, *And if you were involved in Leo's death, ain't that exactly what I'd expect you to say?*

Suddenly she felt uneasy, as if she'd thoughtlessly leapt into a situation that she ought not to have placed herself in at all. She cursed herself for being so weak, for caving in after the trauma of the shooting and falling into bed with Nick when really she should have stayed away. Kept it business-like. Nick had a good reason for killing Leo, and she was stupid to have let her attraction to him override that.

'Look,' he said, swiping an agitated hand through his hair, his expression tense with irritation as he half turned and looked at her. 'Why not move in here? Or back into the safe flat?'

'You're joking.'

'Do I *look* like I'm joking?'

'Why, so you can keep an eye on me? Make sure I don't talk to anyone I shouldn't?'

'Something like that, yes.'

Lily nodded slowly, biting her lip. Fury was building in her. She threw back the sheet and stood up, started hunting around for her clothes.

'You know what, Nick?' She rounded on him suddenly. 'I've *been* locked up for twelve years. Before *that* I was locked into a loveless marriage, just making the best of it. Before *that* my parents made me feel a failure and – when I got pregnant – a slut. Do you *really* think I need to be locked up again, kept safe, kept *under control? Do you?*'

'Lily, for God's sake . . .'

'No! Don't say another word. I've heard enough. Now where the *fuck* are my shoes?'

42

'She tried to get the security company to change it all back,' said Oli accusingly, her eyes resting on her sullen-faced sister.

They were sitting in the kitchen when Lily got back from Nick's. Lily came in through the back door and experienced a strong sense of déjà vu. Here were her two girls, replaying a scene from their youth. Saz trying to seize control, and Oli complaining to their mother about it. Same old, same old.

She felt weary and confused. The drive-by attempt, her angry parting from Nick, had left her drained. She looked at Oli. Looked at Saz.

'I'm going up for a bath,' she said, and walked through the kitchen, away from them both.

'Hey!' Saz had followed her out into the hall.

Lily walked on, heading for the stairs. She couldn't face another showdown with Saz, not now.

'Hey!' Saz caught her arm, spun her around.

Lily looked at her daughter. Registered the intense hatred on her face, saw her own features in that face that was so twisted with anger. Felt sad, and tired.

'Where's Richard?' asked Lily.

'What?' Saz frowned, wrong-footed.

'Your husband. Richard.'

'Out. Golf.'

That boy's no fool, thought Lily. Saz in a bad mood was not something anyone would want to encounter close up. Again, she felt a pang of pity for Richard. It would take a very strong man to stand up to Saz – or a very weak one to accommodate her.

'And I don't see what the hell that's got to do with anything,' said Saz, recovering her angry stance.

Lily looked down at Saz's hand, still gripping her forearm with bruising force.

'You can let me go now,' said Lily mildly. 'You want to talk? Okay, let's talk.'

'I don't want to talk to you,' snapped Saz.

Over her shoulder, Lily saw Oli come out and stand in the kitchen doorway, watching them anxiously. She'd foreseen problems and, sure enough, here they were, staring them all in the face.

'You just want to shout the odds,' said Lily.

'No! Not even that! I just want you to get the *fuck* out of our home,' bellowed Saz, releasing her arm with a furious flick of disdain.

'Saz phoned up the security company and asked them to come back and reprogramme everything,' said Oli from the doorway. 'Just like you said she would. Only she didn't have the new passwords or anything, so they wouldn't do it.'

'Why don't you shut *up*, you little snitch,' said Saz angrily to Oli. Oli went pale. Lily could see how much she hated being at odds with her sister.

Saz turned back to Lily. 'I want you *out* of here.'

Lily stared hard at Saz's face, pinched up, ugly and suffused with rage. She knew Saz. Knew that change rattled her. Knew that once she took up a stance on an issue, she'd stick to it regardless of any evidence that she could be mistaken. But for fuck's sake – she was this girl's *mother.*

'Why are you so sure I did it?' Lily asked her. 'Why do you want to believe the worst of me?'

Saz was silent, fuming.

'What is it, Saz?' asked Lily quietly. 'Is it that you've hated me for twelve years, and if it's true that I didn't kill your dad, you've been proved wrong and you've hated me for nothing? Is that it? What, are you going to lose face if you change your mind?'

'You killed him,' sneered Saz, nodding her head for emphasis.

Lily turned away, finding it too painful even to look at her daughter right now.

'Yeah, you go right on believing that,' she sighed, and went on up the stairs.

'You killed him!' yelled Saz after her.

The bath helped. Luxury again. She'd always been a girl with a taste for that, and it had made prison all the harder. She soaked for a long, lazy time in lavender-scented bubbles, relishing the hot water, the time she could spend just wallowing, just day-dreaming . . . and, despite herself, thinking of Nick.

She was trying so hard *not* to think of Nick, but there he was in her mind, intruding, his eyes boring into her own, first fierce and then gentle . . . and there was a faint echo of his scent still on her body, a welcome soreness that the warm water eased. Her breasts were tender from the pressure of his lips and teeth. There were finger-shaped bruises forming on her thighs. She felt . . . good; physically satisfied in a way that she had never been with Leo.

But she had parted with Nick on bad terms. He didn't want her to contact Julia. But she knew she must, even though it was the last thing she really wanted to do. Every fresh discovery about Leo was making her feel more debilitated, more ground down. Still, she wanted to know, *ached* to know, who had let her stew inside for all those years. And when she found out who that someone was, she was going to make them suffer, too.

After an hour or so she got out of the bath, dressed, applied make-up, combed her hair and looked at herself in the mirror and thought, *I could be dead right now.*

Someone had tried to kill her. Her gut feeling was that she had been the target, not Nick. She was pretty sure Freddy or Si King were behind it too. Or . . . she paused, staring at her reflection with a frown. Maybe she had other enemies too. Maybe people had been talking and someone knew she was looking around for answers. Maybe someone thought she was getting too close.

She shuddered, because when she thought of *enemies*, it was *Saz's* face she saw in her brain, twisted with hatred for her own mother. Saz believed Lily had killed Leo, and refused to be swayed from that opinion.

But I'm her mother. We were close once.

Hopefully soon Saz would begin to see that Lily was not the monster she believed her to be. And Lily had to go on with what she'd started. She picked up the phone and dialled out.

It rang and rang. No answer.

She dialled again.

Come on. Pick up.

'Hello?' said a female voice, just as Lily was about to put the phone down.

Lily jumped, startled. The woman's voice on the other end was loud, aggressive.

'Who's that?' demanded the voice. 'Come on, who is it?'

'Julia? Is that you?' asked Lily.

'Who's that? What do you want?'

Now Lily could hear the edge of fear in the voice. Not aggression; fear. 'It's Lily. Lily King. I'm . . . I'm out, Julia. And I'd like to talk to you.'

There was dead silence from the other end. In the background, there was a rhythmic noise, like a distant motor.

'Julia?' prompted Lily. 'You there?'

'Yeah. I'm here. I'm not talking to you,' she said, and put the phone down.

Lily dialled again, but Julia didn't pick up.

She put the phone aside. Then she snatched it up again and phoned Becks.

'Jesus! Lily! I wondered where you'd got to,' said Becks, sounding breezy but with an undercurrent of awkwardness. Lily knew Becks must feel really bad about having to turn her out. But she wasn't going to hold a grudge over that.

'I'm still here,' said Lily.

'Where's here?' said Becks, giving a half-laugh. 'Joe said he heard you were staying at The Fort? I said you couldn't be.'

'Well I am.'

'But Si . . . and Maeve . . .' said Becks falteringly.

'The girls are here with me. Oli. And Saz.'

'Right.' Becks was quiet again. 'It's . . . nice to hear from you, Lils.'

'Yeah.'

Becks didn't sound as if it was nice to hear from her old friend Lily. She sounded like Lily had just put the kibosh on her whole day. Desperation seized Lily suddenly. She wanted to go back to a time when their friendship had been an easy, cosy thing; back before Leo had died and she had been sent down. She wanted to feel *normal* again.

'Maybe we could meet up?' she suggested. 'Do lunch with the girls, like we used to?'

Lunch with the girls. *The ladies who lunched.* That's what they had all been, back in the day. Blowing their husbands' ill-gotten gains before the taxman got wind of too much cash hanging about the place. How carefree and shallow and *stupid* they had been, living the high life with all their designer gear and moody sports cars and spa treatments, but without a doubt it had been fun. Lily had bought into the luxury lifestyle big-time. After the upbringing she'd had, that chilly, repressive, hand-to-mouth life of proud poverty, it had been like release from a cage. But now . . . oh, now she knew she'd just exchanged one cage for another. It had been a comfortable one, but a cage nevertheless.

'Monday?' suggested Lily, hearing the eagerness in her own voice but unable to suppress it. 'We always met on a Monday, didn't we, at Luigi's?'

'Um,' said Becks, 'Luigi's closed down.'

'Oh!' Lily felt foolish, wrong-footed. 'So where do the girls meet now?'

'Well . . . Le Soleil,' said Becks doubtfully. 'In Cheap Street.'

'There, then,' said Lily. 'One o'clock? All the girls? You, me, Hairy Mary . . .'

'What about Maeve?'

It was true that Maeve had once been among Lily's circle of friends. Now she was among her circle of enemies.

'Does she usually come?'

'Yeah, she does. Usually.' *But if you're there, it's going to be tricky.*

Lily heard the unspoken words as clearly as if they had been telegraphed to her over the wires.

'Um . . . Becks. I don't think she'll want to come if I'm there. And . . . I don't really want to see Adrienne there, if that's okay with you?'

'Oh yeah. Sure,' said Becks quickly. 'I understand, Lils. Totally.'

'That's a date then, yeah?' asked Lily, trying to ignore the part about Maeve, trying to ignore Becks's obvious unease with this call. She was trying to start afresh; why would no one let her start over like she wanted to?

'Yeah,' said Becks, clearly making an effort. 'Yeah. Great. Sure.'

Lily rang off, wondering if it was really safe to go out and about after what had happened with Nick outside the restaurant. But bollocks to it. She'd done with all that, skulking in corners, hiding away from the world. Now she was going to come out in the open.

Then the phone rang, and she picked up.

'Hello?' It was probably Becks again, wanting to alter something.

Breathing.

'Hello?' said Lily again, her heart starting to speed up, her mouth drying to dust. 'Who is that?'

But they didn't answer.

Lily put the phone down with a shaking hand and sat there staring at it.

It rang again.

This time, she didn't answer.

43

Alice was feeling a bit better. The staff were pleased with her; she was talking to them, just a bit. She even talked to her mother – she despised her mother – when the old witch visited, and to her hated brother too. She doled out a few words to them, made her mother happy that she was 'coming along', made her brother jealous of the attention; it was all fine, no problems.

Mostly she talked to Jem, one of the cleaners, who was Malaysian and had come over here to be near her boyfriend. With Jem, she could rattle on a little, because Jem wasn't interested in anything she had to say, not really. Jem just smiled a lot, and understood only bits of what Alice was saying to her, and that was just fine as far as Alice was concerned.

'This is *my* boyfriend,' she said to Jem, and showed her the crumpled photo of Leo that Lily had left with her when she visited.

'He handsome man,' said Jem obligingly, glancing at the shot while mopping the floor.

'Yes, he is.' Alice ran her fingers lovingly over the photo.

Jail Bird

'He's so good to me, he buys me presents.' Alice felt that this was true, but she couldn't really remember them. There had been a Tiffany bracelet . . . hadn't there? But she didn't know where that was.

'Yeah,' said Jem with a brilliant smile, remaking the bed.

'He used to take me to his club. He *owned* a club,' said Alice thoughtfully.

What had the club been called? She couldn't think. Only that they had been there together, and all the girls had flocked around Leo, but he had been with *her*, Alice. So many lovely women, and his wife was lovely too, she knew this, she had seen Lily . . . King.

Lily King.

The club was called Kings.

And Lily, his wife's name was Lily, and wasn't that strange, because the woman who had called to see her, who had brought her his photo, her name had been Lily too.

The buxom nurse came in, frowning at the cleaner, who was taking her damned time; she should have been *way* along the hall by now.

'We went to his club, called Kings,' said Alice to the nurse, brandishing the photo at her.

The nurse glanced at it and then away. She was up to her ears in work, and suddenly Alice had stopped being silent and started chattering on to anyone and everyone. She *preferred* Alice silent, really.

'Did you,' she said. 'You done the loo yet?' she snapped at Jem.

Jem shook her head, no.

'Well, get a bloody move on, chop-chop, yeah?'

'All the women wanted him, but he only wanted me,' said Alice. She remembered all the women, even the one who

255

had come on to Leo while she was there with him, the one he had laughed at; oh, how they had laughed at the silly cow . . .

But Leo . . . wasn't he dead?

Hadn't she heard that somewhere?

Alice fell silent, and turned and stared out of the window at the lake. Later, maybe after lunch, maybe sometime today, she wasn't sure, she would go for a walk by the lake. She liked that.

Alice was down there in the evening. It was chilly, she'd put on her cardigan. She liked this time of day; everything was quiet. The light was starting to fade into dusk and the sky was tinged with soft, peachy pink. It would be a fine day tomorrow. She walked around, getting her trainers muddy again, the nurse would complain, but to hell with her. She walked along to the lake's farthest edge, out of sight of the main building; once it had been a private home, a mansion; a wealthy family had owned it before it became a psychiatric clinic. The lake had been excavated way back in the past, and it was beautiful: big plants there, leaves big as umbrellas, rushes whispering in the breeze, coots and ducks squabbling for territory, and she remembered, she remembered now, yes, Leo *was* dead; and she pulled out the photo from her pockets, fingered it, caressed his face.

A tear slipped down her sunken cheek.

Leo was *dead*.

A woman was walking toward her. Blonde. Smiling.

Lily King . . . ?

No. Not her.

'I think he's dead,' said Alice, and she started to cry in earnest.

The woman came up close, and put an arm around Alice's bony shoulders. 'He is, Alice. I'm afraid he is. And you wish you were with him, don't you?'

Alice nodded. Oh, to be with Leo. They'd had such fun. *Such* fun. She looked at the woman. She *knew* the woman's face.

'I know you . . . don't I?' she asked uncertainly.

'Don't worry about that now, Alice. You know what? You *can* be with him,' said the woman comfortingly.

'How? Can you tell me how?' Alice asked her desperately.

'I'll show you,' said the woman, and bent and picked up a handful of stones.

Now Alice wept again, this time with gratitude.

44

Lily could see it on their faces, as soon as she entered the restaurant, as soon as she approached the table where they were sitting, waiting. Becks and Mary and another woman she didn't know. But then Becks and Mary had had twelve years to make new friendships. No Maeve, thank God. And no Adrienne; Becks had taken note of what she'd said on the phone.

What she saw on their faces was *curiosity*. They were looking at her as you might look at a two-headed dog or a dinosaur brought back to life after a million years in a peat bog. She was a freak, and this was a freak show.

'Lils!' Becks stood up and got a smile on her face. She leaned over and air-kissed Lily.

Little dark-haired Mary did the same.

'Good to see you again, girl,' said Mary, going a bit red in the face. Mary had never visited her inside – but Lily understood. She'd have been intimidated by visiting an inmate in prison if she'd been in Mary's shoes. Only bolder souls like Becks would tough it out.

'You too,' Lily told Mary with a smile.

'And this is Vanda,' said Becks, and Vanda, a snooty-faced ultra-skinny blonde stood up and greeted her politely. 'Vanda, this is Lily.'

'Hi Vanda,' said Lily. Vanda nodded frostily, as if someone had just given her a dog turd for a present.

Lily's conviction that this was a mistake deepened as they ordered. Vanda kept shooting odd looks at her, and Mary seemed uneasy. Becks was babbling nineteen-to-the-dozen, trying to keep it light, but the atmosphere at the table was tainted, and Lily quickly realized that it was *her* who had tainted it, simply by showing up. She was out of place here among the girls, stuck here like an interesting exhibit in a tent at a funfair.

Roll up, roll up. Come and see the amazing Jail Bird, fresh out of prison!

The starters came, and the wine, and they ate and drank, the others talking about inconsequential things: hemlines, Botox, the latest decorating trend, who was sleeping with who. By the time the mains arrived, Lily was wishing she'd never pushed for this. And when Vanda turned to her and opened her mouth, she just *knew* that she shouldn't have done it.

'So . . . I hope you don't mind my asking . . . but what's it like? Inside, I mean.'

Lily'd been waiting for the question. It had been simmering under the surface of all the other conversation for a while now, and here it was, finally, bursting to the surface, boiling over at last like lava.

She sipped her wine and looked around at their faces. At Vanda's, coldly curious. At Mary's, embarrassed but curious too. At Becks, who looked back at her with a hint of desperation in her eyes as if to say, *Hey, this was your idea. I didn't want to do it.*

'Only I heard,' Vanda was going on, 'that the culture shock of coming out – particularly after a long sentence – is so intense, so hard to cope with, that many – no, *most* – people who come out go back inside within a year. Did you know that?'

'But that ain't going to happen to you, is it, Lils?' said Becks quickly, with a nervous little laugh. 'Because you didn't do it – right?'

'Yeah, but even so. All that time in there,' said Mary, her dark eyes, fringed with thick black lash extensions, resting on Lily's face. 'Must have been awful.'

Lily pursed her lips and looked around the three of them. Reminded herself that they meant no harm, and that their reaction was probably a natural one. 'It's a big adjustment,' she said.

'And you're back at home now,' said Becks. 'With the girls. Jesus, I bet Maeve was happy about *that*.'

'Seems like she couldn't have her own kids, so she was keen to have yours instead,' said Mary.

Lily gave a thin smile. 'She only had 'em on loan,' she said.

'Oh fuck, talk of the devil . . .' said Becks, her eyes on the big window at the front of the restaurant, beside the pavement. They all turned and looked. Maeve King was walking by, strutting with her usual bossy little fat woman's walk, her flicked-up blonde hairdo catching the sun. She glanced into the darkness of the restaurant as she went past, and probably saw nothing because of the reflections of the cars passing by in the big sheet of glass, but the expression on her face was pure poison. She knew they were in there. Knew Lily was there with them.

'Oh shit,' said Mary.

Lily looked at Becks. 'Does she know we're meeting up today?'

Becks shrugged awkwardly. 'I had to tell her you'd be here. Couldn't just let her show up, now could I?'

'And she said . . .?' prompted Lily.

'She *said*,' Becks sighed, 'no way would she want to come if you were here.'

'And I bet that's the polite version.'

'It's difficult, Lils,' said Becks, her expression unhappy. 'I got to try to keep Maeve sweet, you know that. Joe does work for Si sometimes, I can't rock the boat too much.'

'Looks like you're rocking it now.'

'Yeah, but . . . I can't do it too much or too often, Lils. You're my best mate and I love you, but I can't. Sorry.'

There was a tight silence.

'Your daughters must have grown very attached to Maeve,' piped up Vanda. 'It was good of her to step in. For twelve years, after all.'

Twelve years was time enough to turn an impressionable young brain any way you wanted it to go, Lily knew that. She sat there and wondered how often in the course of a day Maeve had bad-mouthed her to the girls. How often they'd been told Mummy was a killer, Mummy didn't love them, Mummy never remembered their birthdays or Christmas or any fucking thing, that she was in jail with scum and that was where she belonged because *she* was scum too.

Lily had switched her attention from Becks to Vanda. 'You close to Maeve?' she asked.

'We're all friends of Maeve's,' jumped in Becks quickly. Her pale blue eyes held Lily's and said, *Please Lils, don't start anything.* 'We're friends of yours too, Lils. Me and Mary anyway. Vanda don't know you.'

Yeah, and she ain't going to know me either, thought Lily, who had taken against the chilly-looking woman big-style.

'It's hard, Lily,' Becks went on. 'We're all friends, and this feud between you and Maeve is awkward for us.'

And you might have to pick sides? Lily wondered, looking around the table at them. They all dropped their eyes, got busy with cutlery, napkins, any fucking thing. Well, Vanda was already on the Maeve team of cheerleaders: that much was obvious. But she had thought that Becks – and Mary – would be on her side. Maybe she was wrong about that.

Maybe she was wrong about a lot of things.

Suddenly she felt like even another mouthful of food would choke her. She threw her fork down on the plate and stood up.

'Look, it's been fun, but I have to go,' she said, wanting only to get away now. 'Got to see my probation officer – as you do. I s'pose I'm lucky they didn't fit me with a Peckham Rolex.' Lily gave Vanda a cold smile. 'That's an electronic tag, Vanda. Something they sometimes like to fit on us ex-cons, keep track of them. Otherwise I guess there's no telling where us bastards'll end up or what mischief we'll get up to, is there?'

Vanda went red. 'Really . . .' she sniffed.

'You look a bit hot, Vanda, allow me to cool you down.' And Lily grabbed the water jug and dumped the contents over Vanda's expensive hairdo.

Vanda shrieked and surged to her feet in fury.

Other diners turned and stared.

Water was dripping off Vanda's couture suit, cascading in runnels over her heavily made-up face.

'Oh Lils don't . . .' started Becks, but Lily was already striding off across the restaurant to the foyer, furious tears pricking her eyes.

God, she'd been such a bloody fool. You couldn't reclaim the past, make it whole and clean again. Too much dirty water had washed under the bridge; it was no good trying to pretend it hadn't. She didn't fit into this – *their* world – any longer. She didn't give a toss whether the rug in her hall matched her hair colour or whether the kitchen worktops were granite or marble or even fucking cardboard. She used to care. She didn't now. She'd changed, moved on. They hadn't.

She was at the door when Becks caught up with her, grabbed her arm.

'Lils! I'm sorry, I didn't know Vanda was going to come out with all that,' she said.

Lily gulped down a calming breath and forced a smile. 'Don't worry, Becks. Not your fault.'

'Are you all right?'

All right? Yeah. Dispossessed, hated, cast out into the wilderness for something I didn't do, but all right.

'I'm fine,' said Lily. 'Going to look up another old friend this afternoon.'

'Oh. Who?'

'Julia.'

'*Julia?*' Becks's jaw actually dropped. 'But you . . . ain't you heard what happened to Julia?'

Lily was frowning. 'I know she married Nick, and they divorced. I know she was humping Leo.'

'Yeah, but wait. There's something you don't know,' said Becks.

'Oh yeah? What?'

Becks told her. Later Lily went off to see her probation officer, like the good little lifer out on licence that she was, but for hours afterwards she couldn't get Becks's words out of her head.

45

Lily was still feeling staggered by Becks's revelations about Julia when Jack phoned her at home that afternoon. She felt *safe* at home, despite all the difficulties, despite Saz's ongoing hostility. Here she was barricaded inside behind her state-of-the-art security system. Nowhere else felt truly secure now, not really. This was what the King brothers had reduced her to. Or *would* reduce her to, if she let them. Her thoughts strayed again to Julia, to what Becks had said.

'She won't see you. She don't see anyone. Not now.'

And after that, the explanation. The dawning horror of it. And why, *why* in God's name hadn't Nick told her about this? Was this the reason he hadn't wanted her to see Julia? Was he . . . oh God . . . was he in some way implicated in what had happened to Julia? Was that why he'd hidden these facts from Lily?

Maybe he was hiding more than that, she thought, and felt sick, and afraid.

Nick.

He'd been her first love. Once, she had believed they were

meant to be together. But it hadn't worked out that way. Leo had snatched her away from him, and worse, far worse than that, he had *let* Leo do it. And then Leo had snatched Julia. Lily tried but she could not stop herself from seeing all sorts of awful patterns emerging here, and they all converged on Nick. Nick her lover. Nick who might be her friend, but who could also be, in that covert and concealed way of his, her enemy.

She and poor bloody Julia had Nick and Leo in common. They had mixed, up close and personal, with these bad, hard men, and somehow it had destroyed them. Would she too become like that – shut away from the world because the world was too dangerous, too frightening to engage with? Already she felt it in herself, her reluctance to leave the safety of home again.

No.

They weren't going to corral her with fear. They weren't going to fence her in, make her mind her mouth. *No way.*

Then Nick phoned.

'Hi,' she said, feeling flustered at the sound of his voice, bewildered with all that was spinning around in her head about him.

'Hi to you too,' he said, and she could tell that he was smiling. 'I want to see you.'

She felt a shiver of sheer lust rocket through her. But then . . . oh God, all these things in her mind, tormenting her. What Becks had told her about Julia. And Nick had been evasive, even angry, when she had raised the subject of Julia to him.

'I . . . I'm really busy,' she said lamely, unsure. Then, hearing the stony silence that greeted this she added: 'Maybe in a few days . . .?'

'A few *days?*' There was a mixture of laughter and irritation in his voice. 'Hey, lady. I can get women any day of the week, you know. I just have to click my fingers, and there they are.'

He was only teasing, she knew that, but still she felt annoyed. 'Then why don't you bugger off and do that?' she snapped.

Silence. Then he said: 'What's going on, Lily? Has something happened?'

'No. Nothing,' she lied.

'Only the last time I saw you, you were a lot warmer than *this*.'

'Bad day,' shrugged Lily.

'Well . . . call me when you're having a good one,' he said, and hung up.

Shit, thought Lily, slamming the phone down, feeling sad and bewildered.

Immediately it rang again. She picked it up quickly, thinking it was him, apologizing, but it was Jack, who lost no time in adding his bit to the shit-storm that she already sensed was blowing her way.

'It's Alice Blunt,' he said.

'Alice? What about her?'

'You sitting down?'

'No.'

'Well, do it.'

Lily sat down. Her heart was racing. Whatever this was, it wasn't going to be good news.

'Is she all right?' she asked, dry-mouthed.

'No. She ain't. I'm sorry as fuck, Lily,' said Jack on a heavy sigh, and then he told her the news.

* * *

They weren't pleased to see Jack and Lily at the clinic, but no change there. They hadn't been pleased last time, and *this* time when Lily asked to see the manager, she and Jack were ushered straight into a small office where a large, red-faced woman with a bad perm and a well-filled black twinset sat behind a desk. She didn't waste a moment.

'You're Mrs King, you visited Alice?' she rapped out.

'Yeah, that's me. Lily King.'

'You told a member of my staff that you'd been in Australia, but that wasn't true, was it? You've been in prison.'

'Yeah,' admitted Lily.

'And is this yours? Did you leave this with Alice?' The woman pushed the crumpled photo of Leo across the desk to her. Lily picked it up. It was damp, the image turned faintly green.

'I thought it might . . . I don't know. Jog her out of it. Or something,' said Lily.

'I was told by the nurses that your visit upset her. That she started acting strangely at that point. When you came here, gave her *that*.'

'I didn't intend any harm,' said Lily, feeling nauseous. She didn't want to start believing that *she* had been responsible in some way for Alice doing what she'd done. 'How . . .? I mean, what happened?'

The woman sat back, her eyes still hostile but slightly less so. 'She drowned herself. In the lake.'

Lily's feeling of sickness intensified. She thought of Alice's room up on the first floor, with its outstanding lakeside view. Of Alice, sitting there day after day, looking out at the cold green waters and plotting her own demise.

'We found the photo on her body,' said the woman.

Maybe it comforted her, thought Lily. But she couldn't

get past the remembered image of Alice screaming and screaming when she'd shown her the photo. Oh Jesus. Maybe it didn't comfort her at all, seeing his image. Perhaps it brought home to the poor demented cow all the more that he was lost to her. It could be that the photo had set about this chain of events and led straight to Alice's death at her own hands.

At her own hands. Alice had killed herself – so why then was Lily sitting here feeling like a murderer?

'Of course incidents like this look very bad for us,' said the woman.

Lily stared at her blankly. *And is that all you care about?* she wondered. It wasn't the best of times to ask, but Lily thought, what the hell?

'Can you tell me,' she said hesitantly, 'who paid the fees for Alice's care?'

'No,' said the woman, going even redder in the face. 'I can't. And now, if you'll excuse me . . .'

'Well . . . when's the funeral?' The least she could do was send some flowers.

The woman's eyes were openly hostile. 'I don't think that need concern *you.*'

'So much for that,' said Jack when they stood out in the foyer.

Alice's brother Malcolm was coming down the stairs, carrying a cardboard box. *Alice's belongings*, thought Lily. He spotted her standing there and bustled over, all truculent attitude and low intelligence, just like before.

'Tell me you're not thinking of going to the funeral,' said Jack, eyeing the approaching man beadily. 'You'd get lynched.'

'No, I'm not going within a mile of that,' said Lily with a shudder. She'd felt cold and shaky ever since Jack's call.

She couldn't help it. Alice. Poor bloody Alice . . . 'Jack, I still want to know who paid her fees.'

'Don't sweat about it. I'll find out, one way or another,' said Jack, and then Alice's brother was suddenly there in front of them, radiating aggression.

'They said you upset her,' he started in, dumping the box on the floor and stabbing with one pudgy finger at Lily.

Jack stepped forward. 'Ease up, pal,' he advised.

The brother subsided, but only slightly. He was breathing hard, pumped, eager to take his rage out on someone, anyone. 'They said this silly mare showed her a photo of that git Leo King. Made her flip. Our mum's in bits over this.'

Jesus, what if that's true? thought Lily in anguish. *What if I really did push her over the edge?*

She was aware of people moving in the background, nursing staff pausing, their eyes anxious. Did they have security here during the day? They must have. But right now, there were no reassuring uniforms in sight.

'You need to cool down,' said Jack.

'*You* cool down, arsehole,' spat Malcolm, his eyes still fastened with hate on Lily's face. 'This is *your* fault. My mum's been admitted to hospital with pains in her chest, and it's all down to *you*.'

The mother bothers him, thought Lily. *Not the fact that his sister's just killed herself.*

He wasn't just angry at Lily. He was angry that his mother cared enough about his sister to mourn her death. She had that strong impression again, of this troubled man hanging on to his mother like a prize – *Look, she's all mine!* – and wondered what would happen to him when the mother finally died. What then? Madness, she suspected. He looked more than a little mad already.

'You need sorting out,' said the brother, and surged, red-faced and bulging-eyed, toward Lily.

Jack lashed out fast and punched him right-handed. Malcolm dropped like a sack of shit and hit the floor. He lay there, eyes open but dazed and unfocused.

'No,' said Jack, pointing down at him. '*You* do.'

'I think we ought to get out of here,' said Lily as a chorus of protesting shrieks went up from the nurses.

'Seconded,' said Jack, and they stepped over Alice's brother and hurried from the building.

46

'Someone tried to kill me,' said Lily.

They'd fled the clinic and now they were sitting in the car outside Julia's house. When Lily blurted that out, Jack looked at her like she'd flipped.

'You *what?*' he said.

'I think someone tried to kill me.'

'Are you serious?'

'I think they did.'

'Um . . . how?'

'Drive-by. Obviously they missed. But I'm not absolutely sure I was the target. They could have been aiming at who I was with.'

'Who *were* you with?'

'Nick O'Rourke. Made a mess of his car.'

'Nick O'Rourke.'

'You've heard of him?'

'Who hasn't? He's a face. Maybe they *were* after him. Not you.'

Lily shook her head, unsnapped her seat belt. 'I don't think so.'

'And what makes you say that?'

'The King brothers. They've threatened me. They want to even the score over Leo. They won't believe I didn't do it.'

Jack sat back, ran a hand through his dirty-blond hair. Looked at her with bright, inquisitive blue eyes. 'Now come on, girl. This is shit or bust now. Having told me all *that*, are you really sure you want to go on with all this? See this Julia bird, and these two others? Are you *sure*?'

'What else can I do? Once I find out who did it . . .'

Jack was shaking his head. 'Fuck me,' he said suddenly, 'listen to yourself! What else can you do? I'll tell you what else. You can fuck off out of here, go far, far away, sit on a sunny beach and sip pina bloody coladas. You can go and keep pedigree chickens down on the farm. You can do whatever the hell you like, enjoy your freedom, forget about all this shit. If the Kings are serious, they won't let up.'

'Neither will I,' said Lily.

'No, maybe not – until they finally stick a bullet in your stupid brain. Lily – don't be a fool. Give it up. Pay me off and say goodbye.'

'You want paying off?' Lily threw open the passenger door and got out. She looked back in at Jack sitting there behind the steering wheel. 'Okay, I'll pay you off. Job done. You can bail out of this; you don't have to keep going. You can fuck off back to your office, go back to your normal line of work peering in bedroom windows or filming someone nicking paperclips – nice, safe, normal things like that. Get back in sweet with Monica, you know you want to.'

'I told you. I'll deal with Monica when this is sorted.'

'Sure you will.'

'I will.'

'Fine. But listen up, Jack. I'm not stopping. I'm seeing this through to the finish.'

'Lily – it could be the finish of *you*.'

'What do you care?' asked Lily, slamming the door closed and walking around the car. She opened the gate and went up the black-and-white chequer-tiled pathway before knocking on the door of the little Victorian villa, one of a huge long road of identical houses.

'Hey!' Jack had come up behind her. 'Now don't go getting in a strop with me. I'm just telling you like it is, that's all.'

'I know how it is, Jack. I know it's stupid and I know it's dangerous. But it's just something *I have to do*.'

'No,' said Jack, catching her shoulder, squeezing it hard. 'You *don't*. I've told you the options. There *are* options.'

'Not for me.'

Jack let out a sigh. 'Jesus, I knew you were trouble from the first moment I clapped eyes on you.'

Lily knocked harder at the door. Why was nobody answering the damned door?

'As I told you, Jack,' she said, 'you can bail out.'

Jack looked at her. Crazy tart. But admirable, too. She had a focus and a determination he'd encountered in very few women, as well as being tall and blonde and pretty fucking good-looking. He'd start fancying the daft bint if he wasn't very careful. And usually he was *very* careful. He knew of the King brothers. Knew of Nick O'Rourke. He believed it would be a really, really bad idea to get mixed up in anything involving them. But still . . . there was Lily. Her name sounded soft and pliable. But she wasn't like that. She had the strongest will, she was like iron. She was so bloody *stubborn*. And struggling through all this shit alone, if he backed away.

He really, really wanted to back away.

But the truth was, she needed his help, and he'd feel like shit if he didn't give it. So he stepped forward and hammered hard on the door.

'She expecting you?' he asked, peering into the window beside the door. It hadn't been cleaned in some time. The turquoise paint on the door was peeling, and down at the base of the door were deep scratch marks, exposing the wood completely.

Lily was shaking her head. 'I phoned her, but she said she didn't want to talk to me. I have to speak to her.'

'This is another one of those things you just have to do,' said Jack, sighing.

'It is.'

'All right then. Let's try round the back.'

They went down the alleyway at the side of the house and looked at the ramshackle back garden. There was a clothes-line in the centre of a stretch of unmown grass. A cheap white plastic chair and a small table. Two cats were sitting on the step in front of a scruffy-looking back door with a cat-flap set in it. Jack went and looked in through the window. There was a sink in there, from what he could see – though that wasn't much: the windows at the back were as filthy as those at the front. Lily joined him, looking in. And then something loomed into view inside, something like a Halloween mask. Jack fell back.

'Shit!' he blurted, stumbling over a white cat that yelled in protest and scooted away.

Lily looked aghast at the face hovering there. *Oh hell*, she thought. She raised a hand and tapped softly on the glass.

'Julia?' she called out. 'Come on, Julia. Let me in.'
And they heard the bolt shoot back on the door.

The shock of Julia's face was even greater because she'd once been so beautiful. Hell, on one side of her face she still was. The sunlight caught her as she opened the door and peered out at them. From *this* side, the side she was now being so careful to present to her unwanted callers, she was still the beauteous Julia. There was a finely arched brow, a stunning, almond-shaped violet-blue eye, silken white skin, a mouth that would give Angelina Jolie's a run for its money.

Julia kept the right-hand side of her face turned away from them as she let them in. She was walking ahead of them into a small, scruffy living room that stank of cat piss. Slinking shapes moved about in the semi-darkness, brushing up against Lily's legs. There was purring, arching of backs, sinuous move-ment, the hot silky brush of fur.

'Fuck me,' muttered Jack under his breath.

Lily wasn't breathing, not much. She was trying not to. The place was filthy, and the stench was eye-watering. As her eyes adjusted to the gloom – the curtains were half pulled over the window – she was able actually to see outlines in the room. There were eight or nine cats in here. Old Berber rugs thrown over sofas. Dusty African masks on the walls. A tired-looking aspidistra in a bowl on a table that was strewn with cups and plates. A tabby cat sat in the middle of the dirty crockery, licking one paw with dainty precision.

'I don't know what you want,' said Julia, moving ahead of them. She slumped down on one of the sofas. Dust plumed and danced in a shaft of faint sunlight that had managed to creep in through the window. She pulled a ginger cat onto her knee and held it there like a comforter, her hand smoothing quickly over its fur. It started to purr loudly.

The noise on the phone, thought Lily. *Like a motor.*

Lily sat down opposite Julia. The trick was to breathe through your mouth and not even to consider what you might be sitting on. Jack sat down too, making a face.

'I don't *want* anything,' said Lily. 'Just to talk to you about things.'

Does Nick know she lives this way? wondered Lily.

But then – Nick hadn't wanted her to contact Julia. To spare her the pain of seeing this? Or to hide away a dirty secret?

Julia was eyeing Jack with cold suspicion.

'This is Jack Rackland,' said Lily. 'He's a friend of mine. A private investigator.'

'Yeah? What's he investigating then? Me?' Julia shot back.

Lily looked at her with pity. The hair was almost the same – a thick, wheat-coloured mane, lustrous, wonderful – but now rendered paler by strands of grey. Julia had been one of the few pure natural blondes in their group. Lily had been born mouse-coloured. Hell, she'd *been* a mouse in every way in her younger years. Blonding her look up had given her a bit of confidence. She'd gone in for streaks, highlights, whatever – they all had, except Mary who had always been and probably always would be relentlessly brunette. Only Julia hadn't needed to resort to the dye bottle.

But her face. Her poor face. Even with Julia's best efforts to keep her head turned to one side, still the damage to the right side of her face was shocking, repellent.

'Jack's helping me look into what happened with Leo,' said Lily.

Julia nodded slowly. *Her poor face*, thought Lily again,

seeing the angry red weals and . . . oh fuck, it looked as if that whole half of her face had *melted*. It was hideous. The eyebrow was gone on that side, the eye was half closed. Even the corner of the mouth was deformed, making Julia's speech slurry.

'Everyone said back in the day that you reckoned you didn't do it,' said Julia, looking down at the cat purring away there in her lap.

'That's true. I didn't.'

Julia glanced up, a hank of hair throwing a concealing shadow over the ruined side of her face. 'Yeah, right. Then who did?' she asked.

'That's what we want to find out,' said Jack.

'We know about you and Leo,' said Lily.

'Oh?' Julia gave them that careful, sideways look.

'We know you weren't the only one, either.'

Julia was silent for a moment. 'Well, he wouldn't want me *now*, would he?' she laughed mirthlessly.

Jack said nothing.

Lily said: 'What happened to your face, Julia?'

'Oh, so you've decided to talk about the elephant in the room,' said Julia, half smirking.'So . . . what happened?' Lily asked again.

'Someone threw acid in my face.'

Lily took a breath. Wished she hadn't. But for fuck's sake, this was horrible. That someone could have done this to beautiful Julia. She'd been the best-looking girl in their crowd. They'd all admired her looks, would have *killed* for her looks. And now . . . here she was. Disfigured for life. Wearing shapeless clothes, because what was the point of doing otherwise? No one would look at her now. Not Leo. Not Nick. No one.

'Who did it, Julia?'

'I never knew.' She shook her head. Her lovely long white hands were exactly as they had always been, smoothing over the cat's back. Its eyes were closed in bliss. A deep purring was emanating from it. 'I came in one night after I'd been at a party. Got out of the cab, and someone rushed up to me – I couldn't see who, it was just a dark shape . . . and flung this liquid. They ran off. And after a little while, it started to sting. And then to burn. And I . . . I got my key out somehow, came in, splashed water all over my face, but it was burning, I was screaming, it was agony . . .' Julia gulped, caught her breath, the stress of remembering that awful night causing her to falter. 'I . . . my neighbour heard me. Came running round, phoned the ambulance, I think I passed out with the pain. They got me to hospital . . . but the damage was done.'

'Is there . . . is there nothing they can do?' asked Lily. 'Reconstruction?'

'Oh.' Julia forced a smile, shook her head. 'They wanted to. But I couldn't face it. They couldn't promise the end result was going to be worth a damn anyway, so why put yourself through all that? Anyway.' Her mouth set in a grim, twisted line. 'I'm happy here. I've got my cats. Animals don't care what you look like, you know. You love them and you feed them; they don't judge you. They don't turn away if they see you in the street.'

'But you must go out sometimes,' said Lily hopefully.

'Internet shopping. It's great.' Julia was smiling again, but it was wearing thin. She glanced towards the window. 'It's dangerous out there.'

Yeah, thought Lily. *Tell me about it.*

She thought of her own situation, of the Kings and what they would love to do to her, and suddenly she could see

279

how a person could end up this way – shut in, *imprisoned*. She couldn't let that happen to her. She *wouldn't*.

'Does Nick know what happened?' she asked.

'About my face? Yeah, he knows. I suppose he thinks it serves me right. After the Leo thing.' One bright and beautiful eye stared straight at Lily. 'I'm sorry about Leo. Our fling, I mean.'

'Yesterday's news,' said Lily. *So Nick had been trying to spare her this.*

'Yeah, only it ain't,' said Julia. 'You didn't do it. So who the fuck *did*?'

'That's what we want to know,' said Lily.

'You know what I'd do, if I was in your shoes?'

'No. What?'

'I'd leave it. Go far, far away. That's what I'd do.'

'I told her,' said Jack.

Julia looked at him briefly, then turned her attention back to Lily. 'And you didn't listen, I suppose,' she said. 'You always were the stubborn one. Quiet and stubborn, that was you in a nutshell. Look . . . can you go now? Please? I've got things to do.'

Yeah, like what? thought Lily. *Order in twenty tins of cat food and a microwave meal or two – anything rather than set foot out there again?*

Lily felt a stab of anger. That someone could have reduced the poor cow to this, living in fear behind closed doors, only her cats for company. Did Nick look out for her, help her? She supposed not. Julia had cheated on him. And Nick really wasn't the forgiving type.

So is he the type to throw acid in the face of a deceiving woman? she wondered. She didn't know. Not for certain. That bothered her. Shit, *everything* about Nick bothered her.

'Do you see Nick at all?' asked Lily as they stood up to leave. 'These days?'

'Nick?' Julia stood up too, scooping the ginger cat up into her arms and somehow contriving to keep the right side of her face concealed beneath the long fall of her hair and the bulky body of the cat. 'God, no. Why should I?'

'Well, you were married. Once.'

'Not for long,' said Julia, ushering them towards the front door, where she stooped awkwardly, cat still clutched to her, and unbolted, unlocked, unlatched.

It's like Fort Knox, thought Lily. And again, she was reminded of her own set-up. Living at The Fort, which was rigged out like a high-security outpost – or a prison.

Maybe Julia was right to feel under threat from the outside world. In here, she felt safe. Out there, monsters lurked.

Poor bitch.

'And anyway,' said Julia, as she opened the door and the sunlight fell upon her ruined face, 'it wasn't much of a marriage.'

Lily and Jack stepped out onto the pavement. Julia moved back, into the deeper shadows of the hall, her hand already on the door to shut the world out.

'Why do you say that?' asked Lily, curious.

'Because he married me on the rebound, didn't he?' she said with a dry crackle of laughter. 'After you took off with Leo. It was *you* Nick really wanted. It was always you.'

Jack and Lily got back in the car outside Julia's. Lily fastened her seat belt, but Jack just sat there behind the steering wheel, his face blank, his eyes thoughtful as he stared straight ahead at the car parked in front.

'Jack?' said Lily. Why wasn't he starting the damned car?

After a moment he turned his head and stared at her for so long that she began to feel more than a bit uncomfortable. Then he said: 'What's going on, Lily?'

Lily looked at him blankly. 'What do you mean?'

Jack was silent, still staring. It was starting to worry her.

'I *mean*, what the fuck's happening here?' he said, and he was looking at her like she was a total stranger.

'No, you've lost me,' said Lily. 'Sorry.'

'Oh, well let me just *find* you again,' he said. 'Alice drowned. Julia scarred. What's going to happen next, Lily? What's going to happen to the others, the others *you've* just insisted you have to track down and confront?'

Lily's mouth dropped open in shock at what he was saying.

'What – you think *I* had something to do with Alice's death?' Lily let out a wild laugh of disbelief. 'Oh come on. Alice was unhinged. She committed suicide.'

'That's just a supposition. No one knows that for sure yet.'

Lily was shaking her head at him, her face disbelieving. 'You can't be flaming serious. And what about Julia? I don't know when that maniac decided to have a go at her, but you know I was inside when it happened. Banged up. No *way* could I have done it.'

Jack sat back, his expression dubious.

'Come off it, Lily. You were married to Leo bloody King. One of the biggest crooks in the East End, one of the best-known faces in the whole of Essex. One thing he had – and one thing I guess you'd have too – was *connections*. Inside or out, he could have ordered anything done. And so . . .'

'And so you think I could too?' Lily really was laughing now: it was too ridiculous for words. 'Wrong, Jack. I never had that sort of clout. I was just the little woman indoors; the one who everyone thinks finally flipped and planted a bullet in her cheating husband's brain. I didn't have the contacts; I didn't have the connections. Leo had it all. Not me.'

'Yeah? Because I'm sort of puzzled by something.'

'Go on,' said Lily, feeling hurt and confused by this sudden and unexpected attack. 'Let's have this out in the open.'

'Si King and Freddy want to do you damage, so you say.'

'I say it, Jack. Because it's true.'

'Then why didn't they get to you while you were inside? Perfect alibi for them: you in stir and them out in the open. If they wanted your arse so badly.'

Lily slumped back in the passenger seat. He had a point. She knew he did.

She passed a weary hand over her face. 'I don't have the answer to that, Jack.'

'No, neither do I, and that sort of bothers me. And what bothers me even more is that I might be helping you with some crazy sort of vendetta. What bothers me is what's going to happen to those other poor cows who've crossed you.'

'Jack . . .' started Lily desperately.

'No, listen. You told me you wanted revenge. Is this it, Lily?' Now he was staring at her face as if looking for the truth there. 'Is this all you, Lily? Julia scarred. Alice drowned. What are you doing here, picking them off one by one?'

Lily was silent, fuming. How could he think that?

Easily, she reasoned with herself. He didn't really know her.

'What, you got nothing to say?' challenged Jack.

'No,' said Lily. 'Just drive the damned car, will you? I think we've just about said it all.'

47

'You *cunt*,' said Freddy King, red-faced with rage.

'There's no harm done, Mr King,' said Jase quickly, trying to get his arse out of the fire while he still could; talking rapidly, persuasively. 'It was a near miss. Nick O'Rourke was with her, that's true, but I missed. I missed them both. Next time, I'll get the cow.'

'You bloody fool,' snapped Freddy. 'You soft-headed . . . what the fuck you done now?'

They were up in the office above the club, and Freddy was going berserk. Jase was looking shame-faced at the carpet, feeling like seven different kinds of shit was raining down upon his head.

He knew he'd fucked up. Should have looked more care-fully, should have got her when she left the house in the taxi rather than waiting until she came out of the restaurant, but he hadn't been feeling well; actually he'd been feeling like shit, his head aching, his chest hurting. Jesus, he was going to have to let up on those fucking pills and he *would*, just as soon as he'd got the door back, just as soon as he'd got back in sweet with Si and Freddy.

But now, this. He'd screwed up. Knew he had to take a caning over it. So he stood there and took the abuse Freddy was heaping upon him and thought, *Okay, get it out of your system, you arsehole, call me any fucking thing you like, and then simmer down and forget it.*

Only Freddy didn't seem to be simmering down. And, as for forgetting it, Jase didn't think so.

'Look, I've been straight with you, ain't I?' asked Jase desperately after the arse-kicking had gone on for what he felt was long enough.

'Oh, that's all bloody right then,' said Freddy, thumping a meaty fist down on the desk. 'That's just sodding well *fine*. But see – I really hate to piss on your fireworks – you think Nick O'Rourke's going to stand for this? Nah. He's gonna be combing the streets to find the little git who had the *nerve* to try a stunt like that. And how long before he gets back to you, you stupid tosser, and then to me?'

'There's no way it can be traced back,' said Jase quickly. 'I torched it out in the middle of nowhere. There's *no way*, I promise you.'

'You promise me!' Freddy stood up, came around the desk, and although Jase stood a head taller than him he grabbed him around the throat and in an instant had shoved him back over the desk.

Freddy's leering crazy face was inches from Jase's own as Freddy put all his considerable weight upon Jase's chest. Jase didn't move. Intimidation wasn't about size, it was about attitude – and Christ did Freddy have that. Not as much as Si, but still, he had it. Jase could hardly breathe, but he didn't moan on. Best not to. Best to just keep it buttoned and take this, get it over with. Wasn't it?

But he *hated* being treated like this. He was the main man, or he had been until Si had kicked him into touch. It had all been going so good, then wallop! Back down the snake. On his arse.

'Don't you go giving out promises, you little shite,' snarled Freddy, with his knee up on Jase's chest.

Couldn't *breathe* . . .

'Your fucking promises ain't worth *that*,' Freddy snapped the fingers of one hand derisively in Jase's face. Jase flinched. Felt the anger building. Treating him like this. *Him*. After he'd worked his bollocks off to get where he was today.

'Mr King . . .' Jase started, unsure of what he was going to say, only knowing that he couldn't take this, it was too much. He'd thought he could handle it, do the crime, do the time, ain't that what the bitch Lily had done? Kept her head down, taken her punishment? But he couldn't do that. All right, he'd made mistakes. But that door downstairs was *his* door, and he wanted it back. He was losing cred among his mates on the streets, and now Freddy was kneeling on his chest and he couldn't *breathe* . . .

Suddenly – violently – he flung Freddy off. He saw Freddy's mad eyes widen in surprise and he liked that, his blood was up. He gave Freddy a hard smack across the jaw that sent him thudding back into the door.

Bliss.

For an instant, anyway. Then the red haze of rage fell away and sanity returned. Jase realized what he'd done. You didn't take a poke at one of the King brothers and get away with it. Freddy straightened and put a hand to his jaw. His eyes were on Jase and they were murderous.

Jase had to think, and think fast.

'What if I told Nick you ordered it done?' he flung out just as Freddy was launching himself forward.

Freddy froze. 'You *what?*'

Jase's eyes took on a crazy light as true inspiration hit him. That was it. 'Yeah,' he said, bouncing on his toes, his knuckles smarting from the punch he'd doled out to Freddy *Jesus, he'd hit Freddy King*, a sane part of his brain was hollering, but he wasn't listening; the blood was singing in his ears and he felt as high as a kite because he had it, this was it, this was his way back in.

'You get me my door back okay? Or when Nick O'Rourke comes looking, I tell him you asked me to do it. How'd you like *that?* After all, it's the fucking truth. Ain't it?'

Freddy was silent, his eyes fastened on Jase, one hand cupping his throbbing jaw. Then he dropped his hand. Nodded.

'You're right,' he said. 'It's the truth. Even if you *did* make a complete balls of it.'

'I can put it right,' said Jase, wanting to be helpful here. If Freddy was magnanimous enough to concede a point, then damn sure he could too. 'No charge.'

'No charge except the *door*, right?' asked Freddy with a slight smile. Then he winced. 'Jesus, kid, that's a good right hand you got there. A real haymaker.'

'I'm sorry I hit you, Mr King,' said Jase. 'Really I am.'

Freddy made a *so what* gesture and went back around the desk. He sat in the chair and looked up at Jase. 'I like someone who can handle themselves. Someone who can dish it out as well as take it. Forget it.'

'That's very big of you, Mr King,' said Jase. 'Will you talk to Si? About the door? And we can work something out

287

about Mrs King, no sweat. I'll sort it. Best to do her *inside* the house, really. Make it look accidental. Nice and easy.'

'Sure, sure,' said Freddy. *The door, the door.* They were in the middle of a serious fuck-up here, and he was moaning on about the fucking *door?* Freddy didn't want a ruck with Nick O'Rourke; Nick didn't take any prisoners. Leave it to this arsehole and they'd soon find themselves up to their necks in a gang war. No, it was better that he did Lily King himself. He could see that now. Up close and personal was best.

Jase was thinking that this had gone far better than he'd hoped. He had screwed up, taken a swing at the boss, but he was persuasive. He had talked Freddy round to his way of seeing things. Now he was going to get his door back, restart the charm offensive on Oli and everything would be right back on track, like he wanted.

'Go down and get yourself a drink,' said Freddy with a smile. 'On the house. We'll sort this out okay? No worries.'

Jase went off downstairs.

Freddy's smile dropped from his face like a mask.

The little fucker had *hit* him. Rage flooded into Freddy like a hot, bitter tide. And the bastard seriously thought he was going to get another chance after that, screw things up even worse? That little shit had a lesson coming. Freddy sat there, his jaw aching and throbbing, and stared at the closed door. Jase Conway was all out of chances. He'd just used up his very last one.

48

One day, unannounced, the cellmates Lily had grown used to were moved. Mercy was one of them. She had become a mainstay of Lily's life, and there had been no time to say goodbye. She sat down on her bunk, wondering who she was going to find to talk to now, when she heard a yell. Standing up, she went over to the cell window.

'LILY! LILY KING!'

Mercy's huge, bellowing voice was drifting up from the outside courtyard.

'LILY KING!' Mercy was yodelling out there somewhere.

'MERCY?' Lily yelled back from the gap in the window.

'WAVE, GIRL. CAN'T SEE YOU!'

Lily waved and peered out. Across the yard she saw a robust brown arm, waving back.

'GETTIN' SHIPPED OUT OF THIS SHIT-HOLE!' shouted Mercy.

'HOME? HOME TO JAMAICA?' bawled Lily.

Jessie Keane

'YEAH. SOON.'
'GOOD LUCK!'
'YOU TOO!'
That was the last she ever saw of Mercy.

49

Lily was surprised when Jack Rackland phoned her a day after their visit to Julia. She'd thought she wouldn't hear from him again. Oh, she'd get an invoice, but that would be that. And if that was the case, she'd pay his damned invoice and be done with it. Fuck him.

But here he was, phoning her.

'Oh. Hi,' she said, still feeling furious with him.

'I phoned Reba Stuart,' he said.

Lily counted to ten. 'Why?' she said at last. 'You think I poisoned her?'

'Lily—'

'And what about Adrienne, don't tell me you ain't checked up on *her* yet? I could have done the brakes on her car, anything. You're taking a chance.'

'Lily, will you shut the fuck up and listen?' said Jack, and she could hear reluctant laughter in his voice now. 'I'm sorry for what I said. I don't think you're a killer. It just . . .' he paused, sorting out his words. '. . . It spooked me, that's all. Seeing Julia all scarred like that. Started me thinking all sorts.

D'you know, I could still smell those damned cats on me even after I got home and took a shower. I had to bin my clothes.'

He was apologizing, that was something. But Lily still felt angry. The damned unfairness. After all the shit she'd been through since Leo's death, still people were ready to think, *Oh yes, she's the woman who did her husband. So yeah, of course she could do this too.*

'I'm apologizing here,' said Jack when Lily said nothing.

'I know you are. Okay. Apology accepted.'

'Reba was fine.'

'Why wouldn't she be?'

'Oh and I *did* check on Adrienne.'

'Thanks for the vote of confidence.'

'You sure you want to go on with this? Find the last two?'

'You sure I can be *trusted* with the last two?'

'I thought we'd just covered that.'

'*You* did, Jack.' Lily felt like putting the phone down on him but, apology or not, she wanted to speak to the last two. She took a breath. Calmed down a notch. 'Oh, all right. Yeah, let's press on. Why the hell not?'

'I'll be there in an hour,' he said. 'Pick you up and we'll go see Bev and Suki Carmody. They're a double act – or they were.'

'What, entertainers?'

'Strippers. And I ought to warn you, the double act didn't end on stage, either.'

Oh my God, thought Lily, and put the phone down. It rang again almost immediately.

'Hello?'

There was only breathing.

Someone was there.

'Hello?' she asked again.

Breathing.

Lily put the phone down, swallowing hard.

Someone trying to scare her. And succeeding, too.

She stood up. The phone started ringing again, but this time she ignored it and focused on Bev and Suki Carmody, and finally the damned thing stopped ringing.

Bev and Suki.

Bad enough Leo'd been boffing all these tarts one at a time. Now, if she'd understood Jack correctly, it turned out he'd been doing them mob-handed, too.

'You still here?' said a harsh female voice.

Lily looked up. Saz was standing just inside the kitchen door, wearing figure-hugging Versace jeans and a tight white t-shirt. She was looking at her mother with stark dislike.

Lily stood up. She really wasn't in the mood for another run-in with Saz.

'Yeah. Still here. And still waiting for a civil word to come out of your mouth, Saz,' she said quietly.

'You'll wait a long time for *that*.'

'Pity,' said Lily, 'because I didn't kill your dad. And I tried to get in touch with you and Oli too many times to count. Both those things are true. And so is this, Saz – you're my daughter and I love you very much.'

Saz's face twitched.

That hit home, thought Lily.

'Well, *I* don't love *you*,' said Saz, recovering quickly.

Lily smiled wryly. 'That's a shame. But you know what, Saz?' Her eyes held her daughter's with earnest appeal.

Saz was eyeing Lily suspiciously. 'No. What?'

'You're going to have to learn to get used to me being

here, and sometime – whenever you're ready – the gloves are going to have to come off, and we are going to have to talk to each other, properly. Because I'm here to stay. And you're going to have to get over it.'

Saz said nothing.

Lily walked past her daughter and headed for the stairs.

Jack had got it right; Bev and Suki were still a double act. They lived together in a poky little flat in Shoreditch, and seemed to share the attentions of a large, handsome black guy who, throughout Jack and Lily's visit, hovered in the kitchen with the door open, cooking. The fragrant scent of frying plantains was drifting out, and reggae was chugging away from the radio. In the lounge, the sweet scent of recently smoked weed was nearly overpowering the aroma of frying plantains.

'You're Lily King?' Suki asked, wide-eyed and smiling, as if she was meeting an old pal, not the wife of the man she and her sister had been shagging over a decade ago. 'I heard you was out.'

Time had been kind to Bev and Suki. They were still very good-looking women, and each of them had a curious spaced-out innocence about them. They were both curly-haired pale blondes, both dressed in hippy-chic gear – fringed buckskin waistcoats, floral peasant blouses, skin-tight jeans and Ugg boots – and they both wore a lot of jangling, silver-coloured jewellery.

Suki settled Lily and Jack down on a shawl-strewn couch.

Meanwhile, Bev was busy taking calls on her mobile and leaving the room a lot.

'She don't do this much,' said Suki when Bev had hurried off into the bedroom clutching her phone for the fourth time.

'Oh?' queried Jack.

Suki dropped him a wink. 'Don't want the benefit snoops round, now do we?' she grinned. 'And who does it hurt? She earns a bit of pin money talking to a few wankers on the end of the phone.'

'Chatlines are *big* business, man,' chimed in the man from the kitchen. Lily recognized the warm, syrupy echo of Mercy's Jamaican *patois* when he spoke.

'That's Winston,' said Suki. 'He drives. Man and van for hire, that kind of stuff, you know. And I do the tarot.'

Suki looked at Lily and Jack's faces.

'For real,' she added, and smiled. 'I got the gift.'

'Mrs King wanted to meet you,' said Jack, getting down to business. 'She knows you were knocking off her old man back in the day.'

'Ah.' Suki didn't look particularly chastened at that. 'Yeah, well. Can't tell a lie, me and Bev *did* know Leo King pretty well.' She looked at Lily. 'Men, eh?'

'Yeah,' said Lily. 'Men.'

'We were strippers back then. Met Leo. It wasn't a *love* sort of thing, don't go thinking that. It was just fun, that's all. Nothing serious.'

And that makes it okay? thought Lily.

'Why did you want to meet us, anyway?' asked Suki, tilting her head to one side and peering at Lily closely.

'Curiosity,' said Lily, but it was more, much more, than that. One of these women could have killed Leo. One of these women could be responsible for her doing twelve years inside. For driving a wedge between her daughters and herself. For causing her all this grief, all this pain.

'Nah, there's something else.'

'I didn't kill Leo,' said Lily. 'I want to find out who did.'

Suki's eyes widened. 'Get outta here!'

'It's the truth,' said Lily.

'What, you done time for someone else?'

'Got it in one.'

Suki was silent for a moment, taking it in. 'And what now?' she said at last. 'You want – what – revenge? Is that it?' Suki was shaking her head. 'Let me tell you, girl, let it go. You let that sort of stuff into your heart, what you gonna get except more heartache?'

Oh Jesus, we've got us a philosopher here, thought Lily.

Now Suki pulled out a pack of cards. 'Let me do you a reading? Free of charge.'

'No thanks,' said Lily. Tarot cards! She didn't believe in ghosts and ghouls, angels and devils. She'd *seen* hell close up, and it had bars.

'Shuffle the cards, anyway,' said Suki, holding them out.

Lily took the pack with an impatient sigh. Shuffled them. Suki took them back and started laying them out on the low table between them.

'Look,' said Lily after Suki had laid out the first card, 'I told you. I don't want a reading.'

'Oh come on,' smiled Suki.

'No!' snapped Lily, her face suddenly like thunder. 'Listen up. Just because you sucked my husband's dick, that *don't* make us bosom pals, you got that?'

Suki's smile dropped from her face in shock.

'*Got* it?' reiterated Lily.

Suki nodded.

'Good. All I want to know is, can you think why anyone would have wanted to kill Leo?'

Suki let out a shaky laugh. 'How long you got? Seems to me *you* had the best reason of all, and the Bill seemed to think the same. But there were probably others.'

'Did *you* want to kill Leo? Or the call-centre queen in there, how about her?'

'Jesus, why would we want to do that? Leo was *fun*. I was sorry when I heard he'd got done. Really sorry. And when they sent you down for it, I was glad. Because I thought they'd got the one who'd done it. You *really* didn't . . .?'

'I really didn't.'

'This is gonna burn in a sec,' shouted Winston from the kitchen.

Suki was staring at Lily. 'Let me do the reading, girl,' she said. 'Winston can stick the dinner in the oven, keep it warm.'

Lily stood up. 'I told you. I don't want your bloody reading. Come on, Jack.'

Jack passed Suki his business card. 'If you think of anything . . .' he said, and she nodded.

They piled off down the stairs. Nothing gained at all. *Now I've met them all face to face*, thought Lily as they went out into the chilly night. *Every one of them. And so what? It's got me precisely nowhere.*

Inside the flat, Suki started clearing the table. Winston was a keen cook; he didn't really like to be kept waiting when he was ready to dish up. Bev was still in the bedroom, busy with another caller. Suki cleared away the bowl of potpourri, the stack of amethyst crystal, a much-thumbed copy of *Heat* magazine – and the single card she'd selected for Lily. Now she paused and after a second she flipped it over.

She gasped. Then she looked at the deck that Lily had just shuffled. After a moment's hesitation, she started laying out more cards.

50

'Hey babe,' said Jase cheerily, standing there at the back door of The Fort clutching a huge bouquet of flowers.

Oli stared at him dubiously. She wasn't returning his smile. Actually, her face *ached* too much for that, where he'd struck her. She'd never forget that he'd done that. And she really, really hadn't wanted to let him in the gate. She should just have told him to go fuck himself, and she had been tempted to do that. But old habits died hard. So she'd let him in, and now he was standing there, giving her the big apologetic grin, laying on the famous Jase charm with a trowel.

All forgotten, right?

Wrong.

'Only the best,' he said, pushing forward into the kitchen so that Oli had to step back, 'for my best girl.'

He held out the bouquet, the most gorgeous thing. All reds and purples, her favourite colours. Roses and lilies, it was exquisite. Lots of acid-green fern, a lavish length of scarlet satin ribbon, and a card with two linked hearts on the front of it.

Reluctantly, Oli took the peace offering.

She went over to the sink, put in the plug, ran in cold water, and plunged the stems into it. She didn't look at the card.

Jase was closing the door behind him, coming to her, smiling, holding out something else. Oli looked at it. It was a large heart-shaped box of Godiva chocolates.

'You like these, I know you do. The violet things.'

'Violet creams,' said Oli dully.

'That's the ones.'

And now he was coming closer, pulling her into his arms, nuzzling at her neck.

Oli stood there like wood.

Jesus, this was going to be tricky, thought Jase. He drew back, smiling down into her eyes, trying to work the old magic. He could see the yellowing bruise around her mouth. Shit, he shouldn't have done that, what had he been thinking? But it would be okay. He was going to work this out, get everything back on track again.

'You smell good,' he said huskily.

'Just had a bath,' said Oli.

'I should have come earlier, I could have scrubbed your back.' He kissed her. 'And other things.'

'Jase...' said Oli. She half turned in his grip, put the chocolates on the worktop.

'Hush,' he said, and kissed her. She felt his tongue pushing into her mouth. But it hurt. She pulled back, turned her head away.

'What is it?' asked Jase and, despite himself, he heard the anger in his own voice, felt it building up inside.

All right, he knew he shouldn't have hit her. His old man had whacked his mum a few times, and it was bad, he *knew* it was bad. But Oli had been giving it all that, yacking on and on, and he had cracked and whopped her one, so it was more her fault than his really, wasn't it? But he didn't say that, he *wouldn't* say that. It was time to be magnanimous, take the blame, grovel – which he hated to do; but he'd do it, he *had* to do it to make things right again.

'Jase, I want to talk to you,' said Oli, easing herself out of his arms.

'Oh?' Oh crap, now with the talking again. Why did women insist on talking all the time? But he had to humour her. Taking a breath and calming down a bit he said: 'Okay, let's talk then.'

Oli folded her arms over her body and stared at him. Not warmly, he noted. Her eyes were cold. This was not a good sign.

'I could have just told you this over the intercom, but I don't think that would be fair,' she said, then paused and bit her lip. 'I don't want to see you any more, Jase. I'm sorry. It's over.'

Jase nearly rocked back on his heels, so great was the shock of what he was hearing. Over? But for fuck's sake, he'd apologized. He'd *crawled*. He'd brought her flowers and shit. And now she was saying it was over?

'Oh come on,' he said, and laughed, and gave her the hundred-megawatt grin that always made the girls drop their drawers. 'You don't mean that.'

'Yeah, I do,' said Oli. 'It's over, Jase. Finished.'

'No.'

'*Yes,* Jase. I just don't feel the same way about you any more.'

'Is this . . .' He turned away from her, feeling angry, thwarted, fucking *furious*. '. . . Is this about that little *tap* I gave you?'

It was Oli's turn to laugh. 'You *what?* Don't call it that, as if it was nothing. It was something all right. You *hit* me, Jase. And I don't find that acceptable behaviour. And it's done, okay? It's finished.'

'Listen,' said Jase, stabbing at her with an accusing finger. 'If you hadn't been so fucking *mouthy*, I wouldn't have been forced to do it.'

'Forced?' Oli's eyes widened. She couldn't believe what she was hearing. He had lost control. He had *hit* her. And he was trying to make out it was all her fault?

'You just kept on and on at me, Oli,' he said, and she couldn't believe it but he was now standing there looking pissed off, even hurt. 'What was I supposed to do, just take it?'

Oli took a calming breath. She could see he was getting steamed up, and she didn't like that. She remembered all too vividly what had happened the last time. But inside she felt sore, and sad. She'd thought it was love. She had *adored* him. And he'd killed it, stone-dead.

'Maybe you should have just walked away,' she said, turning from him with a shrug and a sigh. 'Cooled down a bit.'

'Yeah?' Suddenly his hand was on her shoulder, spinning her around. His fingers dug into her flesh, hurting her, and she winced. 'And maybe *you* should have just shut your fat mouth for once, Oli. How about *that?*'

There was rage in his eyes. The instant he released her, Oli backed away from him, feeling a chill of fear creep up her spine. Her shoulder stung; there'd be bruises. She swallowed. She should have done this the easy way. She could have dumped him by text. She could have told him over the intercom. But she had wanted to do this the right way, the civilized way, because there would have to be at the very least civility between them, seeing as they were certain to come into contact with each other. They went to the same places, moved in the same circles; there were things that they would have to address. She had wanted to do this *right*.

Now she saw that it was a mistake.

Jase raised his hands and clutched at his head and stared at her. 'You silly bitch, this is a big deal for me,' he spat out. 'I . . .' he seemed about to say something, then he changed his mind and thought again. '. . . I *love* you, Oli. Honest to God.'

'No,' said Oli quickly. 'I don't think you love me. I think you love the *idea* of me. Of getting in good with Uncle Si, and I'm a major part of that, ain't that right? Get in with me, and Uncle Si will sweeten towards you. I know you've been having troubles, Jase, I hear the rumours, do you think I don't? You've fallen out with Uncle Si, and Freddy's mad at you over something.'

'No. No! We sorted that,' said Jase hurriedly, wondering what the hell was happening here, wondering why it was all falling apart in front of him, when he'd had it all planned out, all neat and tidy.

'Yeah? Only what I'm thinking is, *I'm* your ticket back into the inner circle.'

'No.'

'Yeah, Jase. At least be honest with me.'

'I'm being honest. I'm telling you, Oli, you're breaking my damned heart here. I love you.'

'You hit me.'

Jase let out a roar and turned away from her, closing his eyes. The dumb *bitch*! 'I *explained* that. It was a lapse. A silly mistake.'

'Yeah,' said Oli coldly. 'It was that all right. And how would you excuse the next time, Jase?'

He rushed towards her, exasperated. 'There won't *be* a next time,' he yelled full in her face.

'What's going on here?' asked a voice from the hall doorway.

They both turned. Lily was standing there. Oli felt her stomach unclench with relief. Jase just stared blankly at Lily for a moment, then turned back to Oli.

'Ols . . .' he murmured. The rage had dropped from him like a cloak. He'd gone from ballistic to normal in the blink of an eye.

Oli knew she was doing the right thing. She should have done this before; she should never have let things get as far as they had.

'I'd like you to go now, Jase,' she said quietly.

Lily moved further into the kitchen, her eyes glued to Jase. She'd wondered what the hell was kicking off, all that shouting and screaming, and she'd heard . . . Jesus, she'd heard them shouting about him hitting Oli. That bruise on Oli's face was as she suspected. She hadn't slipped on the drive. This bolshy little fucker had *hit* her.

'Yeah,' added Lily, and went over to the back door and opened it wide. 'Off you go.'

Jase gave Oli one last despairing look, sent Lily a glance of pure hatred, and stormed past her out of the door. She shut it behind her, locked it. They heard his car starting up with an angry roar. The wheels threw up gravel as he sped off down the drive. After a moment, Oli walked over like an automaton to the intercom and opened the gates. They watched the screen as he sped out, swerved onto the lane, and with a screech of tyres he was gone. Oli pressed the button to close the gates. Her hand was shaking. She looked at Lily and suddenly her eyes were full of tears.

'You all right?' asked Lily, opening her arms wide.

Oli nodded, and after a moment's hesitation she gave a gasp and flung herself into Lily's warm embrace. 'I've got to talk to you,' she sobbed. 'I've got to tell you.'

'Shh,' said Lily, smoothing a hand over her daughter's hair. 'Later, sweetie. Tell me later.'

'No! I want to tell you now.' Oli gulped and drew back a little, her eyes swimming with tears.

'All right then. What is it?'

'Mum . . . oh God, I've been so stupid. I think I could be pregnant.'

Jase sped off down the road, crashing through the gears, his brain a whirl. Behind him, he saw the gates closing. Saw his *future* vanishing in front of his eyes. Christ, his chest hurt. It really hurt now. Had to cut down on the steroids soon. First, he had to find a way round this. *Had* to do it, get the King bitch, had to drop Lily King dead at Freddy's feet like a dog dropping a gift for its owner. But now Oli had kicked him into touch. Now he couldn't just stroll in the house and get the cow, like he'd wanted. He'd tried getting her outside the house, but inside was best. Inside was where she felt safe, relaxed. Getting back in Oli's good books had been key to that. But now he didn't have an easy way in at all, because Oli had blown him out.

Bloody Oli. Stupid little mare. One small tap and she went apeshit. He knew he shouldn't have done it, but he'd never do it again. Of course he wouldn't. *Never.*

He had to find a way through this. *Had* to.

But Christ – his chest hurt.

51

Lily was in the indoor pool in the early evening, doing laps back and forth, revelling in the luxury of it now that it was warm and silky on her skin, just the way she liked it. But there wasn't much else about her situation that she liked.

She was so sad about Saz – broken-hearted really – because Saz didn't seem to be weakening, not even by an inch. Saz and Richard were out this evening, playing squash or something, and she was glad. The atmosphere in the house when Saz was here was just awful.

She was really worried about Oli, but glad that she'd split with Jase. From the moment she'd first seen him, she'd had a bad feeling about Jase. And now this. She was still trying to get her head around it.

Oli could be pregnant.

Oli had poured her heart out to her mother, telling her everything, that Jase had persuaded her not to take precautions but she should have *insisted*. She was late for her period; she was never late. And she knew she should have taken a test already, made sure one way or another, but she had been too frightened, too worried.

Lily was furious with that jumped-up little bastard. She hoped that it was a false alarm. She even hoped there was someone else on the scene, someone who'd make better father material than one of Si King's heavies. She said this to Oli.

'No,' Oli had told her tearfully. 'There's no one else. I was in love with him, Mum. Really in love, but when he did that . . .'

Hit her, thought Lily, feeling a choking, icy rage taking hold of her.

When he did that, Oli had seen the light. Thank God. But . . . now there could be a child.

'Do you . . .' Lily had spoken slowly, choosing her words with care. '. . . If you *are*, do you want to go on with the pregnancy, Oli? And have you told Jase you could be?'

'No, I ain't told him yet,' said Oli, discarding another wad of sodden tissues.

Lily patted her arm, passed her more.

'But I'll have to, sooner or later. 'Cos if I am, I'm keeping the baby.' Oli looked at her mother with anxious, red-rimmed eyes.

'It's your decision, Oli,' said Lily.

'I know. I've thought about it a lot. I'd want to keep it.'

Lily forced a smile onto her face and thought: *Holy shit, I could be a grandmother.*

She wasn't even forty, and her daughter was maybe going to have a baby.

'It'll be fine,' she told Oli firmly.

Oli sniffed and blew her nose loudly. 'You know what? I can't believe I'm saying this, but . . . I'm so glad you're back,' she said.

Lily felt a warm glow as Oli said that. Lily knew she'd patched things up with Oli, and she was grateful for it. Saz's early return had cooled things down a bit – Oli was clearly torn between loyalty to her sister and to her mum, and it showed. But Oli had turned to her in this time of crisis; Oli was on her side. Whether her relationship with Saz was beyond saving or not – well, that was in the lap of the gods. All she could do was *be* here, much as Saz didn't want that. All she could do was be ready to welcome Saz with open arms when the moment came. *If* it did.

There were other things to concern her too, and she was busy mulling them over as she swam. She'd met all Leo's girls now. And a fat lot of good it had done her. She listed them in her head.

Adrienne Thomson, wife of dull, worthy accountant Matt. Easy to see why Adrienne had embraced a tasty bit of rough like Leo.

Alice Blunt. Poor, demented girl, obsessed with Leo and ready to self-harm to force him closer. Now she was dead, drowned at her own hand.

Reba Stuart. Hard as nails and twice as nasty. On the bash for a living in those days, but now a madam. Maybe Reba was the sort of woman Leo *should* have married, not quiet, mousy Lily. A woman as tough as he was.

Then there was Julia. Poor scarred, once-beautiful Julia, hiding away from the world that judged her and found her ugly.

And the last two – Suki and Bev. A double act. She was willing to bet Leo had found that a huge turn-on, having two nearly identical women at once.

But the question was – had one of Leo's whores killed him? Had one of them – just as a 'for instance' – disliked him boffing half the country, and kicked off on a grand scale?

It was a question to which she still didn't have an answer. However, as she floated, thoughts drifted through her head. *Adrienne* drifted through; Adrienne who had kept a list of all Leo's other women, who had been so proprietorial about Leo that she had hired Jack to trace them. But then, Adrienne had been a bit older than Leo, and just that bit more eager to hang onto him when the alternative was married life with Matt – or 'Door-Matt', as their circle of friends had called him behind his back all those years ago. Adrienne had walked all over the poor git, that was a fact, but he'd soaked it up, more fool him. He'd even stuck with her when it all blew up over Leo's killing and her involvement with him.

Matt, the poor bastard, toiling away over his books and adding up columns of figures for the firm to keep Adrienne in clover. Had she been grateful? Lily didn't think so. She'd mocked him to her friends. Laughed publicly about the size of his prick. Really, that wasn't nice. And maybe – *maybe* – Matt had been more aware of his wife's behaviour than any of them had realized. Studious Matt, wearing thick glasses; not bad looking but, oh *God*, such a boring little man. Small wonder Adrienne had looked elsewhere for her excitement, and wanted to cling to it – and keep it to herself.

Jack had done his bit. He'd traced Leo's other women for a second time, presented them to Lily on a plate. And now . . . what? She'd got nowhere, really. All she'd done was make herself feel sick to her stomach at the thought of what a meek, silly little homebody she had been, while Leo had been out on the lash, indulging his huge sex drive with all these other women.

Lily swam to the edge of the pool and hauled herself out.

She was tired. Christ, it had been a quieter life in jail. Nothing to think about; nothing much to worry over. Whereas out here, she was overwhelmed with it all. And, feeling overwhelmed, she longed to call Nick, longed to see him.

But that looks too needy, she thought.

Although she *felt* needy, she knew she couldn't show it. And she still wasn't sure whether he could be truly trusted or not – after all, he'd kept Julia's disfigurement from her, hadn't he?

God, she was tired. She climbed out of the pool, planning to grab a quick shower and then get an early night.

She awoke in darkness with the usual sense of displacement. In prison? No. No noises of the druggies banging around in their cages, no soft tread of the screws passing by. It took her a moment or two to place herself, to remember where she was. She was *home*. But not in the master bedroom, not in *their* bedroom.

Something had woken her up.

Someone talking? Maybe Saz or Oli passing by on the landing . . . but the landing light was off, she could see nothing but darkness when she looked towards the door. There was no telltale crack of light at the base of it.

Lily sat up, switched on the bedside light. *Something* had disturbed her, jolted her out of sleep. She looked at the clock. It was a quarter to four in the morning. Someone moving about? Voices. Someone talking. A woman's voice? Then someone tapped at the door and her heart kicked into a gallop.

'Who is it?' she called out.

'It's me,' came back the quiet reply. 'Richard.'

Ah. The semi-invisible bridegroom. And what the hell was he doing tiptoeing around the place in the dead of night?

She could hear the voice again, droning out the same thing over and over.

A female voice, high with distress . . . or was it a child's voice? She felt a shiver of fear. What the *hell*?

She threw on a robe and hurried over to the door and opened it.

Richard was standing there in sleeping shorts and nothing else. He was bleary-eyed, his hair sticking up all over the place. He had one hand to his head. He looked worried.

'I saw your light go on,' he said.

'What's up?' asked Lily.

'It's . . .'

And now Lily could hear the voice more clearly, and she could hear snatches of what it was saying. *Daddy?*

'. . . It's Saz. She's done this before, a couple of times. Before we got married, I'd stay over sometimes, and she did this then: it freaked me out.'

'Where is she?' Now Lily felt anxiety grip her. What was wrong, was Saz ill? Delirious?

'In the master suite,' said Richard, and started to walk that way.

'What the hell's she doing in there?' asked Lily as she followed. 'That room's locked.'

'She went down and got the key from the study. I followed her.'

Oli's door came open across the hall. She peered out, her tousled hair like a wild dark halo around her sleepy face. 'What's going on?' she yawned.

'Saz is in the master suite,' said Lily, and Richard pushed open the door.

'*Oh Daddy, I'm so sorry. I'm sorry, Daddy, I'm so sorry,*' *Saz was saying loudly in that weird singsong voice.*

311

'Jesus,' said Oli, coming out into the hall.

She followed Richard into the master suite, with Lily behind her.

Saz was kneeling by the bed, her hands clasped as if in prayer. The wall behind the bed was pink with fresh plaster.

Richard said gently: 'Saz? Honey?'

Lily stepped around the bed so that she could see Saz's face. It was turned up to the ceiling, and her eyes were open . . . but seeing nothing.

'She's sleepwalking,' said Oli softly. 'She's asleep.'

Lily looked at Saz. It was spooky. She was there . . . but not there at all. She wasn't aware that they were standing around her. Her brain was playing out some private movie scene that they weren't a part of.

'Oh Daddy, please forgive me, I'm so sorry,' Saz was intoning, like a prayer.

Forgive her for what? wondered Lily.

'You said you've heard voices in here before,' said Lily to Oli.

'Yeah, I . . .' Oli put a hand to her mouth. 'Jesus! It was Saz, it was *this*. She scared me shitless, the silly mare. I thought I was losing it.'

So did I, thought Lily.

'Look,' said Oli, suddenly brisk. 'You mustn't wake her up. I read that about sleepwalkers. You have to just guide them back to bed.'

Richard bent over his wife and gently gripped her shoulders. Saz fell silent.

The silence was even spookier than her endless droning, *Sorry, sorry Daddy, sorry.*

Saz was now standing up and Richard was guiding her

back to the door. Her eyes were open, but she still wasn't seeing them.

Sorry for what? thought Lily again, and into her mind came a vision of long-ago happy days, of Leo teaching Saz to shoot clays out in the grounds. Saz had become a really good shot.

Sorry for what?

Saz could easily lift a shotgun, even as a child.

Lily watched Richard guide Saz tenderly back to their room. She kissed Oli a brief goodnight, and then stood there in the hall and thought, *Oh fuck me, no, it can't be.*

But . . . sorry for *what?*

52

She dreamed again that night. Mercy going back to Kingston, back to her home and kids. It was a happy scene, but Lily knew that the flowers, the party, the giggles, the fond reunions, were all a lie because she had heard on the prison grapevine that Mercy had been shot dead within a week of arriving home, killed by the same dealer she'd once been a reluctant drug mule for.

For Mercy, there had been no happy ending.

For Lily, there was just the daily grind, the endless grind . . . but it would end, wouldn't it, one day? In her heart she couldn't believe it, but in her head she knew it had to be true.

Rumours abounded in Holloway, and besides the sad news about Mercy she heard other things, scary things: that the remaining King brothers were going to get her while she was in stir, make her pay in blood for Leo's death.

So it was a relief rather than a sadness when they moved her to Durham. All right, Becks couldn't visit any more; but she hoped – maybe vainly – that Si and Freddy's influence *was weaker up north than down south. She did more years there in Durham, watching a new procession of cellmates go by – girls with boyfriends, women with husbands – who had all for one reason or another become embezzlers, crackheads, killers. Girls on suicide watch, others catatonic with fear at being banged up inside. Bullies. Bitches. Bull dykes. Brasses. All human life was there; Lily saw it all.*

Time wore on, and sometimes Lily thought that this was reality, here, inside; that outside was the dream, something her mind had cooked up to torment her. Outside was the myth, the cruel illusion. Her home, her life, her girls – all fantasy. This was the only reality. Prison.

Finally she was moved to New Hall in Yorkshire, and then there was the staggering luxury of day-release for her last year at Askham Grange. The photo – that precious photo of her and the girls – was dog-eared and faded, but still safely tucked away in her bum bag. Every morning and every night she lay in her bunk and stared at it; it gave her comfort. And time wore on, and on, sunrise, sunset, just like the song . . . until one day, at last, she was released. She was free. Free to find out who had done this to her, and the girls.

53

Going back to bed after Saz's escapade, Lily tossed and turned, but eventually fell into a troubled sleep peppered with the same old dreams of stir. She awoke with an aching head and a heavy heart. Cold rain was beating against the window-pane. The weather was an apt reflection of her mood.

She got up, showered, went down to the kitchen and made coffee, then took it into the study with her. The house was quiet and she was glad of that. She didn't want to talk, only to try and make sense of all the things spinning around in her brain. She closed the study door behind her, and went over to the TV. She plugged it in, switched on, loaded the tape in the old VCR. Pressed 'play'.

Leo was there.

'Well babe, if you're playing this then I'm dead,' said his voice. On screen, he looked healthy, tanned, prosperous. The old Leo she had known so well.

No, Lily – you just thought *you did.*

'You've found the stash and the gun. Keep 'em both safe, girl. Just a bit of life insurance for you. Look after the girls.

If you need a hand, there's always Si and Freddy.' He hesitated, glanced down. 'If you're *really* in the shit, call on Nick. Okay? The boys'll help you.'

Oh really? She wondered about that. Leo had crossed Nick twice – once with Lily, and then with Julia – as if everything Nick had, Leo wanted to snatch away. Had he wanted other things, too, apart from women? A bigger slice of business, maybe?

She wasn't sure and it was all starting to drive her crazy. Her thoughts about Nick were muddled, her suspicions about him tangled up with that old powerful sexual attraction. She longed to call him, to be on good terms with him again. Their last conversation had rattled her. She'd forced herself to take a step back from him, cool it down, and he'd clearly got the message . . . but she hated not being in contact with him.

'What the hell's this?' said Oli's voice from behind her.

Lily sprang to her feet, clapped a hand to her chest.

'Jesus! I thought you were still asleep,' she gasped.

'After Saz's little floor show last night?' Oli said, crossing the room and standing there, staring at her father on the screen.

Lily turned down the volume. Leo was mouthing something. Oli was still staring at the screen, awestruck. 'That's Dad,' she murmured.

'Yeah,' said Lily. 'It is. He left the tape for me to find. In case of emergency.'

Oli turned and Lily could see the bright gleam of tears in her dark eyes. 'I loved him so much,' she said softly.

'I know, Ols.' Lily thought about Oli's news of her possible pregnancy. If it was true, if she really was, then this would be Leo's grandchild, a grandchild he would never play with, never see, never throw laughing into the air. She felt sadness grip her, and anger. All right, he hadn't been the best of husbands, but someone had snatched his life away, and that someone had yet to pay for it.

But Saz, she thought suddenly. *What about Saz, muttering apologies to her dead father in her sleep? What about Saz, who even as a child had been used to handling guns . . .*

And now another thought occurred. Saz had hated the smell of guns when they were fired, hated to get the oil and cordite on her hands, so Leo had bought her a small pair of gloves and she had worn them whenever she was shooting with him.

There were only my fingerprints on the gun.

No, it was rubbish. Lily told herself firmly. Saz and Oli had been out that night, Maeve had been babysitting them. But Saz *had* been used to handling guns. And last night Saz's tormented brain had sent her into this study to get the key and then up to the master suite to apologize. For what?

Lily had a sudden flashback to that awful night. She felt again the shock, the horror. Leo lying dead with his head blown away. The blood. The gun. The horrid, cold slippery weight of it. For a moment she felt a wild leap of hope as she considered that. The weight of it. But she had *seen* Saz lift that gun when she was a child; she knew it wasn't beyond her. *Oh Jesus, so much blood . . .*

'You all right, Mum?' asked Oli, looking at Lily's face.

Lily shook herself. 'Yeah. Fine.' She sat down quickly.

'Oh my God,' said Saz's voice from the doorway.

This is all I need, thought Lily with an inward wince.

Saz was crossing the room quickly. Now she stood beside Oli and stared at the screen.

'For God's sake, what *is* this?' she demanded.

Not the tearful reaction of Oli. Saz was looking at the screen with something very like horror.

'Leo left this for me to find,' said Lily quietly.

'Did Richard tell you that you were sleepwalking last night?' Oli asked Saz.

Saz seemed to recoil slightly at that. 'Yeah. He did.'

'You were in the master suite.'

'I know. He told me.'

'You were like a bloody zombie. You seen those flicks? They walk like this.' Oli did a stiff-legged zombie stagger.

'Oh shut the fuck up, Oli,' snapped Saz, still staring, as if mesmerized, at the screen.

'Yeah, come on, Oli. Saz can't help it. Cut her some slack,' said Lily, watching Saz's face.

Saz whirled, arms folded, and looked at her.

'And I don't need *you* to defend me,' she said. She turned back to the screen. Stared. Said nothing. Showed not a flicker of emotion.

Lily watched her.

Then, abruptly, Saz turned away from the screen and came over to where Lily was sitting.

'We've been talking, Richard and me, and we've come to a decision,' she said.

'Oh?' *Now what?*

'Yeah. We're leaving. Today.'

Lily sat there, gobsmacked.

Then she rallied. 'Don't go, Saz. Stay. Let's work this out.'

Saz shook her head. Lily thought she saw something, some faint shadow like fear in her daughter's eyes, but maybe she had imagined it. After all, she didn't know her daughter at all. Not any more.

'No, I'm not staying here. I don't want to be here any more. Not with *you* here.'

Lily felt the hurt of that, stabbing into her guts like a knife.

Her lovely Saz hated her. She looked directly at her daughter, her heart feeling as if it was bleeding. Saz had erected an impenetrable wall between them, and she wanted so much to break it down, to find the girl who was hiding behind it. 'Saz . . . what are you sorry about?' she asked gently.

Saz's face went blank: the shutters were down. Everyone – Lily especially – shut out.

'What?' she asked.

'When you were sleepwalking last night in the master suite, you said the same thing over and over again,' Lily went on. 'You said, "I'm sorry, Daddy." You kept on repeating it.'

'For God's sake!' Saz burst out, her eyes angry. 'I was sleepwalking. I do that sometimes. It's none of your business; *nothing* I do is any of your business, you got that?'

'Come on, Saz . . .' started Oli nervously.

'No!' Saz turned on her like a snake. 'Don't tell me to come on. Christ, you're so weak, Oli.'

Lily saw the hurt on Oli's face.

'You've swallowed all her lies whole,' Saz went on. 'Well, *I* ain't. I'm not staying here. You're *welcome* to each other.'

Jack phoned an hour later, while Lily was in the kitchen, alone, feeling miserable. She didn't pick up at first, scared it could be *him*, the breather, but finally she thought *oh sod it* and snatched the phone up.

'Yeah, what?' she asked, relieved to hear Jack's broad Cockney accent.

320

'And a good morning to you, too,' said Jack.

'It ain't a good morning, Jack. But go on, what's the news?'

'Oh, this and that. Found out from one of the nursing home staff that Alice's brother was none the worse for wear after I decked him.'

'Pity.'

'I thought that too,' said Jack, and she could hear the smile in his voice. 'And I had to stump up a ton to get to know who paid her bills. Which will go on *your* bill, naturally.'

'Yeah, sure. And?'

'Purbright Securities. Paid every month, on the first. You know Purbright Securities?'

'No.'

'Me neither. I'll check it out with Companies House.'

'Thanks. Anything else?'

'Oh yeah. That fruitcake phoned.'

'Which fruitcake? I know so many.'

'Suki the tarot lady.'

'Oh, *that* one. What did she want?'

'She's shot away, ain't she? But hard to dislike. Quite nice, really, in a batty sort of way.'

'What did she say?' Lily didn't think Suki was a nice girl. Nice girls didn't shag other women's husbands, not where she came from.

'She said to tell you that you gotta take extra care. She did your reading after you left, and it wasn't good, that's what she told me. Said she turned up the death card and there were other things too. Now the death card, she explained this to me, the death card ain't always a bad thing. It can mean transformation, she said. But it can also mean—'

'Death?' suggested Lily, trying to make light of it. But she felt – ever so slightly – spooked.

'Got it in one. She said you had a troubled aura, very dark, she said she could see—'

'Yeah. Enough, already,' said Lily sharply.

'Just passing on the message,' said Jack.

'Consider it passed. I'll take care.'

She could hear wheels running over a floor, voices. She turned on the stool and looked through the open kitchen doorway into the hall. Saz and Richard were there, dragging their cases towards the front door. Saz paused, and threw her a poisonous glare. Richard didn't look at her at all.

Lily sighed and turned away. 'Was there anything else?' she asked Jack.

'I'll drop the bill in sometime, okay? For services rendered.'

'Yeah. Do that.' She put the phone down.

Behind her, she heard the front door close. Saz was gone.

Lily sat there, feeling like shit. Finally, she picked up the phone and gave in. She called Nick.

54

Winston was singing along to the radio, he was happy. Bob Marley was on there, singing about one love, one heart.

But Winston had *two* loves.

Amen to that. Happy was Winston's default setting, and why not? He lived here rent-free with two beautiful blonde mamas, he drew the social, he did a little man-vanning on the side, smoked a little ganja, got plenty of ciggies from the local tab house, did a few deals here and there, everything was cool, everything really was just fine, yes sir.

He'd been here three years with Bev and Suki, and he loved it. He loved London; he loved the sights and the smells of the big city all around him. His family were back home in the Caribbean, and he loved them, sent home what he could, but he didn't miss that life too much, not right now.

He didn't miss loitering outside the five-star complexes waiting for the rich white females to wander out to shop. He remembered the low wall beside the hotel that he and his mates had targeted, and they sat there smiling big smiles and urging the ladies to join them. They had pieces of foam to place upon the wall so that the ladies could be comfortable, and many did 'take the foam', enticed by buff young bodies and offers of cooling slices of watermelon. As a living, it was pretty okay. The ladies were often lonely and middle-aged, they liked the fit young bucks paying them attention; and the ladies were generous in their gratitude, buying the boys and him meals, drinks, clothes – and dishing out free sex, too.

Here, he didn't have to work *quite* that hard. Here, he'd met Suki and Bev in a club, and before long they had become not a twosome but a threesome. Suki and Bev seemed to like operating that way, and it suited him too.

So he was happy. He bopped along to the radio as he washed up in the kitchen. It was late; the girls were already in bed – one in his, one in the spare. He didn't know who he would get from night to night, he never knew, they said they liked to surprise him. He was just tidying up, bopping along to Bob, and yes, he was happy.

Only there was something niggling away at him. Just a little bit. It wasn't Bev. Bev was no trouble at all with the chatlines, and boy did they pay.

'I just say naughties down the phone and they come, then it's over,' Bev had told him. 'Money for old rope – ker*ching*!' And she'd laugh.

Bev was cool. Detached. He liked that. She was a fine woman, a bit edgier than Suki, you had to give her space, respect. Suki was the emotional one, prone to getting all sorts of airy-fairy ideas about how she was in touch with the spirit world and all that crap.

Spirit world, my fine black arse, thought Winston.

She might believe she had the gift, but that was all bollocks as far as he was concerned. So it was seriously annoying, how the visit from that King woman and her hired help had unsettled poor Suki. *More* than annoying. He'd picked up Jack Rackland's card after him and the King woman had left, tucked it into his shirt pocket out of Suki's way. Winston knew trouble when he smelled it, and any more of this shit with the King woman and he was going to pay a visit, set them straight. He didn't know where to find Lily King, but Jack Rackland was only a stone's throw away – Winston noted the address, committed it to memory. Winston wasn't having anything upsetting his girls, no sir. Jack Rackland would be sorry if he did; that was for sure.

Now Suki was imagining all sorts, talking about Death and how she had gone on to do the full cross spread after Lily had shuffled the cards, and it had been the worst hand she had ever seen.

'The *worst*,' Suki kept telling him, and her eyes were spooked. She was really, really frightened about all this. Having dreams, too. *Nightmares*.

Which only confirmed Winston's opinion that it was all bullshit, and *troublesome* bullshit at that, if it could upset their normally happy home the way it was doing right now. He'd been tolerant of her tarot crap, but now he was thinking it was like all this ouija board stuff like that film he'd seen, scary shit, *The Exorcist*, that was the one – and he was thinking that if he could persuade Suki to hang up her crystals and *burn* those cards, then he would. And why should he care about the King woman's problems?

'Hey, that's *her* worry,' Winston had told Suki. 'Not ours.'

'Yeah,' said Suki, but she looked unconvinced. She had seen something in the cards that had rattled her.

He really hated to see her or Bev upset. They had such a good life here, the three of them. He loved both his women

325

with a passion, and would protect them with his own life if necessary.

'You want to talk about this?' asked Winston, keen to play the supporting role, although it was a pain in the arse.

Suki only shook her head, which surprised him. He was used to Suki running off at the mouth like there was no tomorrow, telling him all about swords and cups and auras and shit.

She'd get over it. Winston cast an eye around the little kitchenette, checked he'd turned off the gas, then put the tea towel on its hook, silenced Bob with regret, switched off the lights, and took himself off to bed.

Hey, nice surprise. Bev tonight, who welcomed him with open arms as he snuggled down naked with her beneath the crisp white sheets. The sex was good, like always. Bev was uninhibited after a toke or two, would do anything, venture anywhere, to give pleasure. So it was cool. And finally they slept, wrapped in each other's arms. They never heard the dull thud of the lit rag as it dropped onto the doormat downstairs.

55

Nick thought that if Freddy was mad enough to get Tiger Wu under contract to do Lily this soon, then a drive-by wasn't beyond the bounds of possibility either. One of his and Si's gofers was favourite. He suspected Jase Conway, because there had been talk on the street that Jase had fallen from grace, lost the door on the club, and was keen to ingratiate himself with the brothers. And how better than to do what they had long promised – to off Lily?

He had no proof, but his gut was telling him that Lily outside was in far greater danger than Lily inside. He drove over to see her, stopping at the electronic gates to use the intercom. He was aware of the camera above, tracking him. That was good. He was pleased about The Fort's good security, because by Christ she certainly needed it.

She was waiting for him at the open kitchen door as he drove up, looking fine. She was wearing figure-hugging jeans and a turquoise t-shirt, her blonde hair falling around her shoulders. She looked ridiculously young, and her eyes smouldered at him as he got out of the car and walked over.

'Hi,' he said huskily, and leaned in and took her in his arms and kissed her.

'Hi,' breathed Lily against his mouth, relishing the hard male feel of him, the heat, the strength. She'd missed that. She'd missed *him*. This was the man she should have married. The man she should have been with all these long, cold years. Not Leo.

She caught herself thinking these things and then thought, *Oh Jesus I can't go here again . . . can I?*

But maybe it was too late for second thoughts. Because she'd slept with him, and it had been wonderful. And she wanted to sleep with him again. She was sad to think that they'd lost all those years . . . but what good were regrets? You could only start from *now*. The past was dead. The future was uncertain. Only now mattered.

She clung to him, and just for a moment she forgot about Julia, forgot all her suspicions, that *he* could be the one who had let her rot inside . . . but only for a moment.

'Something wrong?' he asked.

Everything. She was glad she'd called him. But now he was here . . . now she wasn't sure. She looked at his face, such a strong face: the dark hair, the deep and dark eyes staring into hers.

Lily shook her head and looked away. She led him into the kitchen. Oli was there, chatting on her mobile. She gave him a wave and a mouthed *hi*, but she looked wan, pale, not her usual bubbly self.

Lily knew why.

Oli had finally taken the pregnancy test this morning. Together they had stood, clutching each other, and watched the single blue line appear. Oli was going to have Jase's baby. It was definite now.

Oli left the room, still talking on the phone.

'I wanted to have a word with you,' said Nick.

'Okay,' said Lily, trying to compose herself, trying not to behave like an overexcited teenager around this man. 'I'm listening.'

'About Jase Conway,' he said.

Lily sat down and gestured for Nick to sit, too. He seemed to take up a lot of room in the kitchen. His sheer presence was overwhelming. 'What about him?'

'I heard a rumour that Oli's been seeing him. Is that still the case?'

Lily shook her head. 'No. It ain't. She's dumped him.'

'Tell her to make sure he stays dumped.'

'Why?'

Nick looked around him. 'He's been right here? Inside the house?'

'Yeah. Sure he has. Seeing Oli.'

'Don't let him in again. Under any circumstances.'

He was frightening her. Lily stared at him anxiously. 'Why?' She wanted to tell him about Oli's pregnancy, she wanted to confide in him, but she knew she couldn't. She was still unsure about him. And she couldn't subject Oli's private life to public scrutiny.

'Freddy set Tiger Wu on you. If he'd do that, he wouldn't draw the line at a drive-by.'

Lily's mouth dropped open. 'What, you think *Jase* could have been in that car?'

Nick shrugged. 'Can't prove it. Yet.'

'But you think it was him.'

'Yeah. I do. He's looking to regain favour with Si and Freddy. How better than to get to you? I'm telling you, Lily, you don't ever let him in here again. Not *ever*, you got me?'

This was all getting messy. *Too* messy. She thought again of what Jack had said. Fuck off to a distant shore and sip pina coladas. It was looking more and more appealing. Saz still hated her. Leo had boffed a whole tribe of women, any one of which could have taken it into her screwy head to kill him. The Kings were trying their damnedest to see her in hell. And now this.

All right, she'd never liked Jase. She thought he was muscle-bound, thick-headed and handsome, nothing more. When he'd hit Oli, he'd screwed any chance of making Lily alter that opinion. But now . . . now she was supposed to believe that he was in that car, shooting at her, trying to kill her?

But I'm Oli's mother.

Would Jase for a single moment baulk at causing Oli pain? The bastard had *hit* her. Impregnated her too. What *else* had he done to her, Lily wondered? And the thought of how Oli's life could have panned out made Lily's blood turn to ice. Married to an aggressive oik like that. Tied to him. Used and abused as a punchbag when his temper boiled over – as inevitably it would.

'He's never coming in here again,' she said to Nick.

Nick let out a breath. 'Good.'

Oli came back into the kitchen. She was off the phone at last.

'Hi, Nick,' she said with a smile.

'Hiya, Oli,' returned Nick.

'I'm gonna have to love you and leave you,' said Oli, giving Lily a peck on the cheek. She glanced at her watch. 'I'm late already. Bye.'

She was gone, out the back door, revving up her little car and shooting off down the drive.

'She don't seem broken-hearted,' said Nick.

'She ain't, and I'm pleased about that. I think . . .' Lily caught herself.

'You think what?' Nick was looking at her curiously.

Lily stared at his face. Finally she decided to say it. 'I think she got over him the moment he hit her.'

'He *what?*'

Lily nodded. 'When he did that, she switched off. It was finished.'

'The jumped-up little tick,' said Nick.

'I never liked him.'

'Well, thank God she saw the light.'

Silence fell between them. They were inches apart. Around them, the house was silent, waiting. The phone started ringing. Lily stiffened, let it ring.

'You want to get that?' he asked.

'No,' she said, because it could be the breather again, saying nothing, trying to frighten her. Fucking well *succeeding*, too. He'd called several times now. It could be Freddy. Could be anyone. No, she didn't want to get it.

'Nick . . . did you know about Julia? About what happened to her face?' asked Lily.

He stared at her for long moments. Then he let out a breath. Nodded.

'Is that why you didn't want me seeing her?'

'I thought . . .' He paused, his nearly black eyes holding hers. '. . . I thought it would distress you. And maybe make you doubt me. Make you think I had something to do with it.'

'I didn't think that,' said Lily. 'I don't think you'd do something so fucking cowardly.'

'Don't they say poison and acid are a woman's tools?'

'God, do they?' Lily shuddered.

'Tell me you've stopped looking into all this troublesome shit,' he said, and took her hand.

'All right. I've stopped looking into all this troublesome shit.'

Nick sighed. 'Now tell me the truth.'

'I can't stop. Not until I know the answer.'

'The answer to who killed Leo.'

'Right.'

'Look, if you're going on with this, at least take me with you on your next escapade.'

'Tell me again that it wasn't you who did it.'

'What?'

'Killed Leo.'

'It wasn't me who killed Leo, Lily. Are you mad? And let you stew inside all those years? Are you crazy? No, Lily – it wasn't me.' He was smiling slightly. He leaned forward and kissed her again, parting her lips with his tongue, invading her, taking her over. Lily actually felt her head start to spin. He pulled back a little, looked deep into her eyes. 'Kill Leo and inflict all that on you? Never. Let's go to bed.'

'It's ten o'clock in the morning.'

'Perfect,' he said, and kissed her again.

Lily was asleep when the phone started ringing. She sprang up in the bed, alarmed, bewildered, wondering what was going on, where she was ... then it came back to her. Nick had been here, and after a couple of blissful hours he'd left, and she had fallen asleep and now it was one o'clock, her stomach was growling with hunger and the damned phone was ringing again.

The breather, she thought, looking at it as if it might be about to bite her. It rang and rang, and then she thought, *Fuck this.*

Lily picked up. 'Hello?' she asked, feeling her chest constrict, dreading the sound she just knew she was going to hear.

'Lily?' asked a masculine voice on the other end of the line.

'Jack?' She thought it was him, but he sounded odd. Not his usual chirpy self.

'Lily, turn on the BBC news. Turn it on *right now.*'

Lily scrabbled under the pillow for the remote. She aimed it at the little TV over on the dresser, and the set hummed into life. She pressed one. The reporter telling the nation about what had happened. Saw the picture, the little arcade of shops cordoned off with police tapes, the blackened front door, the upstairs windows all blown out from the heat of the blaze . . .

Jesus!

'Where are you?' she managed to say to Jack at last.

'At the office. Lily, I'm getting a bad feeling about all this. Julia. Alice. Now *this.*'

Lily felt sick to her stomach. She thought of Saz, saying over and over, *I'm sorry, Daddy.* Thought of her and Leo out in the grounds, shooting clays. Thought of Adrienne and her list of rivals for Leo's affection.

'Look, I'll come over,' she said, although she didn't want to, she didn't want to set foot outside the house now. She was safe in here. Out there . . . who knew? She thought of Leo's Magnum, tucked safely away. *This is what it's like for Julia*, she thought, and her whole being rebelled at that. She *would not* become like Julia, caged by her fears. *No way.*

'Jack . . .?' she said.

But there was a brief noise in the background and then Jack was gone.

* * *

Jack dropped the phone. A very large black man with dread-locks and a machete had just kicked open his office door. He thought, *Winston, the plantain man at Suki and Bev's place*, and then Winston launched himself at Jack, screaming, yelling about how they'd brought death to his home, him and the King woman, and death was all they deserved in return, and he thought, *Oh shit, this is it, gonna die*, and Winston waded in and there was only pain, pain, pain.

Lily quickly switched off the TV. She tried Jack's number, but only got the engaged signal. She swore and dialled a different number.

'Come on, come on, pick up,' she muttered.

'Hello?'

'Adrienne?'

'Yeah.' Caution in her voice now. 'Who's that?'

'It's Lily. Adrienne, did you ever discuss that list of yours with Saz or Oli?'

'What, the list of tarts Leo was bedding?'

You were one of them, thought Lily, but bit it back. No good riling Adrienne up. 'Is there any other fucking list?' she snapped.

'No. Of course I didn't. Why would I want to upset them? It had nothing to do with them, they never hurt a soul.'

Oh God, please let her be right about that, prayed Lily.

'Adrienne,' said Lily, and then paused, unsure of what she wanted to say.

'Yeah?'

'Take care.' She didn't know what was kicking off here, and she didn't want to run around *spooking* anyone, but Jack was right, this was all starting to look very odd indeed.

That blackened front door was burned into her brain. Oh God. Suki and her death card . . .

'What?'

'Look, just take care. People on that list are coming to grief. So . . . just be careful, will you?'

Before Adrienne could reply, Lily put the phone down. She was going to have to go out again. But she was frightened. She thought of Julia, locked inside by fear, and her own fear ate at her. She went upstairs and fetched the Magnum, loaded it and slipped it into her bag. She wouldn't use it. She *daren't*. But just carrying it would make her feel safer. She came back downstairs and dialled out again. Nick picked up straight away.

'I need you to come with me somewhere,' she said.

'Okay. I'll come back over.'

'Thanks.'

'Pleasure,' he said, and hung up.

56

Nick was there in his Mercedes within the hour, and boy was Lily glad to see him. He asked where she wanted to go and without fuss he drove her there. She'd had time to get washed and dressed, but she'd been too shaken to eat. Anything she swallowed would just come straight back up, she was sure of that.

In her mind's eye she saw again the blackened door beside the little shopping arcade, the drone of the newsman's voice. A woman dead in a house fire. But the police suspected arson. And the dead person was Suki Carmody, who had seen something bad in Lily's cards, who had been afraid and had tried to warn Lily to take care.

Well, here I am, taking care, thought Lily as Nick drove with casual grace through the streets.

And now she was here, at Jack's office.

'You want me to come in with you?' asked Nick, setting her down in the side road just off the High Street.

'No, I'll be fine.' She didn't want Nick loitering around

Jack's office, listening in and disapproving about what they were discussing.

Lily got out and walked over to the office. The door was half open.

'Hey, Jack?' she called out to silence. She felt a shiver of apprehension creeping up her spine.

She was just rattled over Suki, that was all. Suki was dead. Bev was in intensive care. Winston was fuck-knew-where.

She pushed forward, went into the office where she and Jack had sat and chewed the fat over Adrienne's list.

'Hey . . .' she started, and then she sagged against the door as a dizzying spiral of shock travelled all the way up from her toes to the roots of her hair.

There was a bloodied bag of bones sitting in Jack's chair.

It was just blood, and sinew, and . . . well, it had a head, but even that was covered in gore. There were splashes of blood up the walls, and there was blood coming out of a big cut on the thing's left arm, it was pumping, it was pumping, oh fuck it was *arterial* blood, of course it was. She saw the dirty-blonde tufts of hair sticking up, stiffened with gouts of blood, on the thing's head. The phone dangled loose on its cord, brushing the bloodied floor.

She felt vomit rise hot and sour into her mouth and turned to one side, half choking on it.

Oh my God, Jack.

She stood there, swaying on her feet, aware that someone some distance away was moaning, and then she realized that it was *her*.

'God – Jack . . .' she groaned out.

And then the door swung slowly shut behind her. Lily half turned, all the hair on the back of her neck standing up, a hot spasm of fear clutching at her. Winston was standing there, big as a barn door and clutching a bloody machete against his soiled grey t-shirt. He was staring at her, and he was weeping.

'Winston . . . ?' Lily gasped out. 'Oh Jesus, Winston, why . . . ?'

The death woman was there. That was all Winston knew. She was standing right there in front of him, the one who had brought death to their happy home. Suki was dead, and Bev . . . who knew? She might not pull through either. Their home was wrecked. Their *life* was wrecked. And all because they had opened the door to the death woman and her helper.

'You didn't have to go an' do that,' he sobbed. 'Not jus' 'cos she slept with your man. Why'd you have to go and do a thing like that?'

'Winston,' said Lily, aware that her voice was shaking, aware that she was in extreme danger here. He thought *she* was responsible for the fire . . . ? 'Winston, listen. No. I didn't . . .'

Shockingly suddenly, he lifted the machete and charged at her.

Lily pulled out Leo's Magnum from her bag without the slightest intention of doing so. It was slick, automatic – self-preservation. She didn't want to die, oh shit, she couldn't end up like poor bloody Jack, cut to ribbons . . . so she held the Magnum steady and pointed it two-handed, straight at Winston's huge barrel of a chest, and shouted: 'Hold it!' in a voice she didn't even recognize as her own.

He stopped in his tracks, snorting like a bull, tears and sweat and snot pouring down his face, the machete raised ready to strike her down.

Jesus, Winston, don't make me have to shoot you, thought Lily, nearly paralysed with shock, fear clawing at her and making her light-headed.

She was holding the Magnum steady, although it was heavy and she was scared of it going off. Leo's gift to her – *thanks Leo* – but oh God she didn't want to have to use the bloody thing, she didn't want to have to shoot anyone, she didn't, she didn't.

She'd have to go back inside if she did. She *couldn't* go back inside . . .

But Winston stood still, crying, staring at her. The machete dropped from his hands, adding another scarlet splatter to the ruined carpet. Then he turned on his heel and half ran, half fell out of the door and was gone.

Lily stood there like she'd been turned to stone.

Then, behind her, she heard a groan.

She turned.

Blood was still pumping out of the thing in the chair, and she thought, *Wait. Dead bodies don't pump blood because the heart ain't beating.*

Jack was *alive*.

And now he was stirring, trying to move.

She put the Magnum away and leaned out of the open door, looking for Nick's Mercedes. She spotted it parked up a hundred yards away and shrieked at the top of her lungs. 'Nick! Nick!'

Nick was out of the car like a shot.

He came at a run, surging in through the door, nearly knocking her flat on her arse. He looked at the thing in the chair, which was now trying to speak, bloody froth bubbling on its lips.

'Fucking *hell*,' said Nick, as Lily took out the old mobile she'd borrowed off Oli and started with shaking fingers to call for an ambulance.

He snatched it out of her hand, shoved it into his jacket pocket and pulled out a pair of leather driving gloves and pulled one of them on. He gave Lily the other one. 'Don't leave your prints anywhere, okay? And *not* your mobile phone, dummy. Use his landline, but we're going to do this first. Now what we're going to need,' said Nick, 'is your tights. Get them off. We got to tie off that arm before he bleeds out. Then we fuck off. Quick.'

'Is he going to die?' Lily asked shakily, pulling on the glove.

'Maybe,' said Nick with crushing brutality. 'We'll do what we can.'

57

Kings was buzzing and Si and Freddy were happy with their new Head of Security, Brendan Gibbs. He was a tough bastard but not a loose cannon like that fucking Jase – who was still hanging around like a bad smell, propping up the bar, acting like he was still cock of the walk. Freddy watched him and promised himself he was going to sort him, very soon.

'Saz is in with the new hubby,' Freddy told Si as they sat upstairs in the office throwing back a few single malts.

The news that his niece was in was not particularly welcome to Si. He had plenty of punters in here, the evening was going with a swing, and he knew most of them were high as kites on E and cocaine. Which was fine, but he didn't want to hear that about his own niece. She was better than that – or she fucking well should be.

'Have Brendan keep an eye out,' said Si.

Freddy nodded. Maeve came bustling in with the books; she helped Matt out sometimes in the office. Freddy couldn't stand the stroppy cow, sister-in-law or not. He gave her a curt nod, threw back the last of his malt and went off down-stairs.

Jase pushed through the writhing punters and got to the bar and caught sight of Saz. She had that limp dick Richard standing sullenly alongside her. Saz was wearing a brown polka-dotted halter-neck dress that was way up her arse and plunging to show off her boobs. She looked hot, but he wasn't interested in that. He felt down tonight, and he kept shooting edgy looks at Brendan, who was patrolling the place in DJ and bow tie, patrolling *Jase's* place, ordering *Jase's* boys around. The boys kept their heads down and just did as he said, their eyes never meeting Jase's. It was as if he had ceased to exist.

Christ, that made him furious.

Not long ago *he* had been in charge here. Now Jase was being treated like wallpaper. But all that would change, he *knew* it would change, the minute he came through for Freddy and did Lily King like he'd promised. Freddy and Si would fall all over him then; they'd be so bloody grateful, he could write his own cheque, have his door back, anything.

If only he could *get* to the bitch. He frowned. When she wasn't safely tucked inside The Fort now, she was being squired around by bloody Nick O'Rourke, and he'd already had one near-miss in *that* department, so how to do it? He was driving himself apeshit, trying to think of a way. And Oli could never know. He'd make sure of that. After he'd offed the old girl, Oli would need a shoulder to cry on, she'd be back on side in no time. But . . . *how?* How was he going to get to Lily King?

As the strobes zoomed and flickered and the DJ cranked up Lily Allen's latest, he looked at Saz standing there jiggling her bits at the bar. He elbowed through the punters and pitched up at her side. She glanced at him, gave him a spaced-out smile. She'd been on the old happy pills, he saw straight away.

'Hiya, Jase!' she yelled, and leaned over and gave him a smacker straight on the lips.

'Hi, Saz,' returned Jase, trying not to laugh out loud at the expression on Richard's face as he witnessed the clinch. Jase gave the wuss a look that said, *Want to make something of it?* and Richard looked away.

Jase tried to catch the barman's eye. Yeah, he was *invisible*. He'd become the invisible man in here.

'How are you, sweetie?' Saz asked him, sipping her drink.

He leaned in close to her so as to make himself heard. 'Cool. Don't usually see you in here.'

'Wanted a night out,' said Saz. She cast a disparaging look at her husband. 'Richie hates it here.'

And you don't give a shit about that, thought Jase.

He'd never liked Saz. Saz was everything Oli was not – snooty, shallow, a real pain in the rear. If *he* was Richard, he'd yank her out of here right now and take her home and give her a stiff talking-to.

Saz's eyes were glassy. 'Heard Oli and you had a bit of a row.'

'Yeah. A bit.' He didn't want to discuss that with her. He tried again to catch the barman's eye. *Another* one ignored him.

'I heard you'd split,' said Saz. 'Jeez, get me another drink, Richard, will you? I'm parched.'

Her loving husband gave her a look that said, *You've had enough*.

'Look, I can't stand this bloody racket, I'm going home,'

said Richard, giving her a cold stare and Jase a look of blank dislike.

'Okay. You go. Uncle Si'll drop me home later.'

Richard looked taken aback. *He thought she'd go with him*, thought Jase. How little the poor sap knew his own wife.

Richard gave Jase an uneasy glance. Then he looked at Saz.

'Oh go *on*, Richie. I'll be fine.' She flapped a dismissive hand at him.

He nodded and reluctantly turned away and was suddenly lost in the surging crowds.

'Let me get that,' said Jase, what the hell, and he signalled for the barman and was again ignored.

'I'll get 'em in,' said Saz. She held up a hand and the barman was there like lightning. Jase stared at the tosser while she placed the order, voddy and orange for her, a lager for him.

'Oli and I ain't really split up,' he said.

'Oh?'

'We had a fight, that's all.'

The drinks came and Saz fell on the voddy and orange. The E was making her so thirsty.

The barman was turning away when Jase said: 'Hey.'

The man's eyes wouldn't meet Jase's. Jase saw red. He leaned over and caught the dipstick's tie and yanked him forward, over the bar, cracking his forehead hard into the man's nose.

The barman let out a yell and fell back, blood pouring out of his hooter like Niagara Falls. He was staggering, blinking, eyes watering, blood sploshing all down the front of him.

'Next time you see me, you fucking well *serve* me, yeah?' snapped Jase.

The barman weaved unsteadily away. Jase glanced around, feeling buzzed. A couple of the bouncers – *his* men – were watching him. As he stared back, they looked away. He turned his attention back to Saz.

'Whew!' she said with a laugh. '*Very* macho.'

Silly tart.

'Oli's stupid,' said Saz, her eyes playing with Jase's. 'You're gorgeous.'

'Tell her that, will you?' The state Saz was in, he could make *her* drop her drawers if he chose to. Which he didn't. But while she was here . . . Jase was thinking busily. He spun out a hopeful line. 'It'd be nice to surprise her with something,' he said. 'Something real special. I may as well tell you, Saz, I want to propose to her.'

'That's so *romantic*,' sighed Saz with a smile, leaning into Jase, her hand caressing the hard muscles of his forearm.

'Yeah, I know she'd like that,' said Jase. 'But it ain't possible, is it? The place is in lockdown, I heard.'

'Oh. Yeah,' said Saz, shrugging regretfully.

'It's a pity, because she'd love it.'

Saz glugged back the last of her drink. 'Fill me up again, Jase, will you?'

Jesus – at this rate he was going to have to carry her out of here. He reordered for her, not for himself. It was a different barman, and this one didn't ignore him. *Better*, he thought.

'It'd make Oli so happy,' he went on. 'But there's no way, I guess.'

'Yeah. That's right.'

Saz was frowning now, peering at Jase. She felt a little sick, to be honest. And suddenly she felt uncertain too,

sorry that she'd let Richard go. Richard was sweet, dependable, the best. Either you had the type of man you could
rely on, the plodder, the unambitious one, who bored the
arse off you most of the time if you were honest but who
at least never tried laying the law down, or you had the
type who excited you, who wanted to dominate you, who
thrilled you but caused you tears and a world of hurt, a
lion of a man.

Her dad had been a lion of a man. Named for the lion
that had been his star sign. *Leo King*. She thought of her
wedding day, the day when her dad should have walked her
down the aisle, but he hadn't been there.

Saz's eyes filled with tears.

Uncle Si had stood in, but it wasn't the same. It had *never*
been the same, ever since . . . oh shit, ever since that awful
night.

'But I guess it's out of the question, right? All locked up
tight,' Jase was saying.

'What?' Saz asked vaguely.

'The house. Locked up. That right?'

'Oh! Locked up, yeah,' said Saz, and grabbed at the drink
the new barman had placed in front of her.

'Pity,' said Jase. 'That's a terrible pity, don't you think?'

'It is, it is.'

'Oli would have loved a surprise like that.'

'Well, she would.' Saz turned to him, tears forgotten,
bright-eyed, smiling now. She nodded and tapped her nose.
She nearly missed it.

Jesus, talk about rat-arsed, thought Jase. 'And why not,
yeah? You can do it, Jase, and you know *why* you can do it?'

Jase shook his head.

'You can do it, because there's a way in.' Saz frowned, as

if some stray thought had troubled her. She turned her face up to him and suddenly she looked sober, solemn.

'What?' Jase hardly dared breathe. What was she saying?

Saz shrugged. 'I loosened some bricks in the wall when I was little. When it was first built and the mortar was soft. The security system's always switched off on Thursday afternoons because the gardener's in the grounds. I could always come in and out without anyone knowing, and I still can. Only on Thursdays, though.' She looked at him and half smiled. 'So it's lucky that's tomorrow. Right?'

58

When Lily got home she was sick at heart and shaking like a leaf. She double-checked all the doors and windows, then went straight into the sitting room, thankful that Oli was out and not able to see the state her mother was in and to start demanding explanations. Lily poured out a brandy and knocked it back in one. Her eyes watered. She slumped down on the couch. Shit, she never wanted to go through anything like that again, not ever.

Oh God. Jack.

All she could see was Jack propped up there in the chair behind his desk, a Jack that was unrecognizable, covered in blood, wrecked, dying . . . and then when she heard the noise and turned and Winston was there.

She'd thought right then that she was dead, too, all hope gone – just like Jack.

But *maybe* there was a sliver of hope for Jack. She and Nick had legged it after they'd applied the tourniquet to his arm to stem the bleeding and called the ambulance from Jack's own phone.

There were CCTV cameras on the High Street but not on the smaller side road where Jack's office was located, but even so they'd gone out carefully, separately, one at a time and no running, no calling attention to themselves. Even so, Lily was braced for a call from the Bill. There would be stuff in Jack's office to link her to him, she'd been inside, she was ... oh Jesus, she couldn't go inside again.

She fetched another brandy and threw that one back too. Felt a tiny bit warmer, an iota calmer. Her hands shook a little less. She felt slightly less likely to vomit.

No. Nick had assured her. Had said that there was no way the Bill could put them together with this: they'd wiped any trace of themselves away.

'But your car,' said Lily as they stood in the blood-spattered office, 'the car. The CCTV. They'll see the plates.'

'They're fake, stupid.'

Stupid. Even in the depths of her terror and bewilderment, that had rankled. But maybe that's exactly what she was. Probing around in things she didn't understand. Nick had warned her, and he was right, as usual. It would have been bad enough if it had been her hacked to pieces. But Jack. Poor bloody Jack, who'd doubted her a few times, who'd advised her to call the whole thing off, but who had still stood by her, staunchly supporting her; and look where that had got him.

He could die.

He probably *would* die.

Oh God, please don't let me have Jack's death on my conscience, she thought in anguish. But she knew that it was a faint hope her prayers would be answered. God hadn't listened to her in a long, long time.

She sat there and her eyes fell on her bag. She put the

empty glass to one side and pulled the bag onto her lap. She took out the Magnum and sat there dumbly, looking at the gun and thinking, *I could have killed someone today.*

When the situation in Jack's office had arisen, her own reactions had both stunned and appalled her. Survival mode had kicked in almost instantaneously. She was not a violent person. She had *never* been that. But she had seen Winston there, bloodied, demented, looking at her, and the machete, and immediately the synapses in her brain had started screaming, *Threat, threat, threat!*

The Magnum had been in her hand before she had even been aware of her intention to draw it. That was the seriously scary part. She sat there and stared at the gun with the same hypnotic fascination as if she was staring at a poisonous snake. She had to put the thing away now, stow it somewhere safe, somewhere neither she nor anyone else could snatch it up with deadly intent. She sat there for a long time in the silence of the big house, thinking, thinking. And then she had it. She stood up, tottered a little on her feet. The brandy and the fear had all rolled into one big battering ram and now it hit her, full force. But she wasn't going to put this off. She went and got some masking tape from the cupboard under the stairs where a few household tools were kept. Then she trotted off, staggering only slightly, to put the Magnum away.

Later, she made a couple of phone calls. She knew it was late, but what the hell. The first was to Adrienne.

'What do you want?' asked Adrienne when Lily told her who it was.

'Nothing, Adrienne. I just wanted to say I hope you're being careful, that's all.'

There was silence. Then Adrienne said: 'What, is that a threat?'

Lily looked at the phone in exasperation. 'No, for fuck's sake, of course it's not a threat. Look, things have been happening to the women on that list of yours.'

'You *said* that. What the hell do you mean?'

Lily told her about Alice Blunt's apparent suicide, and Bev who was in intensive care having inhaled more smoke than ten thousand test beagles, and Suki who hadn't survived the fire at all, the poor cow. 'You knew about Julia, I suppose?'

'Her getting marked like that? Yeah, I knew.' Adrienne sounded worried now. As well she might. 'That was bloody nasty, that.'

'Adrienne, are you *sure* you've never shown anyone else that list? Apart from Jack – ' who was now either dead or dying, and she couldn't face telling Adrienne that – 'and me?'

Adrienne was quiet for a moment on the other end of the line. 'No. Look, I told you. I was telling the truth. Of course I haven't. Why would I?'

'No, you're right, why would you?' Lily frowned. 'But it looks as if someone's getting to the women on it. Wouldn't you say that's what it looks like?'

'Yeah,' said Adrienne, and now her voice reflected her fears. 'Yeah. I would.'

'So take care, Adrienne. That's all I'm saying. This is just a heads-up. Watch out, okay?'

'You started all this trouble,' said Adrienne suddenly.

'Hey – *you* kept the list,' flung back Lily, stung.

'I wish to God I'd never set eyes on you, Lily King, *or* your cheating rat of a husband,' said Adrienne, and the line went dead.

Lily sighed and dialled again.

The phone was snatched up on the first ring.

'Hello?' demanded a female voice, very aggressively.

'Reba? Reba Stuart?' asked Lily, picturing the brassy madam in her mind, leathery skin and hair bleached to fuck. Mean, baleful eyes glaring out at the world.

'Who wants her?'

'This is Lily King.'

'You *bitch*,' snarled Reba.

'What?'

'Oh, don't come the fucking innocent with me. You want to gloat now, I suppose. Ain't that it?'

Lily looked at the phone. '*What?*' she echoed faintly.

'Oh yeah.' Reba sounded seriously pissed off. 'This is you. I *know* this is you, you rotten little mare. You can deny it all you like, but I know what I know.'

'Hey, Reba – why don't you tell *me* what you know? Because I'm in the dark here.'

'We've been raided. We've been shut down. I'm looking at a stretch inside. But then you *know* all this. You grassed me up to the cops. Didn't you?'

She'd only phoned Reba to warn her to watch herself. But something had obviously already kicked off.

'Reba—' she started.

'No! I don't want to hear another damned thing from you.'

'Take care, Reba,' said Lily quickly, before the madam could hang up on her.

'You *what?*'

'I *said* you've got to take care. There's a list of Leo's mistresses. And I think someone's picking them off.'

There was silence on the other end of the phone. 'You *serious?*' said Reba, more quietly.

'That's what I phoned for, to warn you.'

'What the f . . .' breathed Reba.

Lily told her then. Laid it all out about Alice, Bev, Suki – and Julia.

'Jesus,' said Reba.

'And if you've been raided, it had nothing to do with me. I've never grassed up anyone, Reba. You can believe it or not believe it, but it's the truth.'

'All right. Suppose I *do* believe you about that – which I fucking don't. But this other thing. What the hell . . .?'

'Believe that too, Reba. Keep safe, okay?'

'All right. I will,' said Reba, and hung up.

59

Coming to this point on the perimeter always filled Saz with a dreamy, nightmarish sense of déjà vu. It was nearly five o'clock on Thursday afternoon, and she and Jase were standing on the grass verge outside the wall surrounding the grounds of The Fort. Hardly any cars passed by, and that was good as far as Jase was concerned; that was *excellent*.

Maybe this wasn't such a good idea, thought Saz. Just being here again made her feel faintly sick. And she'd never liked Jase. She knew the feeling was mutual. She'd been doped up and pretty drunk when she had agreed to this last night. Now she wished she hadn't, but she couldn't very well go back on her word. Jase wouldn't like it, and he was so uncertain of temper that you wouldn't want to upset him, not ever.

She reckoned that Jase had been OD-ing on the steroids, he was so pumped up and aggressive. A lot of the guys in Uncle Si and Freddy's orbit did that, big bulging muscles and an attack-dog attitude earned their keep, after all. But it was too late for second thoughts.

'You're sure it's off now?' Jase was asking her.

'Yeah,' she said, still feeling unhappy about this.

All around the wall there were sensors. The grounds themselves were crisscrossed with electric beams that would trigger an alarm if anything crossed them. But, between two and six every Thursday, it was all switched off, because the gardener was in the grounds.

She was sure all right. How many times as a kid had she come in and out of here on a Thursday afternoon, finding this little section of wall where the bricks were. All you had to do then was avoid the gardener, use your key to get into the house – she still had a key – and bingo, there you were, inside. It was a game, beating the system, proving how clever she was. Like *Mission Impossible*.

Her mother had come back and so she'd had to leave, but this was her home, she couldn't be banished from it just like that, so she hadn't handed back the new key. *Fuck you, Mother dear.*

'I can't see why you want to get into the house, though,' she said to Jase.

'I explained all that,' said Jase with a theatrical sigh. 'I'm going to wait until dark, okay? And I don't want to risk being spotted by the gardener, see? He'd get spooked and I'd have to explain; it would all get too complicated and it would ruin the surprise. So I wait inside the house somewhere, in one of the spare rooms or some damned thing, until it's dark – and then I sneak out and propose to her, ain't that romantic?'

Yeah. It was. Very. Saz wondered if Richard would ever do such a thing, but she knew he never would. For a moment she was envious of Oli with the passionate Jase wooing her back after an argument. All she ever got from Richard after they'd rowed was sulks and the silent treatment for days on end: it really wore a person down. But then, Richard would never turn really nasty, and she had a feeling that Jase could do that in an instant.

She couldn't back out now.

But coming here disturbed her. Brought back so many memories, of happy days and of hideous ones too. Happy times, sneaking around, hugging her secret to herself. Happy memories, and hideous ones. That night. Oh, that night. Coming back to see Dad, because he was there alone, Mum was away. Saz was Dad's Best Girl, his favourite, so she sneaked back in to see him, surprise him. *Surprise, Dad! Surprise!*

And he had been surprised.

Very surprised indeed.

60

He watched them from along the road. He was tucked into the shadows of the woodland opposite the house, and he was thinking that this would be just fine if only he could lose Saz somewhere. No need to involve the poor little cow in all this – it was a shame but a man had to do what a man had to do. He'd do it, too. He'd work it out. He *had* to. He'd waited so long for this.

Inside prison, Lily King had been protected by an invisible ring of steel. Outside, she was more vulnerable, but Leo had done this gaff up like Fort Knox, which had been a problem when she had retreated inside the house, which she had done more and more, lately. She was getting nervous of coming out. He knew that.

She was *right* to be nervous, because given half a chance he was going to do it, have his revenge. Fuck Si and what he said all the time – wait, just wait; well, fuck that, and fuck Si too and fuck the horse he rode in on. Freddy was *done* with waiting. He'd been watching Jase chatting up Saz,

357

and wondered what the hell all that was about, but now he knew, now he could see, and he was triumphant.

Saz had a way in. She was going to show Jase the way, probably to make up with Oli.

Oh, Jase boy, you are wasting your time, thought Freddy. Because he wasn't going to get a chance to patch it up with Oli; he wasn't going to get a chance for anything. Jase was long overdue a lesson, and tonight he was going to get it. Two birds with one stone, wallop. It would be *sweet*.

Freddy watched with satisfaction as Jase and Saz bent to the wall and started moving the bricks to one side.

Yes.

61

Nick phoned at just after six. Lily had paid the gardener at half past five, and then he'd left. She'd put the security system back on, and she was in the sitting room; the light was fading just a little outside. She went and pulled the drapes, switched on a light. A warm glow filled the room.

'Hi,' said Nick. 'You okay?'

'Shouldn't I be?'

'It shook you up, that happening to Jack Rackland.'

Yeah, and it was all my fault, thought Lily. Nick was right. She *was* stupid.

'I'm just going to phone the hospital,' she said.

'Is that wise?'

Lily felt an edge of annoyance. 'No. Probably not. But I can't just let the poor bastard lie there and die.'

'He might not be dead, yet.'

'It looked pretty bad.'

'Leave it to his family. Keep your head down. He's in good hands.'

'He don't have a family. Well . . . only an ex-wife.' Mouthy little Monica, whom Lily thought Jack was still in love with.

'Even so. Leave it.'

Lily flopped down on the couch, drooping, her spirits low. She'd liked Jack; she'd appreciated his dedication and his humour. To see him like that . . . broken, bloody . . . had been horrible; it had left her shaken and sick. But Nick was right, she didn't dare enquire about him at the hospital. If the police traced the attack back to Winston, it might not be long, despite all Nick's assurances, before they came knocking at her door.

And then what?

She was terrified of going back inside; she'd rather top herself first. To be caged up again would be beyond awful, now that she'd had a taste of freedom. All right, she'd made no headway at all with Saz; but she was hoping that would change, given time.

I'm sorry, Daddy, I'm so sorry.

Sorry for what?

That refrain from Saz's sleepwalking kept echoing through her brain.

Now she had to confront it. She had to face the possibility that it had been Saz, her own daughter, who had done that to Leo. And if it *was* Saz, where did that leave her? Where did it leave any of them?

Up shit creek, she thought miserably. *Without a paddle and without a shred of hope that life would ever be normal again.*

Lily wrenched her wandering mind away from the massive problem that was Saz, and instead she thought of Oli. Her little Oli had grown into a sweet and funny young woman; she loved spending time with her. And there would be Oli's baby soon to spoil. If she had to go down again, she would miss yet more years with her precious girls. She couldn't – wouldn't – endure that.

And there was Nick, too.

Nick, who had been her first love. Nick, the man she *should* have married. She was – to her own shock – still head over heels in love with him; she could admit it to herself if to no one else. Just hearing his deep, gravelly voice on the phone gave her the shivers. If she got banged up again, where would that leave her and Nick?

Yet she had come within an inch of risking jail. Had pulled out the Magnum, and if Winston had kept coming she knew she would have used it. Blown him away – and blown away her own chances of freedom, too.

'You still there?' Nick was asking.

'Yeah.'

'You *sure* you're okay? I could come over.'

'No, I'm all right. I'm not good company right now. Think I'll just get an early night.'

She could hear the Kaiser Chiefs being played loudly upstairs. Oli was in her room. Oli, who was pregnant with Lily's first grandchild. That was something to be celebrated, even though the circumstances were far from ideal. But Lily didn't feel in the mood for that, either. She felt a gnawing anxiety about Jack. Wanted to know he was okay. Or dead. Or *something*. She just wanted to *know*, either way.

'You get some sleep. Okay?' said Nick.

'Okay.'

And he was gone. And it was then that Lily heard voices, a man's and a woman's, arguing in whispers in the hall.

62

Lily stood up and went to the half-open door of the sitting room, both curious and concerned. No one should be in here . . . unless Oli had invited some friends round? But Oli would have told her; she knew Lily didn't like strangers wandering around the house.

Lily paused, just a step or two from the door into the hall. She knew the woman's voice, the woman was Saz. Lily frowned. Saz had left, yet here she was, back inside the house. And . . . that wasn't Richard's voice. This voice was harder, harsher. Lily stopped in her tracks, and a buzz of fear went skittering up the back of her neck. She tiptoed to one side of the door, flattened herself to the wall behind it. She heard Saz hiss: 'Look, I don't know about this.'

'You what?' asked the man with her. His voice had risen. He toned it down. 'You *what?*' he whispered.

Lily looked through the gap beside the hinges on the door and saw Jase standing there with Saz.

What the hell . . .? she thought.

'I don't think we should go ahead with this. I'm sorry. But

I don't think Oli's going to be very pleased about it. She don't much like surprises. I really think—'

'You *think?*' Jase laughed at that. The sound echoed out there, bounced off the marble. Lily could see them across the hall, standing near the front door. Jase's body language was confrontational; Saz's was apologetic, head bent, her expression uncertain.

'I'm sorry,' said Saz, and gave an unhappy shrug.

'It's too late for changes of plan now,' hissed Jase.

Saz's head whipped up and she stared at him. Lily watched, wondering what the hell was going on. How had they got inside the house? And surprise Oli with *what*, exactly?

She was getting a bad, bad feeling about this.

'Look, I've decided . . .' whispered Saz.

'No, *you* look,' shot back Jase, his voice rising now, looming over Saz, stabbing at her with a finger to emphasize his point. 'You just fuck off now, take yourself off somewhere, okay? If you know what's good for you, because I got something I gotta do here, and I'm going to do it right now.'

'Oli won't be impressed by this,' said Saz, shrinking back a little.

'Oli?' Now he laughed, and it was an ugly, threatening sound. 'Fuck Oli, the dozy mare. It's your ma I've come to see. Time her and me had a little chat.'

And Lily saw Jase pull out a cosh, wield it in his right hand.

Shit a brick, she thought.

'So where is she?' asked Jase. He wasn't even bothering to talk softly now. He was focused on what he had to do, that was all.

Saz said nothing. She stood there as if paralysed, looking at the cosh in Jase's meaty hand.

'*Where is she?*' roared Jase.

Saz flinched and cowered back.

Jase advanced on her, smacking the cosh into his palm. 'Come *on*, Saz. Tell me where the bitch is.'

'You lied to me,' said Saz shakily, backing away.

Saz, thought Lily in terror. *Oh God, was he going to hurt Saz?*

She wanted to dash out into the hall, throw herself at him, kill him with her bare hands. But her feet were frozen to the floor.

Suddenly Jase swung the cosh. Saz gave a cry and there was a sharp *whack* as the thing hit her cheekbone. She staggered back and fell. Lily clapped her hands over her mouth to stifle the scream of rage and terror that almost escaped her.

'*Where?*' bellowed Jase, standing over the poleaxed Saz. 'You want some more of this? *Do you?*'

Saz was prone, clutching a hand to her bleeding cheek, sobbing. She shook her head wildly.

'Tell me where,' said Jase.

Saz said nothing.

Lily swallowed hard and stepped out, started to move around the door. Fuck it, she couldn't let him hit Saz again. She *couldn't*.

And then Oli's voice from the top of the stairs said: '*Jase? What the hell are you doing here? Oh my God. Saz? What's happened? What's he done to you?*'

Lily heard Oli start down the stairs.

'She up there?' Jase was saying, and she heard his tread, heavier, bulkier, he was going up the stairs. Shit, *Oli* was up there, the cash, oh Christ in heaven, Oli was pregnant and he could hurt her, throw her down the stairs, make her lose the child, anything. He could hurt both her girls, and she couldn't let that happen, she just couldn't.

She stepped out around the door.

Saz spied her instantly. But Jase and Oli couldn't see her, they were on the stairs. Lily looked straight at Saz. *Honey, be quiet. Say nothing*, Lily's eyes said urgently to her daughter.

'You can't come in here just like this. How the fuck did you get in here?' Oli was screaming at Jase as he thundered up the stairs towards her.

Got to do something quick, thought Lily. She crept out into the hall, Saz watching her dazedly, and eased open the cupboard under the stairs. Tools in there. A hammer. She snatched it out of the box.

'You bastard, what are you *doing*?' Oli was shouting.

Lily's eyes fell on the fusebox. She flipped up the cover and looked at the pop-out fuses there. Showers. Ring circuit. Water heaters. Cookers. *Lights*. She pulled out the fuse.

Suddenly, The Fort was plunged into darkness.

63

'Hey!' Jase yelled.

He'd seen her at the edge of his vision as he climbed up the stairs, seen her moving quickly across the hall in that split-second before the lights went out. And now he was on the staircase and Oli was up ahead, at the top of the stairs. He couldn't see fuck-all, he was blind. But he knew she was up ahead and once he had hold of Oli, the King bitch was going to have to toe the line, he knew that much for sure. He started edging up, thinking there were maybe eight or nine steps to go before he reached Oli and grabbed her.

'Oli?' he said, tightening his grip on the cash.

Just speak, you silly cow, because the minute you open your yap, I'll know exactly where you are.

He could feel sweat breaking out all over his body. His chest was a tight, painful knot. He wished he could see. Wished she'd speak. But she was silent.

'Oli?' he said again, more urgently.

And then he felt the impact, something thumping him hard in the chest. No, she wouldn't, she . . . he teetered wildly, trying to keep his balance, his mind's eye supplying him with a dizzying picture of the drop behind him. If he fell, he could break his damned neck.

'*Jesus!*' he roared, furious, because yes, it was Oli. She'd pushed him and he was . . . oh shit, he was pitching backwards, losing it, hands splaying out, the cosh going flying from his fingers. He felt a stunning pain as his head struck a stair, then his shoulder; his arm was wrenched, his leg . . . fuck it, fuck, fuck, this was not how it should be going, this was not meant to *happen*.

Pain exploded in his body and erupted in his head, and he fell, he *plummeted*, backwards into the darkness.

'God, do you think he's dead?' Oli asked in a trembling voice. 'I pushed him; I shouldn't have done that. Oh no, oh Christ, do you think I killed him?'

When Lily had heard Jase going arse over tit down the stairs, she had thought he had merely lost his balance. But Oli had pushed him.

Good going, girl, she thought.

She'd popped the fuse back in. Blinked a bit as the lights flared back on, illuminating the hall to a dazzling degree. She saw that Saz was on her feet, swaying like a drunk, blood dripping steadily from her cut cheek. Jase was on his back at the bottom of the stairs, and Oli was standing three-quarters of the way down them, watching him as if he was going to leap up like a jack-in-the-box, grinning like a maniac and yelling *Surprise!* before killing them all.

Lily, still clutching the hammer, went over to where Jase lay. His neck wasn't at an awkward angle; she didn't think he'd broken it, which was a pity. His chest was rising and falling, Oli hadn't killed him, *also* a pity. The cosh was feet away, but she didn't want him coming round and grabbing that again, so she kicked it across the hall, well out of his reach. Then she went back to the cupboard under the stairs, speaking quickly over her shoulder.

'Oli, take your sister upstairs,' she said.

She was peering in the box. No rope, no string. Fuse wire. That would do. She grabbed it and was turning when suddenly Oli said: 'Uncle Freddy . . .?'

Then Lily knew their troubles had only just begun.

64

Lily whirled around. Freddy was walking across the hall to where Jason lay. He'd picked up the cosh. He flicked a look at Saz, at Oli. Then he focused his attention on Lily, and grinned.

Lily felt all her bones turn to water. Freddy's eyes said it all. His intentions were very clear. But she still thought of the girls, her girls; she had to keep them safe, but how was she supposed to do that? She looked over at Saz, who was now near where Jase lay, just a step or two away from the stairs.

'Oli!' said Lily sharply, because Oli was staring at Freddy as if hypnotized. Oli's head flicked round and she looked at her mother. 'Take your sister up to the master suite. Right now. Go on.'

'No.' Oli was looking at Freddy, seeing that all his attention was focused on Lily.

'*Yes*. Go on, Oli. Move it,' said Lily.

And finally Oli moved. Saz staggered toward her and Oli put a supporting arm around her shoulders. Together, they started up the stairs. Lily watched them go. There was a lock on the master suite. It wouldn't stop Freddy, but it would certainly slow him down if he went after them.

And he has to do that, doesn't he?

Because he was going to kill her, and he couldn't leave witnesses. Even if they didn't see him do the deed, they'd know he was here and that Jase couldn't have done it because Jase was out of commission. They'd *know*.

What the hell am I going to do? wondered Lily wildly.

She was still holding the hammer.

She wasn't a killer, and Freddy was built like a brick shit-house. Even if she could get past his guard – and that was a laughable idea – would she truly be able to beat his thick skull in with the hammer? Would she be able to find that strength in herself? She didn't know. To protect the girls, maybe. But as she watched Freddy leaning over the fallen Jase, as she saw the girls reach the landing at the top of the stairs, all she could think was, *I am in terrible trouble here.*

Oli got Saz into the master suite. Saz lay back on the big bed, groaning. Oli hurried into the en suite and came back with a towel.

'Here,' she said, and pressed it gently to Saz's face. Then she turned and looked at the open door and wondered what the hell to do. She couldn't call the police. It was part of the King creed: you *never* called the police. An ambulance then, for Saz? But something was kicking off downstairs, something serious; call an ambulance and before very long the police would be here too.

But who to call? She needed help. *Lily* needed help. She thought of Nick O'Rourke, but she didn't have his number. Then she thought of Uncle Si. If anyone could control Freddy, it was Uncle Si. But then . . . she really wasn't too certain about Uncle Si, either. She could remember all too clearly that day when her mother had been in the pool, and Si had been there, ostensibly helping her out, but she didn't think he had been doing that at all; she was pretty sure he was just trying to keep Mum in there until . . . until she *died*.

But she had to do something. And Uncle Si *could* control Freddy. No one else could.

She picked up her mobile with shaking hands and phoned Uncle Si's number. Aunt Maeve answered.

'Aunt Maeve? It's Oli. Can you get Uncle Si to come over to the house please? Right now? Uncle Freddy's here . . .' Uncle Si could be here in moments; he only lived up the road. She would let him in, and he would make everything all right . . . wouldn't he? 'Can you tell him to hurry? Please . . .?' Oli's voice cracked, dried up, her mouth was like dust, she couldn't get another word out, she was panicking too much.

'Oli? Calm down,' said Maeve. 'What's going on? Is your mother there?'

'Yeah. She's here. Uncle Freddy's after her. I can't . . . please, just please will you get Uncle Si here, Aunt Maeve? Please make him *come*.'

65

'He hit Saz,' said Lily. 'Can you imagine that?'

This was beyond surreal. Lily was standing here in her hallway, talking to Freddy King as if he was normal. Mostly because she *wished* he was behaving normally. Fat chance of that. Her voice was high with anxiety. High with fear. Because there was one thing *everyone* knew about Freddy King, and that was that he was a psycho; he wasn't normal at all.

'Really?'

Freddy was staring at her like a cat gloating over the cream. He couldn't believe his luck; he had her cornered at last. She knew that he'd wanted this for a long, long time, and somehow Saz had let Jase in, and that had provided Freddy with an entry too. Now she was toast. She was finished. He stood there, staring at her, smiling, Jase's cosh held casually in one hand. He slapped it lightly into his palm, looking at her, grinning.

Here it comes for you, bitch.

Then Jase groaned.

Lily's eyes skittered away from Freddy and fell on Jase.

Yeah, come on, Jase. Come on you meat-headed, thick-skulled pile of shit, wake up! thought Lily urgently. *Wake up and give this lunatic something different to think about.*

Freddy dropped his gaze, looking down at Jase.

Jase groaned again, his face creasing. He lifted one arm, turned over onto his side.

'They must have been arguing over something,' said Lily hurriedly. *What to do, what to do . . .?* Keep him talking for now. Keep him busy. Keep him focused on Jase, not me.

'Yeah?' said Freddy without interest.

'He was going to surprise Oli or some silly thing.'

'Oh. Yeah?' Where had she put the hammer? It was over there, on the floor by the cupboard.

Shit, he's going to kill me.

'Only they argued,' Lily rattled on. 'I heard them arguing out here, I came out to see what was going on, and he hit her with the cosh, can you believe that?'

'No. That's unbelievable,' agreed Freddy.

Jase's legs were making weak movements now. He was within an inch of full consciousness, and then Lily was going to have two of them to worry about instead of one. My God, what was she going to *do*?

'Big bastard like this hitting a young girl?' Freddy was pursing his lips, shaking his head. 'We can't have that, now can we?'

He was putting the cosh down on the floor.

I'm too far away to reach it, thought Lily. And anyway, trying to reach it would be a fool's errand. Try to reach it and she would put herself within striking distance of Freddy, and that would probably be the last thing she ever did. She should have taken hold of the damned thing herself, not just kicked it out of Jase's way.

'We *certainly* can't have that,' Freddy was saying almost to himself. He knelt down beside Jase and tapped his cheek lightly. 'Hey boy. You there?'

Only a groan from Jase. Then his eyes flickered open and he saw Freddy looming over him.

Lily saw Jase try to grin. It was a faltering effort, and soon vanished.

'I'm . . . putting i'right for you, Fred . . .' he murmured. 'I'm putting it right.'

'Yeah,' said Freddy, smiling softly down at Jase, his expression as tender as a fond father with a baby. 'Sure you are.'

All at once the smile was gone. Freddy put his arm around Jase's neck. Lily heard a half-strangled gasp escape Jase and she recoiled in horror, thinking, *Oh my God, oh shit, oh no*, and then Freddy had his other hand on Jase's skull.

Freddy's face went brick-red with effort as he applied pressure. A noise that was halfway between a scream and a gurgle went up from Jase then. His arms thrashed. There was a loud, sickening *crack*, and suddenly Jase was limp and still. Freddy released him, and he slumped back onto the hard floor like a rag doll.

'Tosser,' said Freddy contemptuously, and stood up, grabbing the cosh. He looked down at Jase's dead body and suddenly gave it a vicious kick. The body twitched like a marionette. 'Fucking *tosser*,' he growled.

Lily's bowels felt as if they were about to let go. He'd killed Jase, killed him in cold blood. Thank God the girls hadn't been down here to see that. And now . . . oh shit, now his head was rising, and his eyes were on her again. He was starting to move.

Lily moved too, quickly, throwing herself so that she went skidding across the marble tiles, hitting the cupboard by the stairs, aiming for the hammer. She missed it. Freddy pistoned into the back of her and she felt herself go down like a sack of shit, Freddy scrabbling about on top of her – *Jesus, the weight of him!* – and her head hit the tiles, she saw flashing lights, her head spun, but the cupboard door was half open and oh, if she could only reach inside, just an inch, two inches, she'd be there.

Freddy was trying to get a swing at her with the cosh. She squirmed, aimed a knee at his balls but missed. Someone was gasping and yelling, and only distantly did she realize that it was her.

Maybe the girls would come, grab the hammer – shit, where was the hammer? – and do for him before he managed to whack her with the cosh.

She could hear Oli shouting something, saying, *Please please come,* but no one was coming. As usual she was on her fucking own here, and Freddy had her, he had her, there was no hope.

Then her scrabbling fingers touched the hammer.

Oh thank you, God!

She grabbed it, aimed it straight at Freddy's bulk, hit him as hard as she could.

He reeled back with a shout of pain, clutching his jaw. Maybe she'd broken it. She hoped so. Her aim hadn't been good, she'd been half pinioned beneath him. But she had shaken him, hurt him a little, she knew she had – and now she was loose. For a moment, only. A moment when everything seemed to slow to a crawl.

She saw Freddy half stagger to his feet and come back at her. Saw her own hand hovering alongside the fusebox, and then he grabbed her again, roaring, shrieking that she was a bitch, she'd killed his brother, and by fuck now he was going to kill *her*, and then her quivering fingers were yanked back, away from the fusebox and she thought: *No, no, this can't be happening.*

She strained away from him, and then her fingers found what they were searching for. The lights went out for a second time. Surprise made his grip on her relax. With one last desperate effort, Lily kicked free of him, and sprinted off into the darkness.

66

She knew every inch of this house. There were fifty steps on the staircase, it was five strides to the master suite upstairs, take ten steps along the hall and there was the door to the indoor swimming pool room. She was through it, slamming it closed behind her; there was no lock. She could picture Freddy still at the cupboard, scrabbling to get the fuse back in, but he'd take time because he didn't know this house and she did. She had *dreamed* of this house when she'd been in prison.

In darkness she skirted the echoing blue vastness of the pool, heading for the changing cubicle at its far end. She knew she didn't have a choice any more. It was kill or be killed: her or Freddy. And by Christ, it wasn't going to be Freddy who came out of this, not if she had anything to do with it.

It *had* to be her. If Freddy got her, then he would have to get the girls too. So fuck the Firearms Act. Fuck assault with a deadly weapon. They'd have to throw the bloody key away this time, and if they did, then at least she would know that it was because she was truly guilty, not the innocent patsy she had been before. Her girls were here, and she couldn't let anything happen to them. She *would* not.

She was almost outside the cubicle, breathing fast in the humid atmosphere of the pool room, when the lights went back on. She yanked open the door and stepped in, closing the door behind her. She lifted the seat and there it was, Leo's Magnum, taped to the inside. She tore off the tape and was straightening up to check it was still properly loaded when she heard the door from the hall open and softly close.

Shit, she thought, her heart thundering sickly in her chest. *Here comes Freddy.*

67

She couldn't see him coming, but she could hear him, treading soft-footed alongside the pool. She would have to wait until he opened the door into the changing cubicle. She could hear him coming closer, closer.

Her mouth was dry but there was the sweat of sheer terror rolling down her face, making her eyes sting. Her bowels felt like mush, her heart was clattering away at a gallop.

So this is it, she thought. *Shit or bust. I kill him or he kills me and the girls.*

She was holding her breath.

The steps were close now, so close.

Her hands were slippery on the gun. She rubbed one damp hand down her jeans, then the other, then she tightened her double-handed grip on it and aimed at the door.

The steps stopped, right outside.

She was going to wait until he opened it and then – *oh shit* – she was going to blast him into the next world. Lily steeled herself, teeth gritted, concentrating everything on just holding the heavy gun steady, making the first shot count.

The handle on the door was going down.

Oh Jesus oh God in heaven help me.

She braced herself for the recoil. It would have a big kick, this gun. It was a hand-cannon. That's what Leo had called it. A hand-cannon. And insurance. The ultimate backup plan. Now, she was going to cash in the insurance. Leo'd told her all about this gun, had told her it was so powerful that even a glancing shot could kill because it could rip a limb off.

'And if this baby hits your mid-section your guts are going to end up in a tree in the next county,' he had told her, and she had cringed at that.

But now she was going to have to do it. Blast Freddy fucking King to hell, where he belonged.

She was trembling, shaking, feeling that she was going to puke now.

She thought of him casually breaking Jase's neck. She'd never forget it. That hideous *crack* as Jase's neck gave way.

Focus, she told herself. She was so stressed her mind was wandering off. *Shoot him now, through the door.*

But she couldn't do it. She had to look him straight in the eye, she had to *know* that he was dead; this was one dragon that had needed slaying for a long, long time, and she was going to make sure she did it. She *had* to.

The door was pushing in. She held her breath.

The door was opening.

Oh help . . .

Lily blinked, trying to clear the salt-sting of sweat from her eyes.

Come on then, you bastard, come and get it . . .

The door opened wide.

Lily's finger tightened on the trigger, here we go, here it comes, you bastard...

And then she froze.

It wasn't Freddy standing there; it was Maeve.

68

'Lily? What the hell . . .?' asked Maeve, her eyes not on Lily's face but on the huge gun in her hand. 'What are you *doing*?'

Lily stared at her, open-mouthed. *Shit. She'd nearly blown her sister-in-law to kingdom come.*

But Freddy! Where was Freddy?

'Where is he? Where the hell is he?' she blurted out.

'For God's sake! Could you point that thing somewhere else?' cringed Maeve.

Lily looked at the gun in her hand. Shuddered. She put it down on the seat. She dragged both hands through her hair. She was sweaty with fear. She could smell the stench of it on herself. 'Jesus, Maeve, I could have killed you.'

'Oli phoned and we came on over. She let us in. She was in a state.'

Maeve was still watching Lily as if she might snatch up the gun again, might take it into her head to start shooting.

Can't blame her, thought Lily. She knew she must look demented.

'She . . .' Now her voice wasn't working. A cracked, hag-like noise came out of her mouth. She swallowed, tried to compose herself . . . 'She's a good girl.'

But where the hell was Freddy?

She was living in a nightmare. Freddy was stalking about the place, there was Jase lying dead in the hall, and now Maeve was standing here looking at her as if she was crazy, which at the moment she probably *was*, and her girls were here, at risk, one of them pregnant with a dead man's child, the other guilty of patricide.

There. She'd admitted it to herself.

She hated the thought, but everything was pointing Saz's way. Even Saz's anger against her mother could be nothing more than her own guilt eating away at her.

Shaking, she walked to the edge of the pool and slumped down before she fell down. She crouched there with her head in her hands, thinking, *Please, no. Not Saz*. She felt devoid of energy, all the fight had gone out of her. If Freddy barged in right now and throttled her, she wouldn't care. Saz had killed Leo. She knew it. It made her sick to her stomach to even think it, but there it was, staring her in the face.

Saz had the means to get in somehow. Saz could handle Leo's shotgun. Saz was exhibiting signs of unbearable guilt.

Wake up and smell the coffee, you silly cow, she thought in despair. *Saz did it*.

Oh God. Lily straightened, pulled her hands through her hair, wondered if she was going to throw up. Blinking back tears of weariness and distress and terror, she looked up at Maeve and did a double-take.

Maeve was holding the Magnum, and it was pointing straight at Lily.

69

Lily was so shocked that she could only stare, her mouth open, her eyes wide with disbelief.

'What the . . .?' she managed to get out at last.

'Freddy's out in the hall. With Si. Sorting out that loser.'

Not good news. Freddy was bad enough, but Si was deadly. Why weren't they in here, finishing her off? They had their chance now. All her defences were down. But then – they knew she was cornered. They had time enough to get rid of Jase's body while Maeve held her down here. They could afford to be leisurely about all this. She was trapped. And here was Maeve – dumpy, rather laughable, little Maeve – pointing Leo's gun at Lily's head.

'Maeve, what on earth are you doing?' asked Lily faintly, standing up shakily.

Maeve gave a little laugh. 'Taking this gun off you. You tried to shoot me with it, we struggled, and I shot you. By accident.'

'What?'

'You just had to go stirring things up, didn't you?' Maeve

went on, as if Lily hadn't spoken at all. 'You just had to do it, even though everyone told you not to.'

Lily's eyes were glued to the gun. The great black maw of the Magnum's barrel seemed to yawn at her like a chasm. 'I don't know what you're on about,' she said.

What the hell was happening here?

'I'm on about that silly cow Adrienne, and her list.'

'But . . .' Lily was frowning, trying to make her panicking brain think about anything other than the fact that Maeve was standing there, rock steady, pointing the Magnum at her head. She gulped and tried again . . . 'But Adrienne didn't tell anyone about that list. I asked her twice. She *swore*. How the fuck do you know about it?'

Maeve smirked. 'Matt told me. He was working from home, and he went looking for some paper and he found the list, tucked away in Adrienne's desk drawer. He came in to work all upset next day and I wheedled it out of him, asked him what was wrong. Boy, was I in for a surprise! He showed me a copy he'd taken. Showing all the *tarts* Leo was shagging. And why would Adrienne have such a thing? Matt put two and two together – he's an accountant, after all – and he came up with the correct number. Adrienne was boffing Leo and she was jealous of these others: so jealous she'd had them tracked down. Of course I said that him and Adrienne were sound, so why start stirring things up? And he agreed. He's such a loser, he worships the ground that daft bint walks on. I said it was best to just trash his copy of the damned list and forget it; and I screwed it up and binned it right in front of him. Of course, the minute he was out of the office I was in that bin like a long dog, getting it back out again.'

'What are you telling me, Maeve?' Lily asked, dry-mouthed. 'When did all this happen?'

Maeve was silent for a beat, watching Lily.

Then she said: 'Nineteen ninety-six. Not too long before Leo went off to the great golf course in the sky. The bastard.'

But she'd always thought that Maeve *liked* Leo. Lily stood there, shaking, watching this woman who she thought she knew and yet was suddenly strange, different.

'He laughed at me, you know,' said Maeve.

'What?' Lily shook her head, tried to clear her thoughts. It was hard to think with that thing pointing at her. And now, over Maeve's shoulder, she saw Saz step through the hall door into the pool room. Saw her start forward, her mouth opening, eyes widening, as she saw her aunt Maeve holding a gun on her mother.

No, Saz, thought Lily desperately. *Go away. Keep out of it.*

But then Si appeared behind her. Saw the two women at the far end of the pool. Grabbed Saz's arm, held her still.

'He had you, and he had all these others,' Maeve was ranting on. 'A whole fucking procession of them. You know what? I was going to leave it. But then I saw the list, I saw that *fucking* list and I couldn't bloody well believe it. He had all of *them*, and yet . . . when I approached him, *me*, one night in the club, you know what he did? He laughed in my face. Called me a fat little nobody; said he wouldn't screw me even in the dark. He said he would *never* screw around with his brother's wife, you *never* touched kin, what was I thinking of, what sort of slut was I? Which is funny, because he seemed to *like* sluts. And then he said I was ugly, and did I think he was desperate or something? He was a cruel bastard, your husband.'

Lily kept her eyes on Maeve, although she was terribly aware of Saz standing there in horrified silence at the other end of the pool; aware too that Si was hearing this, hearing how his wife had propositioned his own brother – and been rejected.

She couldn't take this in. Maeve had seen the list, had *known* Leo was fucking around. And she had been jealous of the women on the list. Pretty women, all of them. Sleek, blonde creatures, not dumpy little self-important Plain-Janes like Maeve.

'You always looked down on me,' said Maeve. 'You all did. You. Becks. Mary. Adrienne. Julia. All of you.'

'That ain't true.'

'Yeah it is. And you were all so good looking. Not like me. I even had my hair done like yours, Lily King. Tinted to the same shade, cut in the same style. I even started to dress like you. I wanted to *be* you. But that still wasn't enough for him. You had Leo. He had the looks, the real sparkle. Si's a dull bugger. He didn't ever care about me. I was just the wife, her indoors, helping out with the books sometimes. We had no kids, no nothing. And Freddy's a fool. Leo was the real prize and by God didn't he bloody know it?'

'You don't have to tell me any of this, Maeve.' Lily could feel Si's presence there, taking all this in. *A dull bugger.* He and Saz had drawn closer; they were halfway down the side of the pool now.

'Yeah, I *do*. I want you to know what sort of a shit you were married to. And that all he got, he fucking well deserved.'

Lily stared at her sister-in-law in horror as it all sank in. 'For fuck's sake. *You* killed him. I was talking to his mistresses, I even . . . good God, I even suspected my own daughter, and all the time it was you.'

It was beyond belief. *Maeve* had done it. *Maeve* had left her to stew inside for twelve years. This woman, this stroppy little cow, *she* was the one responsible for Lily's suffering;

she was the one who had robbed the girls of their father and convinced them of their mother's guilt.

She'd been jealous of Leo's mistresses, and jealous of Lily's life. She'd *wanted* Lily's life, Lily could see that now. She'd wanted her husband, for starters, and when she couldn't have him she had killed him instead. Then, unable to have children herself, she had happily grabbed Lily's girls, played the doting aunt. She'd made them depend on her while their mother served time for doing their father. Poor little mites. How skilfully she must have poisoned their minds against Lily.

Lily thought of Saz coming in here tonight. Saz had somehow bypassed the security systems. There was a way in. Saz knew it; maybe she had known it even as a child. Maybe she had even told Maeve about it. Lily knew that Maeve had been at The Fort often on Sundays; she knew Maeve had seen Leo get the key to the gun cabinet from the desk drawer on several occasions. Leo had loved showing off the Purdeys to Si, and they had enjoyed shooting clays together in the grounds some weekends.

Then she thought about Leo's mistresses. Thought about Alice. Clapped a hand to her mouth. 'Oh my God. Alice. You didn't . . .'

Maeve's expression was sneering. 'You see? That's a prime example of what I'm talking about. If you hadn't started arsing about with that list, none of this would have had to happen. You went and saw that nutter in the home, didn't you? Somehow seeing you made her come out of whatever cloud-cuckoo-land she's been in for all these years.'

Not me, thought Lily. *Leo. The picture of Leo.*

'And she started talking. Alice Blunt was in the club the night I talked to Leo, the night I . . . came on to him. She heard. She *saw*. She was hanging off his arm and grinning; they were both laughing at me. She knew he'd turned me down, and you had to go and see her and start her talking, and I thought, what if she talks about *that*? How long then before you started putting it all together?'

'You killed Alice,' said Lily, horrified.

Maeve gave a 'so what?' shrug. 'She was wandering about the place. I just led her into the lake, that was all. It was easy. Told her she was going to be with Leo again. Looked just like she'd drowned herself. Of course, *I* was the one who put the stones in her cardigan pockets, not her.'

Lily was thinking frantically now. *Jesus*. She was thinking about Reba getting raided. She was thinking about Suki, killed in the fire at the flat, and Bev, who was still in intensive care suffering the effects of smoke inhalation.

Lily's stomach lurched with realization as it hit her. 'You're doing them all. You're making it look as if it's me.'

Maeve gave a tight little smile.

'You *are*,' said Lily with sudden ferocity. 'You torched Bev and Suki's place.' Which had led on to Winston freaking out and attacking Jack. 'You grassed Reba Stuart up to the police – didn't you?'

'See? You *can* work it out, if you try.'

'But what about Julia? Someone threw acid at her when I was inside – you couldn't pin that on me.'

'I never intended to.'

'Then why do it to the poor bitch?'

'Why do it to beautiful, *exquisite* Julia?' Maeve looked thoughtful. 'Oh, let me see. Her head was so fucking big she could hardly get it through a door. She knew how good she looked; she *knew* that she only had to enter a room and every man in it was gobsmacked. She was on that fucking list. I knew she was doing Leo behind Nick's back. I thought I might tell him . . . but then I thought, no. Then she came to our tenth anniversary party and she was bragging, actually *bragging* about how men chased after her. And I thought, lady, I'm going to take you down a peg or two. And I did.'

Lily felt red-hot rage envelop her then. That poor cow Julia. All right, she'd been a pain in the arse in her younger days, she *was* vain; she was arrogant and proud of her beauty. But what Maeve had done to her had been cruel beyond belief.

'And what about Adrienne?' So far as Lily knew, Adrienne was fine.

'Saving her until last,' said Maeve gloatingly. 'I *like* Matt. He's a nice man. He don't deserve a slapper like her for a wife.'

Jesus, the price they'd all paid just because Leo wouldn't give Maeve a leg-over. 'You stupid, malicious cow,' Lily spat out, unable to stop herself.

'Hey!' snapped Maeve, raising the gun. 'Pot, kettle, black,' she said, and pulled the trigger.

70

Lily dived sideways, into the pool. The gun went off, a huge explosion of noise that set her ears ringing, and she had a feeling that it had been *this* close, that bullet, too close for comfort. Then she was under the blue, blue water, and she thought, *Oh shit she's going to fire at me again, I'm a sitting duck in here*, and she swam off under water, waiting for the fatal impact.

She tried to stay under, stay deep. Under the water, bullets would be slowed – wouldn't they? – and Maeve's visual perception of her exact whereabouts would be distorted. That was the plan.

It was a *good* plan.

Only . . . she was running out of breath. Her lungs felt as though they were bursting. She was getting a feeling, a powerful feeling that she just *had* to take in air, or water, or something, but she had to open her mouth, her body was telling her: breathe or die.

She kicked further down the pool, as far as she could go, cringing, expecting at any moment to feel the shocking pain of a gunshot, but she knew she was going to have to come up for air.

Lily broke the surface of the pool near the shallow end, the end at which Si and Saz had been standing. She whooped in lungfuls of air, her head whipping round. Si was gone. Saz was gone. There was shouting going on at the other end of the pool, Saz and Maeve grappling . . .

Then Lily saw what had happened, saw why Maeve had missed her when she fired.

Saz had made a run for it and grabbed her. Saz had tried to protect her mother from Maeve. She saw Maeve push Saz roughly aside, saw the gun swinging around towards Saz.

'No!' Lily shrieked.

But Si was there, pushing Saz aside. Husband and wife confronted each other. The gun in Maeve's hand was steady, aimed at Si's chest. Saz stepped back nervously. Lily froze.

Si was staring at his wife as if he had never seen her before. Finally he said: 'You did it.'

Maeve's chin tilted upwards. 'Yeah. It was me. I did it.'

'You killed my brother, just because he wouldn't betray me? Wouldn't jump my wife like she wanted?' Si was shaking his head; he couldn't take it in.

Maeve was silent, but she had grown pale.

'And all these years, *all these years*, you let us think it was *her*? You let her take the rap for you? You were going to just stand back and let us get even for what she'd done, when all the time she *hadn't fucking well done it*?'

Now Maeve looked uncertain. Si's rage was not something anyone would want to incur, and he was visibly trembling with fury now. 'He had all these women,' said Maeve weakly.

'*That was Leo!*' shouted Si. 'That was who he was: we all knew that. What was it you said? Si's a dull bugger, Freddy's a loose cannon, but Leo had the sparkle. You got that right. Leo *did*. He charmed the knickers off more birds than you could count – that was *him*. You came on to my brother, and because he didn't bite you just *killed* him.' Si raised a hand and clutched at his head as if it ached. '*Shit,*' he moaned.

'He had all these women,' repeated Maeve.

Si straightened. 'Give me that bloody gun,' he said.

For a moment Maeve's face tightened. Her hand was gripping the Magnum so hard that her knuckles were white. Lily thought: *She's going to shoot him; she's going to shoot Si right now.* She saw Saz standing near to the couple, tense with dread, shivering as if with cold, and mentally willed her daughter not to intervene again, not to risk it.

But then Maeve's hand dropped. Si stepped forward, and took the gun from her. They were nose to nose, eye to eye. Si grabbed Maeve's arm with one hand. He pocketed the Magnum and then half turned away. Suddenly he turned back, and smacked her full-force across the face. Maeve's head jerked back and she let out a pitiful cry.

'You stupid *cunt*,' snarled Si.

She saw Saz's head turn, saw the uncertainty in her face. Her eyes caught Lily's. *No sweetheart, keep still, keep out of it, for the love of God don't come in between them*, thought Lily desperately, and shook her head.

Saz kept still.

Maeve was crying now, great fat tears rolling down her face. Si kept hold of her arm and started walking her back to where Lily was still in the pool, half submerged in the water. Maeve's feet were dragging, but Si was yanking her after him, and now she was saying, *Please Si, I didn't mean to do it, I didn't mean it.*

Twelve years too late. Lily stood there waist-deep in water, her hair plastered to her head, her clothes sodden. Si stopped walking and looked down at her in the pool. His face looked gaunt, grey. All of a sudden she knew what Si King was going to look like when he was an old, old man.

'I didn't mean to do it, Si, I didn't,' Maeve was gabbling on, tears pouring down her face.

'Shut the fuck up,' said Si.

Maeve fell silent.

Si looked down at Lily.

Shit, he's not going to say sorry, is he? wondered Lily, and she felt a freakish desire to laugh, or cry. She wasn't quite sure which.

'I'll sort this,' he said instead. He stared down at Lily for long moments. 'Okay?'

Lily gulped down a breath, aware suddenly that she hadn't dared breathe at all for some time. She looked up at Si, who had been her enemy for so long that she had almost become accustomed to the fact. The last time they had been like this – her in the pool, Si looking down on her – he had been trying to drown her. Si had hated her just about forever. But now they both knew the truth.

Lily nodded. 'Okay,' she said.

And Si King, brother of the late lamented Leo, pulled his wife from the pool room. He didn't leave Leo's Magnum behind, and Lily was glad about that. Let the damned thing go now, what did she care?

The door slammed shut behind them.

71

Feeling close to collapse, Lily swam to the side of the pool and dragged herself out. She sat there, exhausted, slowly getting her breath back. She was aware of Saz moving at the other end of the pool, but she couldn't focus on anything right now. Saz came and sat down beside her, handing her a towel. Lily nodded. She didn't feel she could speak. Not yet.

'Are you all right?' asked Saz. 'I thought she was going to kill you.'

Lily let out a mirthless laugh. 'You know what? So did I.' She started drying her face and hair.

'What d'you think's going to happen to her?' asked Saz quietly.

'How the hell should I know?' snapped Lily, and now she did feel like speaking, she felt angry, she felt *furious*. She had to spit some of this bile out, or bust. 'How did you get back in here, Saz? Come on. Tell me. How the fuck did you get in here, and lead all *that* straight in after you?'

Saz shrugged and her face clouded. 'I'm sorry,' she said.

'*Stuff* your sorry, Saz.'

'I . . . I always had a way in. It was like a game, beating the security systems.'

'A *game?*' Lily turned her head and stared hard at her daughter. Her cheek wasn't bleeding any more, but there was a lump the size of an egg coming up there that was going to be one hell of a bruise. 'You brought Jase in.'

'Only because he said he wanted to surprise Oli, propose to her!' Saz's face was naked, pleading. 'They'd had a row and he told me he wanted to get back in her good books. I couldn't see any harm in it.'

Lily was silent, thinking. 'Is Oli okay?' she said at last.

Saz nodded. Then her face grew troubled. 'I think . . . I think Jase is dead.'

Lily had a brief horror-flick running in her brain when Saz said that. Freddy grabbing Jase's neck and wrenching it round. The noise. *Crack!*

She shuddered. Then she looked at Saz. 'Tell me what you were sorry about,' she said.

'What?'

'When you were sleepwalking. You kept saying over and over, "I'm sorry, Daddy." What was that about? Do you know?'

Saz lowered her head. 'I came in that night. The night he died.'

I'm sorry, Daddy . . .

The words echoed in Lily's brain, Saz's voice, the voice of a nine-year-old girl coming from the mouth of a woman.

Leo with one of his tarts in the master suite, Saz coming up the stairs. *Surprise, daddy!* And then seeing what was happening on the bed, seeing and maybe even understanding; thinking, *But I'm his best girl. And that ain't Mummy.*

Lily could see it in her mind's eye. Saz creeping back downstairs to the study, slipping on those special gloves Leo had bought for her, getting the key to the gun cabinet out of the desk drawer, opening the cabinet, loading the gun, she was *used* to loading the gun, Leo had taught her how. And then going back upstairs . . . and blowing Leo away.

'I was going to surprise him,' Saz said. 'I climbed up the stairs, and I thought I would surprise him, I loved him so much.' Her eyes filled with tears. After a moment's hesitation, Lily reached out a hand and squeezed her daughter's hand.

'But,' Saz went on, heaving a heavy sigh, 'he wasn't alone.'

'Oh Saz,' said Lily mournfully. 'Did you see him in bed with another woman?'

'No. I saw . . .' Saz's head whipped round and she stared into Lily's eyes. Then she closed her eyes tight, blocking the memory, her face screwing up with pain.

'It's okay. Go on,' said Lily reassuringly. She was holding Saz's hand tight now. 'What did you see, Saz?'

'Oh God,' said Saz, and she started to cry. 'I saw *you.*'

Lily stared at Saz. '*What?*' she said faintly.

'I saw you,' sobbed Saz. 'I . . . I saw you. But it wasn't you, was it? I've been so stupid. I saw a blonde woman in a dark suit, holding the gun. It was smoking; there was the smell of the stuff, cordite, and I could see that Daddy was on the floor. The woman was in the doorway of the master suite; she was facing away from me. It was *your* hairstyle, and you always wore those dark suits, you remember?'

Lily remembered.

I wanted your life, Maeve had said.

'But it wasn't you at all, was it? I thought it was you, but it was *Aunt Maeve.*'

'Shh,' said Lily, and put an arm around Saz's shuddering shoulders. 'Hush, it's all right. It's all over now. Tell me why you were sorry, Saz. Just tell me that.'

'I was sorry because I . . . I didn't protect him,' wailed Saz. 'You'd been arguing a lot in the weeks before that, do you remember?'

Oh yeah, Lily remembered. She'd thought Leo was playing around, taking the piss. And he'd said she was going off her head. She had actually started to believe him, had started to think she *was* going crazy. She remembered the rows. Remembered them well. But she had tried – they had *both* tried – to keep all that shit away from the girls. Obviously they hadn't tried hard enough.

'I thought you'd finally lost it and killed him. I *saw* you there. So I was glad when they locked you away. I was *glad*.'

Saz started to cry again, but more softly now. 'I'm sorry,' she said. 'I'm so sorry, Mum. And I've been phoning you, and saying nothing. Trying to freak you. I've been a total bitch, I'm so sorry.'

Lily's, eyes filled with tears too. For the first time in twelve years, Saz had called her Mum. It was a moment she would never forget.

'Don't be sorry,' she said gently, and she pulled Saz's head down onto her shoulder and stroked her silky hair. She was crying herself now, but they were tears of joy; at last, *at last*, she had her daughter back. 'Don't be sorry, baby. It's all gone now; it's all over. We'll start from here, okay? We'll start all over again.'

72

'Purbright Securities,' said Jack Rackland.

'Oh for God's sake, don't worry about all that now,' said Lily, wishing she could have brought Jack flowers, but they didn't like flowers on this hospital ward because of MRSA. 'Look at the state of you. Jack, you look like shit.'

'Oh, thank you,' croaked Jack, and lay back on the pillows.

He'd come out of intensive care three days ago, spent a day in high care and then been transferred onto a normal ward. He'd had a lot of transfusions. He was a mess of bruises, bandages and bloody stapled cuts, and he was just about as white as the pillowcase his mussed-up dirty-blond head rested on. But he was *alive*, and Lily had been sure she'd been looking at a corpse the day Winston had gone for him with that machete.

'I'm not *worried* about it, I'm just telling you, that's all,' said Jack.

'Can I get you anything. A glucose drink? A bottle to pee in?' She smiled. She was just so damned pleased to see him there in one piece.

'Look, this is undignified enough, without you taking the
. . . Let's get back to the case. Purbright Securities.'

'Yeah, okay, who runs that? Who was paying for Alice's
care?' Lily thought she already knew the answer, but she
didn't want to steal Jack's thunder.

'Can you hear something?' asked Jack.

Lily could. There were raised voices in the corridor, coming
closer.

'What do you mean I can't take flowers in?' yelled a female
voice.

'Uh-oh,' said Jack.

Lily poked her head out the door. A very short, angry-looking
woman carrying a huge bouquet of flowers was tip-tapping
imperiously down the corridor, heading for Jack's room, while
a couple of nurses tried to detain her.

'What does Monica look like?' Lily asked him.

'Don't bother to ask. That's what she *sounds* like. They
notified her when I was brought in – she's still my wife after
all, my next of kin. She's been in and out ever since, and
every time she gives the nurses all that about the sodding
flowers. They've *told* her, and still she keeps bringing the
bloody things in. That woman is a *nightmare*. Look, as I
was saying – Purbright Securities.'

'Yeah, go on.' Lily was bright-eyed with interest.

'Purbright Securities is a division of Sunstyle Security
Systems.'

Lily remembered the security guy in the kitchen altering
the codes, and Oli telling her he was from Sunstyle Securities.

'Directors?' she asked.

'Now that's the interesting part . . .' He hesitated, aiming
for impact.

'Oh, cut to the chase, Jack.'

So he did. Lily looked gobsmacked, then she laughed out loud. 'That other thing I asked you to look into . . .'

'Jesus, have a heart! I'm in hospital, for Christ's sake.'

'But did you get a chance . . .?'

'Yeah, I got a chance. Checked the birth certificate. You were right, his old man's name's not on there.'

'Terrific.'

Monica arrived at the door. She took one look at Jack.

'Oh Jack – *baby*!' she crooned, and ran forward and flung herself upon him, flowers and all. 'How are you today? Are you feeling any better?' Monica was dropping kisses and pollen and petals all over Jack's bruised and bloodied face.

'Ow! Fuck me, girl, have a heart,' he complained, but he was nearly smiling.

'Um . . . I'd better go,' said Lily, edging towards the door.

At that, Monica extricated herself from Jack's bed of pain and fastened a gorgon-like glare upon Lily. 'And who the fuck are *you*?' she demanded.

'Just a friend,' said Lily. She gave Jack one last smile. 'Thanks, Jack. For everything.' She had already decided that she was going to slip a little bonus in for Jack sometime soon – by God, he'd earned it.

'Pleasure,' said Jack, and managed a wink.

Lily went on home, and left Jack to Monica.

73

Some days later they visited the grave together, all three of them; Lily and her two daughters, arm in arm. And although Lily hadn't been able to take flowers to the living, now she took flowers to the dead. They stood there solemnly in the graveyard and looked down at the beautifully carved and embellished black marble headstone.

Here Rests Leo King
Died 1996
Beloved Brother and Father
Sadly missed

There were a few red roses wilting in the urn. Lily took them out, replaced them with fresh ones – white this time.

'Who put these here?' she asked the girls, curious.

'Nick comes every week,' said Saz. 'He leaves the roses. I've seen him here a couple of times. He must have loved Dad a lot; they were such good friends.'

Lily stood up and they were silent again, staring at the headstone.

'Do you think Aunt Maeve really went abroad?' asked Saz.

Lily nodded, *sure I do*. A few days after Maeve had pointed the Magnum at Lily's head, Becks had told her that Maeve had phoned and said she was flying out to her and Si's villa in Marbella for a long break.

Lily had said nothing, only expressed mild interest. But secretly, she thought that this was the deal: if you took a plane out to Malaga, and if you then booked a taxi ride to Marbella and pitched up at the villa door, Maeve would not be there to open it. Wherever she was, whatever had happened to her, was between her and Si. Lily knew she had to let that go now.

'I still miss him,' said Saz. Lily looked at her. Saz was shaping up now; she was even being nicer to that poor tolerant sap Richard.

'Yeah, me too,' said Oli sadly.

Lily wondered if Oli missed Jase, too. That night, that horrible night when she had thought Maeve was going to shoot her dead, came back to her full-force then. She remembered that she and Saz had staggered out into the hall, supporting each other, to find Oli sitting alone in a state of shock on the bottom stair.

There had been no Si, no Maeve. No Freddy. And no Jase. Only Oli, and when she'd seen them coming out of the swimming pool room she had cried out and run to them and they had stood there, the three of them, for a long time, clutching at each other, hugging each other tight, knowing that they had by some miracle come through something fearful, something that could have ended very differently indeed.

Now Lily put an arm around each of her daughters, relishing the warm feel of them, unable to quite believe her luck. She was out of prison. Si had taken care of Maeve, Lily was free, and the King boys were off her back. It had to be enough for her. Hell, it *was*.

She was back with her girls, and they really were *her* girls again. Her beloved daughters, her *family*. Thoughts of family took Lily's mind to her mother. The girls didn't know their grandmother at all, and she felt bad about that. She couldn't let her own difficult relationship with her mother ruin the girls' chances of knowing their only surviving grandparent, could she? She decided that she would try again with the cantankerous old witch, introduce her to the girls, see what unfolded. Family was *important*.

She thought again of Leo – big, ebullient, laughing Leo, who could fill a room with the sheer immensity of his personality. He'd given her the gift of these two lovely girls, and – finally – she found that she could forgive him for all the rest. She knew she hadn't been blameless; she'd never loved him as a wife should: he must have known it. He wasn't a fool.

'He'd be so proud of you both,' she said, knowing it was true. Leo had loved his girls. He had even, in his slightly skewed way, loved her. *Bye Leo*, she thought with a faint pang of sadness.

Then Saz said to Lily: 'Mum, Oli and me have been thinking. Um . . . about selling the house.'

Lily looked in surprise at Saz. Then at Oli. Then she shrugged. 'Well, I think it's probably a good thing. It's . . . sort of a sad place now, ain't that the truth?'

'Yeah, it is,' said Oli.

It was over. And – yes – it was time to move on.

'Saz?' she asked her elder daughter. 'Is that what you really want? To sell?'

Saz was nodding. 'Yeah, and we also thought that, maybe, we could split the proceeds three ways. Matt could help us sort out the details. A share for you, me and Oli. What do you think?'

Lily looked at each of them in turn. They both looked faintly embarrassed, a little worried. 'I think you're a pair of bloody diamonds, that's what I think,' said Lily with a smile.

Saz relaxed. She sighed, looked again at the headstone. 'Oli's right. It's been sad there.'

'We'll have one last blow-out,' said Lily. 'A big party. Then we go. Okay?'

Saz and Oli nodded.

'Okay,' said Lily, and led her girls away from their father's grave.

74

That evening she sat alone in the study at The Fort and watched the tape again. There was Leo, larger than life, talking to her, telling her that if she was watching this, then he was dead.

'Oh Leo,' said Lily, and she cried a bit for the loss of him then, the big bruiser who was the father of her girls, the one who could always make them all laugh; Leo the wide boy, the crook, the charmer, the philanderer – just like his dear old dad Bubba King had been.

One more time she watched it right to the end.

'The boys will look after you. I love you, Lils,' he said, and then there was nothing but white noise, and Leo was gone.

'You bastard,' she said softly, and then laughed through her tears. *The boys will look after you.* He had said that again and again throughout the tape.

She couldn't even raise an ironic laugh at that any more, it was too sad. Oh, she didn't doubt her troubles with Si and that lunatic Freddy were at an end. They had their culprit;

she was in the clear. But look after her? No. She was on her own.

She thought again about Purbright Securities, a division of Sunstyle. She thought of one of the directors whose name Jack had given her; it was that firm that had paid for Alice's care and fitted The Fort's security system. She thought: *The boys will look after you*. Thought of Bubba King, Leo's father, and Leo's 'boys'.

The house was silent all around her. The wall had been repaired, there was no way in now, no way out except through the gates. The security system was working. If you breached it, the alarm would go off – somewhere. Leo had always said it didn't go off here, what was the point of it clanging away out here in the arse end of nowhere? It went off . . . well, he hadn't specified. But she had always *assumed* it went straight to the local cop shop.

But wait a minute.

Would Leo *really* have wired his gaff up to a cop shop? Answer: no. Surely not.

So when the alarm went off, *if* it went off, where was the alarm actually raised?

Lily had a suspicion, just a faint suspicion, that she knew the answer to that. She switched off the tape, and went out into the hall. Went to the security panel beside the door. Looked at it. And started to smile.

Leaving the system on, she walked out into the grounds, tripping sensors left, right and centre. She breached all the crisscrossing beams, and somewhere – she knew – an alarm was sounding, loud and clear.

It didn't take him long to get there – she was timing it on her watch. Soon she heard a powerful car approaching, roaring along as if speeding to an emergency. She stood there, leaning against one of the wide-open gates, and then the headlight beams caught her in a dazzling field of light and the Mercedes screeched to a halt three feet from her. Someone tall and dark got out of the driver's seat and stalked across the gravel towards her.

'Twelve and a half minutes,' said Lily. 'That's pretty good, although I believe new guidelines for the emergency services require . . .'

'What the *fuck* are you doing?' demanded Nick O'Rourke, breathing heavily and looking, now they were *both* caught in the headlights' glare, pretty damned angry and alarmed. Which was fitting, really.

'Testing the system,' said Lily.

'*Which* system?'

'The one Leo and you put in place, the *alarm* system that's connected straight to your house.'

Nick was silent.

'And I know about Purbright Securities being a division of Sunstyle, who fitted the system – oh, and that you're on the board, as was Leo when he was alive – oh yeah, and that Purbright paid for Alice Blunt's care.'

'Ah.'

'*And* I know why Si and Freddy didn't get to me inside.'

Nick looked at her. Placed both hands on his hips, let out a breath, looked at the ground, then back at her face. 'Now come on. You *can't* know that.'

'All right, then. I guessed. Bearing in mind everything else that I know for sure, and are you going to tell me I got it wrong? Because I know I haven't, Nick. You put a ring of steel around me when I was inside. Because I was Leo's wife, and because you knew me and loved me and you couldn't believe I'd done him but if I *had*, then I must have been provoked beyond reason. I guess you know by now that it was Maeve?'

'I heard.'

Lily nodded. 'Leo left me an old tape and on it he said the boys would look after me. He kept on saying that, the boys would look after me, but he didn't mean Si and Freddy, and he didn't mean any of the boys who worked for him, either.' She paused. 'He meant *you*, didn't he, Nick?'

Nick was silent again for long moments. He was staring at Lily's face.

'You know what?' he said at last.

'What?'

'You're devious.'

Lily shrugged. 'It's been said.'

'And you had the front to tell me dumb blonde jokes.'

'You and Leo had a very special relationship, ain't that right?' said Lily softly.

Nick sighed. 'Let's go in,' he said, taking her arm. 'And talk about it.'

75

Bobby 'Bubba' King had been a player, just like his son Leo. He had played . . .

'With my mother,' said Nick as they sat in the sitting room.

Lily looked at him. She twined her fingers into his. He squeezed her hand. 'I had Jack check the birth records,' she said. 'Your dad's name wasn't on it.'

'Can't actually blame him for that,' sighed Nick. 'When he found out Bubba King had been poaching on his territory, he kicked off and divorced Mum. Took off for the States when I was about a year old. Never saw him or heard from him again. Leo's dad stepped in, looked after Mum and me. She didn't marry again and I was an only child. She died when I was twelve.'

'I knew that, but Jesus, I can't get over this. You're their half-brother. Si and Freddy and Leo.'

'Yeah, but Si and Freddy don't know that. Bubba was closest to Leo, and Leo was the only one he told.'

'*When* did he tell Leo?'

'When Mum died.'

By the age of fourteen, Lily knew that Nick and Leo had been a team, standing together on the streets, into all sorts. By seventeen, they had been driving around in hot cars and pushing the boundaries in all sorts of ways, working their way up in crim circles, two good-looking boys who attracted girls without any effort at all. Nick had attracted Lily... but when Leo stepped in, Nick had stepped back. Because *you don't touch kin or anything that belongs to them.*

'I always wondered why you didn't fight harder for me,' said Lily.

Nick turned his head and looked at her with those dark, dark eyes. Nothing like Leo's. Thank God. But maybe if they *had* been, she'd have wised up that much sooner.

'What, go up against Leo?' Nick sighed. 'I was angry with him, sure I was. Furious. But I was even angrier with *you*. He was the only blood I had. My mother was dead, I had no grandparents. Bubba always helped me financially, but that was about all. Si and Freddy were kept in ignorance, because I suppose Leo and Bubba knew that there were enough contenders for the King crown as it was, and Si and Freddy might prove a threat to me if they thought I was closer than they'd previously believed me to be.'

'You and Leo were like... blood brothers.'

Now Nick grinned. 'We *were* blood brothers.'

He showed her a white, inch-long scar on his inner wrist.

Lily gasped. 'Leo had one exactly the same,' she said, fingering the whitened skin there.

'That's right, he did. After Bubba told us, we did it. Cut our hands and joined the blood together, swore to be brothers forever.'

The boys will look after you.

'And then you met me...'

411

'Yeah. And then Leo stormed in, and you *let* him storm in, so I stepped back.'

She had been so quiet, so obliging, then. Hurt by Nick's sudden apparent withdrawal, she had allowed herself to be charmed by Leo.

'I was just a dumb girl, Nick. I was snowballed by Leo. I wanted you to step in, and all you did was fucking well step *back*.'

'Now this is bloody ironic, wouldn't you say?' His eyes were dancing with mirth now as he stared at her. 'We both wanted the other to show more resistance to Leo. And we both folded.'

Lily sat back wearily, half laughing, half sad. 'He certainly was a force to be reckoned with.'

'Yeah. That he was.'

They were silent.

Then Nick said: 'I was so fucking miserable when I let you go. So I thought, hey, who cares? I'll date beautiful girls. All cats are grey in the dark. When that didn't make me any happier I thought, what the hell? – and I married Julia.'

'The playboy Nick,' said Lily. She remembered how it had hurt her, seeing him with all those different, glamorous companions. And then when he had married Julia, although she would have denied it, she'd felt low for weeks. 'Poor Julia. Second best even though she was so gorgeous. And being so gorgeous, and so vain . . . she went and upset Maeve.'

Nick was staring at her, drinking in her face.

'What?' asked Lily.

'I thought I knew you. Gentle, quiet Lily. I thought . . . if she'd done that, this awful thing, then she's been provoked beyond all reason. Then it came out at the trial that he'd been hitting you . . .'

'He didn't,' said Lily quickly. 'That was something the brief cooked up to lessen the sentence.'

'Yeah, but I didn't know that. And I wondered what *else* he might have done to you, because I knew Leo. I knew his appetites. So I thought you must have been *forced* to it. So when it all came to a head, I was torn in two. I loved Leo. I loved *you*. And Leo had always said, look after Lily if anything ever happens to me. He'd give me one of those big bear hugs of his and he'd say that, time and again: *always look after Lily*. So . . . I looked after you. Kept you safe inside. Si did try to get to you in there, but I put things in place.'

Lily remembered the rumours she'd heard in stir – that someone was out to get her. Yeah – *Si* was out to get her.

But not any more.

'Ah, what the hell? It's all water under the bridge,' he said, and leaned over and kissed her.

'Yeah,' said Lily, and put her arms around his neck and pulled him in close.

All that wasted time, she thought.

But no. It hadn't been wasted. She had her girls. And she had grown a backbone in prison; it had toughened her up, made her strong.

'You've caused me a hell of a lot of anxiety,' said Nick against her mouth.

'You broke my heart,' said Lily.

'You broke mine.'

'Oh come on – do you actually have one?' Lily scoffed with a smile.

Nick pulled open his shirt and put Lily's hand in there, over his heart. His chest was hot, the skin there like silk over steel. 'Feel that? It's beating, yes?'

'Then it's not broken.'

413

'Just a hairline crack, maybe,' said Nick, his eyes playing with hers.

Lily sighed happily. 'I love you, Nick O'Rourke. I always have and I think I probably always will.'

'You *think*?' His lips hovered over hers now.

She didn't need to ask if he loved her too. Hadn't he proved that, a thousand times over? Guarding her in prison, and outside too. And stepping back when he thought she was in love with Leo.

She had been overwhelmed by Leo. But *this* was love, faithful and enduring love. The type every woman craved, deep down.

'I love you too, Lily King. And I think . . . you know what I think?'

Lily shook her head.

'I think it's *way* past your bedtime.'

Epilogue

The party for Lily King's fortieth birthday was held in the grounds of The Fort the following April. The Fort sale was agreed. The recession had delayed the sale and whacked twenty-five grand off the asking price of two million, but there was still going to be plenty left for Lily and the girls.

There was a huge marquee, a guest list of villains and wives a mile long, fairy lights strung up in all the trees. Kylie was giving 'I Just Can't Get You Outta My Head' her all from the huge sound system the DJ had set up beside the outdoor pool. Saz was dancing with Richard, Oli was rocking her new baby son in her arms, and Lily was looking at her birthday cake's single lit candle and thinking: *Thank Christ they didn't try to get forty of the buggers on there. The sprinklers would have drowned the lot of us.*

The party organizer, a posh twenty-year-old girl with a clipboard and fixed smile, came up to Lily.

'Ten minutes, then we cut the cake, Mrs King, yah? I'll start getting everyone into the marquee.'

'Fine.' Just time to nip to the loo, check her make-up.

Lily went indoors, attended to her ablutions, and was coming back outside when suddenly Si was there, blocking her way.

Lily made as if to step around him.

Si blocked her path again.

She looked into his eyes. *What the fuck now?* she wondered.

'Hi, Lily.' He was staring at her face. 'Happy birthday.'

Lily gulped. Si always had and always would make her nervous. 'Thanks,' she said. He didn't move aside. He was still blocking her exit like a brick wall.

'I wanted to tell you that it's been sorted. As promised.'

'You mean . . .'

'I mean Maeve.' He paused for a beat. He was telling her he'd disposed of his wife and he looked as calm as a millpond. Lily felt a shudder run through her. 'But there was something I thought you should know about. Something odd.'

'Oh? What?' She didn't want to know. *Whatever* it was, she just didn't.

'It troubled me, this thing. Do you know what that's like, when something keeps niggling away at you?'

Lily nodded. *What the hell's he on about?*

'She said . . . *Maeve* admitted she was there on the night Leo got done.'

'I know that. *She* did it.'

But Si was shaking his head. 'She told me she followed the girls in, through the breach in the wall.'

Lily was frowning now. 'Saz was there. She saw Maeve standing over Leo with the gun in her hands. She thought Maeve was me.' But he'd said *girls*. Plural. 'She's not saying Oli was there too?'

Si looked tired all of a sudden. He sighed. 'It's true Maeve

416

came on to Leo and he turned her down. It's true she was attacking Leo's women. But – Lily – I have to tell you this. With her dying breath she kept saying it. Both the girls were there. She followed them in. And it was Saz that fired the gun. Maybe she meant to just threaten him with it and it went off, I don't know. The girls knew what Leo had been up to with the women, they knew you were upset.' Si was staring at Lily. 'Maeve saw it happen. She *swore*. She got the girls back out. And then you came home early, and you got fitted up for it, and she thought, better you than the girls.'

Lily was standing there, open-mouthed with shock. 'But . . . she told me she'd done it,' she managed to get out.

'She wanted to hurt you. She hated you. She *wanted* Leo dead after he mocked her. And when you think about it, everything worked out just fine for Maeve. She had your life. She had your girls. All right, she didn't have Leo. But what she did have was *revenge*.'

'No . . .' said Lily.

'Why would anyone lie with their dying breath?' Si asked her, shaking his head. '*That's* what bugs me. I don't think they would. So . . . I had to tell you.'

'But Saz . . . Saz was furious with me, as if she really believed I'd killed Leo.'

'I thought about that,' said Si. 'Jesus, it's all I've been thinking about for months. Oli must have witnessed the killing, and after that I think she just blanked it out . . .'

Oli had told Lily that she couldn't remember anything about what had happened around that time. Lily felt her guts lurch as she thought of that. Everything Si was saying . . . oh God, it made sense. She didn't want it to, but it did.

'Her mind just shut down; she couldn't accept what had happened,' Si was going on. 'Maybe for a while she actually

417

did believe that you'd killed Leo. And Saz . . . well, who the fuck knows. Did she pull that trigger deliberately, or did the gun go off by accident?'

'But Si, she would have *loaded* the damned thing,' said Lily.

'Lily,' said Si, his gaze flat as he stared at her. 'We're talking a nine-year-old kid here, playing up to her little sister. She may have loaded it, played the whole charade out to the full, with no real intention of firing it. Who the fuck knows?'

Lily was shaking her head. 'Maeve could have fired it, wiped her prints off afterwards.'

Si was silent for a moment. 'Her dying *breath*, Lily. She swore it was Saz. Saz with her special little gloves on. No prints to remove. Think about it. The poor kid must have been eaten up with guilt after that. She'd killed her dad. Caused you to do twelve years inside. When she saw you again, it must have crucified her, brought it all back. Don't you think?'

'Mrs King!' The party organizer was pushing past Si's bulk in the doorway. She looked at Lily, standing there pale with shock, and gave her a bright-eyed, efficient smile. '*There* you are. Come on, Mrs King. Time to cut the cake.'

Si and Lily exchanged a long look. Si stepped aside. After one faltering moment, Lily hurried past.

Si caught her arm, halting her progress. Lily's head turned and she stared into his eyes. 'What are you going to do? About what I told you?'

Their gazes locked.

Lily took a long, quivering breath. Then she straightened and pasted a smile on her face.

'What did you tell me, Si?' she asked him with a slight, puzzled frown. 'I can't seem to remember.'

Si looked at her for a long moment. Then he nodded and freed her arm. 'You're right,' he said. 'It was nothing. Nothing at all.'

Lily hurried on into the marquee. Everyone was clustering inside now. She looked around.

Si was there, edging in at the back of the crowd. So was Freddy. And there were her girls, Saz and Oli, Saz laughing at something Richard had just said to her, Oli cradling baby Leo.

Baby Leo.

Leo would have been chuffed to nuts if he could see his grandson and know that Oli had not hesitated for a second over a name choice. Baby Leo was already very visibly a King, with a mop of dark hair, black eyebrows and long girly black lashes. And, of course, navy blue eyes.

'Don't all babies have dark blue eyes?' Oli – exhausted but serenely happy – had asked Lily when she first held her grandson after the birth.

'Do they? I don't know. God, he's beautiful though. Isn't he?' Jase's child.

Lily looked across at Oli and the baby now, held tight in his mother's arms, and put thoughts of Jase to one side. And everything that Si had just told her? She was going to forget it. Right now. She took a deep, calming breath. Tonight, she wanted everything to be perfect; let the dead rest in peace, let the living have their fun.

Nick strolled over, smiling. He put an arm around her shoulders. Leaned in. Kissed her.

'Mrs King,' said the organizer, as a hush fell over the watching crowds. 'Would you like to say a few words?' And the woman was off again, urging the waiters to top up everyone's glasses with champagne for the toast.

'Oh, I don't think . . .' Lily glanced at Nick. He nodded. *Go on.*

'Well,' said Lily. She raised her voice, looked around at all the faces. Many of them were the same faces she had confronted at Saz's wedding. But their expressions were different now. Si had put the word out. Lily was in the clear over Leo. All was forgiven. She was being watched with smiles, with anticipation – not with hatred.

She saw Becks, all in pink – her favourite colour, standing in the crowd, beaming from ear to ear, with Joe. Adrienne was there, but what the fuck, what was the use of bearing grudges? And Matt – dull old dependable Matt, the company accountant – was at her side. Hairy Mary was there with her East End hard boy.

Everyone who was anyone was there.

And *she* was the star of the evening. Lily King. No longer the jail bird. Accepted again. Back in business.

She took a breath and said: 'Hi, everyone.'

Then she thought again of what Si had told her. She swallowed, hesitated. Pushed it once again to the back of her mind. She was going to forget he ever said it. One day soon, she would. She'd forget. She promised herself that she would. She took a quick gulp of champagne and went on, her voice growing stronger with every word.

'Hi! Nice to be with you all again. Thanks for coming. We'll be leaving this house soon, I think quite a few of you already know that. Once this was a great family home, but now I guess it's time we all moved on, put some of the past behind us. I've got a new grandchild.' Lily smiled across at Oli and baby Leo, and a faint cheer went up from the crowds. 'So we've got a lot to look forward to. And now I'm going to blow out this bloody candle, and make a wish.'

Everyone clapped and cheered. Lily blew out the candle.

'What did you wish for?' asked Nick in her ear.

'A new life,' said Lily.

'Oh, I think we can manage that,' said Nick with a smile. He held up his glass. 'A toast!' he said loudly. 'To Lily King!'

And they drank to her, all her enemies; now – at last – her friends.

What's next?

Tell us the name of an author you love

Jessie Keane

Go ▶

and we'll find your next great book.

www.bookarmy.com